"Ranne

A Knight in Peril

When Sebastian, Earl of Langlinais, became ensnared in his villainous brother's plots, he had no choice but to turn to his virgin bride for help—a wife he had not seen since the day they had wed as children. He had planned for her to remain his wife in name only, yet Sebastian had not counted on being enchanted by her beauty. But could he really tell her the secret reason why their love could never be . . . ?

A Bride-in-Waiting

Convent-bred Julianna had spent her days learning the wifely arts . . . and her nights longing for the man she had wed so long ago. Summoned to join him, the naïve bride came face-to-face with a man so virile, so powerful, she trembled in his presence. And although he asked her to go against everything she held true, she could not resist surrendering . . . even if it meant losing her soul.

"A writer of rare intelligence and sensitivity . . .
a powerful story."
Mary Jo Putney

KAREN RANNEY

My Beloved

An Avon Romantic Treasure

AVON BOOKS  NEW YORK

AVON BOOKS, INC.
1350 Avenue of the Americas
New York, New York 10019

Copyright © 1999 by Karen Ranney
Inside cover author photo by Susan Riley Photography
Published by arrangement with the author
Library of Congress Catalog Card Number: 99-94775
ISBN: 0-380-80590-1
www.avonbooks.com/romance

First Avon Books Printing: August 1999

AVON TRADEMARK REG. U.S. PAT. OFF. AND IN OTHER COUNTRIES, MARCA REGIS-
TRADA, HECHO EN U.S.A.

Printed in the U.S.A.

WCD 10 9 8 7 6 5 4 3 2 1

To my son, John,
for a thousand reasons,
among them love and pride

Prologue

Templar Headquarters
Cyprus, 1249

What were they going to demand for his freedom?

Sebastian of Langlinais sat on the low shelf chiseled from the rock wall. It had served as a bed for past occupants of this monastic cell, but he vowed not to spend one more night in this place. The monastery was a way station of sorts, a place the Templars brought injured pilgrims and rescued prisoners. A place for healing and contemplative silence.

He'd had enough of silence and nothing could heal him.

His hands were tucked into the wide sleeves of his monk's robe. But his head was not bowed in piety; instead, his gaze was directed at the wooden door. A year of imprisonment had rendered his face gaunt, and that same confinement now made him impatient.

The man who entered the room an hour later was dressed in the distinctive white tunic and red-embroidered cross of the Poor Knights of the Temple of Solomon. Only the elite wore such a uniform;

1

most of the warrior monks wore black or brown mantles.

The resemblance he bore to Sebastian was not surprising. Each had his mother's eyes, his father's strength.

"You are fortunate, brother. A great many prisoners die before they can be ransomed," the Templar said in greeting.

"Is that why they've sent you here, Gregory? To remind me to be grateful for my survival?" Sebastian's voice was a mere rasp of words. He'd had no cause to speak in prison, isolated as he had been from the other men.

"Are you?" Gregory of Langlinais smiled, but the expression appeared flavored with irony. "The expression on your face is not one I would liken to gratitude, brother. Nor do you seem surprised to see me. Even after all this time."

A small table and one chair filled a corner of the small chamber. Upon the table sat a pitcher of wine, a loaf of bread, some goat's cheese. Gregory kicked out the small chair with his foot, rearranging his sword with an absent gesture as he sat. He reached for the pitcher, tipped it to inspect the contents. "Come, won't you join me? The monastery's wine is better than most. Let's celebrate our reunion. How long has it been? Six years?"

"Forgive me if I decline. I prefer to sup alone."

Gregory nodded, set the pitcher back down. "My Templar brothers tell me you are reclusive, Sebastian. I've never known you to be so."

"Imprisonment will change a great deal about a man, Gregory."

"Even your choice of clothing?" His gaze surveyed the garment Sebastian wore. "I remember your dressing in a more secular fashion."

"And I recall that you joined the Templars as a pro fraternitate. Why take orders when you could have remained a lay member?"

Gregory's smile illuminated a face tanned brown by the sun. His hair, once as dark as his brother's, was now tinted with golden highlights. "Inducements, Sebastian. The Templars needed leaders. Knights are always welcome in their ranks."

"And power is a heady lure."

"My position is less one of influence than it is of endless details."

"When may I leave?" Sebastian's question sliced through the conversational patter.

Gregory's smile vanished. "When you have agreed to certain terms."

"What do the Templars want from me, Gregory? My oath? I was never asked to abjure my beliefs. I will swear to that."

"Your freedom was not easily obtained, Sebastian." Gregory traced a finger along the rim of one earthenware mug.

"So, it's money. How much was my ransom?"

He named a sum that caused Sebastian to draw in his breath sharply.

"I've pledged Langlinais in your name. It was the only way to obtain your release."

"I was valued more highly than I thought. Pity my worth was never demonstrated during my imprisonment."

The finger paused in its journey. "I never knew, Sebastian. Not until the arrangements were being made to free you."

Sebastian could only offer him silence in response. Once there had been only laughter or good-spirited rivalry between them. Too many years separated them, too many unshared memories lay between them. They could never become confidants again.

"How do you propose I repay that sum, Gregory?"

"That is your concern. Consider yourself fortunate that you are heir to a demesne rich enough to finance your release. You have a year to repay the Order, Sebastian, the term of your imprisonment."

They each knew to do so would be nearly impossible, even for the Lord of Langlinais.

Gregory stood, walked to the door. With his hand upon the rope handle, he turned. "Why did you go on crusade, Sebastian? It's a question that I've wished answered ever since I learned you were made prisoner of the Egyptian pasha."

"Why does any man go on a quest?" The words sounded tired, as if they had been often repeated. In truth, it was the first time they had been spoken.

"Not you, Sebastian. Had you not won so many tourneys, I would have thought you fearful of battle."

"Any man of sense avoids war."

"Even when right is on our side?"

"A view no doubt espoused equally as passionately by infidels," Sebastian said dryly.

"Your words border on heresy." Gregory stared at Sebastian as if to engrave his face upon his memory. "Were you at Montvichet, Sebastian?"

Sebastian narrowed his eyes. "Is that why you are really here, Gregory? Not to demonstrate filial affection, but to have this question answered? How did you know?"

Gregory shrugged again. "One of the villagers no doubt contributed the information."

"Was he prodded to recall with torture, Gregory?"

"Why were you there, Sebastian?"

"Another question that has bothered you all this time, Gregory? Magdalene sent for me."

Sebastian watched as the look in Gregory's eyes changed. Was there only surprise there? No hint of grief?

"She had become a Cathar. Didn't you know?"

Gregory shook his head.

"She died well, I'm told. But then, they all did."

"They were heretics," Gregory said, his voice sharp.

"She was the only mother you and I knew. Does your role as a Templar not allow you to remember that, Gregory?"

Gregory opened the door. "Pay your ransom, brother. Or Langlinais will be beset with Templars." He hesitated a moment as if to give his words more import. "And Magdalene was only a whore."

The door closed soundlessly behind him.

Sebastian sat staring into the shadows. Gregory had not asked the one question for which he'd been prepared. Not with the truth, but with a carefully fashioned lie.

Where is the Cathar treasure?

The omission disturbed him.

Chapter 1

Langlinais Castle
England, 1251

Were all brides as terrified?

Her hands felt icy, despite the fact that the air was heavy with the summer heat. How odd that her palms should feel cold and wet at the same time. Juliana wiped them surreptitiously on her surcoat. The embroidered cotte she wore was too heavy for the warm weather. A veil was attached to the toque on her unbound hair; the chin band felt as if it were strangling her.

She had dreaded this day for years. She had only been five when she'd been led by her mother's hand to her father's side in the solar. The room had been hot and stuffy and crowded with people. They had spoken words she'd barely understood, about vassals and oaths and territories and land. "Do you understand, Juliana?" she'd been asked. She had nodded, and said the words as she'd been instructed. Then, she'd seen the boy there, the tall one with the brown hair and impatient tapping foot. He'd smiled at her, but she'd only scowled at him, then thrust herself behind her mother's skirts again.

6

She had not seen him again after she'd been led from the room. Only later did she learn it had been her wedding day, and the boy her husband.

At the convent she was known as the Langlinais Bride, for all that she'd never seen the castle before, and her husband only once. For most of her life, she'd lived at the Sisters of Charity, preparing for the role of chatelaine of this sprawling demesne. Years had been spent inside gray walls, waiting for this very day.

She had another name bestowed upon her by the girls fostered at the convent. Juliana the Timid. Juliana the Mouse. "*They are jealous of your position*," the abbess had told her. Ignore their words. Pay them no heed. She had never told the abbess that their teasing rang with undeniable truth. She *was* frightened of the dark, disliked the height reached even when standing upon a stool, avoided the pond on the convent property. On the journey here, she'd discovered that horses could be added to that list of things she'd choose to avoid if she could.

But it hadn't always been so. Once, she had been brave and daring. The day she'd made a face at the boy who'd stared at her. The same boy who was now a man, and the husband she awaited.

She had lived in an agreeable limbo, married but not forced to be a wife. Ten years had passed, then twelve. At a time most brides would have joined their husbands, she'd been sent word that Sebastian, Earl of Langlinais, had gone on crusade. Two years later, he'd returned. A week ago word had come, explaining that her husband had been imprisoned by the infidels, ransomed, then released. There was no further reason to delay joining him.

Her journey from the convent of the Sisters of Charity had taken no more than a few hours, the

procession of twenty men-at-arms escorting her a
show of honor and force expected for a knight's
bride, a lord's wife. At dusk they had ridden
through the gates of Langlinais. An hour ago she
had been escorted to the great hall and left there
beside the fireplace. She could hear a faint summer
breeze sigh through it now, as if calling her name.
Juliana. It was more a warning than a welcome.

The great hall at Langlinais was easily three times
larger than her childhood home and decorated more
lavishly. She traced the painted outline of one stone
block on the wall beside her. Her fingertip came
away shaded red, and she hurriedly wiped her hand
on her skirt once more. Her head was still bowed,
but she glanced from beneath her lashes to see if her
actions had been observed. Three men were setting
up tables, and a servant girl had placed a large plat-
ter upon the head table, but they paid no attention
to her.

It seemed no one knew she was here. Should she
stand and announce her presence? The idea of calling attention to herself was daunting. It would be
more fitting to simply wait until she was greeted.
She returned to her covert perusal of the hall.

She could not recognize all of the different flowers
painted on the wall. She had had little experience in
the convent gardens. Sister Helena had merely
pointed to the weeds and Juliana had obediently
pulled them from the soil.

Her skill lay in the scriptorium. Her joy there, too.
With her husband's blessing, she might be able to
continue her work here, in this new and imposing
home.

The fireplace beside her was one of two structures
in the great hall. They were built into the walls, the
stones curving over the hearth in a wide arc. Com-

fort was evidently a priority to her husband. The iron brackets upon the wall were filled with a profusion of oil lamps and candles. The night was being pushed back by such brightness. The rushes beneath her feet were clean, strewn with daisy and rose petals. *And perhaps lavender*, she thought, taking a deep breath.

A dwelling not in dire need of a chatelaine.

All of the tables, the bustle of activity, and the smell of roasting meat made her wonder if there was to be a celebration to mark the occasion of her arrival at Langlinais. If so, she would sit at the dais with her husband. She would share a trencher with him, and be expected to smile and act pleased to be married to a man she'd met only once in her life when she was barely out of infancy. He had been possessed of a kind smile and an impatience to be done with it.

Will he feel the same tonight—our wedding night?

A soft knock was prelude to the call. "My lord?" Sebastian ignored both.

He stood in the master's chambers looking west, toward a sun that had already reached its zenith and was slowly descending into night. He knew what his steward was about to tell him. She had arrived. His bride.

"My lord?" Jerard was not going to go away, it seemed.

Sebastian went to the door, braced his hand against the thick oak studded with iron braces. This portal had stood for generations, bulwark against intrusion, but it could not protect him now.

"She is here?"

"Yes, my lord."

What kind of woman would agree to the bargain

he was about to make? A question to which he'd found no answer. For months, he'd wanted to avoid this moment. Had delayed it until it would have been dangerous to continue to do so.

He'd seen her only once, on the occasion of their wedding. As her father had sat at the desk signing the documents that would pass her and her dower lands into the keeping of the earls of Langlinais, she'd peeked from behind her mother's skirts, her green eyes as bright as a new leaf. She'd had her fist in her mouth. Her mother had slapped her hand away, but it had only crept back a moment later. He'd winked at her, and like a wise little owl, she'd stared back, her eyes widening at such irreverence. Finally, she'd stuck her tongue out at him, and he'd laughed, charmed.

Their marriage had been a union of their fathers. Hers had been a vassal of his, and proud to align his family, by way of his daughter, with the Langlinais earls. Before her father left on crusade, he'd wanted her future assured, so the five-year-old bride had been roused from her nap to wed him. Sebastian would have done anything for his father, including marrying a child he wouldn't see again until she matured. The bargain had been made and the Langlinais coffers increased by her dower lands in Merton. He found it ironic that he'd had to sacrifice those same lands to the Templars in order to pay a portion of his ransom.

He'd not been so prepossessing back then, only a twelve-year-old boy. Years had added muscle to his arms and legs, and height to his frame. Would she see him as different?

He almost laughed then. Of course she would see him as changed. He would be fortunate, indeed, if she didn't run screaming from the castle.

Another knock. His summons then to the moment of truth. He opened the door only a few inches.

"Bring her upstairs." Now he would speak the words that would put into motion this great and glorious farce. What would she say? Would she be a danger or a blessing? He would know in a few moments.

Chapter 2

"My lady?" A soft voice at her side. Juliana turned and a man smiled down at her. "I am Jerard, my lady, your husband's steward. I have been sent to fetch you."

The speaker was very tall and thin, dressed in burgundy tunic and hose. One hand rested on the hilt of a short sword buckled to his waist with a leather belt. His blond hair was cropped short, framing a face that was angular and tanned, set now into stern lines. It was a face that gave her, strangely, the impression of humor. As if the serious expression he wore at this moment was forced upon him and was not his natural countenance.

Her stomach clenched, but Juliana stood, followed him through the great hall. There were people there, the sound of talking, a laugh, but other than that, she did not notice. Her attention was on her composure and the fact that her knees felt as if they wobbled when she walked.

The steward led her to the far end of the hall, where a steep flight of stairs led to a covered interior corridor.

A small oil lamp illuminated a painting of a glade, heavily forested and deeply green. In the middle of the mural, a pool shone with such glistening brilliance that she touched the wall to test whether her fingers would come away wet.

Jerard threw open the second of three doors. She reluctantly left the mural and stood on the threshold as he turned, walked to the opposite door, and rapped his fist sharply against the iron-banded wood.

"She is here, my lord," he said to the closed door.

Not your bride, not Juliana, not lady. Only she. Simply she. It relegated her to her exact position in life. The female to his male. She was only a vessel to her husband, whose contempt for her must be fierce indeed that he had not even greeted her himself, but had sent his steward to fetch her.

She turned, squared her shoulders, and entered the room. An oil lamp, its flickering flame casting shadows over the walls, illuminated the room, revealed her chests neatly arranged at the end of the bed.

The chamber was as beautifully decorated as the great hall, made bright by the white wainscoting with red roses painted above it. Juliana sat down on the bed, sinking into the thick feather mattress with surprise. Her fingers rubbed over the snowy white sheets, expecting them to be rough to the touch. Instead, they were soft, as if they had been laundered often. She stood and opened the tall chest placed against the wall. It was empty, and smelled of new wood. A bench and two chairs made up the remainder of the furniture.

It was the window, however, that captured her attention. It was not merely a narrow slit, but wide and nearly her height, topped by an arch whose stones were decoratively carved. But it was not its size that amazed her. The window was glazed with glass not the usual greenish white tint but as clear as water. When she looked down she could see an inner courtyard, its outlines blurred by darkness. During the daylight hours the sun must flood into the room. She brushed her fingers against the surface of the glass, discovered that it was still warm to the touch.

She turned and stifled a sound of fright.

A specter stood there watching her. A shadow limned in light. No, only a man garbed in monk's habit. But he seemed so tall, so broad of chest, that he filled the doorway. Indeed, he looked to be more than a mortal man.

"Are you Death?" she asked in a tremulous whisper.

"Come to judge you in your final hour?" His voice was low, a rumble of sound. Had he spoken, or had she just imagined the words? "What would you confess if I were? Or does your silence indicate a pure soul?"

Not Death then. Death did not speak in a voice that hinted at irony. She felt absurdly weak, as if her knees wished to give out beneath her.

"Are you a zealot, then?" she asked, hearing the tremble in her voice and wishing she was capable of hiding it.

"No."

His cowl shadowed his face so well that she could see no hint of his features. She clenched her hands together at her waist, forced herself to take a deep breath, ask yet another question.

"A monk?"

The words came softly, seemed tinted with kindness. "I am your husband, my lady wife."

*   *   *

Her hand reached out and rested at her throat as if to keep her heart from leaping there.

She was a stranger to him, yet there was a resemblance to the child he'd seen once before. The shape of her lips, the symmetry of her face, the color of her eyes, her hair. But whereas the child had viewed him without fear, it was all too evident that this woman was afraid. Her eyes had not veered from him, as if hoping to pin him in place and halt his advancement.

Enchantment. He should not feel it. Or a host of other emotions, all out of place for this moment: bemusement leavened with a slice of curiosity and the oddest amusement. The hand that carefully bracketed her neck, thumb and fingers splayed, was blotched with ink.

As he watched, her skin seemed to grow whiter, so fragile a hue it was as if snow had been given life. Such paleness set into relief the plump pinkness of her lips, the startling brilliance of eyes the shade of spring grass, her hair the color of a Saracen night. She blinked a few times, rapidly, her mouth fell open, her hand still touching her throat as if to measure the beats of a struggling heart.

He almost reached out with his hand, his fingers braced to feel her skin before he remembered.

He had no doubt of how he appeared to her. A frightening vision of a cloaked and garbed monk. A cleric in appearance but not in soul. His cowl had been slipped forward a few inches in front of his face, a shadow was all that anyone could see of him. The rest was covered adequately by the black wool and gauntlets crafted of leather. *Hardly a sight to reassure her, Sebastian.*

But somehow, he must. She must agree, else his future, and that of Langlinais, was in jeopardy.

*   *   *

No fire burned in the fireplace, but she wished, improvidently, that there was one. She might have turned and extended her hands toward the warmth of the blaze. Allowed some time to elapse during which she might be able to think, do something other than stare at the black-robed figure of her husband.

"Will you not sit?" he asked, and she sat heavily on the bench.

Of all the thoughts she'd had of her marriage, of all the fears and trepidation, she had never imagined herself confronted by such a vision. A man, cowled and wrapped in black, draped in the color of night with a voice that sounded like muted thunder.

Her heart beat so hard her chest trembled with it.

He sat in the corner on a chair constructed with an X for a base. His monk's habit pulled back from his arms, exposing gloved hands. He linked his hands together and folded them beneath the cloth. A gesture done so quickly it seemed second nature to him.

"I submit to you an agreement, my lady wife, about which you must decide before I leave this room."

She spread her hands at her waist, wished she could rid herself of their dampness. "We have already forged one bond, my lord, that of marriage. What other understanding would you wish?"

Silence, while he seemed to weigh her words. Was he surprised by them? She had shocked herself by voicing her thoughts. She did not often do so. It was easier to remain silent. That way, she could only be ridiculed for being timid, not for the thoughts of her mind.

Sebastian studied her. "If you will agree to pose

as my wife, you will have Langlinais as a reward."

Juliana stared at him in shock and confusion. "I am not posing, my lord. I am your wife."

"Without consummation," he explained softly. "Or hope of it."

The Church endorsed two ways of marriage, the first that of declaring "words of the future" uttered by young children. Such a marriage was valid only as long as it was later consummated. Vows considered "words of the present" could be exchanged when the bridegroom was at least fourteen, the bride twelve.

They had been put through a marriage ceremony when they were children, in order to effect a peaceful transfer of her dower lands in Merton. But by his words he was saying that their wedding would never be considered legal and binding.

"You wish me to pretend that I'm no longer a maiden." The bluntness of her speech surprised her again. She was not given to such candor. Perhaps the reason for it was simply that this meeting was too abrupt, the questioning too odd, the bargain he offered strange and disconcerting.

"Yes," he said. Simply that. No more explanation than that. Just yes.

"And if I do not agree?"

"Then you will be returned to the convent tomorrow."

He was garbed in shadows, but she had the impression that he studied her closely. "Why should I agree to such a thing, my lord?"

"Why should you not? I offer you the freedom of Langlinais to do with as you will."

She looked down at her hands. Freedom? To a villein it meant the ability to own his life. What did such a thing mean for her? No marriage bed, evidently. But what else comprised this spurious freedom he offered?

"Have you a man of letters living here? And a library, perhaps?" Her question popped free before she could think it through.

"Would you like a tour of Langlinais before you decide?" There was humor there, if only a small bit of it, a dry husk of amusement.

She stared in front of her, wishing that she was not offered a view of herself in the night-darkened window. Her toque shone whitely, her skin as pale as her headdress. She looked away. She should think on this bargain he wished between them rather than noting her appearance.

"You would have me lie about our marriage."

His shadowed face turned in her direction again. "Who would dare ask such a question of you? Who would want to know if you lay with your husband? No one at Langlinais."

"May I have some time in which to decide, my lord?"

"No."

There was no hesitation in his voice, as if this plan had been long considered and he was impatient with her participation in it.

"You wish me to choose this moment?"

"Yes."

"To be a wife without knowledge of her husband?" She clasped her hands tightly in her lap.

"Yes."

"Or return to the convent?"

"Yes."

Would he say nothing more? Give her some reason? Or was she simply to be content with his assent? Yes and yes and yes.

"Why will there be no true marriage between us, my lord?"

Her hands twisted together, a habit she thought she'd outgrown when she was a little child. She'd been cured of it by having her hands tied behind her back. She no longer twirled her hair around her finger either, another habit she'd been weaned of when one of the nuns had simply cut her hair to within an inch of her scalp. She had cried for a week, but she'd never adopted the habit again, not even when her hair had finally grown back to its former length.

"I regret that I cannot answer your question," he said.

There, a few more words from him, but not an answer.

She looked down at her hands. If she returned to the Sisters of Charity, she would forever be a wife without a husband. She knew neither of them could have their marriage annulled. To do so it would have to be proven that they were related closer than the fourth degree or that each had submitted to the marriage against his consent. They had both been children, eager to please their parents. Nor was there any relation between them. Only one of service; her father had been a loyal vassal to his. Yet, surely her marriage would be set aside if he did not wish to bed her? The laws governing such things were not known to her, but she doubted that her life would be made better by the simple dissolution of this marriage. She would simply be wed again, her dower lands taken back and given to another man. The fact that she had been wed to her father's liege lord meant that the king would have to adjudicate such a thing. Timid Juliana, petitioning the king. Where would she find the courage?

At the convent she would be able to do her work

again, but only within the confines of gray walls, subject to a regimented schedule. At Langlinais there would not be the tolling of a bell. She would not have to wake before dawn and retire at dusk. She would not ever have to weed a garden again.

She studied him in the silence. "*Who would ask?*" he had said. Indeed, he may be correct. She might never be forced to seek the king's counsel or to lie. In fact, a life here might well be a blessing.

"Whatever decision you make now, my lady wife, cannot be repealed." It seemed an ominous warning.

"Are you certain you are not an ascetic?" she asked softly.

For a long moment he didn't answer.

"An ascetic?" Was he discomfited by her question? "You believe me to be a penitent, then?" His voice oddly toned for a man. Too deep and yet soft. As if he'd not used it often enough and was just now becoming accustomed to it.

"It is the only thing I can imagine, my lord."

He looked away, the deep cowl pointed in the direction of the window. "I wear no hair shirt, and my attire is for one purpose only, but not that of self-abasement. If anything, circumstance has done that to me." He jerked, as if startled by his own words.

"Were you wounded in the Holy Land, my lord?"

"You must not do this, you know," he said, his low voice sounding almost kind. "You are trying to find explanations where there can be none."

"But I do not understand."

"I know that." His words were soft, almost sorrowful. "And I cannot make it more clear, Juliana."

She looked at him, startled. It was the first time he'd said her name. It had never seemed so lovely before, a word comprised of rolling syllables. It flowed from his mouth like a brook might tumble over round and polished stones. She flushed and looked away, surveying the chamber so obviously meant to be hers. But not shared. Alone. No man's hands would touch her. For that alone she should not fear him, and yet, he was perhaps the most fearsome man of any she'd met.

He offered her freedom. But it was too much a gift, one dappled in sunlight and extended on a plate of gold. Why did he do it? Was he incapable of siring a child? She felt her cheeks warm. Too many questions, after all, and he sat waiting for the answer to the most important one of all.

Would she pretend the union? A strange request from a bridegroom she did not know, a husband wed for so many years but seen only once.

He stood and moved to the other side of the window, on the same side of the room as the bench upon which she sat. They were close enough to touch.

A sweet smell seemed to emanate from his clothing, a hint of cinnamon. She wondered if he carried the costly spice in the little silver ball at the end of his corded belt. He was not the man she'd fashioned him to be. She knew him less now than when she'd entered the great hall.

Word had spread of his exploits, the number of tournaments he'd won, his father's death, his own departure for the Holy Land. Even the convent had not been exempt from tales of Sebastian of Langlinais.

Before today she'd imagined his appearance, had taken the knowledge of his exploits and paired it with what she knew of the world, rendering him almost solid in her mind. He would be strong. Knights must be, in order to carry a lance and armor and sword. He would be tall. The boy she'd seen but once had seemed to tower over her. He would be handsome. Again, that young man who'd grinned at her had been graced with a flashing smile and a comely face.

She had created a rich and detailed picture of her husband. Except that he had rendered all of her thoughts oddly black, muddied them with the reality of his presence. The man who stood beside her hinted at mystery and secrets she might not wish revealed. There was something about him that cautioned her not to explore further, something buried in his softly voiced words. She knew, without testing the point, that he would not answer any more of her questions.

It would be safer to return to the convent, to live among the nuns and do her work. It would be wiser to heed these currents she felt in the air, the hint of danger and the lure of a voice that made her tremble.

She stood, certain she would refuse him. Sure of it. They faced each other, strangers united. She opened her mouth to speak the words to refuse his strange bond, but the words would not come. The ghostly echo of girlish voices taunted her for her lack of courage, her fright at the click of branches against the roof, a looming shadow. Into the silence came their laughter, the echoes of their derision. As she stood watching him, she remembered all those times she felt frightened. Had it been in preparation for this moment, this decision?

But she could not remain Juliana the Timid forever. Her life had been measured by her fears. Was her future to be limited by them? She was, after all, the Langlinais Bride. She straightened her shoulders, determined this once not to be afraid.

"I will remain, my lord," she said, and somehow managed a smile.

Chapter 3

A short woman in a deep blue surcoat over a pale yellow cotte bustled into the room within minutes of Sebastian's departure. Her immaculate white wimple accentuated the roundness of her face, her friendly brown eyes set into the wrinkles there.

"I am Grazide, my lady. I have been assigned to be your attendant."

Juliana was not used to having someone wait upon her, but she smiled.

Grazide busied herself unpacking Juliana's trunks. "My lady, I have never seen such beautiful work." She moved the oil lamp closer to the gowns strewn on the bed, the better to examine the workmanship.

"The convent is renowned for its embroidery, Grazide. I am fortunate in that my father was generous in providing for me."

"I would wish to be half this talented, my lady." Her look was rueful. "But then we cannot all be bluebirds, can we? There are some among us who must remain sparrows."

Grazide's comment prompted a smile. Her next actions, however, shocked her. The woman untied the linen binding of her toque and removed it from Juliana's coronet of braids, then bent and gathered up the material of her surcoat and began to drag it over her head.

Juliana's protest was nothing more than a small whimper, but she jerked back the material, clutching it with tight fists.

Grazide frowned in confusion. "My lady, you must change from your journey."

"I can do it myself."

"If you wish, my lady," she said, but at the same time she jerked the wadded cloth from Juliana's hands. "We shall work together." She smiled a bright and friendly smile.

Juliana felt like a leaf in a gale.

"We have been waiting for you, my lady," she said as she pulled the cotte over Juliana's head. "It's been a long time since the castle was blessed with a young couple. Why, the last was when my lady was alive and she's been dead these many years. Sir John—he was the lord's father—was an old man when he died five years ago."

The discarded cotte was placed gently on the bed. "Langlinais is a beautiful place, my lady. I am sure you will enjoy it here. Why, our lord is the kindest and most generous overseer. My own son was allowed a trade and now acts as carpenter for the castle." She ceased her talking only long enough to ask Juliana which garment she preferred to wear. Juliana pointed to it.

"And the celebration." Grazide's hands fluttered in the air. "Well, everyone has been invited. All fifty of the people assigned to the castle. There are to be jongleurs and musicians, my lady, and a feast to rival anything in Sir John's time. Oh, those were the days, Lady Juliana. We had a celebration for almost any occasion. The grandest was when Sir John knighted his two sons." She sighed, placed her hands upon her hips, and stared into the air as if to witness the grand event again.

The respite of silence did not last long.

"But I fear those days are gone. The lord does not encourage visitors to Langlinais. He keeps to himself. But you can always find him atop the east tower, looking down on us." She smiled and shook her head.

By the time Grazide finally helped her into her clean cotte Juliana was suffused in blushes. The cloth felt cool against her heated skin. She had not been naked before another person since she was five and tended by her mother.

"Nothing happens at Langlinais that he does not know of, from the number of hens laying to the roofs needing new thatch. But, he was always that way, my lady, being concerned as he was for his people. Well, at least he was when he stopped being so wild. They were well doted upon, he and his brother. Neither was sent away to foster, no doubt because so many children had been lost before those two came of age." Grazide sighed. "Their own father taught them how to be knights, and there were many girls in those days who would find reason enough to be near the quintain when they were practicing."

Grazide set a circlet upon her hair, stepped back to admire her handiwork.

"But it's time you came to Langlinais, my lady. I think, sometimes, that he is of too serious a nature. A new bride is just what he needs. I know this may sound odd, my lady, but he might be too devout. We rarely see him, other than to view him on the tower. But I know he spends a great deal of time in the chapel."

The agreement, only an hour old, lay like lead in

Juliana's chest. Had he lied, then? Was he indeed a zealot?

She stood, allowing Grazide to fasten the sleeveless train to her shoulders. The embroidery of scarlet-and-gold flowers was so stiff the garment could stand without support.

"You look like a princess, my lady," Grazide said. She smiled at her, evidently pleased.

In a matter of moments, Grazide was gone, and the room blessedly silent. Juliana sat on the bench in front of the window, the train folding stiffly as she sat.

She was dressed for the celebration to be held in the great hall below. There, the lord and his new lady would accept the congratulations of the villeins, the castle knights, those dignitaries and guests invited for just such a momentous occasion as this. Would he come to escort her? Or would he simply allow the speculation as to their absence to grow? Would lusty ballads be sung about Sebastian of Langlinais and his impatience to make valid his marriage?

Juliana looked toward the bed. What was the reason her husband would not bed her?

She wished, now, that she had never read Ovid's *Ars Amatoria*. She had told herself it had been to prepare for her wedding night. Instead, the poem on the art of love had only added to her questions. So, too, the other ancient poetry she'd read and marveled at, that such words could stir the senses even after so many years.

Come to me, beloved, and smile at me. For sweet is the turn of your lips. Place my hand upon your chest that I may feel the life of you, and sigh with it.

The oil lamp was pitiful comfort against the night. She walked to the window, looked down at the garden. A torch was stuck upon a stand and illuminated a walkway. Light and music, add to that a tincture of laughter and the night welcomed the reveler.

It was a taste of loneliness she had not expected. Something in this odd bargain she had not considered, after all.

It would have been so much easier if she had simply been left at the convent. There, she'd been allowed to spend an hour a day in the scriptorium, and on rare but special occasions was able to coax the abbess into a game of chess. In the convent, men were not required. Women did not wonder about love. Or be afraid at the hint of mystery.

It would be somehow fitting if she sat alone in the night and contemplated her future. But she was Juliana the Mouse and afraid of the dark. She returned to the bench and wished the oil lamp was brighter.

Sebastian knelt in the chapel. One lone candle resting upon the stone altar softly illuminated his figure. His head was bowed, his forehead against the wooden rail that surrounded the sanctuary. His arms were outstretched, hands tightly gripping the rough-hewn wood. His coarse monk's robe of black wool extended past his wrists and pooled on the stone floor.

Behind him the small chapel was empty and silent. The sound of laughter beyond the iron-studded door was the purest irony. A celebration to honor the union of the Lord of Langlinais. But they would never be truly joined.

The wood cut into his forehead, splinters sliced into his skin. "Please," he said. Nothing answered him. There was no response. God was silent. So too, his creatures. The owls that nested nearby were solemn and mute. If a mouse made its home in the

Langlinais chapel, its presence was not noted.

The cowl lay on his shoulders, his face bare. Only the shadows, deep and comforting, protected him from prying eyes. He bowed his head again, forced into humility not by faith or devotion but by a despair as wordless and deep as a night sky.

For what should he pray? Absolution for the sin of killing, even in the name of faith? For the sins of the flesh? Or for once enjoying them so heartily? Perhaps he should pray only for death, oblivion rendered fast and just. A swift end, like those he'd meted out in battle. This was nothing less than war, wasn't it? One fought in solitary, with Death on one side and him on the other, the adversaries so unevenly matched that the outcome was certain.

He had always been able to hold Death at arm's length. With each passing day, the distance lessened a hairsbreadth, until one morning he and Death would stand nose to nose and Sebastian would inhale the nothingness of his own breath.

But he did not wish to meet his old nemesis crawling and weeping and grateful for his appearance. He had ridden into battle with no more than a moment's thought to terror. He had stood with sword raised high in both hands and planned when to deliver the fatal blow. That is the way he would have preferred to die. Not this way.

"Please." A guttural plea.

Both fists gripped the altar rail, his head was bowed in supplication. He was no martyr, no believer in suffering for the sake of his soul. Yet, was it not for the sake of his soul that he was here at all? A soulless husk would have ended his life long since. He could have fallen upon his sword or simply marched into the sea, his chain mail weighting him down. He could have availed himself of poisoned mushrooms or a hundred plants that promised sweet dreams with no awakening. Or thrown himself screaming and cursing from the east tower.

It was too late to regret that he had not done so. Too late to wish he'd never seen his wife. Seen Juliana.

He crossed his arms and leaned his face against them. The wool scratched his cheek. Sensation. He would lose that. His days were measured now, carefully marked against the loss of feeling. Each morning he awoke and tested himself, the stroke of a finger against the cloth of his sheets reassured him that he could still feel. One day, he would begin to note the difference. On that day, he would leave the world he knew. A few years later, he would let it be known that he had died. A mysterious death, one that would leave Juliana protected without the taint of rumor to mar her future. A virgin widow.

"Please," he said once more, and this time his prayer was not for himself, but for the sake of the young woman he'd summoned to his side. He wished her shielded from the sight of him, protected from the might of the Templars, guarded from harm.

It was a small thing to ask, in view of his greater prayer.

Chapter 4

The soft knock upon the door made Juliana sigh and long to ignore it. The morning had been so peaceful, filled with occupation. Grazide would be like a verbal whirlwind in this calm. But obedience had long been instilled in her and was not easily ignored. She called out, and the door opened slowly.

Spread before her was the horn in which she stored the ink she'd already prepared and two sheets of parchment, one still attached to its wooden stretcher. The original of the encyclopedia she was transcribing was cradled reverently in her lap. She had promised the abbess she would finish her work on the Chronicon. In the trunk were various leather pouches containing her ink, the powder that created the blue color she used for her illuminations. She had no vermilion and could not, therefore, write the name of God since it could only be inscribed in red. Therefore, she would leave the gaps for the word, so that the abbess could complete the manuscript.

The true light from the large window in her chamber was glorious. Her only dissatisfaction was the fact she had no proper surface upon which to write. A scribe's desk needed to fit certain requirements, none of which was met by the few pieces of furniture in the room. Therefore, she did the only thing she could in order to continue her delicate work. She sat on the floor and used the flat-topped lid of her trunk.

The abbess would not have caviled at her posture, nor at the fact that the costly embroidered gown she wore would likely be damaged by the rough wood floor. The abbess had often forgotten her own role in favor of her cherished occupation.

"Juliana?"

She turned her head, her gaze traveling from his boots to the top of his cowl, a lightning journey considering his height.

"Are the chairs not to your liking?" His voice, deep and low, shivered through her.

She set aside the encyclopedia and stood.

He bowed his head, seemed to study her belongings as they lay scattered on the floor. "You did not tell me you were a scribe, Juliana. Is that why you wished to know if there was a man of letters here?"

She folded her hands together. "Hildegard of Bingen was a scribe, my lord, a very famous one. There have been women of great talent all throughout history, although their names have often been removed from their manuscripts."

"You defend where there is no need. But tell me, why were you sitting on the floor?"

"I required a surface on which to write."

He turned, and walked through the doorway, then halted and turned back to her. "Perhaps there is a solution," he said. "Will you come with me?"

Juliana followed him to where the hallway made a sharp angle. At the end was a door she had not noticed last night.

Even her childhood home had not boasted of a

separate floor of private chambers, and an internal pentice. Most dwellings had a covered external passageway that joined chambers. In winter it made the traveling from one place to another miserable, but at Langlinais there was no need to be subjected to the elements. Also, here each chamber did not lead into one another, but to a hallway. It was privacy to a degree she'd never imagined.

"It is an oriel," he explained, opening the door. "We have no priest," he said, "but the room was originally constructed for his use."

"Is there no mass at Langlinais?"

"We have no priest," he said again, offering no further explanation.

Nor did she seek one after she'd peered into the room.

The oriel possessed a stillness that was sure to guarantee her future contentment. He removed the iron bar across the shutters. The morning sun streamed into the tiny space from the archery slit. But that was not the greatest delight. Stretching from wall to wall, a distance of no more than four feet, was a great oak timber, planed to a smooth finish and placed so that it would act as a perfect surface upon which to write.

"Will this be acceptable to you?"

She nodded, still in awe.

"It is high enough that you might sit on a stool, Juliana."

"I have never had such a place, my lord. Or such a desk upon which to write. Not even at the convent."

"There must be some compensations for living at Langlinais."

A reminder, then, of the bargain between them. She looked up at him, just now noticing how close he was. The small oriel seemed dwarfed by his presence.

"I will send Jerard to help transfer your writings and tools," he said suddenly.

He left her then. Only moments later, Jerard appeared with her trunk and a stool from her chamber. Still another trip provided her with all the items she'd left strewn on the floor.

The steward helped her to unpack all of her supplies, stack them neatly upon the shelf. He asked no questions, but she could see that he was curious.

"My inks," she said, when he handed her two small leather pouches.

"It looks like dust."

She smiled brightly. "It is, until it is mixed with water. My favorite ink is made with wine as an ingredient."

"Do you like this? Being a scribe?"

"Yes," she said simply. It was her only talent and her greatest joy.

What she did not say was that she had not known what to do with herself this morning. She had been beset with questions. Should she leave her chamber? Remain inside? If she had truly spent the night with her husband, would she have been changed in some way that would be visible to others? There was no one of whom she could ask these questions. Only a husband might know, and he had made it clear that he would never fulfill that role.

Therefore, trapped within her chamber by a ruse, she had sought comfort in those things familiar and normal.

She left the oriel and returned to her room. Her husband was there in the middle of the room, standing beside her bed. When she entered, he turned, the gloom of his attire made even more somber by the light from the window. He did not belong, this shadow, in a room brightened by the sun.

"Why did you seek me out, my lord? Was it to change your mind?"

"No, Juliana."

She looked away then, her hope extinguished. Yet, for a moment, bright and fevered, it had existed. A union with this stranger would have been a daunting thing, but one of less mystery than the agreement he wished between them.

She had expected to end her maidenhood last night, had feared the intrusion of a husband's touch. She had spent days dreading the idea of lying beside a stranger and having his hands on her. He had the right to do so, to kiss her, and know her body even more intimately than she did.

Surely it was not disappointment she felt?

He pulled the sheets back from her bed, dislodging the careful way she had tucked them in, pulled them tight. She might be the Lady of Langlinais, but she'd been taught to see to herself. Servants were for those who were infirm or aged, and she was neither.

He opened a small vial and held it over the bed. She watched as the blood dotted the sheet, stood in silence as it soaked into the mattress.

"Is that necessary, my lord?" Her cheeks warmed as comprehension dawned.

"There must not be any question of the validity of our marriage, Juliana."

She had no response to that. Only too many questions, none of which he seemed disposed to answer.

Chapter 5

By the second week at Langlinais, Juliana's routine was established. Her days began at dawn, when she was roused, not by the clamor of a bell, but by gentle stirrings as the castle began to awake.

Grazide drew the water for her morning wash, and was then banished from the room while she dressed. She had accomplished Grazide's removal only after days of being suffused in blushes. Her true embarrassment had done what her words could not. After she dressed, Grazide entered the room again to braid her hair. This morning she was as voluble as ever.

"Oh, how very pretty you look, my lady," she gushed. "Just like the lady should appear. Will you and the lord be joining us at dinner this eve?" Her look was comprised of a measure of hope and what passed for subtlety with Grazide.

Juliana never knew how to respond to such pointed questions, one of which she received each morning. Most times she found refuge in silence.

"Well, perhaps he is too busy being a bridegroom, my lady." Grazide tilted her head and smiled at her, a look of speculation on her face.

"I would not be surprised if he was a rogue, my lady. As a child, he was ever so. One time he and Gregory went hand over hand across the river bridge. He and Gregory nearly drowned when they both fell into the rushing water. Why, I remember how upset Magdalene was when she learned. She boxed their ears and sent them to bed without their dinner."

"Magdalene?"

"His father's concubine. A lovely woman, she was. And why she turned down the old lord's offer of marriage, I'll never know."

Grazide tucked in the braids at the top of her head like a coronet. "After he died, poor thing, she left for her own homeland." Grazide bent her head around until she could see Juliana's face. "She was French, you know."

"Who is Gregory?"

Grazide laughed. "Well, I can tell you two haven't had time to talk much. Gregory is the lord's only brother. Not that there weren't plenty of children at first, bless all their little souls. And his mother's of course. Poor thing died giving birth to another son. But they were all lost for one reason or another." She patted Juliana reassuringly on the shoulder. "But we've no reason to think that will happen to you, my lady."

Another statement Juliana had no comment for, but as usual, Grazide didn't seem to expect one. It was doubtful if she could have remained silent long enough to hear it.

"He and Gregory were always trying to defeat the other at some game or some such. Where one was, the other could be found. In fact it was because of that the lord broke his leg."

"Why do you never speak of Sebastian as an

adult, Grazide? Even at the convent we'd heard tales of all the tourneys he'd won." Indeed, it had been the single bright spot in her life. A paradox that the man she did not know could bring her such fame. The other girls at the convent had whispered about him, had asked her questions about her husband, and had acted oddly disappointed when she refused to speak of him. What could she have told them? That the man they spoke of with such girlish awe was also a stranger to her?

"Indeed, my lady, he is a great warrior. But those days of his tourneys were sad days, too. With his father so ill and him away and Gregory having left home to find his fortune, there are more sad memories than there are happy ones." Grazide's hands stilled on the crown of her hair as if she stared off into the past. "Perhaps it is just that I like to remember the good times, my lady, when he was young and so, too, my little Ned. Both grown to men now." She patted Juliana's shoulder again. "But what am I saying? The good times are here again, are they not? And you and the lord will fill the castle with children." She smiled brightly.

The truth, however, was that there would never be children at Langlinais. Not hers, at least. Juliana stood and dismissed Grazide, the pleasant moments of the morning having abruptly dissipated like fog.

She entered the oriel and closed the door behind her. This tiny space provided the only comfort from the questions that ate at her.

Juliana discovered that it was no great feat to pretend herself blissfully wed. There was no one, after all, she needed to convince. Everyone assumed she was pleased to be the wife of Sebastian of Langlinais, to be living in such a beautiful place. There were no duties she was expected to perform, no acts as chatelaine. There was nothing about the castle that was lacking, nothing that required her presence or her participation.

For hours she was allowed to do what she loved, existing not as the ultimate barter by her father, for the glory of the convent, or the use of a husband she did not know.

She had been told by the abbess that she was a good student. To please her, Juliana had studied even harder. The abbess was a woman of great talent, who believed that knowledge was to be shared; therefore, Juliana was allowed to read any of the manuscripts in the convent's possession. Consequently, her education had strengths and weaknesses. She was well versed in the Latin poets and philosophers, but less so in contemporary thought and not at all in Greek.

The great thinkers wrote of ignorance and knowledge, love, and morality. But they rarely dwelled upon happiness. None of the writings she'd read had spoken of joy, so intense that it could alter the mind and make pure the soul.

Juliana, for all her youth and seclusion, had known moments of pure happiness. The seasons gave her pleasure. The perfect song of the first robin of spring, the sound of a frog croaking on a summer night. A flurry of wind breathing through the leaves of a shedding tree. The first snow. All these moments of bliss had been encapsulated in her mind, to be extracted on those days of punishment when she knelt before the altar or was forbidden the scriptorium. She became adept at isolating those moments that pleased her the most. She could place a perfect moment into her memory simply by closing her eyes and pressing her fists to her chest and saying to herself, *"This, this I will remember."*

Her days in the oriel were like that, memories she would never forget.

The parchment lay blank before her, the sun illuminating the fine grain. She'd prepared it herself, scraping the hide, then liming, and then scraping it again. There were to be no hairs present on her writing surface, no signs that it had not been prepared correctly or that she accepted less than the best effort from herself.

There was something about the blankness of a parchment not yet touched, the emptiness of it that stirred her imagination. The words had not been copied, no illumination colored the page or attracted the eye.

One day, perhaps, she would work with gold. She imagined what it would be like to lay the gold leaf upon a blank page, pressing it into the fibers of the parchment. Then, slowly, the part that would need to be colored would be scraped away. She'd never had the opportunity to work with gold leaf, it being as expensive as the vermilion ink only the abbess was allowed to use.

In a moment, her own ink would be cured enough to start, the color changing from clear to a pale blue. It would be coaxed three letters at a time from the quills she'd prepared from duck feathers. On the parchment, it would first show blue, then gradually darken to black. Then, the words she transcribed would be set to permanence.

On each initial letter of a new chapter, she left her mark, a small drawing of herself. She was not blond and delicate, but the girl in her glyph was. Her own hair was as black as a sinner's heart, her eyes such an odd shade she'd been teased about the color since she was a child. Each time she drew the small girl, hanging from the tail of a Q or sitting upon the crossbeam of an A a smile accompanied her work. Perhaps leaving her glyph upon such important pages was a vain thing to do, but it was the only signature allowed her. In such a way scribes had, over the centuries, left a vestige of themselves in the work they did. This way, if her marginal notes were obliterated, there would be a trace of her remaining in the books she'd laboriously copied.

A sound interrupted her reverie, the soft stroke that comprised the capital B. She halted, quill suspended, not over the parchment in case a drop of ink marred the surface and made her erase all her day's work, but over the shallow earthenware dish set aside for such a purpose.

How long had she been working? She stared straight ahead, noticing the view before her for the first time. Rolling hills and a hazed valley. From her perch in the oriel, the height did not look as frightening. But it was evident the day was well advanced.

She blinked, just now aware of the ache between her shoulders. Thanks to Jerard she did not feel an answering twinge in her lower back. The stool on which she sat had been trimmed to the exact height. She stood and stretched, flexing her fingers.

Then, as she did every day, she took measure of her supplies, noting that her reed quills would need to be replaced soon; two of them were becoming frayed. One of her parchments curled on the corner, either from dampness or improper scraping She would rectify that tomorrow. It was the supply of ink that concerned her the most, however. If she did not begin a new batch soon, she would find herself having to wait until it was cured in order to work.

Tomorrow morning, then, she would begin her search of supplies.

Would each day be as sweet as the one just passed? If so, she could bear her marriage well.

Chapter 6

Sebastian stood and walked to the arched window that overlooked his demesne. His chamber was identical to Juliana's, the only difference being that his window was neither glazed nor as wide, since it overlooked the countryside. It would be foolish to expend so much money on something that could easily be destroyed in the defending of Langlinais. Even though the castle had not seen a siege in more than two hundred years, it was difficult to forget that they lived in a lawless era, in tumultuous times.

It was his favorite time of day. The birds were still; it was that hour before dawn when the sky had lightened but the sun had not yet made an appearance over the horizon. This morning the mist had vanished, leaving behind a clarity to the air that was usually found only after a heavy rain.

His home had been a lodestar, a goal he'd thought about all those long lonely months he'd been imprisoned. His father gone, his mother long dead, his brother in the service of the Templars, there had only been himself left to guard and protect Langlinais.

He had been wise to send Jerard back to England

after he was released. His squire turned steward had proven as loyal to his home as he had been to Sebastian. It had been Jerard who had kept Langlinais prosperous during his imprisonment. And when the time had come to return home, Langlinais had sat like a white beacon upon the landscape, welcoming Sebastian as if he had been whole and strong and worthy of the title lord.

He tucked his hands within his sleeves, turned toward the east to watch the sun begin its journey over the hills of Langlinais. Another ritual, this. One that marked the tenor of his days. He watched the unfolding panorama with appreciation born anew each morning.

To his left was the small village. Before it, a common pasture, a mill, and sheep fields. A few strips of land had been set aside for the villagers. The people who lived there were accountable to him just as he was responsible to them. It was for both his sake and theirs that he'd put into motion the plan to protect this world. He would not have it compressed and held tight in the fist of the Templars. The warrior-monks would banish his people and occupy his home. Unless he stopped them from coming.

Today the fields would be weeded again. The thistles had not been cut before Midsummer Day in the belief that they would grow back threefold if pruned too early. It had become a custom in the village to mark the day with a drawing of straws. The winning boys would circle the fields with blazing torches, in order to chase away dragons. He doubted any of the villagers truly believed in the long-tailed, fire-breathing creatures. It was more likely they simply enjoyed the celebration. The next to come, however, would be September's celebration of the harvest. Until then, there were backbreaking weeks ahead as the hay was gathered, then the rye and wheat.

The people of Langlinais would bring his portion to his granaries with great fanfare, the occasion marked with solemnity. And he would send Jerard to meet them and thank them on their lord's behalf. They would remember when his father entertained them with stories of the Crusades, when there was ale and red wine in abundance, when the occasion of the tithing was a ceremony replete with song and dance and merriment.

His father had been a fierce man, one who had added to the family's wealth by winning countless tournaments over the years, ransoming the armor and horses won or simply selling them outright. Yet, he also had a reputation for fairness. He had married well, a woman of Poitou, and had brought to his home a great thirst for a dynasty. But of the eleven children he'd sired, seven of them sons, only two were alive when he'd died, and neither at his bedside.

They had not been fostered out as was customary. John of Langlinais had told his sons once that he believed himself the only one capable of guiding them correctly. "You were young lions," he'd said. "Why would I subject one of my friends to your presence?" Their duties under their father's watchful eye had been heavy, the days long for a dual purpose. First, to teach them all the duties in which they must be proficient, then to give them a taste of humility.

Sebastian smiled, thinking of his father's proud grin the day he was knighted. He had been twenty, eager to test his prowess in battle. Even more eager to see the world. He had, and returned to his home with this secret, one his people had not yet discovered.

His father had died not of a broken heart as much as an aged one. Even though the effigy carved upon his tomb reflected the customary appearance of a man of thirty-three, John of Langlinais had been sixty-eight when he'd died.

And Sebastian had been in Paris, unaware.

A furl of movement in the corner of his vision distracted him. He turned his head and saw her. His bride walked toward the east gate, a basket in her hand. She wore neither toque nor wimple, only her hair braided in a coronet. Her stride was long, one that decreed purpose and destination in each step.

A woman who had charmed the residents of Langlinais, if Jerard was correct. She rarely gave orders, treated everyone with the same degree of kind bemusement, as if surprised at their presence. She involved herself, he'd been told, almost wholly in her work.

He watched her, grateful for the distance between them. The morning breeze cavorted around her ankles, swirling her skirt playfully, delineating the shape of her legs beneath the fabric. Did she think to leave him? Leave Langlinais? A small smile ridiculed that thought. How, Sebastian? Equipped with a basket and nothing more? His curiosity was piqued, even as she pushed open the gate and entered the forest.

The basket had been found in the buttery. It was not exactly what she needed, but a cursory examination had not revealed any spare jars or crocks. She would have to improvise, but then she was used to doing so. The Sisters of Charity were a parsimonious lot. Having taken their vows seriously, they not only begrudged waste, but were often without the rudimentary supplies needed in a scriptorium. But Juliana had found that being poor could be a very valuable experience. She never wasted parchment, and she could brew at least three colors of ink. It was a rather heady feeling to know that, at least in these two instances, she could do for herself.

The gatekeeper was fast asleep, leaning against the high wooden fence, his neck at an odd angle. Old Simon had given her a small carved wooden cat as a welcoming gift to Langlinais. She smiled and tiptoed past him, closed the gate with a small click, and headed into the woods.

At the base of a venerable oak she stopped, circled the trunk for several minutes, inspecting the ground. She moved off to a second tree, then a third. At the fourth she found what she needed. She began gathering the oak galls, piling them into her basket. She could boil acorn caps, but it was the oak galls that would produce the kind of ink she needed, the blue-black mixture that wore well and did not fade.

She bent and retrieved another gall and placed it in her basket. She was lucky to have found a tree so infested. Otherwise, she would have had to strip the bark, an action that could sometimes damage a tree. She chastised herself for her slowness. The quicker she finished this process, the quicker she could begin her work again.

He told himself that it was foolish to be here. But she was not inside the keep, and he was infused with curiosity about this woman circumstance had made his wife. He stood in the middle of the oriel with his eyes closed, scenting the air like a wolf seeking its mate. Roses. Faint, as if the breeze blew the scent in from the window. But it came from a woman who perfumed herself.

She was tidy in the arrangement of her tools.

There was a pile of quills, some carved and ready, some not yet curved to the necessary point. A small saucer held a drop of drying ink, a horn the powder that produced it. In the center of the space was a book bound in wood, its worn leather hinges testament not only to its age but its use. Next to it, a piece of parchment, half the page completed, the letters carefully inscribed.

He had learned to read the way he'd done most things as a boy, with a great show of reluctance and a secret joy. Magdalene had taught him Latin and Greek and his numbers, so that he would need no scribe to write or read for him. But more than that, she had made his lessons interesting. He'd discovered that he loved to learn, enjoyed exploring the abilities of his own mind.

Why did he think of Magdalene so strongly right at this moment? Because she had been a woman of learning? Or because she would have felt the same as he did now? Impressed at the skill of the writer who had transcribed the words on the parchment before him.

He did not touch anything, merely lowered his hand, covered in a leather gauntlet, until it was only an inch from those implements Juliana used every day. It hovered there as if to absorb the warmth of a hand not present, touch a finger that would lightly press against the parchment the next day.

A sound, no louder than a brush of wind, stilled his movement. He breathed silently, each sense alert to danger. Too many years had been given up to survival not to be alert. Even at Langlinais.

He should have moved, left the room, but he did not. He wondered, later, if he had deliberately ignored the warning in order to see her again.

She entered the room in a rush, but abruptly halted at the sight of him.

The moment was ripe for apology, for telling her that he had not meant to startle her, or to satisfy his curiosity so overtly. But his words were muffled by his own sense of wonderment. He had not imagined her, then, nor made of her something she was not. Too tall to be considered delicate, too brightly colored to be called a lady fair. Still, she reminded him of spring. Or perhaps something more elemental. Her hair was piled in braids atop her head. He wanted to see it tumbled to her shoulders, a mass of untamed, ebony curls.

"Why were you in the forest?" The question slipped from his lips before he knew it was there, yet curiosity was the safest of all the feelings he had at this moment.

Her eyes opened wider, as if she was surprised by his knowledge of her movements. Both her hands moved to grip the handle of the basket tight, as if guarding the slab of lichen inside.

"I was harvesting oak galls," she said. Her voice echoed with a soft quaver. Shy? Or terrified? More like the latter. He had not become less frightening with a second glimpse.

"And what is an oak gall?"

She glanced up at him. "The egg of a gall wasp. Laid in the bark of an oak tree. The gall forms around the egg."

"For what purpose do you want such things?"

She looked down at the basket. "To make ink." She extracted one from beneath the lichen. It looked like a small ball of bark with a protrusion on one end. That was not what fascinated him. It was the visible tremor of her fingers. She *was* frightened, even now.

"What do you do once you have them?"

"Boil them. Then add a quantity of wine, and just the right amount of rust."

"And this ink is stable? It does not change color?"

"Only at first, my lord. But once on the page it remains stable." She did not raise her head as she spoke, but seemed to address the basket.

He turned to leave. It was a kindness he did her. Once, women had smiled at him, had coaxed him into their beds and occasionally into their hearts. He had taken for granted the ease with which he'd enjoyed the carnal sports, the utter delight he'd taken in mitigating his occasional loneliness in the soft willing flesh of a compliant woman. He would never have it again. Memory would have to serve. Or like now, conjecture.

"Have I done something to displease you, my lord?"

He turned. She was looking at him, her green eyes wide and bright.

"Are we to behave as strangers? If we cannot be man and wife, can't we at least be friends?"

"Friends?" he asked.

She took one step toward him, so slowly and hesitantly that he had a chance to move away before she came closer. He did so, even as he damned the necessity of it. Her flush told him she'd noticed the gesture.

"If nothing else, my lord, can we not converse from time to time?" Her words stumbled to a halt. She looked down at the floor.

"You wish to talk with me?" The idea was so novel that he wanted to tip her chin up and see her face again, read the truth of her request in her eyes.

Her nod was a sharp little acknowledgment.

"Is there no one you've found to be your friend at Langlinais?"

"People cease speaking when I enter the great hall," she said. "Or else they wish to serve me."

"This displeases you?"

"I do not feel comfortable with such constant subservience, my lord."

"Yet you show the same to me." She glanced up at him, surprised. "My name is Sebastian."

Silence, while she stood there, mute. He was too patient. He should have left the room, but instead, he questioned her further.

"Are you not afraid of me, Juliana?" Unbidden, his curiosity bobbed free again.

She straightened, but he was aware that her grip upon the basket was even tighter, so punishing he could see the whiteness of her knuckles.

"Yes," she breathed. "I am."

"And yet you would converse with me."

"It is just that I am not used to such solitude." She moved, then, a small step. Not toward him, but away.

"Do you not converse with Grazide?"

"Rather she talks at me, my lord—Sebastian," she said, correcting herself quickly. She looked up then. It was the first time he'd seen a ghost of a smile on her lips. It made her beautiful.

Unexpected amusement quirked his lips. "She has not changed much, then, from the spirited girl I remember," he mused aloud. "If such a thing were to happen, what would we discuss?" He directed the question to her.

Her expression was too open, too vulnerable. He wanted to tell her that the question did not warrant such a look of gratitude. He had not yet decided if making a companion of her would be merely kind or absurdly foolish.

"Are there acceptable topics I should proffer?"

"The weather," he said, without a pause. "And politics, because I enjoy a good argument. Aristotle's *Logic* and *Metaphysics*. Averroes and Maimonides, Charlemagne, the shocking Eleanor of Aquitaine, or even Saladin."

"I've no knowledge of most of those names. Will you tell me about them? All and everything?" She looked down at the floor again. "If we did talk together, that is."

Why was she so timid? What had changed the daring child into the shy woman? A question he should not have asked himself, because it softened his intent, banished his reserve, made him curious in a way that was unwise.

"I will consider it, Juliana," he said, the words pried from him by conscience. In truth, it would be wiser if he did not. He left the room, wondering if her gaze followed him.

Chapter 7

He dreamed of her that night.

The vision and the truth were so tangled in his mind that he could not easily discern what was real and what was only his secret wish. But she visited him in the moments before dawn, a woman of intent and gentleness. He did not, even in his sleep, think to send her away.

She sat on the edge of his bed, her hand cool against his brow. Such a delicate hand, her fingers long and tipped with softly rounded nails. There were ink stains upon her fingers, and she looked away when he commented upon it, smiling. He reached up and allowed his hand to cup her cheek, turn her head back so that her gaze met his. Even in the darkness, he could see the soft flush that enveloped her cheeks, the faint smile tipping her lips.

"Do not be embarrassed. Will you begrudge me my scars?"

She shook her head, then reached over to place her hand upon his chest as if she claimed him as a prize. A possessive gesture, one that he acceded to when he placed his own hand upon hers, pressing down on his skin as if to emblazon her touch, her mark, on him.

In the way of dreams, he could wish and it was made true. Her kiss was that of a woman who yearned to learn her mate, yet had the touch of an innocent still. Her tongue traced the line of his lips, her mouth opened to invite his gentle assault. Her soft murmur enchanted him, led him into the darkness of her kiss. A heady potion, her joy and innocence. An even more addictive brew, her skill and gentle teasing.

The night made her a delicate sketch of charcoal on white, snow and shadow, only faintly graced with a pale rose of cheek and nipples and lips. Even her eyes were dark, shining with emotion.

She knelt beside him, and pushed the sheet off his body. Her fingers traced his battle scars in gentle remonstrance and tender anointing.

The light that surrounded her seemed crafted of a moonbeam. A gentle hue, it seemed designed for Juliana. His night sprite. She bent and kissed his chest, and he shuddered, his flesh never before so sweetly caressed.

She drew her hand down his legs, lingered upon his knees. Then, suddenly she was kneeling between his outstretched legs, her hands running from knee to thigh in a teasing, delicious taunt. For nearly two years he'd felt such hunger to be touched, as if his very skin starved for it. She seemed to know it, pressing her palms up in long strokes, trailing the backs of her hands down as if to acquaint herself with every ridge, every indentation, every muscle of his body. Both of her hands pressed down upon his stomach, then fingers played as they danced lower. He arched upward, yearning for the tender stroke of her fingers in a way he could never articulate.

"Sebastian." Her mouth uttered his name. He wished she would say it over and over, she mouthed it so beautifully. She made of his name something heroic, a pledge of honor. His dream request was granted and she bent closer to him, the ebony waterfall of her hair brushing over his face in a touch as soft as a spider's web, his name on her lips invoking passion.

He was adrift in the cloud of her, sweetly pained and nearly sobbing with gladness. She inhaled his breath and gave him back hers in exchange. Her own sigh echoed his, yet she was him and he was her in that way of dreams.

She was white moon and dark shadow, a creature of the night come to tempt him to forbidden joy. Even her scent acted upon his need, his senses so attuned to her it was almost pain. Whereas he was forbidden and restricted and denied in his waking state, he was allowed and encouraged in this blessed reverie.

His hands, talented with a sword, with the instruments of war, were now imbued with the effortless grace of a lover. His fingers trailed across her skin, each separate and distinct touch causing a shiver in their wake. She was over him now, her head arched back as he cupped a breast in his hand, his thumb brushing its peak. He beckoned her closer and she held herself over him, no longer virgin as much as temptress. The taste of her nipple in his mouth, hot flesh against his tongue was too real to be crafted from mist and need.

She was suddenly around him, over him, enveloping him, the hot passion of her almost as consuming as the words she whispered in his ear, the sound of their names, a chant of desire and repletion in one breath.

His heart beat so loud and so strong it seemed to create a hollow in his stomach. His blood raced and his mind lay dormant. He knew the taste of her. The scent of her was in his nostrils, her soft cries rang in his ears. He became her in that instant, or perhaps it was simply the way of dreams, especially those devoutly wished and forever lost.

Then, it was over. It ended not with satiation, or even physical release. She simply disappeared. One moment she touched him, giving life to all those unvoiced wishes and secret thoughts. The next she was gone, and he awakened abruptly to a room silent in the hours before dawn. Yet he could still hear her voice, that sweet whisper when she spoke his name. It seemed to spiral down into nothingness, a whispered entreaty. Or was that his own cry? In his chest was an odd feeling almost like emptiness.

He sat on the edge of his bed, certain that sleep would not come again this night.

He walked to the table that served as his desk, sat and studied the accounts he kept so diligently in the light of the oil lamp. It was always kept burning, protection against moments such as these when night was too cloying and the walls too close.

Langlinais boasted two stewards. Jerard worked to ensure his orders were followed, Sebastian arranged for the purchase of supplies and calculated the profits gleaned from all his holdings. He did so first to keep himself occupied. Most men hunted, or spent their time in tourneys or as guests at various demesne. But he could no longer be seen among people. His only safety was at Langlinais. The castle was not open to the casual guest either, and while willing to lend the traveler a place in the stable, no stranger was allowed within the great hall. But it was not to stave off his boredom that he knew everything about Langlinais, every coin spent or expended, every profit made. It was because he needed to know, in finite detail, the state of the Langlinais finances, the better to attempt to save his home.

His midnight perusal of the figures did not alter the sum. Even with a good harvest, he would have to petition for more time to repay the balance of his ransom. It might well be a decision that proved unwise. The Templars did not grant extensions without punishing interest. Yet, he wrote the letter, trapped within his responsibility as aptly as he was his body.

The night teetered along on thin legs. At times like these, when he could not sleep, he normally went to stand atop the east tower, carrying a torch to signal that all was well to the men-at-arms in the bailey and aligned on the walls below. They had become accustomed to his shadow, as he sat there for hours, his view of the countryside steeped in darkness.

But instead of going to the tower, he found himself at the door of Juliana's chamber. It was too close, only across the hallway. And at the end of the corridor, a door that led to the chapel. How convenient, to have his soul's nesting place so quick at hand. He should be there, not here.

If he opened the door and went inside, it would be an intrusion as invasive as the visit to the oriel. Yet, he pushed open her door, wondering as he did so if Grazide slept within the chamber. He stood on the threshold, listening, his senses attuned to darkness as if he were a creature of night. There was only the soft sounds of breathing, a hand sliding across a sheet in sleep. But Grazide was not there.

The room was shaded blue from a cloud-covered moon and smelled of roses.

Sebastian stood at the end of the bed, his gaze upon Juliana.

Her hair was a black stain across her pillow. She was curled on her side. A fist rested against her lips, her other hand splayed open upon the sheet. As he watched, her breath seemed to hitch and release, as if she gasped in her sleep.

He'd had no choice but to summon her. He had been excused the delay in claiming his bride by the simple fact he'd been on crusade, and had subsequently been captured and imprisoned. But after he'd returned home to Langlinais, it would have incited suspicion not to have sent for her. As it was, almost a year had elapsed before he'd done so.

She had no idea how vital her role as his wife was, how important her decision to stay had been to him.

She had smiled. In the oriel. A small, sad smile such as one who grieved might wear. That smile had twisted something inside him, something buried and long dead. Or at least he had thought. Her smile, merely an upturn of lips, had sparked it to life again. Urged it to fruition, to completion.

Longing.

They should not have released her from the convent, not an innocent such as she. She nearly had her newborn down upon her cheeks, so naive, so tenderly young she was. It hurt to witness such purity, to be in the same room with it.

If he could pay the remainder of his ransom, then Langlinais would safely be in her hands. One day in the future he would simply remove himself from the world. Juliana's presence would be his safeguard. While they could take Langlinais from him, they could not wrest it from her.

He had given no thought to the woman he would use as his pawn. Yet, now he regretted that he had not considered her. Juliana was too young to be used in this game, too innocent to mingle with players who had long since lost their naïveté and their kindness.

She had trembled before him. Yet, she had stood her ground. An intriguing woman. In another time. Or another place. Perhaps only in his dreams, where his passion was given full rein.

What manner of woman makes ink at dawn? Who looks eager when speaking of rust and wine? Who walked with a jaunty step and bore ink stains upon her fingers. Who smelled of roses and asked if he was Death in a voice that quivered. Who touched him in his mind in his sleeping hours.

He wished he had never brought her here.

Juliana waited until the door closed again and only then did she breathe deeply. She'd slept heavily all her life, but had done so among the company of other girls. Night was not so much a quiet time as it was one of muted sounds. Sister Etherida's snores, the dreamy murmurs of a sleeper, the movement of a body upon a mattress stuffed with hay, a sound of disgust as an old, flat pillow mimicking a brick in softness was pounded into shape.

Nights at Langlinais were filled with silence, as if the great hall and the family chambers were muted beneath a soundless cloud. For this reason, she stirred often and rested less well.

She had known it was him immediately. He did not blend into the shadows as much as he commanded them. Was it just the effect of the monk's robe he wore, or was he truly as large as he appeared?

Her heart still beat wildly, a rhythmic boom no less loud than the sweep of ocean to the shore. She'd seen it on the journey to the convent so many years before, had been transfixed with the crash of waves upon the rocks, and the thundering sound of the power of the sea. Now, her heart sounded much the same.

She could not remember a time in which she'd been so afraid and curious and stirred by pity all at one time. The fear was easy to understand. She was afraid of the circumstance. The curiosity, too. Why had he decreed their marriage to be so strange? The pity she felt because he was so obviously set apart from others. But why?

He had stood silent, a figure shrouded in a black monk's robe. His only ornament a knotted rope. Had he even been real, or just some nightmare from which she had awakened?

When she had first seen him, she'd truly thought him Death, had half expected him to extend a bony finger through the sleeve of his robe and accuse her of all manner of transgressions, most of which she'd no doubt committed. She was convent-bred but too flawed to be as holy as the sisters who'd taught her.

A hint of his face had appeared in the opening of his cowl. Not a spectre, after all, but a man. A face garbed in graduations of color, from black to the barest gray. A strong nose, a firm mouth, a chin that looked to be too stubborn. She could well imagine that face covered with a helm, his body garbed not with a monk's habit, but in armor and tabard, a sword raised high.

She pressed her hand against the cloth that covered her breast, felt the tremor of her heart as it gradually slowed. Perhaps it had been awakening quickly from a dream that had been charming and sweet.

She had not spoken to him. She was more familiar with the solitary communication of the written word. Perhaps if she'd had someone in whom to confide over the years, it might have been easier to remark upon his presence, to question him about it. *"Go to God with your cares,"* the abbess had said, dismissing her wishes for a friend with a compassionate smile but little empathy. Juliana might, if she had known how, asked of his travels in the Holy Land. Or broach more of the questions that sat at the tip of her tongue. Why had he not summoned her earlier? Why was he dressed as he was? Why would he never touch her?

She clutched her pillow to her chest and stared up at the ceiling. Sleep seemed as far away as the answers to her many questions.

Chapter 8

Sebastian turned as the door swung open, and reached for his gloves quickly. Jerard knew his secret, but Sebastian did not wish to bludgeon him with evidence of it every day.

"You look fierce, Jerard."

"I have spent the better part of the afternoon, my lord, arguing with two men." He placed a small carved figure upon the table. Sebastian picked it up, studied it carefully. Old Simon had captured Juliana perfectly in wood.

"Am I to infer that one of your arguments was with Old Simon?"

"The man is stubborn, my lord. I found him asleep again. He sends this to you as an apology for his actions."

"He was always doing so to my father. My brother and I had a legion of knights Old Simon carved." He looked up from his study of the figure. "As long as there are outposts stationed on the hills surrounding Langlinais, it does not matter if he sleeps. Let him. He is an old man, after all. Who else has incurred your wrath?"

"The miller. He wishes his grinding stone replaced."

"Is it necessary?"

"I think the man plays a game," Jerard said with a twist of his lips, "by removing the old stone and setting up his own mill with it."

Sebastian smiled. "He is a man beset with ambition, then. Approach him about it, Jerard. Tell him that we will sponsor a second mill if he will train two boys from Langlinais in his trade. Even an ambitious man must have apprentices."

Jerard frowned. "Do you think he will agree?"

"If he does not, then at least he knows we are aware of his plans."

"I would just as soon banish him, my lord."

"For all your threats, you would not do so. In the years I was gone, I do not believe you banished a single villein."

A ruddy stain appeared on Jerard's cheeks. "It was a time of great uncertainty, my lord. We did not know when, or even if, you were coming home. All of us worked together."

"Then remember those days when those such as the miller begin to vex you, Jerard. It is why men who have fought together become such good friends. A common goal will link even strangers."

Jerard sighed. "I will try to remember, my lord."

Sebastian turned and looked out the window. A long silence while neither spoke. Jerard was occupied with unloading the tray containing Sebastian's noon meal. Sebastian, in turn, was adrift in his own thoughts.

"Do you think it's time I exile myself, Jerard?" He turned.

"No, my lord," Jerard said, his gaze meeting Sebastian's. "It is not yet necessary."

"Yes, but is it wiser?"

"Why do you ask me such things, my lord?"

"She wishes to converse with me, Jerard. To share my thoughts. Is my wife that lonely, do you think?"

"I do not know, my lord." A small shrug emphasized his words.

"Has she made friends with any of the women of Langlinais?"

"In truth, my lord, she is as fixed in her work as you are in yours. I think being a scribe means a great deal to her."

Sebastian had determined the same.

"Are you worried about her becoming ill in your company?"

"It is one of my very great fears, Jerard."

"It will not sicken her, my lord, else I would have succumbed long ago. What harm can it do to spend a few hours with her?"

"It was your stubbornness that made you test that theory, Jerard." He softened his words with a smile.

"Perhaps, my lord." There was an answering smile on Jerard's face.

"Do I appear different to you, Jerard? Different from other men?"

"I do not know how you wish me to respond, my lord."

"With truth and honesty," he said. He held his arms away from his sides. "When you see me as I am, right at this moment, would it appear as if I have a secret to hide?"

Understanding came with a smile. "It does not yet show, my lord. There is nothing that would give her a reason to fear you."

"It is an idiotic thing to contemplate, Jerard. I know this."

"Perhaps some things are not meant to be thought of, my lord, but only acted upon."

"Companionship may well be the worst thing we

could share, you know." He turned back to the window. "I find myself liking her, Jerard."

Sebastian had watched her walk around Langlinais, talking to the people she met. She shared her dinner with no one, seated at the dais with a small smile at anyone who looked in her direction. Somber Juliana, who stopped and petted all the castle dogs and who had made friends of the cats who wandered through Langlinais.

Would it be better if he hid himself away now? Simply to disappear into his solitude? But not yet, surely. The need was not there, yet. *Better now, Sebastian, before your inclination is not to leave at all. Before you are completely charmed and intrigued.* It was already difficult to accept his future. What if it became impossible?

Her hair became dislodged from its sturdy braid by evening. Delicate tendrils framed her face and, more often than not, there was a smudge on her cheek, an indication that she had worked on her encyclopedia for most of the day.

If he was careful, she would never discover his secret. And he knew too well that he could never touch her. But he would want to. He knew this, being a creature of curiosity, being a man who loved learning. He had been tutored in the art of love as a boy of thirteen, had read in Albertus's *On the Secrets of Women* that it was a man's role to give a woman pleasure and had taken that to heart at a young age. He had, of course, continued to gauge his skill throughout his youth, marking his tournament victories with conquests of another, more feminine, sort. His years in Paris and Italy had not been celibate ones.

He found himself wanting to know how her laugh

sounded, what she dreamed about, if she had wit as well as intelligence.

Could he bear it? That was more to the point.

It was an improvident thing to do, to plan on this torture. How could he believe himself exempt from need? He had not touched a woman in too long, let alone one to whom he was bound by God and ceremony. One with skin the color of the palest blossom, whose lips were soft and full.

He'd been shaken at her appearance the morning he'd gone to her room. Light had surrounded her, and she'd sat encapsulated in it, reading the Latin words of her encyclopedia with lips that moved softly.

He would not touch her, his honor and his soul were in jeopardy if he did so. But to sit near her, to converse with her, to smell her scent on her skin and not simply the memory of it lingering in the air, these things seemed necessary. More so, perhaps, than prudence or wisdom.

He would ask her what was her favorite book to transcribe, what were her favorite colors. She could show him how she made those glorious colored inks that colored the frontispage and capital letters. He might, if he were brave enough, tell her a little about these last few years, enough that she would garner the flavor of them, but not enough that she might understand the whole.

He would learn all the nuances of her voice, soft and barely audible as it was. He might see her smile again, or hear her laugh. Had she laughed since coming to Langlinais? Such a solemn creature, his wife, with her serious green eyes, and her full mouth pressed into a prim studiousness. She was an ardent student, an eager learner. Yet, she had acted too much like him, aloof and apart from others.

What would she be like as companion? And was he a fool to want to know?

Chapter 9

"You do not let much disturb you, do you, my lady?" Jerard asked.

She raised her head, blinked a few times, then smiled at her visitor. The oriel was a quiet place, but even so she'd not heard Jerard enter.

"I am very careful. Such things take attention."

"That is why I waited until you moved your hand," he said.

"Thank you. Most people would not have noticed."

"I spent many years as a squire," he said. "Such duties inspire one to notice things others dismiss."

"To protect your lord's back?"

He smiled. "That, and to shine his armor and shield, mend his lance, ensure his horse does not go lame. A thousand duties that a squire must do before he is told. The punishment, otherwise, is not pleasant."

"Were you flogged, Jerard?"

"My lord has a way of looking at you that is worse than a blow, Lady Juliana. I almost wished he would strike me sometimes. It would have been easier than disappointing him."

"I had an abbess who was the same. She had a

67

way of sighing that made my bones ache all the way through."

They exchanged conspiratorial smiles.

"My husband is a man beset by secrets, isn't he?"

"I could not say, my lady." His smile changed to become that infuriating one that warned he would say nothing further.

"I was given something to convey to you, Lady Juliana." He handed her a small silver coffer, an elaborate pattern inscribed on its rounded lid. She opened it slowly, then stared at its contents. It was as if Sebastian had wished to add to his enigma by giving her this odd gift.

Jerard stared down at the box of rusty filings she held in her hand. "Is this something that pleases you, my lady?"

"Yes," she said slowly. "I find that it does."

He left the oriel, which was just as well. Jerard made the small space seem even tinier than it was. But then, Sebastian was larger. But she had rarely noticed how the room had appeared the times he'd entered it. Her attention had been too distracted by the man.

She stared down at the coffer in her hand. It was small enough to fit within her palm. A strange gift. He had remembered the recipe for her ink. She closed the silver box, held her fingers tight over it. Had he touched it? Was the warmth she felt in the metal from his fingers, or from the tightness of her own hold?

Reluctantly, she returned to her work, placing the box in the corner, where she could readily see it. She worked through the midday meal, waving away Grazide when the maidservant would have coaxed her to the great hall. She was determined to finish the Q she had begun nearly a week ago.

The room darkened as she worked, until she realized it was not a cloud over the sun that obscured her writing, but the fall of night. She laid the parchment page to the side so that it might dry completely and poured the ink she had not used into a small bowl. It had darkened too much to be of much use. Mixing ink was more complicated than simply pouring a few ingredients together. Gauging when the time was right to use it was just as important. A pale ink would fade too quickly; one too black would eat through the parchment itself.

She closed the door to the oriel, was walking to her chamber when she heard Sebastian's voice. Curious, she dropped her hand from her door and walked to the end of the passageway.

She placed her palm against the iron-banded wood. The words seeped through the door and into her heart. They summoned her like a child's weeping in the dark. *Intellige clamoren meum.* Know the cries I utter.

She hooked her thumb in the latch, pushed upon the door. It swung open silently. Since it was so dark in the corridor there was no show of light to betray her presence.

The door she opened was the family entrance to the chapel. She'd discovered it the first morning after her arrival at Langlinais. A carved wooden arch led to the altar, above it a large window shaped in the form of a flower, its petals crafted of opaque green glass, now black with night. Upon the white-draped altar sat two lit candles, but no chalice and plate. There were wall hangings depicting biblical scenes, a stone floor painted burgundy and strewn with rushes. But the four sets of benches that sat behind the altar in two rows were not adorned with cushions; nor was there any other sign of wealth.

She moved into the room, pulled the door half-closed behind her. Four fluted pillars supported the roof, domed and strutted to support its pitch. She moved to one side, so that the column did not obstruct her view of the altar.

Sebastian knelt there, head bowed. His words were repeated over and over. "*Sustinui qui simul contristaretur, et non fuit; consolantem me quaesivi et non inveni. Intellige clamoren meum.*"

She'd never heard of a prayer that beseeched as it demanded. *I hoped that someone would weep with me, but there no one. I sought someone to comfort me, but found no one. Know the cries I utter.*

She should not be standing there listening to a man's prayers. The thoughts of a soul verbalized. What she did was invasion of the greatest sort, an intrusion between God and supplicant. Yet, for a long moment she did not move, transfixed by the aura of grief and despair that permeated the room.

For what did he pray?

Her lips echoed the words of the Latin chant he spoke. Moments later, there was another sound, that of a fist striking wood. She jerked, startled. An oath, clear and pure as the morning call of a sparrow, echoed in the room set aside for worship. She clasped her hands together at her chin, her knuckles pressed against dry lips.

A brave woman would go to him, kneel at his side. That woman might even ask him why he prayed the way he did, with entreaty and condemnation coming in one breath. She would place her own fingers against his lips or kneel beside him in anxious prayer in order to beg forgiveness for him. Cursing was a terrible thing to do in a place consecrated to God.

She might yearn to be a woman of fearless courage, but the sad truth was that she failed abysmally at the role. She stepped back as if to press herself into the wall.

A soft sound escaped her. A sigh, perhaps her own prayer. It was not loud enough to be heard, especially by Sebastian, ardent as he was with his own pleas to heaven. Yet, it must have been, because he stopped speaking. A pause in time, in which nothing moved, no words were said. All sound simply ceased, everything but the beat of her own heart and her own barely felt breaths.

Her fingers trembled at the edge of her lips. The silence grew upon itself, one moment maturing into two, then three.

Sebastian stood. He turned, slowly, as if wishing her gone before he looked. As he did so, he pulled the cowl to cover his face again. Not soon enough. Not nearly soon enough. She had viewed him clearly by the light of the candles.

Once, she'd seen a Roman sculpture, found when a farmer was plowing his field. The villagers had brought it to the convent, in hopes that the abbess would be able to tell them if such a thing was valuable or if they should destroy it. The statue, nearly life-size, was of a young man attired in nothing more than a winged helmet. He stood with one leg in front of the other, a hand resting on a thrust-out hip, the other hand behind his back, holding a small orb. The face had been strong, almost insolent. The lips curved and full, the nose proud, the brow broad. High cheekbones descended to a chin softened from sharpness by the hint of cleft. It was the face of a man who, despite his youth, was well aware of his power.

A face not unlike that of Sebastian of Langlinais.

She had prepared herself otherwise, had thought

him wounded or somehow deformed or scarred. She'd not thought him to be beautiful.

They stood staring at each other in silence.

He'd promised her Langlinais, but he'd given her confusion. She was left with endless questions without answers. And now he stood before her unmarked. Another mystery, another riddle.

"Go away, Juliana," he said softly, his voice strangely kind. "Now."

Chapter 10

Every moment of Juliana's life at Sisters of Charity had been precisely regimented. There were bells to mark the hours and the occupations therein, there was the soft entreaty of a sister in charge of a certain duty, the rhythmic chant of Latin as a call to worship.

She was expected to adhere to the rules of the community, even though she was only fostered at the convent while awaiting the summons from her husband. She was watched as closely as any novitiate. All such characteristics of form and self that hinted at waywardness were to be modified or expunged. She was not, for example, allowed beyond the convent gates for any reason. Nor was she allowed in the garden simply to appreciate the scent of growing flowers. Her hour there was set aside for weeding, not for idleness. She had known such regulation of her life that it was odd, if not a bit discomfiting, to experience the sudden freedom of her position as the Lady of Langlinais.

"I feel like walking," she announced to Grazide that afternoon. Instead of protesting, the other woman simply nodded, never ceasing her conversation with the other attendants. Juliana stood there

73

in the great hall, disconcerted. She had marshaled her arguments for her privacy only to have them be unnecessary.

She removed her toque, left her hair in its braid. Her surcoat was light enough that she would not swelter in the heat. The afternoon was bright and still, the drone of a bee was the only sound she heard as she left the great hall. The Terne flowed in a swift movement below the south wall, the gentle breeze rippled the water and cooled the air. From where she stood, she could see the expanse of Langlinais as it curved in a half-moon shape, its walls following the undulation of the river.

She had known only two homes—the one in which she'd spent the first five years of her life and the convent. Neither had adequately prepared her for the castle of Langlinais.

She had discovered in the last weeks that her chamber overlooked the kitchen garden. Its beauty was not merely ornamental. There were fruit trees and huge plots of herbs, in addition to a pond stocked with fish. The flower gardens boasted all sorts of flowers, most of which she didn't recognize. But she knew the poppies, roses, heliotropes, and violets.

She took a deep breath. The air was warm and seemed colored with scent.

Langlinais was always filled with people who appeared to go about their occupations with enthusiasm and few signs of laxity. The young girls who weeded in the kitchen herb garden, the laundress and her helpers, the smith's apprentices, the kitchen workers, all of them appeared industrious and each of them had a ready smile for her as she passed, even though they did not speak. There was not one cross word heard, and if there was criticism doled out, it was the type one friend gives to another in laughing jest. Indeed, laughter was the prevalent sound in the courtyard and bailey, not the muttering of complaints. There was no fear here, no sullenness, only the sound of contentment and from time to time a song joined and carried through the summer morning like the gentle breeze over the Terne.

The path she followed was laid with crushed stone, glittering yellow-brown in the sun. A bee darted in front of her, flew away just as quickly. The air was warmed until it seemed heavy, perfumed by the scent of blossoming flowers and long grasses. The walls along the river were covered with green lichen. She wondered what color it would produce if coaxed to ink.

She smiled at herself. Even now, she could not refrain from thinking of her work. Or of Sebastian.

She'd had a friend at the convent for a short time. Anne had been sent there before her wedding, to learn of such things as the nuns could teach her. She'd been thirteen years old and destined to wed a nobleman. She and Anne had shared, for a few weeks, one of the small stone rooms. Set aside from the rest of the dormitory by a stone wall three feet high, it was a secure place for two giggling girls. Enough that she and Anne had lain awake, sharing their thoughts and fears of marriage.

They had decided that life as a married woman would be a wonderful thing. They had gone so far as to conjecture what their wedding night might truly be like, imagining where there was only mystery. Anne, the young bride, had been wed a long time by now, while Juliana had not yet been taken to wife.

Nor would she be.

She did not understand. How many times had she

thought that in the weeks she'd been at Langlinais? Too many. So far, the extent of her life at Langlinais was the beauty of being able to work all day long in her tiny scriptorium balanced by nights of confusion.

At first, she'd thought her husband one of those men who mortify the flesh as a way of worship. Then she'd reasoned that he must have been wounded in the Holy Land, or badly scarred. But the man she'd seen had been so perfect in face that she'd felt almost shamed to be in his presence. Her own lack of grace seemed to scream at her as she'd left the chapel.

Then what was the reason he wished no true union? Was there something about her he disliked?

She rarely considered her appearance. Vanity was not an attribute at the convent. As long as she was neat and tidy, she was considered acceptable. She was not supposed to know about her body, even her bathing was to be done in the dark, but she supposed she was curved in all the correct places.

Was it her birth? True, her father had not been noble, but he had owned property, and had been a loyal man to the earls of Langlinais. She had brought her dower lands to the Langlinais coffers, and a history of a family that dated prior to the Normans. And if her status had been objectionable, then why had Sir John agreed to the wedding?

Surely Sebastian could forget her appearance or her birth and concentrate upon her personality, instead.

She attempted to be kind, although in truth she found refuge in silence when she could not think of a proper response or a temperate word. She was no healer, but she disliked the suffering of others and aided them where she could. She'd sought out Sister Beatrice and had assisted her in the building of wicker cages for her wounded birds. She believed she was intelligent and she did not think she was of a mean-spirited nature. Was that not enough in a wife?

As to skill, she had only one. She looked down at her fingers. There was a dark stain upon the side of her thumb and another at the tip of her index finger. Regardless of how much she scrubbed her hands, they seemed permanent. The Lady of Langlinais should not be so slovenly.

She could immerse herself for hours upon hours in the thoughts of others. The words spoke to her like the purest notes, a melody made of discourse. She felt that her duty was one of importance, to transcribe these remarks diligently, without adding her own beliefs or interpretation. In this way, she contributed to the world's store of knowledge; she made available to one more person learning that had not been there before. When she'd finished, and written the words *Explicuit*, on the last page, it meant more than "the end." It was the passing of a trust. Surely, that ability was worth something? For that skill, could he not forgive her any other faults?

What color were his eyes? It had been too dark to see, and the child she'd been had taken no note of them. And why, as long as she was wondering about Sebastian, did his voice sound so rough and then so smooth, as if callused and pumiced in one breath? Why did it have the power to make her tremble?

It did not seem quite right to think of him so much, especially since he'd repudiated her so ably. Not only by proscribing their marriage, but by moving aside when she would have touched him, or drawn too close.

Had she made the right choice by remaining at Langlinais? By agreeing to this marriage? What other choice had she? A whisper of her conscience warned that she trod too close to a lie.

For once, she'd wanted to be brave. Now, it seemed, she wanted more. Above all, she wished that all the questions that had begun from the first moment she'd seen Langlinais would be answered.

She was in the lower bailey, now, where the largest of the Langlinais towers commanded the view. Lord Henry's tower it was called, from the first earl granted the property two hundred years ago.

"My lady," Jerard said. His voice startled her, so rapt was she in her own thoughts. He had evidently followed her and stood waiting at her side, his face solemn, his eyes bearing that eternal watchfulness that marked him as loyal and silent. She stopped.

"My lord has asked that you join him, Lady Juliana."

Such simple words should not make her breath halt in her chest. But it was the first time Sebastian had ever summoned her. She continued walking. Jerard did not pressure her, merely kept pace at her side.

"It is a large place, Langlinais." Did Jerard know that she was delaying answering the summons? It appeared he did from the small smile on his face.

"When the keep was given to the first earl, it was very small." he said. "Each earl has added to the castle, my lady. The great hall and barbican were the province of the second earl. The next finished the wall that follows the Terne. Still another added the chapel. My lord's father raised the roof of the great hall, added the family quarters."

They passed through the gate that separated the middle from the lower bailey. She was slowly retracing her steps.

"And what are the masons doing now?" she

asked, shading her eyes with one hand as she watched a group of workmen huddled around the base of the north tower.

"There is always construction of some sort at Langlinais, my lady. They are repairing the foundations of the tower."

The gatehouse loomed before her. A few more minutes and she would be back at the great hall.

"What shall I tell him, my lady?" he asked a few minutes later.

There was no way to delay any longer.

"I will attend him, of course. In his chamber?"

"No, my lady. There." He pointed, and her gaze followed his finger. Up to the top of the east tower, where a black-garbed figure stood. Was he watching them? Had he been watching her all this time?

Fear shivered through her. Mixed with it was another emotion. Anticipation, perhaps. Would he chastise her for coming into the chapel? Or explain, finally, why he clothed himself in a monk's robe and hid himself away?

Jerard did not speak as he led her to a door at the base of the tower. He said nothing, but then, what could he have said? Sebastian was her husband, after all. He had summoned her, and she would come. Men went to war and endured battle. Women were protected and held safe and, for that, were expected to be obedient. It was the way of the world.

Chapter 11

The door revealed an endless spiral of steps that led to the top of the tower. They were not wide, and there was no handhold to grab on to, only the curve of stone blocks as they wound up and up to what seemed to be heaven itself.

Her heart was beating so hard she felt herself shake with it. Her knees trembled, as if they would collapse beneath her at any moment. The initial courage it took to mount the first circle of steps quickly disappeared. By the second, she was certain she was going to tremble to pieces. *"Come down from there, child. You will fall to your death."* Voices from the nuns, from her childhood. An ominous warning that she had no doubt would come true in the next few moments. By the third circle of steps, the only thing that kept her proceeding upward was the fact that it was less frightening than beginning the descent. There was, at last, a handhold. No more than a roughened brick with a worn groove along its length, she gripped it and lifted herself the short distance to the wooden floor of the tower.

At the top, Sebastian did not extend a hand to her to help her up, nor did he seem to notice her presence. She, however, viewed the scene around them and stepped back, nearly falling into the hole of the stairwell.

He turned and watched her, but did not approach. Ah, there was a lesson learned then. He still did not wish to touch her.

"Are you unwell?"

"No," she said, leaning up against the merlon and closing her eyes. She made no move to change her position. "I do not like heights," she confessed.

"Then, why do you come to the top of the tower?"

She raised her head and looked at him. The monk's cowl did nothing to shield his face from view. Or was it simply that she knew it now, and could place nose and eyes and mouth where shadows had before only hinted at features? "You sent for me."

He pushed the cowl back from his head, leaving his face bathed in the sunlight. His eyes were blue. No, not simply blue, but the blue of her ink, just before it changed to black Their look was solemn, but such an expression did not detract from their beauty. Or his.

From this position her view was only of the battlement itself. Sebastian, however, stood too close to the edge. As she watched, he sat upon one of the crenels, his back to the countryside. What would he appear to any who saw him? A huge crow? A pennant? Anything but Sebastian of Langlinais attired in a monk's robe. Was he oblivious to the danger of his perch?

"I would not have asked you here if I had known your dislike of heights, Juliana."

She looked away. From her vantage point, the merlons blocked her view of the countryside, even though she could see well enough through the opening of the crenels. The best view was of her fingers.

The sight of them did not make her stomach lurch.

"This is my favorite place at Langlinais. Perhaps because I can view the entire demesne from here. Or maybe it is because of the year I spent encased in a cell. Some days I cannot bear the confinement of walls."

She sat upon the tower floor, tucking her legs beneath the fabric of her surcoat. Sitting down eased her fear somewhat by hiding the view.

Time seemed to slow as they looked at each other. The sight of his face had the same effect on her as being so high in the air. Maturity had added strength to his face, the delineation of muscle and bone. There was no softness there, no hint of gentleness. A warrior's face. But still arresting. Almost beautiful. Her fingers longed to trace the line of his cheekbone to see if it was that defined or only shadows made it so. And his lips. Should a man's lips be so alluring?

She glanced away, her face heating at such thoughts.

"I thought you scarred, Sebastian. And shy with it." She spoke to the merlon rather than to him. It was easier, somehow.

"You have a great deal of curiosity, Juliana. It stands a scribe in good stead."

"But not a wife?" She turned back to look at him.

His smile was bright yet fleeting. One moment there, the next gone, his face left somber. "Why do you dislike heights so much, Juliana?"

His face was strong and compelling but not unkind. He had asked her a question to indicate that he had no intention of answering hers. The husband she'd feared had been transformed into a handsome man who sat opposite her dressed in the garb of a monk, a small smile playing over his lips. Was she simply to accept his appearance without explanation? Never question him or their odd marriage or the reason for it? It seemed she was, a determination she made in the silence that stretched between them.

"Must one have a reason, Sebastian? Can some people simply not be born with a medley of fears? A man can be born with brown eyes, another blue." She traced the mortar between the stones with one finger, not looking at him.

"And some are brave and others are cowards?"

"Yes," she said, nodding emphatically.

"Yet I remember a child who made a face at me and stuck her tongue out very rudely."

She felt her face warm. "I didn't."

"Oh, you did," he said, smiling. "Enough for me to think you were not timid at all. What happened in the intervening years, Juliana?"

"I don't remember sticking my tongue out at you, Sebastian. I may have frowned a bit." She looked down at her hands. "I was not that rude."

"The child I met wasn't rude. She was daring. It was her wedding day, after all."

She met his gaze, then looked away.

"Did you know there are sixty-one instruments of good works? Abbess Gertrude reminded me of at least twenty of them. I was not to hold a grudge, nor give way to anger. I was to honor all, and patiently to bear wrongs done to me. But in all honesty, Sebastian, I found it difficult."

He did not ask inane questions, but sat there waiting. He seemed to know that the telling of this particular tale was difficult. She'd not repeated it to anyone since it had happened. Even now it seemed odd to do so, as if she disobeyed some celestial dictate.

"A few months after we were married I was sent

to live at the convent. It was chosen, I believe, because of the proximity to Langlinais."

"You were only five years old." His voice sounded absurdly kind. He must not be, or she could not finish this tale. She could hardly bear to think of that child.

"My mother had just died, you see, and I was underfoot. My father wanted to go fighting, and my brothers were all fostered. It was probably the best thing."

"For him." There was a note of disgust in his voice that made her smile. She was not the only child who was unwanted and sent to live with others. At least her father had arranged her future by contracting an advantageous marriage. Even if the deed had been prompted by ambition, it had still benefited her.

"I was lonely, I think, and probably a nuisance to the older girls."

"What did they do?"

"They locked me in the bell-tower."

She glanced over at him. There was an expression on his face that was not at all difficult to read. It was anger, and its presence seemed to warm her heart. Or perhaps it was the heart of that little girl of so many years ago.

"I do not remember going there. Or even why. All I can remember was that it was dark in the bell-tower. Very, very dark."

"Did no one hear your cries?"

She smiled. "I had been counseled to maintain silence, Sebastian. Even though I was frightened, I was almost as afraid of making a sound."

"So you sat in the dark and waited."

"No." She sat up straighter. Even now she could see the ground beneath her feet, so far away. It seemed to rush up at her. She closed her eyes.

"I knew, you see, that it was past dinner, and no one had found me yet. I wasn't sure if anyone would ever come. So, I crawled off the top of the tower and decided to climb down the roof."

He said nothing to her confession. She looked down at her hands. "I slipped and nearly fell, but it was my surcoat that caught on the edge of the roof. I dangled there for what seemed like hours."

"In silence?"

"You sound like the abbess, Sebastian, when she was told. In truth, I forgot the admonitions of silence and screamed a good deal. Enough that a few of the sisters came to investigate. They all wished to rescue me, but I was too high. I fell, finally, into a pile of hay Sister Margaret arranged below me."

"And suffered no broken bones?"

"Perhaps it was not as high as I thought," she admitted.

"But from that day you've hated heights and darkness."

"And horses and water and no doubt a great many other things added to that list," she confessed.

"Yet the child who climbed out on that roof was brave and dauntless."

"Foolish and unthinking," she countered.

"I wonder, Juliana, if it was your fear that marks you, or what you were taught? Which had the more influence?"

She glanced over at him again, startled.

"I've no doubt you were told over and over that you could have been killed by your foolish actions."

She nodded.

"Would you have been as afraid to this day if you'd been congratulated on the bravery of your deed?"

It was an odd thought, one she'd never had before.

"So what I fear is not so much the actuality of a thing, but the consequences of it? Is it not wise to do so?"

"Anything can harm if taken to extremes. Even fear."

"You would have had me become foolishly courageous." She pulled her legs up beneath her surcoat, leaned her arms on them.

"You're too intelligent to be foolish. Your sense would have cautioned you, not the hysterical words of others." Her face warmed at his words.

"Or, it could be that I truly am afraid of heights, Sebastian."

"You asked if some people could not simply be born with fears. I believe so. But to acquire them where none previously existed indicates to me that there is training more than natural-born fear."

"It is an interesting point to ponder." She leaned her chin on her folded arms.

"I would have applauded your courage, and congratulated you on the effort."

"My stay at the convent might well have been marked with punishment, then," she said, smiling up at him.

"Instead of loneliness."

How did he know? "Yes."

"Did the abbess punish those responsible?"

"There were always girls leaving and arriving at the convent. I'm sure they did not stay long after that. In truth, I was there longer than most."

He said nothing to that, only studied her as if he made certain the placement of her features was the same as it had been the day before, that her hair was arranged the same. He looked away, just as she was beginning to warm under his regard.

"I did not mean to pry when I came into the chapel," she said, the words prodded by conscience. He had not questioned her presence there, but she still wished to explain.

He smiled, his gaze returning to her. Surely she was not the first woman to have sighed inwardly at the effect of both that look and that effortless smile. They did not make him appear younger. Instead, they added an aura of wickedness to his strong face.

"I did not summon you here in punishment, Juliana. Did Jerard indicate as much?"

"He did not. I doubt he would ever speak ill of you." In fact, Jerard simply smiled whenever she asked a question he did not choose to answer, not unlike the Lord of Langlinais.

He looked away, to where an early star appeared on the horizon. It winked, like a mischievous cat. "He is," he said, "the most loyal man I've known."

"He is not from Langlinais, though." He had said as much to her one day.

"No," Sebastian said. "I met Jerard on one of my many rounds of tourneys."

"Is it true that King Henry excommunicates those who participate?"

"Perhaps in England, but in France they are still popular. They are, after all, designed to train a man in war, although some are not necessarily mock warfare." A small smile tilted his lips. It was not one of amusement, but rather of recollection. A fond but bittersweet memory touched upon, then as quickly gone. "A knight marks the beginning and end of each tourney with Mass, because there is every possibility that a man might not survive it. Two sets of knights face each other across a level meadow. Then, at the signal, the two armies charge each other. Those who are defeated are held for ransom. That's how a victorious knight wins horses and armor."

"But you were never defeated." She knew that much.

The look he sent her was wry. "I was victorious from my very first tourney, but arrogant. Once, I ransomed the horses I'd won and didn't keep one for my own use. Consequently, I'd not even a decent horse to ride, since my own had gone lame. I was leading him, limping, to the next tourney when I met Jerard. He was working in the stables of his liege lord. He treated my horse so well I was able to fight and win again." He paused, then continued. "I purchased his freedom with my winnings and made him my squire."

"He was a serf?"

He nodded.

"Now he is your steward."

"And has proven himself well in that capacity also," he said.

"I cannot believe it is strictly your horse that claimed you all those prizes."

Her words seemed to embarrass him. He raised his head and watched the sky.

"They were not all prizes," he said, turning once more to her. Evidently, he did not wish to speak of skill with sword or lance. "I was once awarded a fish. A very large pike. And another time, a grove of trees. And in another tourney I won the hand of a very nice lady with a very large nose. I was at great pains to inform her father that I had been married for a goodly number of years to a girl I'd not seen since I was twelve."

"While I learned my letters at Sisters of Charity, unknowing that another wished my husband."

"Oh, I do not think she wished me. She was intent upon another, a German knight with a huge head and nearly as large a nose."

They smiled at each other, content for the moment, both cognizant of the danger they'd skirted in speaking of oaths and childhoods and honor. It was a moment as sweet as the one in which he'd congratulated her on her courage.

Because of that, she asked another question. "Why do you never go outside? Unless it is dark, or dawn and there is no one about?"

"Do you make your own scent?" There were some topics he would not address despite their sudden ease with each other.

"No," she said, bemused by the degree of hurt she felt. At the suddenness of it. It was as if she were a child and someone had offered her a treat, then taken it back just as she reached for it. *No, Juliana, you cannot have it. You do not deserve it.*

Do not ruin this moment, Juliana, by wishing for something you cannot have. Accept what you do have and make it enough. By such logic had she sustained herself during her whole childhood, during those long years in which her father had not come. Only to learn later that he had died two years earlier and no one had thought to inform her.

"I have a large supply of it in my trunks. The abbess sent it with me as a bride gift."

The sight of his half smile made something ache in her chest, some heretofore unknown emotion, comprised of hurt and a sense of her own frailty. She felt almost parchment-thin at that moment, capable of being tossed by the gentle breeze that lifted the corner of the cloth. All because of a smile.

"Is it me?" She tilted her chin up, watched him carefully. Hoping that the answer, when it came, would be kind. "Am I the reason you do not wish a proper marriage?"

He looked surprised for a moment, before his features settled into stern lines.

"I have heard much stupidity in my life, especially during my auctores as a student. But I expected more from you." She heard the harshness of his tone, saw him shake his head as if to negate the question.

"Why did you expect more from me?" She looked up at him, genuine curiosity on her face. "You do not know me. Until this afternoon, we'd barely spoken. You had no way to gauge the way I think. Why would I not believe what I have?"

"Because you are an intelligent woman. Because I've watched you trace your fingers over words as if they were gold. Because you respect the traditions of the scriptorium, honor the learning your skill will promote."

She shifted, pulling in her legs as if to wrap herself into a tight ball. "Yet, you've done nothing to alter my perception. Simply announced it as wrong."

"No, then." The words were soft and tender. "Does that reassure you? No, Juliana, my actions have nothing to do with you."

Again, she experienced the feeling that she was being lured into enchantment. It was not his appearance, or the mystery that surrounded him that enticed her. It was the whole of him. Sebastian of Langlinais.

The child she had been, who had been brave and daring and dauntless, smiled and laughed behind her hand.

Chapter 12

Juliana laid her reed quill down. Today she was coloring in a large area of the initial capital letter, and the work did not necessitate the delicacy of one of her precious duck quills. In truth, the work was going slowly, because she was not able to concentrate. Too often, her gaze was captured by the silver box in the corner of her work space.

She'd stared at a page until she realized she'd allowed a droplet of ink to mar the surface. At least the parchment had been blank. The remainder of the morning had been spent applying pumice to the area and rubbing until it was finally clean.

Normally, hours could pass and she would be barely aware of time. Yet now, time seemed to slow to a pace she'd never felt before, as if every motion took twice as long to complete.

Yesterday loomed in her mind just as it had ever since she'd left the tower. They'd spent hours talking about things that skirted the edges of their odd union. But she had not asked any more of the questions that had been at the forefront of her mind, knowing that he would not answer them.

Below her, the servants worked at their chores, supervised not by her but under Jerard's watchful eye. The laundress was rinsing the tablecloths and sheets, the cook was cooking meat over the cauldron in the bailey, the smith worked at the huge forge. Chamber pots were emptied, rushes were replaced, horses were fed, and floors were swept. All such necessary things.

Juliana found herself listening to the sounds of the castle, becoming so adept at discerning them that she could hear the squeak of a hinge and know it was the door to the mews being opened. She could hear one of her attendants brushing back her sheets in her bedchamber, could hear the soft laughter between cook and helper.

But where was Sebastian? What occupation intrigued him, kept him so silent during the day? If he was no ascetic bound on mortification of the flesh, then why garb himself in a monk's habit and hide himself from the world? She had never seen him in the courtyard, nor had he used the quintain or the tilting field, nor did he ever ride one of the horses she'd seen grazing in the far fields. Or did he sleep when the sun rose and lie awake all night? What was the great secret that held Sebastian almost a prisoner within his castle, and trapped Langlinais in thrall?

Her curiosity was foolish. Whom would she ask? Not the Lord of Langlinais himself. It was as if he were a moated island, separate and apart from every other person with whom he came in contact. She doubted he would divulge the reasons for his reticence and his isolation. Jerard? He would only smile at her and not answer her questions. Grazide? No. She was supposed to be happily wed.

She reached out and picked up the silver coffer, holding it cradled in her hand. Even now, it still felt warm.

Resolutely, she put the coffer down and picked up

the reed again, the habits of a lifetime of service hard to dismiss. She examined the reed for wear and trimmed the edge of it with the small dagger she carried at her waist. It was designed neither for protection nor for eating, but solely for the purpose of trimming her quills and cutting the parchment to size. The abbess had gifted her with it the day word had come that her husband had gone on crusade. At the time, she'd thought nothing of the delay. Now, she wondered what would have happened had Sebastian summoned her before he'd left for the Holy Land. Would he have been different from the man he was now? Would he have worn a black robe and prayed so eloquently?

Her speculations did not matter. He had not summoned her, and wishing would not change the past. Still, she could not help but try to arrange all the separate oddities of the last few weeks into order. She desperately wished for answers, and there were none forthcoming.

"Juliana, you will never succeed if you do not begin," she told herself.

"A worthy admonition."

She turned and he was there. She neither started nor flinched from his sudden appearance. It was as if somehow she'd known he would come, like the tree anticipates a bird's perch upon its branches, or the earth a burrowing rabbit. A small smile tipped her lips at such nonsensical notions. Sebastian, Earl of Langlinais, was neither bird nor rabbit. More a shadow, perhaps, one that fell where it would, as it would, despite placement of sun or cloud.

He entered the small oriel, made even more intimate by his presence.

But she said nothing, nor did she move aside when he stood closer, compelled to by the small size of the room. Her fingers shook as he stood behind her, watching, but saying nothing. They trembled when she opened the small horn that contained her prepared ink, poured a little into a shallow bowl.

"Why is the ink clear?" His voice whispered beside her ear, and by dint of a will she did not know she possessed she did not shudder at the sound of it. Not that it frightened her; it did not. It was no more substantial than a gentle breeze, a hint of sound with just a rasp of emotion.

"It will darken the longer it is exposed to the air," she said, focusing her mind on those necessary things that she must do next. "Or, I can change the color by adding a few flakes of rust."

She turned and looked up at him. "I've never thanked you for my present, Sebastian."

"A small thing."

His smile and hers seemed oddly paired.

He spoke again, the moment gone. "Is it usual to be entrusted with the task of ink maker as well as scribe?"

"The abbess was fond of saying that a good workman knows his tools. I think, myself, that it was a way of making us learn what we needed to know. We did more than copying text. We learned how to do initial letters and other flourishes mostly added by miniators or rubricators. Very rarely does one person do all three tasks."

"But you do all that, make ink, and prepare your parchment as well?"

"I was one of two lay people the abbess allowed into the scriptorium. I was willing to do it all in order to prove I was worthy."

"It requires patience, the work you do."

"And a great deal of good fortune," she said, looking down at her hands. Her fingers were poised at the edge of the work space. She should pick up one of her quills and begin her work. The encyclopedia was not going to be finished if she did not begin.

"Good fortune?"

"Yes," she said softly, her voice almost as gentle as his. There was no need, after all, to shout at each other. They were barely a foot apart. The size of the oriel did not allow for much more separation.

Her fingers trembled and she tightened her grip upon the work surface. The wood, planed and rubbed with oil, felt solid, aged.

She spoke, easing the words past the constriction in her throat. "A drop of ink, too hard a touch upon the quill, a hand that cramps. All these things can ruin a work of months."

He pressed too near, close enough that his robe brushed by her elbow. They were both aware of the touch at the same time. Her indrawn breath heralded his quick movement. A step away and he was no longer so close.

"And has such a thing happened to you?"

"I've my share of experience in rubbing a page clean," she said, smiling down at her hands. "It is impatience that is my greatest sin, I'm afraid."

She looked down at her manuscript. The page was as pristine as if ink had never spilled upon it. She had learned, over the years, how to mask the effects of her own errors so well that the other scribes had come to her when they needed something erased. She had once complained to the abbess that it did not seem fair to be so proficient at mistakes, at which the abbess had simply smiled and decreed that each one of us recognizes her own errors far better than anyone else.

She raised her head and looked out the long, narrow window that showed her the world. She did not need to turn her head to know that he was watching her, studying her in the way she learned those books she was to later transcribe. *Brethren, be ye not lax in your translations, but of alert mind and willing heart.* An admonishment she repeated to herself every morning before taking up her quill.

He carefully turned over a page of the encyclopedia. "Is this what you are transcribing?"

"Yes," she said. "It's not a very long book. But its author is quite verbose, and has a great deal to say on all manner of plants. But there are no illustrations, for which I'm grateful. I'm not much of an artist."

"Yet your glyphs are charming." He traced a gloved finger in the air above her Q.

"An elementary talent, I'm afraid."

"You do not give yourself enough credit, Juliana. Is this something you learned again, this self-abasement?" His smile robbed the words of their sting.

"No, rather the truth. I know my skills or lack of them well. The abbess expected a great deal from all of us. *Aut disce aut dicede.*"

"Either learn or leave? And here I thought my father a stern taskmaster. Your abbess sounds like a gorgon."

She smiled. "No. I quite liked her. I think I confused her, however. I truly believe she was always expecting me to be someone other than I was."

"Perhaps she was waiting for the daring child to emerge again."

"She never did," Juliana said softly. "I learned to accept what I was told."

"Do you accept everything you learn, Juliana? Do you never question those things you see and hear and know? What would happen if you ever discovered a truth that made a lie of everything you know?"

She looked up at him then smiled again. "That the sky is green and the grass is blue?"

He nodded.

"Truly?"

"What if you woke up tomorrow morning and saw that the sky was green? That it had always been green, even when you thought it was blue. What would you do?"

She thought for a moment. "I don't know. I would probably question myself first, to see if I had seen it correctly. Then, I would wish to know why people had not told me. And why I had learned that it was blue in the first place."

"Do you know what I think most people would do?" he asked, his smile vanishing. "I think they would say that it was blue still. That the ones who called it green were wrong."

"Is the sky green, Sebastian?"

She had expected him to answer with a laugh, but instead, he said, "I don't know, Juliana."

He turned to go. When he hesitated at the doorway, she reached out one hand as if to forestall his departure. He moved aside from her touch, a repudiation as telling as his earlier one. But his look was kind, and his words surprising.

"I am at the tower most evenings. I would welcome your company. If you come, we shall speak of Saladin and Aristotle," he promised. "Or we can play chess, if you prefer. Jerard thinks the game too slow, while I prefer to consider all aspects of each move."

She smiled, coaxed by his soft words. "When you speak of the game you look as earnestly hopeful as a young troublemaker who wishes his story believed. I confess to being a novice at it, but I enjoy chess.''

"Will you come again to the top of my tower, Juliana?"

She nodded.

He said nothing further, only closed the door behind him, leaving her alone.

Chapter 13

Courcy, France

Gregory of Langlinais had been elevated to the Chapters-General of the Templars for two reasons: his ability to create order even in the midst of chaos and his almost suicidal belief in his own abilities on the battlefield.

His new position was that of a traveling representative whose skill was in determining then solving the administrative weaknesses of each preceptory. It was not as strange a position for a former Commander of Knights as it appeared. The post required a man who was not easily intimidated, one who could issue orders and expect them to be obeyed without question.

For the last two years, he'd begun to note the strengths of the Order as well as its vulnerabilities. What he saw was an organization whose purpose was fast becoming obsolete. The reason for the emergence of the Templars a hundred years ago had been to provide for the common man on his way to worship at Christian shrines. Now the Order was being used as no more than a force united against the enemies of the papacy or to ferret out heretics within Christendom.

In order to endure, their mission must change. They must chisel a future for themselves that was more in keeping with their power. A vision that most of the leaders of the Templars did not, unfortunately, share.

However, one of the men who did share this view was seated across from him now. It was quite possible that he might be Master of the Order one day because of that perception, and because he embodied all of the exemplary ideals of a Templar knight.

Fifty years earlier, the Book of Judges had been translated into the speech of the day, that the brothers might understand the chivalry of biblical times, especially Joshua's conquest of the Holy Land. Gregory had heard a few brothers refer to the man across from him as the new Joshua. Phillipe d'Aubry was the Marshal, a man near the top of the Order's hierarchy, close enough to the Master to be considered his successor.

D'Aubry was the one man who knew of all the correspondence that routinely flowed through the Outremer. He could enumerate each of the Templars' many loans, and routinely concealed the interest they earned. The Order did not, on the surface, betray their oath of poverty. Nor did they wish to be considered moneylenders. The Order's true wealth was hidden in the ownership of their numerous properties throughout Europe.

"Are you sure he knows?" Phillipe asked.

"I suspect as much," Gregory said. "He told me himself that he was at the Cathar stronghold not long after the siege ended."

A look of interest crossed Phillipe's features.

"There is talk about you, Gregory. That you strive to learn even the hidden truths."

Gregory inclined his head, neither confirming nor denying.

"There may be nothing to this treasure, Gregory."

He formed his answer carefully. "Where there is rumor of sufficient duration, Marshal, there is usually some truth."

"You know, of course, that these Cathars surrendered nothing and confessed not one word. They marched into fire singing songs of joy." Phillipe's look was one of gentle speculation.

"Yet there is still talk that they were in possession of relics of the faith."

"Were you one of those who infiltrated their ranks?"

"No. But I've knowledge of what happened." The Templars had sent a few of their brothers to join the Cathars, claiming a religious conversion, in order to determine if rumors of a great treasure were true. The men returned to confirm that the Cathars did, indeed, hold a treasure. Its existence was established, but not its substance.

"You believe your brother has the treasure, Gregory? That his journey to Montvichet was to retrieve it? That he found it when no one else did?"

"Yes, Marshal."

Phillipe leaned back against the chair and ran his fingertip against the earthenware cup in front of him.

"What do you propose?"

"He has less than three months to pay the remainder of his ransom, plus interest on the loan. I have received word from him that he is not able to do it, even if Langlinais produces a bountiful harvest."

"Then why would he not have offered it to us before now?"

"Perhaps he lacked sufficient motivation to do so, Marshal. Or believed he might be able to pay the loan."

"So you would offer Sebastian of Langlinais a trade? Release of his obligation for the treasure of the Cathars?"

Gregory nodded.

Phillipe steepled his fingers, looked beyond his guest to the far wall, as if the treasure of the Cathars rested there. "If it is true," he murmured, "then we might be the guardians of the true relics."

"Power beyond our greatest thoughts."

"To what use would you put this great power, Gregory?"

His smile was as pleasant as the tone of voice used to address him. Gregory was not deceived by such gentleness. A quick mind lay behind the soft voice.

"Act as guarantors of safe passage. Demand fiefs in reward, the maintenance of the fortresses in Latin Syria."

"You would have us change our function?"

"The world is changing, Marshal, and to survive, we must change with it."

"But you would make us kings, Gregory."

"The divine right to rule, Marshal, has been made possible in almost every country by Templar loans."

"I think you are a dangerous man, Gregory. Or an ambitious one."

"If our role is expanded, Marshal, the Order will require men of ability."

"And you see yourself occupying such a post?"

Gregory inclined his head, allowed himself to smile, but only faintly. "Only if I am proven worthy, Marshal."

"A wise leader would keep you close at hand, the better to know your mind. Or banish you from his presence lest you contaminate his thoughts."

"Shall I leave, Marshal?"

The look given him was one of speculation. "Let us proceed first on the matter of your brother, instead, Gregory. Let's see if we cannot flush out the treasure of the Cathars."

Chapter 14

Sebastian brushed back the monk's hood from his head, raised his face to the gentle breeze, and breathed deeply, eyes closed as if to savor the sensation more fully. Langlinais. The air was perfumed with the smell of flowers and grasses.

He rubbed his gloved hands over his face. He preferred to be barefaced. A way to repudiate everything he'd been, everything he'd done. The man he had been had worn his hair short, his beard full. The man he was now was clean-shaven with hair grown longer.

For two weeks they had met on the tower, Juliana conquering her fear of heights while he ignored his instincts that urged more caution. Torchlit night had formed a buffer against the remainder of the world, one that allowed for confession. She had spoken of the girls she'd known at the convent, the various nuns who'd helped to rear her. He learned of the influences that had guided her and her secret love of poetry. He had spoken of the inhabitants of Langlinais and the history of the castle. Small, commonplace words that created a bridge between them.

But one moment in particular still remained in his

memory, because it dictated what their futures would be.

"One of our men-at-arms can be dispatched to the convent, Juliana, to deliver your encyclopedia," he'd said when she had commented that her work was nearly finished. "Perhaps," he had added, "the abbess might have something else she wishes you to transcribe."

She had looked at him with wide eyes.

"Would you not object, then, if I continued my work?"

In her voice he'd heard fear of his answer.

"Would it give you pleasure, Juliana?"

"Yes, Sebastian." She had smiled brilliantly, and he'd been reminded of his dreams of her. Not because of her happiness, but because of the spear of longing he'd felt upon viewing it.

It was to his benefit for her to be content at Langlinais, but he had not told her that. Nor had he explained that one day, perhaps soon, she would have only her work to keep her companion. He would have retreated behind a locked door.

A sound of footsteps jarred him from his reverie. She was coming. He smiled at his eagerness.

Despair was not a visible adversary. It seeped in like moisture in a dungeon. Slow drops, one at a time, until one day the place is damp and moldy. So it was with him. He had not realized how close he was to the end of his tether until it had been reached. He needed the sight of her, the sound of her, the scent of her too much. She kept him sane and made this half-life bearable.

If he had nothing more than verbal companionship, let it be whole and complete. Let her speak and know that nothing she said would be ridiculed. Let her betray all of her secrets. Let her feel secure in this place, so that there was no need of fear, no reason to tremble in his presence. And when he was no longer with her, let her remember these moments with fondness and a smile. She might even come here again, sit in the same place and recall him and his words.

By such things was a man remembered.

The sky was tinted perse, that strange mix of grayish blue and purple. The air smelled sweet until she realized that the scent was not carried by the soft evening breeze, but by the flowers that adorned the cloth Sebastian had spread over the floor. A pillow lay against the stone, in the same position where she had rested the night before.

Sebastian sat on the opposite side of the cloth, his back against the curved wall. He watched her as she climbed free and shook out her skirts. She had not been able to decide which of her many surcoats to wear, and the trembling in her limbs gave the lie to the studied air of nonchalance she tried to assume as she sat on the cloth.

He discomfited her by his very presence. Was that why she had hurried through her meal? No, it was the reason she'd thought of nothing but him for weeks.

An oil lamp in the center of the cloth was lit against the encroaching darkness. She ran a finger at the edge of the deep reservoir of oil. The lamp was made of metal, fashioned in an ornate pattern she'd never seen before, with a curling handle in the shape of a dragon's mouth. The tail formed the light while the dragon's body was curved in a circle to form the bowl.

Night had fallen upon them, wisps of clouds parting to give them a view of the sky. It seemed to press down upon them, so close she might reach out and clutch a glittering bit of it in her fists. She angled her head until all she could see was the night sky and the stars above her.

" 'Blemishes are hid by night and every fault forgiven.' "

His glance followed hers. "Ovid?"

She nodded.

" 'Yet I'll be born, the finer part of me, above the stars immortal, and my name shall never die.' "

They exchanged a conspiratorial look. One such as scholars share, or those with similar interests.

"Your abbess was an unusual woman to allow you to study Ovid." He moved back into the shadows again.

She smiled, still looking at the night sky, "I doubt the abbess knew. But one could never be sure. She seemed to know everything." She sighed. "I suspect she would not have been pleased to know I read Catullus." She looked over at him. "Have you read his works?"

He shook his head.

"The abbess had only recently received a scroll of his poetry. I'd never heard of him either, but he seemed to be able to express his feelings so deeply. *'Lingua sed torpet, sonitu suopte tintinant aures, gemina et teguntur lumina nocte.'* " Words written by the poet that seemed apropos for this moment.

"My tongue is paralyzed, the sound of my body rings in my ears, my eyes close in the darkness." His voice translated the words softly.

Her eyes fluttered shut. Affirmation without a word spoken.

"You have not said if you like your gift."

She opened her eyes and it was only then that she saw the object resting in the corner of the cloth. It was a thin cylinder no larger than a bunch of quills, topped by a square box the width of two fingers. It was made of gold, carved and elaborately decorated. She picked it up and studied the writing. One word repeated over and over—*al-'alim*. The long square tube was empty, but she guessed its use immediately. It would hold a good-sized quill. The small chamber was fitted with a lid that flipped open on tiny hinges, and inside was a glass vial for ink. A dollop of some sticky material affixed to the opening would keep the ink from spilling.

"It is for a traveling scribe. You can wear it attached to your girdle."

Her fingers traced the writing, her fingers stroking against the strange words as if to find reassurance within the curve of them.

"What does the inscription mean?"

When he spoke his voice was as warm as the metal she stroked. "The learned," he said.

"Are they Saracen words?" She frowned as she traced them again.

"Yes. Does it matter to you, Juliana?"

"Do you not hate them?"

"I hated my jailers. But I appreciate their scholars and men of letters. They are not the same. And I've found that hatred is a habit I'd rather avoid, if given the choice."

She held the gold set between her hands, fingers curled around it as if to keep it from being snatched away.

"I have been given only two gifts in my life," she said, the words not easily spoken but necessary. "Both have come from you."

"Are not husbands obligated in such ways? You are my wife. Do you subscribe to the belief that I can only grant you what is on a list?" There was a pause before he began to speak again. "I think I can remember this inventory of acceptable items. A handkerchief, a fillet for your hair, a wreath of gold or silver, a breastpin, a mirror, a girdle, a purse, a tassel, a comb, sleeves, gloves, a ring, a compact, a picture, a washbasin, a flag but only as a souvenir."

She was as bemused by the softness of his voice as by the list he'd intoned.

"A courtly knight would grant you all these things," he said. "But I am no longer a courtly knight."

He enthralled her, this man who spoke so eloquently. He fascinated her as nothing in her life ever had. It was not simply the garment he'd chosen to wear. Nor, truly, was it the soft melody of his voice. It was these things and more, her own yearning, and curiosity, too.

"You did not work today," he said. Would such a statement betray to her that he had looked for her in the oriel? Or that he'd chastised himself for doing so? Other than that last visit, when he'd come too close to telling her one of the secrets he held, he'd not returned to her tiny scriptorium.

She shook her head.

"My hand was cramping. I fear I am guilty of enthusiasm over moderation. But I've never before had such freedom." Her smile was rueful, her amusement directed at herself.

He wished, just once, that he could touch her. Kiss the inside of her wrist and discern if that was the spot where she placed her rose scent. Or touch her temple, or the hollow at the base of her neck. Her breasts lay beneath her surcoat, covered from his gaze, but not from his knowledge. He knew the shape of them, had studied them in the shadows of the tower.

He had been so desirous of her company one day that he'd not been able to wait until nightfall, but had gone to her chamber like a lovesick pup. He'd removed the stopper from her rose scent and inhaled deeply, as if her essence had been captured within the bottle.

He would never be able to test his dreams as to the shape and curves of her. Sometimes, the longing came so hard and so strong that he fisted his hands in order to keep them from reaching for her. Even at this moment, as she sat smiling at him, he ached to smooth his hand beneath her clothing, feel the sweep of her legs. He wanted to lay her down upon the cloth, extinguish the oil lamp, and love her in the light of complacent stars.

He recognized the depth of his lunacy even as he embraced it. He'd begun to envision all sorts of wondrous things, none of them real. He'd seen Juliana amidst a grove of trees, her smile so blinding that it did not matter if the sun had gone behind a cloud. Juliana, her hand in his, her head nestled against his shoulder, her belly swollen with his child. Juliana, standing in her chamber, her chemise puddled at her feet, her skin washed golden by the dawn sun, her long black hair a silken cloud behind which her breasts teased.

There was no reason for hope, but it popped free like a cork on the ocean. But each time it did, he forced himself to face the future as it would be and not as he wished it to be. Such tenacity of truth was acutely painful.

Did he frighten her still? Perhaps he did. Or if not, she surely had questions as to his appearance. A normal man did not appear garbed in monk's robe and silence. If he had been shorn of his clothing, and the reason for it, he might still have terrified her. He was all those things a convent-bred girl was raised to fear. Licentious and virile, man and warrior, husband and lord. All that and more. Pray God she would never learn how much more.

Tonight he'd brought the chessboard to the tower. It sparkled in the light of a fading sun, its gold and silver pieces as priceless as any of the Langlinais treasures. It was among the last of them. Soon, it too would join all the other precious objects collected over a series of lifetimes, sold in order to pay the remainder of his ransom.

Her exclamation of delight was payment enough for his effort. She sat like a child would, in an excess of enthusiasm, tucked her legs and skirts beneath her, and, at his nod, began her first move.

They did not speak until long moments later, when he'd captured her first piece, an action that caused a frown to appear between her brows.

"Tell me about a typical day at the convent," he said.

She looked up, her eyes sparkling. "It does not make for a lively tale, Sebastian. I woke at four every morning and spent two hours at prayers. Then the morning meal, followed by work in the garden. I had no talent at growing things, so I was set to weeding. After the noon meal and prayers, I was allowed into the scriptorium, where I worked for an hour. Then I helped to teach the younger students and performed the duties I was assigned. Then silence for an hour before bed."

"The rule of Benedict, then."

She nodded. "One part of sleep, one part prayer, and one part intellectual and manual labor." At his look, she smiled. "Do you see? It was not at all exciting. The greatest thing that ever happened was the year I was allowed to copy the works of Vergil, Caesar, and Cicero."

"And steal a moment with Ovid or Catullus."

Her cheeks pinked again, and her gaze seemed to search out the sky.

An hour later, he'd won the chess game. He was pleasantly surprised to find that it was more difficult than he'd imagined. For a short time, he'd debated whether or not he should allow her to win, then decided that she was skilled enough to know if he suddenly changed strategy. But the level of her playing made the game interesting. When he mentioned that, she only tightened her lips and promised to win the next time. He did not doubt she would. Even by the light of the oil lamp, her eyes gleamed with the challenge. Timidity had been buried beneath competition. Nor was she diffident when speaking of her work.

She glanced up at him. "Grazide told me that you studied in Paris."

"An accident of place," he said. "I was celebrating a round of tourney victories, not expecting to be engaged in debate."

She looked entranced, but then the extent of her travels had been to journey to the convent and then to Langlinais.

"I found myself watching the masons on the Île de la Cité. They are building a cathedral there, Notre Dame." He smiled. "Did you know that a temple of Jupiter once stood in the very same place?"

She shook her head.

"They were working on what they called the Gallery of Kings. Twenty-eight statues of rulers from Israel and Judah, Juliana, all the size of a man." Once, he'd had dreams of importing a few of such talented men to Langlinais for the purpose of adding more ornamentation to the facade of the castle. Perhaps it would be something that would interest Juliana in the future. "I'd heard a group of people shouting, and turned the corner to discover a crowd of young men. They were yelling at their teacher, who stood there smiling at them as if he were a proud parent." Even now, he could remember that moment, the confusion that had overtaken him and the bemusement that had followed.

"I became intrigued by their arguments, even more so by the way their teachers listened to them. It was a means of learning I'd never experienced before, a disputation that became the essence of my true education."

She sat back against the wall, folded her hands on her lap, and smiled at him encouragingly. He smiled at his own eagerness to tell her all he'd discovered.

"I spent many months there. If I posed an idea, I was also expected to defend it. Logical thought was more important than emotion. Curiosity was considered a valuable trait."

"What brought you home if you loved it so?"

He smiled. "It was time. I'd spent a few years in Paris and Italy, interspersed my studies with tourneys. I was my father's heir and was needed at Langlinais."

"Yet you left again."

"Grazide again?" Sebastian asked wryly.

She nodded.

"What else did she tell you?" There was no anger in his voice. Grazide had been part of his childhood. Her penchant for telling tales held no rancor or viciousness. She was simply interested in people and expressed it through speech. There were times, in fact, that it was simply easier to convey some information to Grazide, knowing that it would quickly find its way through the castle. She was also very fond of him, which was perhaps why he had assigned her as his wife's attendant. He was still a man, despite his future, and wished himself portrayed well. The irony of that thought did not escape him.

"She said you have a brother."

"And you want to know why I've never spoken of him."

"Or of Magdalene. She spoke of her, also." The oil lamp cast shadows that draped around her like a well-met friend. She seemed right in this moment, in this pose.

He stood and walked to the edge of the tower, looking down at the countryside before him. The view was shrouded and covered with darkness. The past was coming closer again. Each day it bumped against him with more force than the day before. He was a creature not merely of the present, but of those lost days and his fixed future.

"Sebastian?"

Her voice called him from his reverie. He turned and looked down at her.

"Did I say something wrong?"

How did he answer her? With enough knowledge to quell her curiosity? Or with more, to hint at the man beneath? He wished her to know the truth, but not the full measure of it.

He sat on the crenel of the tower, his back wedged against the stone. His gaze was fixed, not upon the countryside he knew so well, but rather upon days he chose not to recall often. Why did he now? Because there were so many secrets between them that he would reveal those truths he could.

"Magdalene was my father's concubine, Juliana.

She was well loved. Langlinais was her home until my father died, and then she left here. She became a Cathar."

He waited, but she made no comment. Her convent had insulated her well, then. "The Cathars did not accept all the tenets of the Church; therefore, they were labeled *infidelis* or not faithful. Heretic."

"You speak of them as if they are dead."

"They are. Or, if any of them still live, they hide from the world." He tapped his fingers against the stone.

"And Magdalene?" Her voice was so soft, almost a whisper. She knew the answer before he spoke it, he was certain.

He could only shake his head. She seemed to realize that he would not speak of that memory. The images of the horror were almost blurred, returned only infrequently in dreams.

"You loved her a great deal, didn't you?"

The image of Magdalene was called up in an instant. "She was a tall woman with a jutting chin and large mouth that was always smiling. Her hair had been laced with gray from my earliest memories, and her voice sounded as if she sang the words." He smiled at Juliana, then returned to his study of the horizon. "She was not at all graceful, being too angular with large limbs, but she walked as if she owned the earth and everything on it. She gave me her friendship first, then her affection. Over the years, I learned to appreciate it, then return it." He glanced over at her again. "She would have liked you, Juliana. And approved of your diligence."

She smiled at him, then looked down at her hands. "Too much diligence I'm afraid." She stretched out her right hand. Three of her fingers looked as if they curled back upon themselves.

He wished he could have taken her hand between his own and rubbed it until it was no longer cramped.

"She sounds like a wonderful woman, Sebastian. I envy you your memories."

"Have you no recollections of your mother?"

"All I remember is that she smelled of flowers, and had warm, soft arms. I cannot even recall her voice. I had a ring of hers, but it disappeared some years ago. Either I misplaced it or it was taken from me. I never knew."

They sat in silence for a moment, each with similar thoughts for the other. An unspoken empathy, it seemed somehow to link them.

"And your brother?" she asked softly a few moments later. "Is that another sad memory?"

"Not a sad one," he said, "but one just as final. Gregory serves with the Templars. His dedication is to them. We were born of the same parents, reared in the same manner. He was my first opponent. I practiced my swordplay against him. Once he was my friend, but now we are strangers." He leaned his arm against the masonry. "I learned that he had taken vows, become a Templar, then later became aide to the Seneschal. Ambition, Gregory has it. How far it will take him is all that's unknown."

"There was a community of Knights Templar located not far from the convent."

"They have many such holdings throughout the country, some dedicated to hospitals, others to act as their domus. The one near you is where they train their English knights."

She looked at him, the frown on her forehead accentuated by the shadow cast by the oil lamp. "How do you know such things, Sebastian?"

"I have made it my duty to learn as much about

them as I can. There are those among the Templars who wish the glory, not of God, but of the Order. For that they will betray women and children and call it faith." He stood, wondering if he trembled over the edge of a cliff by giving her this truth. "I know for they made me their witness."

She silently placed all the pieces back where they belonged on the board. Her deliberation was such he knew she was barely concentrating upon her task.

She stood and came too close. So near that he could smell the scent of her, feel her warmth.

"Will you tell me, Sebastian?" Her voice was filled with compassion.

She reached out one hand. Too close, she was only inches from him. He flinched and drew back. He stepped back, closer to the edge of the crenel. If necessary, he would jump from the tower rather than have her touch him.

"Do not touch me, Juliana. Ever." He should have shouted the command to her, but evidently his hoarse whisper was enough. She dropped her hand and stepped away. By the light of the lamp he could see her surprise. Better she question his rage than be afflicted as he was.

He could not, suddenly, wait to get away.

Chapter 15

"Is my husband well?"

Juliana held her hands tight in her lap, certain that the answer would be in the affirmative. It simply must be.

Jerard nodded. Tonight he sat beside her on the dais, keeping her company as she ate. It was the first time he'd done so. The drone of voices around them encouraged conversation, but she was as disinclined to talk as she was to eat.

Etiquette demanded a certain set of manners at table, and Jerard was the perfect companion, his nails and hands scrupulously clean. He did not pick his teeth with his knife, nor did he use the shared utensils for only his food. He was gracious and courtly and as silent as she. Perhaps he knew that it would be useless to try to charm her from her mood.

The hunters kept the castle in meat, the gardens provided vegetables such as onions, cabbages, leeks, peas, and beans. But, there were no luxuries at the table. There were few spices, although there was mustard in abundance. No loaves of sugar, the food being sweetened with honey, instead. Nor was there rice, or almonds or raisins. Perhaps one day, such an oversight might matter enough to question it. For now, there was a more pressing omission in her life.

"I have not seen him all week," she said, hoping Jerard would contribute the information she needed. Was Sebastian ill? Or had she somehow angered him?

Jerard's sideways glance indicated that it would not be worthwhile to question him further. He would not speak.

"Will you convey this note to him?"

The folded parchment she gave him was a message to Sebastian. Short and private, it consisted of only two sentences. *I concede to your requirements, Sebastian. Will you come to me?* She would never reach out to touch him again. Nor would she ask another question of him. If only he would continue with their conversations. She missed them so. No . . . she missed him. Every night she'd returned to the tower and had waited for him to appear. But he had never come.

The rest of the meal passed slowly. After she left the table, Juliana went again to the top of the tower. She sat there for nearly an hour until it was obvious that Sebastian was not going to come that night, either.

She retired to her room and stood silent while Grazide helped her remove her surcoat. The garment was truly beautiful, one of the loveliest garments she'd ever worn. Of diapered gold cloth, it was adorned with a diamond pattern of blue and embroidered with gold braid and worn over a long cotte of deeper blue. She'd worn it tonight in the hope that Sebastian might agree to see her. Hoping to appear beautiful to him.

Grazide hung the garment in the tall chest. Inside were more beautiful fabrics fashioned into lovely clothing, soft leather shoes embroidered with delicate flowers, toques and chin bands of white linen.

There was nothing she lacked. Except for a husband.

Grazide unbraided and brushed her hair, all the while keeping up her ever-present chatter. It droned over her and around her, but Juliana paid no attention to the words. When her hair was arranged in the loose braid for sleep she stood.

"Is there anything I can do for you, my lady?" Grazide asked.

Juliana shook her head.

"I've left water for your bathing on the bench, and a length of toweling. The new soap is finished, but it burns the skin, my lady, so I would be cautious of it."

She nodded, forcing a smile. "Thank you, Grazide."

Finally, Grazide left the room.

Juliana removed the rest of her clothes, sat naked on the bench and began to bathe. She dipped a cloth into the basin of water. Here, in her chamber, there was only the sound of water pouring over her hands as she washed herself. The slight squeak of a hinge was all the warning she had that she was not alone.

Moments passed like hours. The bench upon which she sat, the basin of cool water, the flickering oil lamp, the cloth now wadded into a ball with one hand, all those things were noted as if she took inventory in her mind.

The shadow on the wall was too large to be hers. Then it moved, even as she remained motionless.

"Forgive me," Sebastian said softly, "I should have announced myself."

She could not look up at him. Her trembling hands smoothed out the cloth and then placed it across her naked breasts. A paltry gesture to hide a small part of her from his gaze. Why did she not move more quickly? Her fingers seemed too slow in their movements, as if playing with time itself.

"You sent me a note, Juliana. To lure me here?"

She shook her head. In truth, she did not know if she could speak. She sat naked before him, her only covering the soft, flickering shadows.

He said nothing further. There was no sound at all in the room except for the drop of water sliding from the rim back into the basin. Her hearing seemed acute enough to hear that, and to note the harshness of Sebastian's breathing.

The light wavered, as if his hand trembled as he held the oil lamp. Her hands fluttered in the air, uncertain as to journey or destination, then came to rest against her naked thighs. She did not speak, however, did not entreat him to come forward or to leave her.

She bowed her head, her hands fisted. Her own breathing was too fast.

He was her husband. This moment proved that. His entrance into her room did not need to be announced. Neither the door nor her inclination could bar him.

The heat of her skin seemed to warm the cloth that stretched damply over her chest. She averted her head, closed her eyes, waited for him to leave the room. A final renunciation. It would come, she was certain. He had refused her as his wife. She waited in silence for him to repudiate her as a woman.

She did not know if he thought her comely. Yet ever since she'd seen him, ever since he'd smiled at her, she'd worried about her own face and form. She wanted him to look at her as if he were captivated. The same way she felt about him. She wanted to see his hands, to have her fingers entwine with his. And his lips upon her brow, that it might cool her skin, and on her neck where her flesh felt especially warm. And if it were not too shocking, upon the curve of her shoulder.

She wanted, most especially, to be beautiful for him.

He still did not speak. Had he been struck dumb with aversion? Or was he shamed that she had not covered herself with the toweling that lay only inches from her fingers? Or was he shocked that she did not protest his appearance even though she trembled in the silence?

"Forgive me," he said.

Why did he beg forgiveness for something that was his right? Or had his chivalry extended even to this room? Such graciousness. Such kindness. She wanted neither. No, that was not true. His kindness cushioned her, made her smile when she was not with him. His thoughtfulness had weaned her from solitude. He had gifted her with oddities, things of such uniqueness that she'd known he had thought of her in the selection.

Please, Sebastian, do not go. Curse me for a sinner, name me a harlot, but do not leave me. She drew a soft breath, listening for the soft slide of the door closing.

Instead, he moved closer, a brush of air against her bare legs told her that. He was behind her now, a still and silent figure. She could see him in her mind's eye as perfectly as if she'd opened her eyes, his figure dark clothed and silent, one gloved hand outstretched and holding the lamp. His beautiful face would be hidden in shadows. Those eyes that so mirrored the evening sky, what emotion did they express?

He said nothing, but the light wavered again. Did he bend closer? Was that the warmth of his breath upon her back or had she only imagined it? She straightened her head, felt another faint sensation upon her skin. No, that surely must be imagination. He'd never ventured this close. A sudden brightness beneath her lids. She opened them a little to peer through her lashes. He had placed the oil lamp on the bench beside her. She closed her eyes again. Where was he?

Her lips felt full, and the pulse beat at her neck as loud as the convent's bells. There were other places where the sensation was just as disconcerting. Her breasts ached. Her skin felt tight. The cloth, drying upon her heated skin, felt abrasive.

A soft footstep alerted her to his location. He was in front of her now. Did he kneel? Was that the explanation for the sound she heard? She could not open her eyes this time, her lids were fused, her breath fueled by heated coals in her stomach.

Was he watching her? Did he look at her sitting there, nude except for a cloth across her breasts? Her knees were pressed together, her hands rested on her upper thighs. She was immobile, but her blood was racing.

"Juliana."

Her name seemed breathed from his lips. A whisper, no more. The sound a breeze might make when dancing through the branches of a tree. A sigh of storm upon the land.

She did not want to answer. He would pull her from this place of secrecy, force her to open her eyes, to face what she was doing. She wanted to remain in this half world, enticing without a word, inviting him to touch her without entreaty. Adrift in sensation that heightened as each moment passed. Imagination coupled with curiosity.

Please, Sebastian, touch me.

"Juliana." Another summons, in a voice that had grown harsh. Still, she did not open her eyes.

"Yes?" She licked her lips as if to cool their heat.

"Remove the cloth."

Time stopped. So, too, her breath. Her hand reached up and flattened itself against the drying cloth. Then her fingers crept to the edge, gripped it and slowly peeled it back. Her skin was cool where it had lain, and her nipples hardened in the sudden surprising chill. Yet, it was as if heat entered her body at the same time.

She opened her eyes to meet his look.

He knelt in front of her, his head bare. His eyes studied her, and wherever they touched she felt as if a tiny flame had been lit. His mouth was compressed into a thin line, his face looked more severe than she'd ever seen it. An ascetic's face, a warrior's mien. She closed her eyes again.

" 'As she waited before me, her clothes cast off her body, no blemish appeared. What shoulders, what arms, what thighs are hers, this youthful beauty. The shape of her breasts are fit for my hands. There is nothing not worthy of praise about her. How I wish to press her up against me.' "

Her eyes opened. "Ovid?" The word passed through the constriction of her throat.

He nodded.

One of his large hands, covered in its eternal glove, reached out, came closer. She could almost feel the heat of his skin through the leather. His palm curved as if to mimic the shape of the breast it would hold in the next moment. Instead, he hesitated an inch from her skin. His hand trembled. She looked up then, to meet his eyes.

"Sebastian." A wisp of sound. Neither admonishment nor question, but rather a plea.

She ached, hurt with the pain of this moment. She wanted him to touch her, wanted his hands on her body. *Please, Sebastian.* Words that were spoken in her heart, in her mind. Instinctively, she knew that he was the answer for this ache she felt, his hand on her would ease this longing.

She extended her hands to him, palms up, a sign of surrender.

He looked at her hands for a long moment, then his eyes lifted until they met her gaze.

From the great hall came the sounds of merriment. Laughter and singing. Voices arranged in harmony, in raucous enjoyment. They would have no idea that their joy was counterpoint to this moment of silence, stretched so thin she could almost see through time. Her chest ached; she could barely breathe, and when she did her breath felt too hot, as if her body was an inferno.

He did not speak, but she could feel the heat of his hand still, even through the leather of his glove. It remained poised an inch from her body. She closed her eyes again.

"Did you lure me here to tempt me, Juliana?"

Her face warmed at the thought.

"If so, you've succeeded at your aim," he asked, his voice rough. "Do you know how badly I want to touch you, I wonder? Do you know how the sight of your body arouses me? No? Of course you can't. You are an innocent, aren't you? Then, innocent Juliana, would you like to know what I wish to do at this moment?"

Her eyes opened, then closed again quickly.

"I would kiss you first, Juliana. I think you would like kissing. Your lower lip especially, it seems almost too full for your mouth. Such things are sometimes an indication of a passionate nature. Is yours, I wonder?"

She looked beneath her lashes at him. He stood.

"I think it is. You've read love poetry in secret. Did the words you read make you hunger, Juliana? Want something you've never had?"

He moved, circling the bench.

"You would become adept at kissing very quickly. I would learn the shape of your lips, the sounds you make as I deepen the kiss. Lovely Juliana, passionate Juliana."

Her lips felt oddly strange, as if they were being kissed. But not simply in passion. In anger. It was there in his words, in the tone of his voice.

"I would touch you, Juliana, on your shoulders, your neck. Kiss you there, where your skin is soft and your pulse beats strong. And at your temple." His voice changed. He was behind her now. He bent and whispered in her ear, as if the words were too intimate to be heard even by the shadows. "I would touch your breasts, Juliana, stroke those lovely nipples of yours. My fingers would make your blood leap."

Her blood seemed on fire, her skin too tight for her body. Her hands were clenched now on her knees. Again, the sensation that his breath brushed her skin. Or was that his hand again, suspended over her body? Why did he not touch her?

"Press your fingers against your lips, Juliana."

She hesitated but a moment, then followed his instructions.

"They are my fingers now, just as your body is mine. You wanted this moment, Juliana. Then experience it."

She shivered at the note in his voice. Not cruel, nor punishing but firm. The tones of a warrior, brooking no refusal. Still, she did not speak to protest his assumption, didn't tell him that his presence here was only an accident. Instead, she felt trapped in the web of his words, entranced, flushed. Wondering.

"I am tracing your lips with my fingers, Juliana." Blindly, she followed his unspoken command.

"Now take your hand and place it on your shoulder." She did so, cradling her right palm against the bulb of her left shoulder. "Touch your skin, Juliana, the smooth slope of your arm."

Her fingers slid slowly down to her wrist. His hand lay only an inch from hers on the slow descent, as if he wished to absorb what she was feeling, touch her without doing so.

"Can you feel me?"

She nodded.

Her body felt as if it were weeping, growing heated and damp. His voice came closer, breathed in her ear, a sorcerer's murmur low and compelling and strangely exciting. "You are trembling, Juliana. Are you afraid?"

She shook her head.

The Latin poetry she'd read had spoken of passion, of a lover's despair, of powerful emotions all churned together. Until this moment she had not understood. Until she'd heard Sebastian's voice filled with anger and need, until she'd felt her own trembling acquiescence to actions that surely must be forbidden, she'd not known that she could feel all these emotions at once. Anticipation and anxiety.

Her body was on fire. *My senses are rooted in eternal torture.* The words of Catullus seemed too fitting.

"Juliana." He spoke her name as if it was a prayer,

a soft invocation of sound. She shivered at the sound of it, bent her head.

"Place your hands beneath your breasts. I wish to touch you there."

She felt as if her heart were racing, as if she'd run to meet him. But she remained pinned to the bench by his presence, by the soft timbre of his voice and a feeling of being ensorceled. No, not sorcery this, but need. A desperate need to know what came after this, what made the poets sing of rapture and bliss.

Her palms cradled her breasts, lifting them. She had never touched herself for the pleasure of it. The sensation startled her.

"You have beautiful breasts, Juliana." His voice was no more than a rough growl. "Rub your thumbs against your nipples, Juliana."

Her head fell back, her eyes closed, but she did as he told her. Her fingers felt abrasive against her sensitive flesh. Her breasts tightened, the skin prickling in response. Her breath came in soft, helpless gusts that matched the cadence of his breath at her ear.

"Do you feel me touching you?"

She nodded, once.

"Tell me."

"Yes," she said, her voice a faint whisper of sound. Even so, it was almost impossible to speak.

She felt empty, aching. Too close to wisdom, too far away from the answers she sought.

"I want you, Juliana. I want to be inside you."

Heat flooded her cheeks, but she did not move.

"I would stretch you gently so that you fit the shape of me. I want to feel your hips move, your body lift to mine. I want to fill you, Juliana. I want to hear you scream in my arms."

Her breasts felt hot, her thumbs stilled as the

pounding of her heart seemed to beat louder in response to his words.

"But it will not happen, Juliana." His voice came from far away.

Only when she heard the door slam did she open her eyes.

Chapter 16

Jerard stood leaning against a staff nearly as tall as he was. As Sebastian's steward, he was supposed to use it as a badge of his authority. Instead, it made him feel awkward. He would never strike an unarmed man. Too many years under the dominion of another man's rule had left him with an abiding distaste for it. However, he was only too aware that everyone had a master, even the Pope. What differed was the degree of power one wielded while attempting to do a master's bidding.

As Sebastian's steward, he had too much authority. Sebastian trusted him to the degree that it was possible to steal from him with impunity, to cheat him without fear of being caught. Not that he would. He owed Sebastian his life and his future. When Sebastian had plucked him from serfdom and asked what it was that he most wanted to be, he had stammered some answer in response. Only later did he realize that he had said, "Free!" Sebastian had made it come true.

The harvest would be in soon, and this occupation of standing at the end of the field pretending to be surveying the work of the villagers would be at an end. The days could not come fast enough.

Yet as onerous as this one duty, he did not wish the passage of time to increase. If he could have slowed it, he would. He'd even wondered if there were spells he might use to do so, not minding the exchange of his mortal soul for Sebastian's health. Would happiness be too great a thing to wish for, in addition?

He used his sleeve to wipe the sweat from his eyes, keeping an amiable smile on his face lest the villagers believe him annoyed or angered. The villagers of Langlinais had a very great respect for their lord, and he, as Sebastian's representative, had to guard his expression.

This harvest might very well pay the rest of Sebastian's ransom. Then, Langlinais could once again become the wealthy demesne it had once been.

Wealth was not a precursor to happiness, however. Just as having a lovely young bride was no guarantee of marital bliss. Jerard was aware of the currents that swirled around both Sebastian and Juliana. They were each so careful not to mention the other. Yet, when he carried news between them about the other, neither cautioned him not to speak. Instead, their demeanor was the same. Watchful, intent, silent, as if trying to hear beyond his words. As if they were creating a picture in their minds of the other and made the picture move, and speak and act according to the words he spoke.

He told Sebastian of Juliana's return to her manuscripts, of her diligence. He spoke of how she did not stop as long as the sun was in the sky, of the two times her hands had cramped so badly she had asked him to fetch some cream from her trunks. But because of Sebastian's reaction to that information, the silence and the stiffness of his shoulders as he'd stood at his window surveying his land, he'd not told Sebastian how she'd been unable to unstop the bottle. Nor had he spoken of how she was not eating well despite how he tried to tempt her at dinner, how her gaze seemed to flit to the empty lord's chair again and again.

To Juliana he was careful not to speak of those moments in which Sebastian stared out the window, how he barely seemed to hear him when he brought news of the villagers, of the inhabitants of Langlinais. He did not tell her how his lord was careful not to ask of her, an omission so obvious that it betrayed his interest.

He acted as messenger and observer, but he was too aware that their union was as doomed as any he'd ever seen.

He had not believed it possible to feel more pain for Sebastian than he had when learning of his affliction. Now, he knew there were only degrees of anguish. His friend and lord had been resolved to his fate, his acceptance hard-won and difficult to witness. Now, it looked as if the battle must be commenced yet again.

The Lord of Langlinais might feel himself alone in his hell, but Jerard would accompany him there willingly, just as he had ever since that day in France. A small enough price for the man but six years his elder, who'd rescued him from starvation, from mutilation, who'd ignored his humble birth and given him a chance to become squire and then steward. He would protect Sebastian with his life. And guard his secret with the same dedication.

She had spent most of her life secluded from the outside world, although anyone who knew of convent life could not say that such an existence sheltered one from practicality. The nuns at Sisters of

Charity worked hard and took pride in the diligence of their labors. They respected both hard work and intelligence. She was the only scribe not exempted from work in the gardens and the fields because of her work at the scriptorium. The abbess had said that she tended to immerse herself too fully in her work and a change of pace was necessary to look at any task cleanly.

How did she look at the task before her now? Not her work, but her life?

She had not seen Sebastian for nearly a week, not since that night he'd come to her room. Memories of those moments lived with her now, and she could recall every word he'd said to her. Especially those at the end. *It will not happen, Juliana.* She felt as if she'd pushed Sebastian away, first with her curiosity, then with her wantonness. It had been an accident of timing, him coming into her room that way. Yet, she had not covered herself, or explained, or asked him to leave.

Sometimes, Juliana wondered if she felt more than other people did. There were times she simply wanted to cry for hours, the pain in her heart felt so great. Or sometimes, she wanted to weep because she was so happy. Did feeling so strongly mark her as a weak woman? Should she guard her emotions with more care?

There was even a difference in the way she worked. Her letters were as correct, her script as precise as any other good scribe, but her illustrations were more poignant. A young girl sat in the window of the letter R, her feet dangling from the crossbar, her gaze pensive. Not a smile to be seen. No winsome look on her face.

Juliana looked out the window at distant clouds. A summer storm was approaching. The wind whipped at her hair, as if to coax her from this place.

She put away the parchment sheet to dry, poured the remaining ink in its container and checked her quills for wear. Then, satisfied that everything was as it should be, she stood and walked out of the oriel, closing the door firmly behind her.

Perhaps if she changed her surroundings, she might also be able to stop thinking about Sebastian.

He'd been aroused and angry, twin emotions that did not deal well in tandem. Sebastian had wanted her to desire him. All he'd accomplished was to feel a measure of shame for his treatment of her. The guilt, however, did not banish his need. It was stronger than before, just as each thought of her seemed more vivid. Juliana. Even the air seemed to breathe her name.

Had she lain awake the whole night as he had? Had her body felt restless and eager for his? His dreams of her had been wild things, but his nighttime visions of her had not eased his daytime need.

He was a man, condemned to die by circumstance and fate. Not, however, before being given a vision of his life as it might have been.

It was as if a celestial voice enumerated all the things that he would never enjoy. Here, the scent of roses, that you might smell it and recall the fragility of her wrists, or wonder at her soft fragrant neck. Here, the sound of her laughter, so that you remember the joy she caused you to feel with a simple smile. Here, the contents of her mind, that you might wonder at what else she knew and how she reasoned. That you might realize she was the companion of your days, that single soul allowed by heaven itself to be your match. Here, the sight most wished, Juliana nude, bathed by gentle light. Juliana, with her eyes closed and her breath coming fast, her skin so delicate and fair. Her toes had curled upon the floor. The sight of them had stirred his heart as her body had stirred his loins. Here, the shadows bedecking her, the curves of her, the sweetness of tight nipples colored pink in the light. His bride, untouched and needing. Her lips open to speak his name, her eyes closed to hide her fear.

Dear God, he'd wanted to touch her. Just with the tip of a finger, to see if her breast would quiver at his touch. Had he imagined it, or had her nipples swelled as he'd watched, lengthening, pouting? A short kiss of benediction had trembled on his lips and had been refused only by the greatest of wills. He'd wanted to brush his hand against her back, the curve of her shoulder, the length of her legs.

Their marriage might have been a gift, a sharing of minds formed alike, of interests strongly similar. And passions? He could only wonder, fuel his hot dreams with imagined sighs and limbs wrapped around him in wonderment. Their nights might have been spent in dalliance, gentle training as he taught her what pleased him and learned what made her weep with joy. He might have come upon her during the course of his day, wound his arm around her shoulders, bent down to give her a kiss upon her nose, nuzzle that spot behind her ear he longed to touch. Or, his fingers might have trailed through her hair in delight, glorying in the touch of it. He might have stopped, and regardless of those around him, enfolded her in his arms, his cheek pressed against her hair, his eyes closed lest tears of contentment leak from his eyes and shame him. She would have nestled close, her head fitting in that spot next to his shoulder seemingly formed for her.

But it was not to be. Her ignorance was a blessing. His knowledge, a curse.

Even as he watched her walk below him, he knew that. For a moment, he'd thought her only a vision fashioned from his longing. For days, he'd not left his room for fear of seeing her. Now she was there, her hair gleaming in the sun, the breeze cavorting playfully amidst her skirts.

She walked too close to the retaining wall. The thought was like a knife pointed at his throat.

Langlinais hugged the Terne's contours like a jealous lover. The castle spanned the river at one point, the surging waters passing directly beneath the lower floor, accessible by a series of mossy steps. Before the river passed beneath the castle, however, it dropped several feet. The descent was marked by a low stone wall, crumbled at one point where the flood of last spring had caused the river to surge over its banks. After the repairs to the north tower were finished, the masons had orders to replace the length of the wall.

All of the inhabitants of Langlinais knew well to skirt the area carefully. Everyone knew it was not safe. Everyone, of course, but Juliana, who rarely ventured so far.

He hardly blinked as he watched her, as if his surveillance of her would lessen her danger.

She stooped to pick something up from the path, examined it carefully, and then tucked it into the small bag attached to her girdle.

He admonished her in his mind, as useless as calling out to her. She could not hear his shout any more than she could hear his thoughts, which commanded her to step back from the edge.

She turned and watched the river in seemingly rapt fascination. The waters were fast, a wet spring had made the level of the river high. High enough that if the ground beneath the wall was eroded, the danger was worse. If the earth crumbled, Juliana would be pitched into the swift-running waters.

There was no one near her. The people in the bailey had their attention on their duties and not on the whereabouts of the Lady of Langlinais.

Damn it, where was Jerard? In the fields, supervising the last of the harvest, a duty he'd remarked about only that morning.

She took one step closer to the edge, lured by something commanding her attention.

He began to run.

Chapter 17

The river had its own voice, effectively muffling every other sound until all Juliana could hear was the roar of swiftly moving water. The Terne flooded from time to time, she'd been told, as if proving that it could not be harnessed. Once even the lower bailey had been submerged.

She stood on the bank of the river, watching the surge of water.

The passing weeks had changed her, altered her in some indecipherable way. How could she live a life in this manner, constantly wishing for more from her marriage when she'd been told from the beginning that nothing would ever come of it?

She felt like a different woman from the woman who had first arrived at Langlinais. The woman who stood here now was not the woman who had agreed to such a union. That woman had been content with her work, with the passage of days marked only by the completion of a difficult passage or an illuminated letter. This woman wanted a true marriage with the Lord of Langlinais. She wanted him to speak with her as he had the nights upon the tower, to talk with her of his dreams, of his past, of the years to come. She wanted him to trust her, and grant her the secret that rendered him inviolate and alone.

The sound of the river comforted her in an odd way, the swift-moving current a chant of nature. Water was another one of her fears. *You must not go near the pond, child. You could drown.* Did she test herself now by walking closer to the edge of the bank as she had tested herself when she sat naked before Sebastian?

One moment she was standing there. The next, the earth crumbled at her feet and she was falling through air. Into nothingness it seemed. A sudden jerk upon her girdle halted her flight, then tightened until she felt like she was being cut in two.

She could hear no sound above the roar of the river. She screamed, her throat scraped raw with terror as she hung suspended over the river. But her screams were silent things. Not even the rumble of the ground crumbling above her could be heard over the rushing waters of the Terne.

She looked down, her eyes widening at the impossible distance below, at the torrent of water beneath her. In that instant, childhood memories melted together, made her five years old again, gave her a child's helplessness and terror. She was going to fall to her death. Her mouth was open, but the sight of the sheer drop below her had silenced her cries completely. The bank crumbled even further, small rocks and roots tumbling over her as the constriction at her waist increased.

She could not swim. The churning water seemed to grow closer and closer as she dropped still further. The discomfort at her waist was increasing. Had she been caught on an outcropping of rock? She must have. No, she was moving, slowly being drawn up by the chain that formed her girdle. Her hands reached out and scrabbled at the side of the bank. Her fingers ground into the soil, the heels of her hands pressing against rock and root in a terrorized attempt to pull herself up to safety.

A rock rolled from the earth above, barely missing her. Then another. The rain of powdery soil was the only warning she had. A slab of retaining wall fell from above, slamming into her, a corner of the heavy stone grazing her arms and hands as she covered her head. The impact stunned her. For long moments she dangled weakly against the earth, breathing in the scent of it, hearing the fall of rocks as they splashed heavily into the river. The pain was everywhere, but her hands felt on fire. Her right hand looked odd, and the flexing of her fingers prompted a surprised yelp of pain. The left was badly cut and bleeding profusely.

Sebastian leaned farther out over the embankment, shouting something to her. She couldn't hear him. The sound of the rushing water was too loud. He leaned out precariously over the eroded bank, only his grip preventing her from falling.

She used her left hand like a claw, grinding into the earth in order to find a hold.

One inch and then another. A foot, then. Long, slow, agonizing minutes later, the neck of her surcoat was pulled taut as Sebastian hauled her up the bank.

"Juliana!" Her name was tossed into the air like a song of survival. Her knees touched solid earth and only then did she make a sound. Small, piteous cries a kitten might make, desperate fear churning inside her, demanding recognition.

Sebastian continued to pull her by girdle and surcoat until she was five feet from the edge of the precipice. The painful squeezing of her waist finally eased, but her hands were on fire with pain. She lay against the ground, blessed earth beneath her back, breathless. She looked up to see the glory of blue sky.

And Sebastian's stark look of horror.

It was difficult to speak, but she felt a need to reassure him. "You saved my life, Sebastian," she said, finally, after catching her breath.

The effort to comfort him did not alter his glance nor cause his eyes to soften their expression. Her gaze followed his. Her left hand gripped his forearm tightly, the fingers of her right lay lightly against his bare skin.

"Merciful God," he whispered.

His gloved hands tenderly lifted her fingers from his skin. Her right hand was swelling; he wondered if it was broken. Both hands were badly torn. Her survival had cost her dearly. Too dearly.

"Sebastian?" His silence worried her. He could hear it in her voice.

Her eyes had the power to unman him. Did she weep? *Please, do not let her weep. Not now.*

The growl of thunder warned of the oncoming storm. The birds that roosted in the castle's embrasures were silent, the breeze that preceded the rain was thick with nature's tears.

"Sebastian?"

Her eyes were filled with confusion. There were several scratches on her cheek, and an angry red spot upon her forehead where it had grazed one of the stones on her way up the bank. The most terrible moment in his life had been when she had suddenly disappeared from view. No, perhaps the most terrible moment was still to come.

He did not answer her unspoken question. He felt curiously numb at this moment. He had been so careful, so damnably careful. Not once had he touched her; he'd never allowed her to come close. He'd seen the look on her face when he'd move away suddenly, had placed distance between them. He had locked himself in his honor, bound himself with restraint, and all of it was for nothing.

Now, she would have to know.

"Will you come with me, Juliana?" The words were forced from his lips.

She smiled tremulously, but rose to her knees, then stood. His people parted for him, the look on his face evidently so severe that it muted their whispers.

He could remain silent, not tell her. But that idea was abhorrent. It would spare him her revulsion, but at what cost? He might as well surrender his honor, his word, all the oaths he'd taken as a knight.

When he reached the forge, he ducked beneath the low-hanging roof and stepped aside for her. The hut was open on two sides, a necessity since the fire was never extinguished. Otherwise, the structure would be too hot in which to work.

He turned to the smith. "Leave us," he said, and the smith and his two apprentices disappeared as quickly as steam from the cooling vat. He turned to the crowd with the same demand, and they were not as silent although they dispersed as rapidly. Unfurling the flaps at either end of the structure, he enshrouded the two of them in heat and privacy.

He stood looking down at Juliana, savoring these silent moments. Her face, so bruised, was still lovely. Her mouth trembled in a timorous smile. She had said nothing since that moment he'd removed her hands from his arms. But the questions remained in her eyes.

How did he tell her?

He'd no cause to smile for years, but those nights on the tower had given that back to him. He could not add up a column of numbers without stopping to think of her. Even the movement of his own fingers around a quill brought to mind her deliberate strokes as she labored in the oriel. He had searched through all the codex and scrolls he owned, looking for comments in the margins, learning the personalities of the monks, or perhaps nuns, who had transcribed them in the long ago past. Nor was his enchantment for her limited to those things of the mind and spirit. He'd wanted her from the moment he'd seen her, trembling and innocent.

A flush appeared on her cheeks. A week ago she'd sat naked before him, coaxed to desire by only his words. She'd blushed so then, and her lips had fallen open the slightest bit. Another similar moment would never come again, and he did not doubt that she would soon wish that one stricken from her memory.

She stood in silence, his Juliana. For these last moments he could call her that. For these puny moments, and those that she had so artlessly given him, would be what he recalled when he was alone. All the moments of her smiling, all the times he'd heard her soft voice, all the recollections he'd had of her would have to last him until the day he died, screaming to God for final deliverance.

But not for her. Not for her.

He knelt on one knee at her feet, bowed his head. It was a similar posture as that of his knighting, or homage to his liege. He had long since won his spurs, and the king was far away, but he knew no one more worthy of his respect than Juliana. She had braved her own fear and given him acceptance with her company. Afraid, she had still come to him, and for a few nights made normal his life.

He could not bear this. His heart beat in steadied, resolute strokes. His mind clamored in the same strong rhythm. It must be done. For her sake. It must be done.

"I warned you never to touch me," he said, the words sounding harsh and raw. "Did you never wonder why?"

Her left hand moved until it rested on his head. A benediction of touch. He closed his eyes, knowing it would be the last time she ever touched him.

It was the most profound moment of his life. The most difficult.

"Yes," she said simply. "Always," she added.

He looked up at her, then away. She stood waiting, patient in the way only Juliana could be, draped in silence and composure. He wanted to hear her laugh, wished to see joy on her face. Not wariness, nor revulsion. But what he would say would only invoke fear. Loathing. Disgust.

The words were almost impossible. He forced himself to meet her gaze, to look into her green eyes even as he delivered the words that would set them apart forever. He gave her the truth, stark and brittle as it was.

"I am leper, Juliana."

Chapter 18

The world reeled, insurgent and heated. Juliana stared at him. On his face was a look she'd never before seen. As if he anticipated the wounds her words would bring him. Did he expect her to repudiate him? It was evident he did. He knelt before her, silent beneath her touch, but separate in spirit.

I am leper.

It was only fitting that the storm descended upon them. First, the scent of rain, then the wind, blowing against the canvas flaps of the forge, swirling her surcoat around her ankles. In moments, they were encapsulated in darkness, the yawning maw of the fire making the small hut appear like the entrance to hell. A thought appropriate for this place and those words.

She could hear the squeals as the laundress and her helper rushed to gather their dried linen. The cook cursed the rain, a door was slammed shut. Laughter, then silence, as all of Langlinais seemed to huddle beneath the storm.

If she closed her eyes, she could almost believe the thunder, great booming waves of it, were happening inside her head. But she did not close her eyes, simply stood there absorbing the storm as if it were penance of a sort.

Juliana, come inside. Do you want to be struck by lightning? Odd that she should realize that the voices were afraid, more so than the childish Juliana had been.

Her hand slid down until it rested upon Sebastian's shoulder. A journey made in pain. Her hand throbbed. She would need to wrap it. But how did she treat her soul? What bandage could she place on it?

He did not move away from her touch, but only closed his eyes. But she should not touch him, should she? There were no words from her past to guide her. No admonishments. Only the cautions of her own mind. But it warred with her heart and her heart won. Her hand remained where it was.

The storm was directly above them now. A flash illuminated the hut, the sudden brilliance pouring over them. Thunder followed instantly, shivering through the ground, through her very body. The earth beneath her feet seemed to shake like a giant beast coming alive after centuries of sleep.

"Intellige clamoren meum." She could invoke the same words now, in the same tone of despair.

"Juliana?"

She blinked and looked down at him. His eyes, those lovely dark blue eyes were filled with . . . what? Her left hand moved from his shoulder to his cheek. The backs of her poor bruised and torn fingers were numb, but they could feel his face. She expected it to be bristly to her touch, but his skin was soft. She traced the line of one eyebrow, smiled as it arched beneath her touch. How utterly beautiful he was, like a rare stone, polished until it was shining. A large obsidian stone.

It was pain she saw in his eyes. She recognized it finally.

"Juliana, did you hear me?"

"Yes, Sebastian, I heard you." Her voice sounded strange even to her. Did it appear so to him? She suspected it did, by the look of concern on his face.

She was adrift in thoughts, as if they were butterflies swirling around in her head, but none of them would remain still long enough to make sense. Sebastian. All her life she'd wished to have someone to confide in, to laugh with, to talk to, and her wish had been granted to her in the guise of this husband. He'd been her friend and the lover she'd thought about, dreamed of. Once, she'd feared him, garbed in the colors of night and hinting of mystery. Where was the fear now? Expunged, drained from her. She could feel nothing but pain at this moment, not simply the physical discomfort of her hands, but a deeper anguish, one of the spirit.

"I would not have such a thing happen to you, Juliana."

She was here but not here. She was standing before Sebastian, attentive to his words.

I am leper.

Oh, dearest God, it all made sense now. All of it. He moved away from her because he'd not wished to contaminate her. *"Do not touch me, Juliana. Ever."* A warning. She'd not heeded it, but only accidentally. She had not meant to touch him.

Without issue. Or hope of it.

Something died within her. Something bright and gleaming and new. Hope? It seemed so. Perhaps she had been pretending all along that such a dictate might be changed. That she might understand his objection to a true marriage and soften him in some way. If so, that notion shivered and succumbed to a final, bloody death.

"*I am leper.*" The words echoed in her mind, like the corridors of the convent were wont to give back sounds. She'd seen a leper only once. He had been a pitiful thing, with hands whittled away to putrid stumps, his face blackened and heavily bandaged.

No, not Sebastian. Please.

"There are those who believe it possible to prevent the disease by fire," Sebastian told her now.

She looked down at him again, startled into awareness by his words. "You would burn my hands, Sebastian?" She looked down at them. She could no longer feel her right hand. Swollen nearly twice its size, it looked almost blue. How strange that it seemed to belong to someone else, not her.

"I would do anything to prevent your suffering as I do, Juliana."

What did she say to such earnestness? To such pain? Another thing they shared, it seemed.

She was someone other than herself at that moment, someone who felt absurdly cold when the forge was an inferno. The throbbing of her hand was fierce, the pain measured her words, rationed her to those she could speak quickly and easily. He wanted to burn her hands. She looked down at them, imagined them without their flesh, singed and raw, bones emerging from beneath her sleeves. It would make her safe, he said. Her vision was graying, the edge of it furred and wavy.

She blinked and focused on him kneeling before her. Sebastian, the brave and noble knight, the husband who would never be her mate. She had gotten what she wanted, hadn't she? All the answers to all the questions.

"No, Sebastian," she softly said, and surrendered to the blackness.

She'd fallen, unconscious, at his feet.

Jerard carried her through the rainswept bailey as Sebastian followed.

She had effectively trapped him with her denial, lanced him to the spot with one word. *No.* There was no cure for her now, only an eternity of watching and waiting and hoping that she did not evince his same symptoms. Fear spread like a fast-growing weed through him.

A spear of lightning lit the sky again, a jagged, omnipotent greeting.

Rain bathed his face as he looked upward, as if to find God in the black sky above Langlinais. Sebastian closed his eyes, felt the stinging slap of wind. The unadorned savagery of this storm was as elemental to him as a prayer. Perhaps it was nature's way of worship.

His own prayer was simple, the intent not for forgiveness, but for Juliana's hands. And most of all for her protection against the leprosy that had so changed his life. He did not want for Juliana what was promised for him.

An Egyptian physician had uttered his death sentence in a voice filled with revulsion. From that day on, he'd been sequestered from the other prisoners, led to a cell barely large enough to accommodate him. There he'd remained, adrift in a horror that recalled every occasion in his life in which he'd seen one of the untouchables, the poor shambling wrecks who were defiled and shunned for their disease.

The Church reasoned that only sinners contracted leprosy, that it was a punishment for lascivious thoughts or lecherous acts. He had never been able

to identify any of his sins as great enough to render
him one of the living dead. His worst transgression
had been a questioning mind, one that asked why it
was permissible to kill in the name of faith and yet
forbidden otherwise. Why did the Church, founded
on the tenets of charity and love, approve of torture
to extract a confession? But why, if he was given a
mind capable of wondering, should he then be punished for it? Surely God would not grant man an
ability that should not be used?

There were no choices then—no vast range of op-
tions between good and evil. He would either be
surrendered to the pits of hell, burning blood red
against the blackness of eternal damnation. Or up-
lifted in a golden chariot, his journey accompanied
by seraphic voices. There were no such careful mark-
ers now. He was neither abject sinner, nor perfect,
but somewhere unremarkably in between.

The thunder growled in agreement.

He stood in the bailey, legs braced, fists outstretched to heaven itself.

Juliana. It was the sound of a storm-tossed wind.
And it was not until he felt the rawness of his own
throat that Sebastian realized he had screamed her
name.

Chapter 19

"I will send Sister Agnes with you," the abbess said. "She has a gift of healing."

"My lord will be grateful for your assistance," Jerard said.

The young man bowed, and she smiled. Twice, she had told him that she required no deference and twice he had nodded but had forgotten just as soon. She frightened him, she knew. Not because of the influence her family wielded—reason enough in her secular years—but because she was the abbess of the Sisters of Charity, a post she'd held for nearly twenty years and had hopes of retaining until her death.

She had been born Gertrude of Bachian, coming to Sisters of Charity initially as a novice uncertain of either her future or her devotion. Thirty years later she was assured of both. She'd found at the convent a place in need of her talents, and in her students the children she'd never bear.

Not all the girls within her care were disposed to accept the guidance she gave them. Yet, with each girl who did, she gave an appreciation for learning, a thirst for knowledge. With each she'd been strict and to each she'd given affection. But the greatest legacy she gave the fostered girls of Sisters of Charity was the gift of self-knowledge. Before they left the convent, they each knew their greatest blessing and how to share it with the world.

Some were possessed of healing abilities, some with the capacity to turn a garden green and lush. Some were endowed with organizational genius and their estates would be managed ably. Too, there were a few who had been blessed with the gift of laughter and little else, but the world could be brightened by humor, she'd reasoned. Sometimes, there was a special girl who passed her time at Sisters of Charity. Her aptitude was such that even Gertrude had been awed. A few years ago it had been Anne Nursia. She had, gentle Anne, been given the ability to create pictures of unimaginable beauty from the most humble of materials. With each girl, the abbess had felt a paradoxical relief and sadness when they'd left the Sisters of Charity.

Juliana had been one of her most miserable failures. Gertrude had never been able to discern the girl's true blessing. Juliana had been possessed of stubbornness, and she had been determined to learn the skills necessary in a scriptorium. It was this strong will, more than natural ability, that had made her a success at it. She was not easily amused, but smiled when coaxed. Gertrude knew that she would chatelaine Langlinais with grace and poise, but it would be because of her training more than inclination. She was too quiet, too reserved, a tapped spring or a dammed brook. A mystery, this girl, and had always been.

Yet she did not hesitate to send aid to her the moment she'd learned of the accident. By such good deeds were the Sisters of Charity known.

Gertrude turned from the grille that separated her

from visitors, and spoke to a novice who stood waiting for direction. Sister Agnes would be summoned and together with her case of unguents and salves and other decoctions of a medicinal nature, sent to Langlinais.

"What is being done for her now?" she asked the young man.

"I do not know, Abbess, I was sent right away to you. But my lord suspects her right hand is broken. It is swollen badly."

She brushed her hands down the front of her habit. "I am not talented in such things, but Sister Agnes is."

"Thank you, Abbess."

She waved him away, turned and went in search of the healing sister.

It was still raining. Moisture sheeted the glass, made it appear as if the room was a watery cave. The light wavered on the floor, even the air seemed misted.

"I thought it was a very brave thing you did, my lord. Everyone saw it," Grazide said. He turned and glanced at her. Her smile twisted something within him. He only nodded in response.

"Her poor hands." Grazide sat on the edge of the bed. Juliana lay beneath the sheet, her hands on the outside, folded at the wrist. Too much like an effigy for his peace of mind.

He could not touch her in order to set her bones and Grazide did not know how. He searched his memory for someone at Langlinais with the degree of skill necessary to aid Juliana.

"I've sent Jerard to the convent," he said, offering the explanation as an excuse for his inaction. His words seemed to satisfy her, a surprising occurrence.

He had rarely spoken to Grazide, or any of his people, for months. Yet her interest was not in him, it was in Juliana's well-being. Such loyalty to his wife only increased his fondness for Grazide.

They watched her together for nearly an hour until he asked that she leave him alone with his wife. She acceded with no further conversation, a rare and well-timed silence on her part.

Juliana sighed, turned her head. Sebastian watched her carefully to ensure it was not just wishful thinking on his part.

He walked to the end of the bed, his arms at his sides. He had, over the last hour, rarely turned his gaze from her, becoming so attuned to the frequency and nature of her breathing that he waited for her next breath. He wondered if she dreamed as she lay insensible. Did she wander through the corridors of a pain-induced nightmare? Her black hair was spread out upon her pillow, her face too pale. There was darkness beneath her eyes, a soft bruising of her flesh that made him want to stroke his finger across her skin, place a kiss there.

Foolish dreams. Even more insane, the wish to lean over her and brush her hair back from her face, place a cool cloth over her brow. Whisper to her that all would be well. He prayed that it would be.

She opened her eyes at that moment. They appeared tired, the whites tinted pink, as if pain had colored them in her sleep.

He felt as he had the moment his father had knighted him. The collee, the accolade against his neck strong enough to topple him to the floor. There was no hatred in Juliana's look. Instead, her eyes seemed to grant him a view of her soul. And in that generous spirit was understanding, compassion, warmth.

Surely he was mistaken. Perhaps he only saw those things because he needed her forgiveness, because his soul ached for it. He had hidden so many things from her. How could she be so open in her emotions? Was it that she was simply befuddled?

He would have said something, but at that moment, Juliana smiled. Not a broad smile, but a soft lifting of pale lips. His vision wavered as if he saw her through the glass of the rain-glistened window.

Then the smile slowly faded. In its place was a furrow above her brow. And a surprising curiosity. "Why did you not tell me?"

"How does one tell a bride such a thing?"

Everything he had done had been to protect Langlinais and himself. The Templars wanted Langlinais for their own, and the Church would have gladly stripped him of the castle. The entire future of Langlinais had balanced on a delicate fulcrum. Because of her, because she'd stayed, he'd banished one fear. Now, there were only the Templars to worry about.

He turned back, determined to give her honesty in this thing at least. "Would you have remained if you had known?"

She seemed to consider it a moment. "I don't know."

"I do," he said. "You would have run screaming for the door."

Her slight smile seemed to lighten some dark place within him.

"Did you send for me only so that no one would question why I was still at the convent after your return?"

He had always thought her intelligent. He smiled at the evidence of it. "It was one of my very great fears. The Church might have sent a cleric to investigate." That representative, had he learned of Sebastian's disease, had the power to banish him from his home. Lepers could not own property.

"But that was only part of it," he said, admitting the whole of the truth. "I wanted to provide for the future of my home and the people here," he said. "My wife could hold Langlinais, protect it from seizure even if the Church tried to take it from me."

"How did such a thing happen to you, Sebastian?"

"Does it matter? There are a thousand answers to that question," he said, "all dependent upon whom you ask. Bad water or goat's milk or the light of a certain moon." He looked away. "By the time I was released from prison, I knew my fate. One I would prevent for you."

"By burning me."

He looked away. "If it would protect you, I would have done it."

"Is there no other way?"

"If there had been, I would have found it. I have made a study of such things."

"And no cure, Sebastian?" The softness in her eyes was his undoing. The sadness in her voice made him want to turn away. But he did not. He stood where he was, looking down at her. Had he thought the scene in the forge the most profound in his life? He'd not foreseen this moment, with Juliana's somber smile and her green eyes hinting at unshed tears.

"None," he said. One word, it told of all his reading and all his research and all the nights when he'd used his education to attempt to find a way to heal himself.

"There is nothing we can do, is there, Sebastian? Nothing at all."

It did not seem to be a question that needed an answer.

*   *   *

Jerard returned from the Sisters of Charity sooner than expected. The abbess had done more than send salves for Juliana; she had sent Sister Agnes, who was supposed to have a healing touch.

Sebastian did not demur as the short and rotund nun bustled into the chamber, her jaw set at an angle that warned any onlooker that she was determined to see success in her mission. He would have done anything at that point to spare Juliana pain, and if the presence of a religieuse would aid her, he did not care that it placed him close to danger. The nun could, if she knew of his condition, banish him to a leprosarium as ably as any friar or priest. But it no longer mattered. His time of freedom was nearly at an end. His seclusion would last the rest of his life. At least during these last days, he could assure himself of Juliana's well-being.

Sister Agnes pointed to the bench with one finger, and Jerard moved it to the side of the bed, then left the room to fetch the warm water she requested. The nun placed her box upon the bench, then sat down, tenderly examining Juliana's hands. Juliana only closed her eyes at the nun's probing, her lips clenched tight. Almost as tight as Sebastian's fists.

Jerard arrived with the water and was immediately sent on another errand, this time to procure a glass of wine.

"I needn't ask if that pains you," Sister Agnes said, when Juliana gasped. "I've no doubt you've broken a few bones in your hand, child." The nun finally released her hands, and reaching inside her box, pulled out a covered jar.

She applied the leeches to Juliana's right hand.

"The swelling prevents any further treatment," she explained, as Sebastian moved closer to the edge of the bed. After the leeches were bloated and had sluggishly dropped off, she lifted Juliana's hands by the wrists, gently placing them in a pan of water into which she'd poured a fragrant mixture that smelled of flowers.

When she removed them, she sprinkled a yellow powder upon the cuts of the left hand and proceeded to bandage it swiftly.

"I will warn you, child, this next will be painful for you."

Sebastian drew closer, glancing down at Juliana. Her face was too pale, but she smiled at his look.

He sat on the edge of the bed opposite the short militant nun.

"I have searched my library for this Catullus of yours and can find nothing of him," he said to Juliana, hoping to take her mind from the pain to come.

"I doubt he is greatly known, Sebastian," she said, keeping her eyes steadily on him. Sister Agnes bent one finger and Juliana's lashes fluttered shut. A gasp, no more than a breath, was all the evidence of the pain she was experiencing.

"I broke my leg once," he said. As a distraction it was a puny offering, but she opened her eyes once more, smiling at him again.

He wanted to tilt her chin up and place a kiss upon her lips. A soft one in reward for her bravery, for the look in her eyes. Not aversion or revulsion, but affection and fondness and something too deep comfortably to name.

"Grazide told me you were a wild child, Sebastian. That breaking your leg changed you." The last two words were nearly gasped. She bit down on her lip as the nun pressed a bone back into place.

He did not think it possible, but she grew even

more pale. He turned to Sister Agnes. "Is there nothing you can do to spare her pain?"

She frowned. "It is God who heals, I only aid Him." The nun looked pointedly at his clothing, as if the wearing of it should have prevented him from asking such an idiotic question. But she did not ask why the Lord of Langlinais was dressed in the rough wool garb of a monk.

"Then can you not aid Him with more gentleness?" He frowned at her and she frowned back.

"She *is* being gentle, Sebastian," Juliana said. "Tell me about how you came to break your leg. Is it a better tale than how I almost fell into the river?" Her smile was wry, his heart seemed to expand as he watched her.

"I was hiding from Gregory," he said. "We were playing some game, no doubt some reenactment of the Punic Wars. I was stationed in the perfect defensive position, waiting for him to attack."

"In the north tower," Juliana added.

He nodded. "Only Gregory was waiting for me to attack him. He never came. I grew tired of waiting for him and decided to find another strategic position. But I took the steps too quickly, and found myself at the bottom of them."

"Rash behavior often leads to rash consequences," Sister Agnes contributed.

He would have said something to the little nun had not Juliana screamed then. Not a full-throated sound, but almost as if she'd been startled into it.

"Do something for her pain!" he demanded, turning to the nun.

"I can do nothing for the pain until I align the bones in her hand. Would you have me leave her crippled?"

They stared at each other. Sebastian recognized

that it was a battle of wills, but she'd said the proper words to silence him. Juliana must be allowed the use of her hands; it was the only thing left her. Her work, and Langlinais.

"Grazide said that you changed then. Was it fear of being lame?" Juliana's voice was a faint wisp of sound.

He turned and faced her again, grateful that her eyes were closed. The better not to see the ruin of her hand. Even now he cringed at the sight of it. He'd seen worse wounds, had suffered more grievous injuries. Except that it seemed different when it was her hand and her pain.

"I had dreams of being the greatest knight in all of England."

"Even then, arrogance," Sister Agnes murmured.

"Can you not hurry?" His temper was being restrained only by a dint of will.

"There are places where the bones of her hand have pierced the skin. It is of importance that they be pushed back in gently. It is delicate work and takes some time." Her tone was surprisingly mild, but her look was not. It chastised with a glance.

"She is in pain." He turned back to watch Juliana, never seeing when the little nun appraised him with another, longer, look.

"My father tied his sword to my leg, telling me that I would decide what my future was to be. Either I would heal as straight and as strong as that sword, or I would be lame and it was the only association I would ever have of it. I was determined to heal, and so I did."

Her wan smile was his only indication that she had heard him.

"Where is that sword?"

"I inherited it upon my father's death and took it on crusade with me."

An agonizingly long time later, Juliana's hand was bandaged. Sister Agnes bathed her face, held her head up and made her sip an infusion she'd mixed with a cup of wine. Then the force of her not inconsiderable will was turned on him.

"She will sleep now. And lord or not, husbands are not needed in this place. Not now, and not until I call."

She moved to the door, flung it open and stood there, defying him. Her look dared him to protest his banishment. Her eyes narrowed when he hesitated.

He glanced at Juliana, who lay with her eyes closed, her face ashen.

"Do you wish me to stay, Juliana?"

She smiled softly, but did not open her eyes. "No, Sebastian."

He stood, oddly disappointed. "Sebastian?"

She was looking at him now, her gaze as steady as before, if just a little more weary. As if the pain had eaten through her composure and her restraint.

"Yes, Juliana?"

"Thank you."

Simple words, but they felt important. He nodded at her. Within moments, he found himself on the other side of the door.

Chapter 20

"Please tell the abbess how much I appreciate your care, Sister," Juliana said a few days later.

"I but did my duty, Juliana." Sister Agnes looked up from packing her box to soften the words with a small smile. "It is now yours to ensure that my work was not in vain. You must have the bandages of your left hand removed twice a day, Juliana, and place another layer of salve upon your hand before having it rebandaged."

Juliana looked down at her bandaged hands. Each separate finger was covered by a length of linen so that they looked large and misshapen. The pain of them had subsided somewhat, or perhaps she had simply grown accustomed to it.

"As to your right hand, Juliana, I've no way of knowing whether you will ever write again. In a few weeks, you may remove the bandages, but I would give it much longer than that before you try to force your fingers to hold a quill."

Juliana nodded.

Sister Agnes came and stood by the bed. "The next weeks will be very difficult. But I've known you since you were a small child, and I know you to be a stubborn girl. That stubbornness will serve you well now."

Juliana nodded. "Sister, is there a cure for leprosy?" She took a chance by asking the nun. Perhaps it was the look in the other woman's eyes, an ever-present compassion, that made her do so.

Sister Agnes turned and continued packing items into her small wooden case. It held the most precious of her healing instruments, vials of precious herbs and unguents made from recipes she was eager to share. Healing, she was fond of saying, was one of those arts that is bettered by contribution. Was she going to answer? Or pretend the question had not been asked?

"I know no one who has ever survived it," she said, finally, not looking at Juliana. "They are poor wretches, truth to tell. But there are things that can be done to bring them comfort. This," she said, placing a small, covered pottery jar on the bed beside Juliana, "softens the skin and has been known to ease the pain of the disease."

Juliana placed her bandaged hand atop the jar.

"Do not allow your kind heart to apply the salve yourself. You must never touch one of them." Her voice was gentle, her look direct. "If there is someone at Langlinais with such a curse, Juliana, it is better that they be taken from here."

Juliana looked down at her hands. He'd wanted to burn her rather than have her suffer the same fate as his. Yet even the most caring nun would have him banished. She forced a smile to her face.

"Thank you, Sister," she softly said, lifting her gaze to the other woman. "I will see to it."

"There are no thanks necessary, Juliana," Sister Agnes said. "I will add the penitent to my prayers.

Is there any word you would have me convey to the abbess?"

"Only that when I regain the use of my hands I will be happy to continue my work."

"Whatever God wills. Perhaps your time will be spent more with the children you will bear."

Juliana managed a smile. There had been enough secrets spilled this morning. She would not tell Sister Agnes that it seemed as if her destiny was pointed in a different direction, but in which way she was not certain. If she could not work, and she would never be a wife, then what was her purpose?

Yet another question that must be answered eventually.

Sebastian stood in the oriel. It was still scented with roses. He carefully turned over the pages Juliana had so carefully inscribed. She had already fastened them together into facing folia, or individual pages, so that they were in proper numerical order. The quaternion, the book containing five sections of pages, would be sent with Sister Agnes to the abbess in the morning.

He read her colophons, those margin notes that indicated the personalities of scribes so acutely. None was as poignant as the message she'd written on the last page. *I have made the letters as properly and perfectly as I could, and attempted to copy without error. It has been my intent to understand the sense of what I have copied, and to concentrate my wandering mind upon this task.*

What had occupied her thoughts?

"My lord?" He turned at the sound of Jerard's voice.

"A message has come for you, my lord. A Templar brought it." Jerard held out the missive, a wax seal across the face of it. Sebastian took it, a feeling not unlike doom stealing over him.

He broke open the seal and scanned the letter. Folding it again, he pushed past Jerard and strode down the hall, Jerard following him. He opened the door of his chamber and tried to force himself to be calm. But anger seemed to churn within him like a whirlpool.

Once inside his room, he thrust the letter to Jerard, waited until the steward read the words.

"How can they refuse an extension, my lord?" There was disbelief coupled with anger on his steward's face.

"Easily, Jerard," he said. "They want something else from me."

Inscribed in Gregory's hand was the reply to his request for more time to pay his ransom. On the surface of it, the letter was a brotherly expression of concern that Sebastian was unable to make the last payment on the loan. Gregory suggested how he might be willing to convince the Templars to discharge the debt. All that Sebastian need do was to surrender anything he might have taken from Montvichet.

"They want the Cathar treasure in exchange for Langlinais." The treasure was no secret from Jerard. His steward had been with him at Montvichet. But the true nature of the Cathar legacy was Sebastian's knowledge alone. He had vowed to keep it hidden and allow it to die with him. The letter, however, altered his wishes.

Jerard laid the letter down on the table as if it were contaminated.

"I know my brother only too well, Jerard. He is happiest when neck deep in intrigue." Sebastian walked to the table and stared down at the letter.

He could almost see Gregory concentrating upon the exact wording. Enough information to alarm, but not enough to reveal the Templar intent.

"What will you do, my lord?"

He could not afford to ignore the veiled threat. He had more than his own future to be concerned about, more than a castle to shield. He had Juliana and the inhabitants of Langlinais to guard. He idly fingered the small carved figure of Juliana given to him by Old Simon.

They wanted the treasure of the Cathars.

The Templars would not raze Langlinais, but they would occupy it. Set the castle up as another of their properties, people it with warrior-monks. His people would be banished, the villagers sent away. Some of the families here could trace their line back to the time of his Norman ancestor. And Juliana? What would they do to his wife? Cast her out? Her welfare, that of his people would not matter to the Templars.

Even if he could pay the remainder of his ransom, he did not doubt there would be another pretext under which they would threaten Langlinais. Some interest he'd not considered, some fine levied. Their hunger for the treasure outweighed any other consideration, even that of fairness.

There was only one thing to be done. He considered how he might offer to the Templars exactly what they wanted, and safeguard both his wife and his home.

"They are going to get exactly what they expect, Jerard," he said. "Take a message to Old Simon for me in the morning. There is some work I need him to perform for me." He spoke the words that would put his plan into motion, then watched as Jerard left the room.

The emotions he felt now surprised him. Relief and rage. The relief was harder to decipher. Did it have at its roots the fact that he knew his plan might work? He understood why he was angry. The Templars had stolen the last of his time with Juliana.

He pulled the robe over his head, reveling in the freedom from its confining folds. His skin chafed where the wool abraded it. He inspected himself, the way he did each day, measuring the progress of his disease like a mother might record a child's growth. There was no fondness in this, however, no touch of kindness a mother might invoke. His condition was progressing, just as he feared. He'd not yet lost the sensation in his limbs, a blessing or a curse, he did not know which. It meant he was not declining as rapidly as he might. Or it could mean that it would be many long and painful years until he died of this.

Until then, he must protect those under his care. First, by giving the Templars what they thought he had. Secondly, by ensuring that they left Juliana and Langlinais in peace.

Chapter 21

"It isn't as if we begrudged her help, my lady." Grazide fixed the end of Juliana's braid with a short piece of blue ribbon. "Nor do I doubt she's a good soul, being a nun and all. But she banished me from your room, and she sent away all of the helpers in the buttery." Grazide sniffed.

"I am sure she didn't mean to be overpowering, Grazide. It's just that Sister Agnes has always been a bit headstrong."

"Pushy. Bossy. Arrogant." Such terseness of speech was unlike Grazide.

Juliana smiled at her, hoping to smooth the other woman's ruffled feathers.

"Then she told me we were a godless bunch, not having a chaplain present at Langlinais. And she said that Cook didn't use enough greens, and that our meat wasn't salted properly."

"I am sorry if she was annoying, Grazide."

The attendant removed the cotte from the cupboard. It had been shorn of its trailing sleeves, the better to accommodate the bandages on Juliana's hands.

Grazide looked up. "It is not your place to apologize, my lady, but hers. Even being a nun does not excuse a body from rudeness, does it?"

Juliana shook her head. Such disputes normally occurred when two strong women were assigned the same task and one looked to be better at it than the other.

Once a great gust of wind had torn the roof from the refectory. She had helped with the cleanup around the convent and discovered that the youngest and most fragile trees had survived, while the strongest, most sturdy oaks had been uprooted. The lesson had not been lost on her. Sometimes the one that willingly bends is the one that remains standing after the storm has passed. She'd found, however, that it was more common for one person to expect the other to bend than willingly to surrender. It was evident that Grazide felt the same.

"I doubt we'll see her again," she said, in an effort to placate her attendant. "Jerard has taken her back to the convent." *Along with the newly copied volume of the encyclopedia.* Juliana wondered if she would ever be able to do such work again.

"Not soon enough, my lady. She lectured us, she did, all about how we were to care for you, and make the salve for your hands. Kept us there for an hour telling us over and over, until I thought of throttling her." There was an odd look on Grazide's face as if she just now realized her words and now wondered at the celestial punishment for wishing to strangle a nun.

"I am sorry, Grazide," she said again. Sister Agnes had left that morning, perhaps by tomorrow, the other woman's anger would have softened.

Grazide draped the cotte over Juliana's head. The voluminous garment served as her night attire, its thin weave masking little of her body. Modesty, however, had been supplanted by necessity. She could do few things for herself now, especially with her hands bandaged so thickly.

"Not that we don't have enough to do," Grazide mumbled, "what with all the preparations for my lord's journey. Twelve men, plus he and Jerard to provide provisions for, too."

"Journey?"

Grazide straightened up, folded her hands at her middle, frowned. "Don't tell me you've no knowledge of the thing, my lady."

Juliana shook her head.

"Off to France he's going. Him and Jerard, with a troop of our men-at-arms."

"When?"

"A sennight or less."

She stood, allowing Grazide to arrange the folds of her cotte around her. Her hands were kept above her waist, to minimize the pain. Sister Agnes had left a draught for her to drink if it became unbearable, but each day the ache seemed less.

What she felt at this moment was pain of another kind. Why had he not told her? And why was he leaving?

There was no knock on the door. It simply opened. He looked up at the interruption, thinking it was Jerard. His steward was his only visitor. Even the talkative Grazide had been convinced early on that he needed none of her care. Never mind that she'd wiped his nose and swatted his backside when he was a boy. No one else would dare invade his privacy. Therefore, it was with surprise that he watched Juliana glide into the room. Between her bandaged hands was a covered vessel. She lowered it gently to the bench. He frowned. She should not be carrying things.

She did not meet his eyes, asked no pardon for the interruption, simply sat beside the jar, her eyes intent upon the black maw where flames leapt in colder days. He knew, in that strange sense that came over him in matters that dealt with her, that her demeanor was studied and calm only through will.

He'd not seen her for two days, had removed himself from her room and her sight. Looking at him could only remind her of what he was. He had enjoyed, for a few hours at least, her acceptance. He did not want to see that emotion transformed into revulsion. But it seemed as if he was to be treated to some strong feeling. She trembled with it.

"Juliana."

"Sebastian," she said, and he wondered fleetingly if she mocked him.

He sat at the other end of the bench and stared ahead, just as she did. Sometimes, it was better not to face one's opponent, but to slice from the side. He waited for the blow.

She turned and looked down at the earthenware jar on the bench. "Promise me you'll use this, Sebastian."

"What is it?"

"Something Sister Agnes says will ease your discomfort. You must spread it on your skin once a day."

"What is it? Bat tongue? Ground-up beetles?"

She shrugged. "I do not know. Does it matter? If it eases you, do you care?"

He did not tell her that there were no potions, no salves, no unguents made that would ease his coming discomfort. He opened the earthenware jar. It smelled of mint, similar to the preparation Sister Agnes had used on her hands.

"Promise me."

He had given her far less than she deserved, he could give her this. He nodded.

"Grazide says you are leaving." It was not a question. Both hands rested on her legs. Heavily bandaged, they looked like white clubs.

He nodded, concentrating his gaze upon the floor. He noted that the timbers were warping in one spot.

"Where do you go, Sebastian? And why? Or do you intend to tell me anything? Shall I aspire to be like Hildegard of Bingen? She was consulted as a prophet, you know. Think of all the conversations we could have without your having to speak. I could think of the question and you could simply think the answer."

His lips quirked at this evidence of her irritation. It was the first time he'd ever seen her angry.

She stood and walked the short distance to where he sat, facing him. She was not a short woman, but he was a tall man. If he had stood, the top of her head would have come to his shoulder. With him seated, she was but a little taller than he, enough to look imperiously down at him. Enough that her chin tilted at an angle that would have been considered regal had he not seen it quiver just the smallest bit.

Her cotte was of linen, finely crafted and too transparent for this moment. Beneath it he could see her lovely body, the swell of breasts, the curve of leg. He did not need to see her to know every inch of her skin. He could too easily recall how she'd looked, naked, in the glow of the lamps. Such recollections were replayed in his mind nightly. He looked away.

"Am I to be left here, then, Sebastian? To weep for you? To yearn? And one day, I will fall into another man's arms and he will console me, and you will sleep your martyr's sleep, content that your plans have been fulfilled?"

If the loneliness was too great to bear, and she took a lover, the world would not condemn her for it. He shied from the idea, his mind skirting the sudden quick image of Juliana being kissed, Juliana with her face flushed with wonder in the arms of another man. He could not think of it without feeling the twin spikes of rage and grief.

Her eyes seemed to deepen, the green of them seen through a sheen of tears. He said nothing as she turned and walked toward the door.

"Fare you well, Sebastian. Go with God." Why did she appear so much more delicate than she had in the past? As if she were no more than a wraith, a faint rendering of herself.

"I cannot take you with me."

"Why, Sebastian?"

He stood and faced her, brushed back the cowl from his head. How he hated this garment, the necessity for its coverage, the shroud of it. It buried him alive, proclaimed the distance necessary between them.

"Because it is dangerous."

She nodded. She accepted his explanation, but she did not understand it. And she would not until he explained the whole of it to her.

Instead of doing so, he asked her another question, one that caused her eyes to widen. "What concessions do you make, Juliana? That night I came upon you in your room. You wrote that you would concede. What did you mean?"

She looked down at the floor, and for a long moment, he did not think she would answer him. Her voice, when it came, was low. "I would ask no more questions and never touch you."

Silence, while he wondered how to respond.

"I never lured you there as you thought, Sebastian."

Another statement to which he could offer no comment.

"The circumstances have not changed much, Juliana. Except that you now know the reasons why."

Her smile was sweet, but he noted that the expression was not mirrored in her eyes. "I will postulate my own question to you, Sebastian." She held up her bandaged hands. "What happens if you've left a leper at Langlinais?"

His scowl was a thundercloud that warned of a storm. She leaned back against the doorframe and watched him. His face took on a ruddy color and twice he opened his mouth to speak and twice shut it as quickly. His gloved hands clenched into fists.

"You cannot come with me."

Calm was the only recourse for his anger. She had not been fair perhaps playing on his fears with her. But had he expected that she would remain here, meek and accepting of whatever fate decreed for her? She had done that once, and been given a marriage that would never be a union. She would not do so again.

Juliana, you must be of a quiet nature, lest you displease others. She forced the voice away.

"The abbess chastised me often, Sebastian. She said that once I had a thought between my teeth, I would not allow it to escape until I had worried it to death. I believe that she even referred to a rat in her description of such tenacity, although I may have been mistaken."

"I thought you were noted more for the timidity of your nature." His eyebrow lifted, his mouth seemed inclined to do so also. Yet, neither gesture seemed one of amusement.

"The two character traits can exist side by side. Should I confess to my fear both at being left behind and of journeying with you?"

"That comment is supposed to convince me?"

"No," she said softly. "This one is. Take me with you, Sebastian. Please."

He seemed to study her, from the expression in her eyes to the bandages upon her hands. What was he thinking? She didn't know.

"To Montvichet, then," he said, finally. "That far and no farther."

She nodded, and said nothing more as she pushed the door closed behind her.

Chapter 22

The middle bailey was crowded with men-at-arms atop their horses. Most of Langlinais was there to bid them farewell, despite the fact their destination was secret, the very nature of their journey hidden.

Juliana remained on the top step. It was barely past dawn, and the sky was beginning to lighten. An air of expectancy seemed to grip the castle and its people. Had it been such when Sebastian had left Langlinais for his round of tourneys?

She sought to find him among the milling men, looked for his distinctive black robe. He was nowhere to be found.

Grazide bubbled along beside her. "Have you ever seen such fine men, my lady? And all of them Langlinais-born and -raised. Why, I knew most of them when they were still babes. And bathed their bottoms myself. That one," she said, pointing to a sandy-haired man standing alongside Jerard, "was my Ned's best friend in childhood days. His sister is now my own dear daughter. But that is enough about me. We should get you on your way. I shall miss you, my dear. Fare you well, and God keep you until we meet again."

Juliana bent and accepted the hug from her attendant, returned it in equal measure. In truth, she had grown fond of Grazide. Indeed, it was impossible not to like the voluble woman.

She straightened up and smiled, looking beyond Grazide to the crowded bailey. It was then that she saw him.

There had been few enough times when her breath had been taken from her. Juliana could count three occasions when she'd been left speechless by events. The occasion of meeting Sebastian for the first time was one; the day she learned his secret another. And then this moment.

"Oh look, my lady, it's him. And mounted on Faeren, too. Isn't he a sight?"

The bailey was lit by glowing orange rays of a slow-rising sun. An ebony horse, his bridle and harness adorned with silver, his saddle dotted with silver insets, danced in the light. His rider effortlessly controlled him, even smiled with the exuberance of one who has been denied a pleasure for too long. His grin flashed in the morning sun as bright as the armor he wore, silvered chain mail that stretched from neck to wrist to ankle, topped with a sleeveless crimson tunic. His sword belt was heavily embroidered in red and silver, and the weapon it held bore a ruby embedded in the center of its hilt.

Sebastian of Langlinais.

This was the man who'd ridden into battle, the knight who'd won so many tourneys. A young warrior with tumbled brown hair that looked gold and red in the sun. A man she'd never before seen. He laughed and she felt her heart fall to her toes to see him this way. No monk wrapped in piety, no man sternly intent upon isolation. A glimpse, perhaps, of the man who'd dwelled side by side with her spirit, the one who'd stolen her heart even as he'd invaded her mind.

Jerard called out to him, and Sebastian responded with a laughing answer. The words they spoke were inconsequential, the meaning unnecessary. The spell that enchanted her grew stronger. At that moment, Sebastian let Faeren have his head, and the horse seemed to fly. Faeren became a winged creature, one crafted of myth and magic. Juliana felt as if she were witnessing an event that would not come again, that Sebastian and Faeren represented all that was good and noble and fine about the world, but that its nobility and shining purpose was both misunderstood and destined to fade.

It was not, she thought, as she watched them race through the north gate, necessary for a man to be pure and virtuous. It was enough for him to wish to be. The knights who traveled on crusade did so with an honorable intent, and had therefore achieved their purpose the moment they left home and hearth behind them. It was not as important to gain back Jerusalem as to wish themselves better men. Yet, even now, men fought and died for ownership of a plot of land, to wrest control while not understanding it was the improvement of themselves that was better sought.

Was such a thought heresy?

A glint of sunlight struck Sebastian's chain mail, a flash of light perfect in its moment. He reined in Faeren, stood upon the hill looking down at Langlinais, a faint figure with hand raised. An odd thought, one that made her take a few steps forward, as if she might be able to reach out and touch him. It was as if they were closer now than they had ever been before. Separated by distance, but not by inclination. Could she feel his thoughts or were they only echoes of her own wishes? They buffeted her as if they were butterflies in a spring breeze. *Come back to me, Sebastian.*

Do not fear, Juliana.

I will be with you.

Forever.

She wanted to weep. Instead, she held the memory of this moment tight to her, vowed to forever remember the sight of him, whole and happy.

"My lady?"

She blinked, pulled from her reverie by Grazide's concern. Jerard stood beside her. How long had they been watching her?

Jerard bowed and preceded her to the wagon in which she was to travel. She turned and bid goodbye to Grazide again, then climbed inside.

She did not look in Sebastian's direction again.

It occurred to Sebastian that keeping Juliana with him might be the best way to protect her. He fully expected there to be treachery ahead, but it had taken a dream, a twisted vision of slashing swords and screaming horses for him to realize that leaving her behind would expose her to more danger than taking her with him.

The Templars' genius lay in political maneuvering. It would be easier for them to use Juliana as hostage to force him to relinquish the Cathar treasure than it would be to lay siege to Langlinais or to capture and torture him.

Not that he thought she would remain behind, even if he'd decided to travel without her. There had been anger on her face, and a surprising stubbornness. He would not have been surprised if she had announced that she would follow him regardless of his decision. But there had been no need for that.

She'd burrowed past his will with her question:
"*What if you've left a leper at Langlinais?*" It was a very
real fear. But was that the only reason he'd decided
to take her with him? Or because he cherished the
time he spent with her? He knew the answer even
as he cursed his own foolishness.

Until they reached the coast, Juliana would be able
to travel in a wagon that would offer her some degree of comfort. After that, she would need to ride
with Jerard, the condition of her hands making it
impossible for her to hold the reins of her own
mount.

By his calculations, it would take them a few
weeks to reach Montvichet. And every mile of their
journey would be eagerly watched, he was certain.

He looked to where the horses stood, to beyond
where Jerard was speaking with another of the men-
at-arms. There were but twelve of them on this journey. A small enough number to embark on a mission
of such danger. He made the signal to mount, and
wives were kissed and children hugged.

The most trusted men-at-arms had been left to
guard Langlinais. A young man who had been selected to train with Jerard was given the task of tal-
lying the harvests, a duty he looked terrified of
assuming. He bid farewell to the people of Langlinais with a wave and a smile. Sebastian rode from
the bailey, and through the gates of Langlinais.

He looked back once, to glance at Langlinais one
final time. It gleamed whitely in the dawn light. His
home. He had left here once for Montvichet, and his
life had been forever changed. What would this pil-
grimage bring him? He turned, focused not on all
his myriad worries, but on the journey ahead, to a
place he had never wanted to see again, even in his
dreams.

Chapter 23

"Why Montvichet?" Juliana asked.

He turned his head, thinking that it was time the question had finally come. They had stopped for the midday meal, and she sat beside him.

He broke off a piece of bread from his loaf. All of his food was kept carefully separated, a precaution that seemed advisable. He chewed idly as he concentrated on his answer.

He drew up one leg, propped his wrist upon it, looked homeward toward Langlinais. "There is something there I find I need." It was the easiest answer.

"We are betrayed and are dying. The siege has lasted too many months and we cannot survive much longer. In the love I bore you, I beg of you to come."

The words Magdalene had written him were emblazoned in his memory. He had not been in time to save her. To save any of them. Yet, he'd discovered that she had not summoned him in order to be rescued, but for another purpose.

His life had changed from that day. His beliefs, sacrosanct and immutable, had been challenged. Even today, he did not know if he accepted what he had found, or simply recognized its potential for destruction.

Juliana said nothing else, but there was a small frown on her face. Was she displeased with his answer? She was looking beyond him, to the sight of the Terne curving like a silver snake in the distance. The earth fell away to the Langlinais valley. Although a fine bright day, a mist seemed to shield the valley, muting the colors until everything blended together, a harmony of nature's hues. The deep green coloring of the trees was borrowed by the tall grasses, passed along to the ground covering beneath the huge oaks. It was as if the world was seen through a gauze veil. A chorus of birds sang in greeting, a sweet melody that signaled the end of summer.

Tendrils of hair at her temples were ruffled by the summer breeze. A touch of sun had tinted the tip of her nose delicately pink. It became more and more difficult to look at her. His own mortality vied with his desire, and there were days in which he toyed too often with the thought of touching her. If only to press his hand against her cheek. His worse nature railed at him, spoke words of temptation into his ear. What would it hurt? She had already touched him, after all. He forced the thought from his mind.

"You do not appear frightened of heights from here, Juliana."

"In truth, I am tired of being afraid, Sebastian. Fear has given me nothing but more fear. I have climbed to the top of a tower and nearly fallen into a river. Perhaps it was those experiences that have made me brave." Juliana turned her head and smiled at him.

She extended her hands before her. She traveled

with no attendants. Their journey was one that dictated as much speed and secrecy as possible. He'd watched her unwrap the bandages earlier, had held himself still so as not flinch as her hand emerged. Some of the larger cuts would always leave scars, but they bore no signs of putrefaction. He had wanted to help her smooth the salve over the cuts, but of course he could not. Instead, he watched as Jerard helped her now, bound her hand again with fresh linen.

"You might be able to use your left hand, Juliana if your right will not be flexible enough to hold a quill."

She sent him a quick smile. "There are those who think that people who use their left hand are creatures of the devil, Sebastian. Have you not read the verse? *'Then shall he say also unto them on the left hand, Depart from me, ye cursed, into everlasting fire, prepared for the devil and his angels'.*"

"Do you ascribe to that thought?"

She didn't speak, only stared at her hands. When she lifted her head and looked at him, her face was somber. "Nothing I used to think seems right, Sebastian."

If she questioned her beliefs before, what he would tell her would only add to her confusion. Why did he suddenly think it important to do so? Because he wanted someone to know what Montvichet meant to him. And who better than a woman who smiled at him and in whose eyes there was a measure of sorrow to equal his?

"Montvichet is a Cathar stronghold," he said. "At least it was before a siege nearly leveled it. It's a place like no other I've seen. It's perched high atop the highest mountain in the region. The only way to reach it a winding road, and then a wooden bridge."

"It sounds as if it could have withstood a siege, Sebastian."

"It did." He tossed the remaining scraps of bread to the gathering birds and watched as two squabbled over a piece of crust. "For nearly two years. An English crusader by the name of De Rutger received the blessing of the Pope to subdue the Cathars. I doubt De Rutger was as interested in the fact that they were heretics as much as he was the rumors of the treasure the Cathars possessed. He set up four catapults at the base of the hill and began the siege."

He stared off into the distance. He had witnessed brutality and horror on the battlefield, and in a way was inured to it. But the carnage at Montvichet had been different. It had been less a religious dispute than a scene of unspeakable cruelty. "The villagers who were not Cathar surrendered almost immediately, but the siege lasted nearly two years. They had water from their well, and were able to get enough food to survive."

She turned to watch him, her hands resting on her knees.

"The men surrendered, finally, in order to spare the women and children. They were given an opportunity to recant their religion. They did not." He kept his voice purposefully without emotion. "The Cathar women and children were treated to the sight of the men being burned alive at the stake. The location of Montvichet made such a spectacle almost impossible to avoid."

He heard her gasp.

"But that is not the worst of it," he said, knowing that he should stop. Knowing he would not. "The women held out under the siege for six more months. Finally, the walls were breached and they were overrun. Three hundred women and children were marched down that mountain, Juliana. They were not even given the opportunity to recant. They were simply huddled in a circle and their clothing set ablaze."

"Is that what you meant, when you said the Templars made you witness?" Her voice was a bare whisper, so faint that the drone of a nearby bee was louder.

He turned to look at her. "De Rutger traveled with Templar guards," he said somberly. "His siege of Montvichet could not have been accomplished without the complicity of the Order. Besides, it is wise to suspect any group with such puissance. Power feeds upon itself. A man might hide his thirst for it there. I know my brother does."

He looked out over the vista, wondered if he could say the rest. He'd never spoken of it.

"I arrived a day later." The square had been solemnly silent. The villagers would not venture from their homes, and Montvichet's attackers had vanished with the dawn, as if ashamed to be seen in the light of a new day. Only the smoldering ashes and blackened forms still huddled together attested to the horror of their deed.

"Why were you even there, Sebastian?"

"I had been summoned by Magdalene."

He glanced at her. Her bandaged hands were at her mouth as if to stifle her gasp. Even now, he wished to comfort her, but he could not. There was nothing he could say to ease the horror of the truth.

"I have two abiding hatreds, Juliana. One is stupidity. Those who will not learn despite their ability to do so. And the other is deliberate cruelty. I saw both at Montvichet."

"Is that how she died, Sebastian?" Had her face grown more pale?

He smiled. "I was told she led the march down the mountain." He could almost see her, her hair blowing in the wind, dark but lightened by silver strands as it had been for all the time he'd known her. Her face would have been composed, that smile playing on her lips. Her eyes would have been shining, and there would have been firmness and resolve in her step.

He stood, called for Jerard so that he might assist Juliana in rising. Their rest was over. So, too, his recollections of the past.

Chapter 24

Courcy, France

The Order was considered one of equality. However, there were limits to how equal a man might be. A strange idea to have in the midst of so many holy brothers, Gregory thought.

The sergeants sat at one table, the squires at another, and the knights still another. A brother who had left the Commandary at night was being forced to eat off the floor in punishment. There were rules for every behavior, and a penalty for each offense.

The dinner meal, served at midday, was adequately attended. The food was plentiful, and included meat unlike the diets found in other monastic orders. The Templars had strict rules against fasting. Warriors did not fight well if they were made ill by austerity.

When he'd first taken the oath of a Templar, he'd been surprised to learn that there were relatively few knights in the Order. The majority of the warrior-monks were sergeants, but a great many brothers served in an ancillary capacity to support those who took up arms.

Dinner was normally eaten in silence, while writings of the Church were read. On this occasion, however, Gregory was determined to speak. He would accept his punishment, but the information he possessed was too important to hold for another two hours.

He waited until the Marshal was seated opposite him, and served by a brother. He drank deeply of the ale and set his tankard down. He nodded only once, and the Marshal lifted one silvered eyebrow.

"He is on the move."

A smile only accentuated the amiable expression on Phillipe's face. But he did not break the dinner silence.

"My sources tell me Sebastian is heading south."

A rise of one eyebrow signaled a question. Gregory answered it with a smile.

"Toward France. It is my guess that he means to travel to Montvichet."

The wagon she traveled in was no more than a wooden box with a door. The only opening was in the ceiling, which meant that she was the target for the hot summer sun. There was only one benefit, and that was that the skies were clear. No rain loomed. The wagon would become a cistern in a storm. By the end of the first day, Juliana had decided that the hard wooden seats were marginally preferable to being on horseback. At the end of the second, she'd realized she was incorrect. A horse was a blessing under certain conditions. Another lesson to learn.

Some excuse was always found to stop frequently. Either the horses were tested for lameness, or the wagon wheel looked wobbly, or Sebastian declared that he needed the time to rest from the heat. But each time her hand was treated and rewrapped, she noted that their journey resumed without delay.

She mentioned this to Jerard on the third day, but he only smiled, his silence in the face of her questions not so much a sign of his loyalty now as it was a source of irritation.

Normally, they would have found shelter in one of the monasteries, or sought accommodation from the lords at one of the strongholds. But because of Sebastian's condition, they dared not. Instead, at nightfall they headed into the wood, set guards to keep a rotating watch while the rest of them slept at the base of the trees. Juliana slept in her wagon, again thankful that it did not rain.

Sebastian seemed to be forever scanning the countryside, paying close attention to the tops of hills and the walled fortresses of two castles. What did he look for?

All of Sebastian's precautions made sense the longer she'd had time to think about them. There had been no chaplain to say Mass at Langlinais for the same reason the village had no priest. The Church often seized the property of those with the disease, cast them out, excommunicated them. Before that occurred, however, they intoned a special mass to render the afflicted one of the living dead.

Would it happen to him? The Mass of Separation was a terrible thing. She had only heard of it happening, had never witnessed it. The penitent was led to a cemetery, where he was forced to stand in an open grave. An altar, no more than a board supported by two trestles, was placed in front of him. While he stood there, his face covered by a black veil, all the strictures of his new life were read to him, all the things now forbidden.

Such a thing would happen to Sebastian if the Church learned his secret. No wonder he'd been so desperate for her to agree to his bargain. Langlinais would be both his home and his jail. One day he would simply go into his chamber and never leave it.

Why, then, did she not fear him? Or truly worry about the disease that even now might be limiting her life? Perhaps because it was hard to believe that Sebastian would ever be laid low. Even now, as he stood before her, she could not reconcile this strong man with the poor beggar to whom she'd given a crust of bread. As to her own fate, perhaps she was filled with a naive optimism. There were worse things than sharing life with Sebastian.

They had come to each other as strangers. Wed by words. She had learned of him the way she might a difficult manuscript to read, the letters obscured, or faded by an imperfect ink. There was the sight of him, once frightening, now understandable. Then, the essence of him. A man who prayed with words that echoed with torment. *Intellige clamoren meum.* Know the cries I utter.

He'd spoken with emotion about Magdalene. In his voice had been no censure for her beliefs, no condemnation of her faith. Only sadness and grief. How did one bear to witness such a thing? And to lose someone you loved this way, it was no wonder Sebastian found it difficult to speak of Magdalene.

The Sisters of Charity convent was comprised of a diverse group of women. They were drawn together by their faith and by their wish to ease the suffering of the world around them. Juliana had never known them to turn aside anyone who needed help, be it in the person of a newborn baby or a woman driven from her home for adultery. She knew nothing of intolerance. Even the priest, who argued with the abbess so vociferously, had been more a figure of fun than one of censure.

Is that why Sebastian had never challenged her work? Because he had learned the horrors of intolerance? Why he was able to delineate his hatred for the Saracens? He condemned his jailers, but not the men of learning. One question merely opened another, like a box within a box. But it had been that way from the beginning. Every time she believed herself to have the knowledge she needed, the world shifted and changed, becoming shadowy again.

She sat, her knees drawn up, her right hand resting upon them. She had eaten a few pieces of bread and cheese and now waited for Jerard to finish his own meal so that her left hand might be wrapped again.

Soon they would begin their journey across the Channel to France. The waves were turbulent, colored the gray of deep shadows. The ocean seemed to stretch on forever, only darkening at the horizon.

Sebastian stood beside a weather beaten oak. A storm had nearly uprooted it and it sat perched on the side of the hill, a spindly, leafless landmark. Idly, he broke off a portion of one small branch, snapping it into smaller segments as he stood watching the ocean before them. He had a habit of doing such things, occupying his hands while he remained silent. A few hardy leaves clung tenaciously to one branch, and there were signs of new growth on upper branches. She had the oddest thought that Sebastian was not unlike that tree, almost destroyed by circumstance, but still fighting for survival.

Jerard walked up to the knoll on which she sat. In his hands he held an earthenware jar that held the unguent Sister Agnes had prepared, and a set of clean linen. She held out her hand and he applied the salve and began to bind it up again with an expert touch.

"You are growing adept at this," she said, smiling.

"I've been a squire, my lady. That alone has taught me how to care for wounds."

"Was Sebastian injured often?"

For a moment she thought he would not speak, that he would remain as carefully silent as he had always been. "In truth, my lady, not very often. But he sent me to assist others. Once we were in the Holy Land any man with skill at healing was needed."

"Neither of you ever speak of those days, Jerard. Why?"

He shrugged. "It is a time that weighs heavily on me." He stepped back, the binding finished. He looked down at the ground. "You do not know how he came to be as he is, do you?"

She shook her head.

His face flushed. He extended his hands, placed them under her elbows, and helped her to rise. She found herself walking beside him, down the road so that they were away from the others. "We were captured and taken prisoner by the Saracens, my lady," he said, his voice low, his words coming fast. "I was not noble, nor a knight. I had no worth, but the Saracens had their own plans for me. Sebastian ransomed me. He saved me from becoming a castrate by using the tourney money he'd won over the years to buy my freedom."

She placed her bandaged hand on his arm. Even as isolated as the Sisters of Charity, they had heard tales of such horrible practices as castration. "But you cannot blame yourself, Jerard, for his being afflicted."

"If he had not been left in prison for all that time, my lady, it is possible he might never have become diseased."

"How was he finally freed?"

"There was no money left to pay his own ransom, my lady. The Templars arranged his release, but not until a full year later. They demanded Langlinais in case he could not pay the loan. Now they want even more." His look was grim, his eyes narrowed.

"What do they want, Jerard?"

For a moment he looked startled, as if he just now realized he'd said too much. But loyalty was evidently balanced against his obvious worry, and the truth won out. "They want the treasure of the Cathars, my lady. And I do not think they would hesitate to kill him in order to obtain it."

Chapter 25

S he should have been more afraid. But then, she'd nearly fallen to her death in the Terne. The rushing waters of the river had prepared her well for the majesty of the ocean. Or perhaps the words she'd said to Sebastian had been more truth than bravado. She truly was tired of being afraid.

She had been escorted to a small bench that occupied most of the rear of the barque. Their ship was small, equipped with two masts strung with heavy canvas. The sails flapped furiously in the wind like an old frightened hen.

Their crossing was to be in a fleet, the horses being transported in the first boat, half of the men-at-arms accompanying them. The third boat would carry their supplies and the rest of the men. Sebastian, Jerard, and she were aboard the second ship. The wagon, because it was too heavy, was left on the shore, to be returned by its driver to Langlinais.

As soon as they left the small dock, Juliana closed her eyes, determined not to look at the pigeon-colored sky and white-flecked waves. It was not fear that made her do so, but a hearty wish that she had not eaten her midday meal of bread and cheese.

The heavy thud of footsteps alerted her. She

opened her eyes to find Sebastian sitting beside her.

"You are looking a little gray, Juliana. Is this your first time on the ocean?"

She nodded, just as the boat rocked with the waves, seeming to gain more momentum sideways than they did going forward. Her eyes widened at the sensation.

"It is all right, Juliana," he said with a smile. "The Channel has a temper, but the crossing won't take that long. You will find that the time passes quickly."

"Have you traveled much on the ocean, Sebastian?"

"Most of my tourneys were in France, so I've a passing knowledge of the Channel. And, of course, my journey to the Holy Land was made over water. The Mediterranean is far more beautiful, being possessed of great ranges of color."

Juliana was quiet for a moment. "Is your disease the reason why you've never spoken of your time on crusade, Sebastian?"

"The journey was not steeped in glory, Juliana, but rather disaster. There was a great deal of profound discussion, but little leadership. In the end, we were outnumbered and overcome. Perhaps the reason I do not speak about it is due more to my anger at being captured. I was shamed because my pride as a knight was bruised." He glanced over at her. "Why are you smiling?"

"You saved my life, and Jerard's. I think you judge yourself too harshly."

"I was taught to fight and win, Juliana. Surrender is anathema to me."

Even now he fought. Another foe this time, but one even more deadly.

She looked up at the sky, turned darker with

storm or night, she didn't know which. A sideways glance showed that he was watching her, his face somber, not a trace of a smile on his lips.

"Is there someone you love?" he asked.

The question so surprised her that she turned her head and stared at him.

"Sebastian, I have lived at the convent for most of my life."

"Were there no gardeners, no visitors you fancied?"

She smiled. "Sister Helena would have assaulted anyone if they'd ventured into the garden without her permission, and the only visitor I recall was the priest. He was old and had only two of his teeth, and was possessed of a most quarrelsome nature. He and the abbess spent most of their time together arguing about the merits of a woman's mind. He did not believe that a woman should be an armarius. The abbess would show him proof of the income our work generated, but otherwise ignore him."

"Did none of the girls have brothers?"

She shrugged. "A few. But they did not introduce me. I was already wed."

"And therefore untouchable? So, you became an outcast like me."

"Perhaps that's why we were brought together, Sebastian. Like matching like."

"Divine mediation? I doubt it, Juliana. You once asked me if I was Death, Juliana. I am, to you."

"It was a silly question from a silly girl."

"But one wiser than this one, who sits beside me and speaks of things best left unsaid."

"About being well matched?" She turned away, faced the open sea. Perhaps it would have been better never to have known him, but she could not imagine such a thing now. He was so much a part of her life, her thoughts, that it was as if he'd always been there.

The wind had picked up; the waves seemed higher. She looked at the horizon, stared into the distance as if the words were written there, where the sea darkened and the sky began. Her hair blew away from her face, a few tendrils whipping free of its braid.

"I've never known love. Not the way you speak of it. I used to wonder about it. Whether it was as powerful as all the poets made it seem. Did men really sacrifice for love, did women wish to die for it? Until I grew to know you, I did not think it possible."

He was so still that she wondered if he had heard her. Would he admonish her for speaking those words? Would he leave her?

For a long moment, he did not answer. When he did, his words came softly.

"You must not love me, Juliana."

She nodded. "I knew you would say that, Sebastian. A wise person would. Perhaps I should even feel that way. But how do we stop the waves? It might be as easy."

She turned to face him. Her cheeks were reddened by the warmth she felt rising through her body. It was as if a flame burned her, spread from someplace within her.

"Why did you ask me if I loved someone?"

He didn't turn away from her, but seemed to search out some truth in her eyes. "Because I wished to know if you might be happy. If there was someone who could bring you joy when I'm no longer there."

She could not speak. Words were insignificant things against this sudden pain. She reached out one hand to touch him, but he pulled away from her.

He turned on her. The sky darkened behind him, a backdrop for his sudden, surprising anger. "Do you think the danger less because you once touched me, Juliana? Do you think yourself exempt from it? I thought the same, once. But do not make light of my fears by refusing to accept them. You are no simpleton."

"Perhaps I am a simpleton after all. I don't fear you, Sebastian. How can I be afraid of a man who saved my life? Who refuses to touch me lest he harm me? I know I should be afraid, but all I can feel is wonder, Sebastian, that you might be my husband, my great and noble knight."

He was conscious of Jerard watching them. Otherwise, Sebastian thought he might keen at the sky like a rabid dog.

He bent his head and took a deep breath to wash away the remnants of his anger, to calm himself. He raised his hand in some movement before he remembered. He wore no gauntlet, he'd given himself a respite from the heat and discomfort of them. She stared at his hand, transfixed. His skin was mottled, the patches thick and scaly. It had darkened in hue over the months until it was deep brown.

She did not say anything, but neither did she recoil in horror. It might have been easier if she had. Instead he saw compassion in her eyes.

"Do you use the unguent Sister Agnes prepared?" Her voice sounded calm.

He admired her restraint. He did not doubt that most women would have run screaming from him. Most women would never have been in his company, let alone saying how much they wanted to touch him.

Please, let the sight of his disease accomplish what

his words had not, induce her to fully realize their fate and to accept it. Otherwise, it was a ripe torment she promised in her eagerness and innocence.

"When I remember," he answered.

"Then I shall remind you, Sebastian." He almost smiled at her then, her chin angled up at him, the stubbornness she'd hinted at once more revealed.

She held too much in her heart, felt too deeply. She would love as fiercely, with obstinacy and resolve. A woman of many facets, all of them bright and shining. At another time, perhaps, they would have been priceless. Now, they promised only to bring them both pain.

He'd suspected ever since she'd learned of his disease that she did not fully comprehend the horror of it. She was capable of remaining in a small room day after day focused upon words, upon the execution of a task. Such a person created worlds in her imagination. Someone who was capable of being such a visionary lived within their thoughts. Thoughts might be shaped and rearranged, but they could not replace the truth. She might not be aware of it, but he did not doubt that she held out hope for him, and while hope was a good and precious thing, it was a burden if it helped to avoid the facts of a matter. When it faded, when she began to believe it, it would not be easy for her. He knew that from experience.

He wished, however, that he might tell her, without causing her pain, how much he cherished these moments with her. He'd asked her if she loved another and had held his breath at her reply. She'd offered a piece of herself, an effortless granting of her own past. A lonely child, a girl in waiting for her life. No wonder she had agreed so easily to their bargain. The conditions were such that her life had not changed. She was still waiting for life.

He stood and left her finally, never having found the words to say that would make her fear what should be feared.

Chapter 26

A Templar was bound to strict obedience to his commander. His word demanded absolute submission. Upon investiture into the Order, a man had to swear to obey the Master of the Temple and any officer his superior. A brother could be imprisoned, exiled, or expulsed from the Templars for using his own initiative. Strict discipline, obedience, absolute faith, all three of these were present in the brothers who surrounded Gregory.

Gregory did not address them, did not explain the purpose of their expedition. It was neither necessary nor required.

Fanatics made good soldiers, Gregory thought, as the column, two wide, proceeded from Courcy. These French brothers had all seen service in the Holy Land, had gained experience fighting the Saracens.

He had trained them hard these past weeks, even being excused from nones and vespers because of it. At compline last night, he'd given them their instructions, and this morning at dawn there had been not one brother missing from the array of mounted men. At midnight, he'd been awake and had attended matins, his own prayers taking shape over the familiar words.

His lookouts had informed him that there were only fourteen accompanying Sebastian, thirteen men-at-arms and a woman. The woman's presence had startled him. His brother, as heir, had been wed as a gawky youth. Was she his bride? On such a dangerous journey? He could not reconcile that knowledge with the Sebastian of his childhood. A careful boy who had looked for attack too often ever to be surprised. Of the two of them, he had been the more impulsive, using his lance in such a way that it overset him, or sometimes thrusting too hard with his blunted sword that he was unbalanced by the weight of it.

How odd that the once impulsive boy would join the Templars, easily take a vow to "preserve chastity, the good usages, and the good customs of the Order." There were other vows he'd sworn to just as serenely, such as those to own no property, never to allow Christians to be murdered, to enlarge the kingdom of Jerusalem, and not to leave the Order without permission.

His reply to Sebastian's request for additional time to pay his ransom had borne fruit, it seemed. It was evident that Sebastian knew of the treasure, or he wouldn't now be returning to Montvichet. He'd evidently hidden it well enough that the initial search by De Rutger and a later one by Templar brothers had not uncovered its existence.

The fact that his brother was on the way to the Cathar fortress was, on the surface of it, acceptance of their bargain. But Sebastian had surprised him by having been at Montvichet soon after the siege had ended, and again by going on crusade. A hint of caution might be wise now. Perhaps he did not

know the man who had become the Lord of Langlinais. It was a good possibility that his memories of
Sebastian might be just that, only memories. The
man his brother had grown to be might prove to be
dangerous.

A word in the ear of a French noble had dispensed
with the problem of Sebastian's retinue. Sebastian
himself could not be harmed until he'd reached
Montvichet. Preferably alone.

Whatever transpired later was the will of God.

"I feel as well guarded as a princess," she said to
Jerard's back.

Her perch behind Jerard was not onerous. He had
placed her hands at his waist with enough nonchalance that she was not embarrassed, and other than
gripping her wrists from time to time when the ter-
rain grew steeper did not touch her. It was, however
precarious a perch, one from which she could see,
and the air, although hot, was not stifling as it had
been in the wagon.

"How so, my lady?"

"It is not bad enough that I have to discommode
you with my presence, but to have all these men
guarding me seems a bit overcautious."

"These are not safe roads, my lady. My lord
would guard you as well as he can."

"I am guarded so well I can barely take a breath,
Jerard."

There was no answer to that, but then, she'd not
expected one.

"Where are we, Jerard?"

Their small fleet had docked at a fishing village
some days earlier, and ever since they'd been on
horseback, traveling deeper into France.

"Brittany, my lady."

Her education had consisted of learning how to be both chatelaine and scribe. She'd had little exposure to atlases, even though she'd once seen a sketch of England. Therefore, Juliana was as unaware as before of their location, and indeed the location of Montvichet.

Sebastian seemed to expect trouble, as measured by the sword he wore. It swung by his side with ease, seeming to disturb him not at all. Yet, it gleamed in the sun as if to call attention to itself, an instrument of death shining brightly and unapologetically.

She had meant to ask Sebastian about the treasure, but the thought had flown from her mind. Instead, her senses had been captivated and her heart had been touched. Then, she had forced herself not to wince when she'd seen his hand.

Weeping would not help.

She fixed her gaze on him riding in front of them. He did not wear a helm. Not because of the heat, she suspected, but because of the freedom. Other men might have chafed at the chain mail, but Sebastian wore it without complaint. It was, no doubt, less onerous to him than the monk's robe he'd worn for so long.

She was not faring quite as well. Her linen headdress was a simple toque, yet the chin strap chafed her skin. By the second day in France, she had discarded it. Her embroidered undersleeves were too hot for this weather, so she'd asked Jerard to trim them on the third day. All that was intact was her sleeveless surcoat, but it was grimy with the dust kicked up by the horses. She felt as though she were caked in dirt, could even taste the grittiness of it in her food and water.

Yet Sebastian smiled through their journey.

"We are making good distances each day, my lady," Jerard said. "We will be at Montvichet within a week."

Jerard had become her only source of information over the last few days. During the day the men-at-arms had no necessity to converse with her, although they spared a few words at evening. The longer they traveled the more distant Sebastian seemed to become, however. He rarely spoke to her and sent messages through Jerard. It was as if his armor had become an inadequate protective device, so he used distance to enhance his isolation as well. Their nights of conversation might never have happened. Or perhaps they had been moments of illusion, something she'd only dreamed.

Each day he watched her mount behind Jerard and each day he wanted to strike his vassal. She would smile her thanks, or say a few words, her lips moving soundlessly. He did not want to hear her words, hear the tenor of her speech, the softness of her voice. Did not want to hear her speak words of gratitude to any man but him.

Mine.

A surge of something feral and angry sped through him. It was ancient and hungry and crazed. It was akin to bloodlust, that need to kill or be killed, that had attacked him on the battlefield.

Mine.

She belonged to no one but him. Her pink cheek was his to cradle in his palm, her hair to be swept aside by his fingers. Her foot to be braced, her arm to be held by him alone. The fact that he had touched her only once was a cruel joke, the fact he could still feel the imprint of her hand a gift. The surprising rage he felt was unleashed by the sight of her pressed against another man. Once, she'd fallen asleep, her cheek resting against Jerard's back. He'd almost killed his squire.

During the last few days, he'd watched her become more comfortable with Jerard, with the other men. Her braid was always neat and tidy in the morning, but by evening it was hanging by a ribbon, tendrils of hair escaping to rest against her cheek. She'd trimmed her sleeves so that they were not so long, and had ceased wearing her toque. The worst of it was when she'd discontinued wearing her undersleeves. In this heat she would have been a fool not to discard them, but still, it meant that there was one less layer of cloth between her and Jerard.

He'd thought himself a strong man, one beset with passions, true, but had always kept them contained. His anger had been saved for the tourney or the battlefield. His lust spent with a willing woman.

He had demanded of himself restraint and strength and thus far had always been able to comply with such grand expectations. Yet, he was expected to restrain himself from a woman who was his wife. Never to hold her in his arms, never to kiss her, never to inhale her breath into his lungs. To watch as other men were the recipient of her smiles and her small but tender favors.

He would rather be outnumbered by Saracens.

It had, oddly enough, been easier to be around her when he had been attired in his monk's garb. Perhaps because it had so readily and constantly reminded him of his plight. There were times, in his armor, that he forgot for hours, when he believed himself whole and the other only a pretense.

A sparkle caught his attention on the far hillside. The sun glinting off a stone or off a Templar's armor? The thought was enough of a chastisement to focus his energy on the task at hand—that of getting them safely to Montvichet. Envisioning his wife in various poses, naked upon his bed, would not ensure that. In fact, it would be better if he did not think of her at all.

A thought he'd had only a moment to ponder before he was attacked.

The first indication Juliana had that something was wrong was Jerard's curse. He swore fluently and with great emotion.

"What is it, Jerard?" He didn't answer her question, only spurred his horse without warning.

He slid from the saddle before she could question his actions. It was then that she looked up and saw Sebastian surrounded by men armored as well as he.

She clasped a bandaged hand over her mouth.

The men-at-arms stationed behind them raced forward, positioned themselves around Juliana. Not one word had been spoken, but they all moved quickly and with unerring certainty into place. Jerard drew his sword, moved to stand in front of his horse. Even Juliana, who had no experience with warfare, knew that such a stance was defensive. It seemed she was to be protected.

The men who attacked them were young and well mounted and possessed of weaponry at least equal to Sebastian's enormous sword. They were dressed for battle, but not united in it. There were no common pennants, no tunics to match. There were at least twenty of them and only Sebastian and six of his men, the others remaining behind to guard her.

Something odd was happening. The men who surrounded Sebastian did not raise their swords to strike him. Faeren turned on a kneed command, Sebastian lunged forward, the thrust of his blade met and held by another sword. But that was all. There was no answering blow. They contained him, but they did not harm him.

There was no such mercy given to their men. They fought valiantly, although they were outnumbered.

"Jerard, will you not aid them?"

She had to shout in order to be heard. The quiet of the afternoon had been supplanted by the sounds of battle, the clang of steel against steel, an oath, a scream.

"I am to protect you, my lady." He did not look in her direction as he spoke, his attention riveted upon the battle scene, just as hers was.

"Then release the rest of our men." That demand was lost in the sounds of battle, or else Jerard ignored it.

Jerard's horse sidestepped, either eager to be in the fray or frightened by it. Jerard remained where he was, stationed at his horse's head, one hand gripping the reins tautly, the other with sword braced, ready to protect her.

Five men separated from the larger group surrounding Sebastian and rushed toward them. One man was cut down by the phalanx of guards; Jerard thrust his sword into the chest of another as he bent to slice at him. The other three managed to wound a few of their men, unhorse another.

It was not until a few moments later that Juliana realized the site of battle had shifted. She was in the middle of it. Swords were raised high, horses were screaming, the faces of the men were sweaty and flushed, their eyes holding a kind of crazed delight.

She could not shut her eyes, transfixed by the sight of blood dripping from a shiny blade. A mailed hand raised the sword high in the air. It came closer. Closer still until it slowly arced toward her. She watched it with a sick horror and wondered why she should meet death in such a way, on a road in France. For what reason was she to be killed? No more important than she simply happened to be here.

That's when she saw him. Faeren must have been equipped with wings. How else could he have reached her side so quickly? One moment, she was looking at death, the next the contorted face of her husband, whose fury had transformed him into a murderous stranger. His face was bronzed, his eyes slitted, a hoarse sound emerged from his throat, a shout born of savage rage.

Had he fought his way free of the circle of men who'd surrounded him? Had she not watched the way he fought, she might have thought it impossible. But a few seconds later she did not doubt it. With one blow, he cut down the man closest to her. The attacker gurgled, spewing blood as he toppled from his horse. Then Sebastian's sword was embedded in the back of the attacker who threatened her. He had been so close that the tip of the man's sword sliced through her tunic as he fell.

Sebastian's glance captured hers easily since her eyes had never veered from him. It was as if the battle slowed, the moment oddly stilled in time. Once again, she had the strange feeling that they spoke without words. Worry for each was transmitted in a glance; reassurance from each was sent back.

Then it was over.

Sebastian's arm sliced down, over and over, his grin was feral and frightening. He used no shield, wore no helmet, was the least protected and yet the most daunting figure on the road made battlefield. He fought like a man to whom losing was an impossibility. But it was possible to perish on this sunny afternoon on a dusty road in France. The men at her feet attested to that.

She learned something else about her nature in those long minutes as she watched him fight. She should have prayed for those men's souls, or to understand why they had been attacked without provocation. But in the deep crevasses of her heart, Juliana knew that she wished no forgiveness for them nor understanding. She wanted Sebastian to win, to overpower them. She wanted each and every one of them to suffer for trying to kill him.

Another sin to wish expunged from her soul. But at the battle's end, as Sebastian sat there surveying the carnage, with his hair sweat-dampened, his breath coming fast, she could not help but be fiercely proud.

Chapter 27

⌒⌒◯◯⌒

"You should not be carrying things, Juliana."

"Sebastian, my left hand is healing nicely. In fact, the bandages should probably be removed from it soon. And if you will note, I am not using my right."

She bent and laid the water jug at his side. Their wounded men lay on the side of a small rise. They had not suffered any casualties, unlike the men who'd attacked them. But there were numerous small cuts and other wounds that could prove troublesome without care. Even now, Jerard was treating a nasty-looking arm wound. In fact, Juliana thought she'd never seen so much blood in her life. She looked quickly away.

Sebastian stood, bent close so that only she could hear him whisper. "If you leave, he will be able to scream, my lady wife. But with you here, he must pretend to be brave." She looked beyond to the man who lay on the ground before her. His gaze was fixed on the evening sky.

The fire burning brightly in the middle of the encampment made her stomach lurch.

"You are going to use fire to seal his wound, aren't you, Sebastian?" Her gaze didn't leave his.

He nodded.

"And the other men, are they as grievously wounded?"

"A few cuts that will heal and a few bruises that will fade. They are used to it."

Unspoken was the thought that she was not.

"Will you send him home, Sebastian?"

"No. He will be safer with us than on his own."

She moved away and he followed her. "He will survive this, Juliana," he said in a tender voice. "He will be bragging of his scar in a few days."

"You speak of such things with ease, Sebastian. You fight bandits while I am sickened at the sight of blood. You are so much more brave than I."

He smiled at her. "I am supposed to be, Juliana. And I doubt they were bandits. They were too well outfitted, for one."

"Were they sent to attack us, Sebastian?"

He looked surprised. "What makes you think that?"

"You scan the hills and watch the valleys too earnestly, Sebastian. It's as if you expect trouble."

"It is only prudence to do so, Juliana. They could be no more than a group of disgruntled young knights. France has been simmering since their king left on crusade. Dissension is common where there is no clear leader."

"Do you believe that is who they were?"

"No." The word chilled her. So, he, too, believed that someone else had a hand in this sudden and unexpected attack.

"You suffered no ill effects, Sebastian? No wounds?"

"A scrape upon my knuckles where a blade sliced against my glove, but that is all. I thank you for the wifely concern."

"It is little enough; I did nothing but sit there."

His smile broadened. "And you feel guilty about that?"

"No," she confessed. "At least I did not scream. It was a great temptation." She looked up at him, shielding her eyes from the rays of a fading sun with one bandaged hand. "You fought very well, Sebastian."

"It was what I was taught to do, my lady wife. Protect what is mine."

He seems to me the equal of a god. He seems, if that may be, the god's superior, who stands face-to-face with me and watches the words that flow from my mouth. The words of Catullus were heretical. She was collecting a bouquet of such thoughts. But she had already been punished ably. The disease that separated them, that kept them forever apart, was a ripe form of hell. Penance enough for her thoughts.

She watched him as he turned away. In a moment, he stood beside Jerard, exchanging words with the injured man.

She was not certain that she knew about love. She'd heard the ballads and read the philosophers and poets. She loved God and had loved her parents. But what she felt for Sebastian was different both from what she'd heard and read and felt in the past.

There was a place in the middle of her chest that felt hollow and achy. It seemed to expand when she saw him, when he came near. Her eyes too easily felt the sting of tears. Her blood raced as if to catch up to her thoughts. She had been forbidden to touch him, yet she felt closer to him than to anyone else. He'd lured her with his words, humbled her with evidence of his honor and sacrifice.

The sun was behind them, the glow of its descent gifting the sky with orange-and-red streaks. Sebastian's armor seemed to be afire. His face was shadowed by a few days' growth of beard. His eyes looked tired, horizon-weary. His chestnut hair was spangled with the eternal dust of the hot summer roads, and his tunic needed to be brushed.

The world might see him as a strange knight, who garbed himself in silence and sorrow. But she knew him for what he was, a man of great dimensions, who grieved, and yearned, who viewed life through eyes of tolerance and acceptance. She knew his loyalty and his protection of those who were weaker.

There was no more honorable man than the one who stood there, his head bared in the light of a setting sun, his hand upon the hilt of his sword. Or one she loved as much.

"Lady Juliana?" A gentle hand upon her shoulder shook her awake. The sky was dark, but she had no idea if it was midnight or the hour before dawn. She yawned and opened her eyes, smiling at Jerard.

Sebastian stood watching her, his arms folded in front of him. She transferred her smile to him. Dawn, then. Time to be about their journey again.

She yawned widely, caught herself and placed her hands over her mouth.

"Do you know, I had the oddest dream," she said a moment later. "All about trees that spoke and flowers that sang. They spoke to me in verse."

"Is that what battle does to you, Juliana?" There was amusement in his tone. "Perhaps you are becoming a prophetess like Hildegard of Bingen."

"Are you teasing me, Sebastian?"

"You sound so amazed at the prospect, Juliana."

She smiled at him, muffling another yawn. "I used to wonder at her visions. She was consulted by kings, did you know? I read a portion of her *Scivias* once. The abbess has a copy."

"Why did you wonder at her visions?" There was still that note of gentle amusement in his voice.

"It does not seem to be a talent for a nun to have, that is all."

"More like a sorcerer?"

"Or a wizard." She tilted her head and looked at him. Jerard had left them, the men-at-arms were some distance away. They were, for the moment, alone.

"What is it you need at Montvichet, Sebastian? Is it the treasure?"

"Did you glean that information from Jerard?" She nodded.

"It is what the Templars are demanding in exchange for Langlinais."

"Instead of your ransom?"

"I cannot help but wonder if it was inflated for just this purpose." He studied the line of sky where it lightened with the coming of dawn.

"It would make sense for them to have fostered the attack upon us, Sebastian. Especially since they did not wish you harmed." She looked up at him, wishing he would sit beside her, knowing that he would not.

"You noticed that, too?" He smiled. "It is, perhaps, not a wise thing to have a wife as intelligent as you."

"Are you a heretic, Sebastian?" Did she ask him that question because of her own recent thoughts?

His smile broadened. "A strange question to ask a crusader."

"I think you see the world from a different place than I," she said. "Neither higher nor lower, simply different. You do not hate all Saracens, and I've seen your pain at the fate of the Cathars. You question the Templars whereas most people are in awe of them. There are some who would chastise you for your tolerance and others for your doubts. Was it your education in Paris that makes you think as you do?"

"Yet it is you who question nuns with visions," he said with a smile.

She returned his smile. "Well, then perhaps we are better matched than we both thought."

"A greater tragedy if it is so."

"Is it, Sebastian? Or a sign that I should always be with you?"

"We have been wed since you were a child, Juliana. All your life has been spent in preparation for linking it with mine. I am a habit to you, nothing more. A refuge, perhaps, for the loneliness of the convent."

Her laughter seemed to startle him. "Oh, Sebastian, I spent fourteen years preparing myself for misery. I dreaded our marriage, was eternally grateful for those years you went on crusade. The day I learned of your summons was the worst of my life."

She had surprised him, she could tell.

"I had never thought of your fearing the day I would send for you."

"It was our union that frightened me, Sebastian but I have found only joy with you."

"Joy? Even with what you know, you can say such a thing?"

She nodded.

"Did you know that the word heretic comes from the Greek *hairetikos*, meaning able to choose?"

It was such an awkward attempt to change the subject that she could only smile at him.

"Perhaps it is not a wise thing to have a husband who studied at the great universities."

He smiled back at her.

"The men, Sebastian. Are they well enough to travel?" She'd heard the muffled screams of the man who'd been burned the night before, and wondered at his courage. She would not have been as brave.

"Indeed, they would be insulted at the notion that they are not."

"You are not going to tell me about the treasure, are you?"

"A little of it, perhaps. Magdalene left me a message," he said. "In the care of an elderly villager. He cried all during the time he delivered it to me. Evidently, Magdalene was as kind and as gentle to this old man as she had always been to me. I was to go to her room, and find a small basket. It was a gift, not to me, but for me to do with as I would. It took two days to find the basket, but I've still not decided what to do with it."

"What was inside?"

"For that answer you must wait until we reach Montvichet," he said, smiling.

"And after that, Sebastian?"

He glanced away.

"After that, Sebastian?" she repeated. The beating of her heart accompanied each word.

She looked up at him. Once again, she had the feeling that they spoke without words. Words that might be improvident to speak, but were felt regardless. Declarations of emotion that circumstance had made impossible. Love and longing so strong that they could almost be felt in the air between them.

You will be forever in my heart wherever I am.

Do not leave me, Sebastian.

I must, Juliana.

Chapter 28

Sebastian was solicitous from that day forward, but he rarely looked at her. Where before she'd thought him aloof, now it was as if he were separating himself physically not only from her but from all of them. Had he truly decided not to return to Langlinais? She didn't know when the thought had occurred to her. She couldn't measure the moment, or hold still the hour. But she felt it, a strong and certain knowledge as if he'd already said good-bye.

You must not love me, Juliana.

Was that the reason? Because he wished to spare her pain? He was preparing her. It was an intrinsic knowledge, one she fought against even as she recognized it. The moment was uncertain, the day was unknown, but one day soon he would simply disappear from her life.

Montvichet was their destination. Beyond that, she didn't know. He had not spoken of what he would do after he'd procured the treasure, whether he would travel to the Templars or have Jerard take it for him. Would he see her home to Langlinais, and then disappear?

Yet however much she might recognize the fact of his leaving, her heart could not bear the cost. She walled off the pain, bid the door be closed and barred against that precise hour he left her.

She watched him now as he sat on the other side of the encampment, staring off into the distance, searching the impenetrable line of forest or examining the night sky.

"May I serve you, my lady?"

Juliana started, so involved in her study of Sebastian that she'd not heard Jerard approach.

She nodded, holding out her left hand. She only wore the bandage when she applied the salve now. She was healing well, the sharp lines in her flesh knitting together. She might not be as fortunate with her writing hand.

The game had been plentiful on their journey, the roasted hare she was offered now as finely cooked as any she might have eaten from the Langlinais kitchens.

Jerard stood in front of her, staring at something in back of her. The expression on his face was lit by the fire, and it hinted at revulsion or disgust.

"What are you looking at, Jerard?" She glanced over her shoulder, but only darkness met her gaze.

He didn't turn his attention to her as he answered, just remained staring at the mountaintop. "Montvichet, my lady."

"That's Montvichet?" Her heart seemed to plummet to her toes as she raised her head, her eyes scanning the height of the mountain.

Jerard nodded. He turned his eyes to her.

"I hate that place, my lady. It is one of ghosts and sorrow."

She had no words in response, surprised at the depth of feeling in his voice. She'd rarely seen Jerard stirred from his usual pleasant equanimity.

"Were you there, then? With Sebastian?"

He nodded.

"The memories, my lady, remain with me even now."

His eyes looked haunted as he stared at the mountain's summit.

The approach to Montvichet was steep and winding. The distance to the valley below seemed to be magnified by the fact that there was a sheer drop off one side of the road and a cliff face on the other.

The horses appeared nervous as Jerard led them up the summit, Faeren's reins held tight in his right hand while his left held the lead to his own mount.

The stunted olive trees were made smaller the higher they climbed. The lake in the distance with its odd-colored red bank, the holm oaks with their dark green and white leaves—they all seemed like tiny replicas of the real world.

Juliana walked with one hand upon the sheer rock face. But she did not seem frightened. Hadn't she told him that she was tired of being afraid? She had sat silent and pale as men had died around her. And then had surprised him with her assessment of their circumstances. A Templar plot and his own surreptitious observations—none of these things had escaped her.

He closed his mind to the thought that her courage would be needed in full force in the coming years. The people of Langlinais would need her.

The top of the mountain split apart, as if a massive sword had cleaved the stone in two. Montvichet was situated on the larger of these two sections, reachable only by a suspended wooden bridge that swung over the gorge. It had been left intact during the siege, De Rutger realizing that he would need some way across the divide.

The village, scarcely more than a few daub-and-wattle huts, lay on the other side of the mountain and was accessible by a branch of the road they'd taken. Sebastian sent Jerard and a few of the men there to learn what they could.

Sebastian crossed the wooden bridge, Juliana behind him. He heard her gasp, but did not turn to reassure her. To do so would be to set the bridge swinging. Once he was on the other side, however, he turned and smiled reassuringly. Her face was pale, but her smile was anchored in place as she crossed.

He walked toward the gateway, Juliana at his side, and entered the stronghold of the Cathars.

Montvichet was carved from the mountain itself, its massive stone blocks tinted yellow by nature, bleached white by the glare of a late-August sun. The fortress now lay like a great animal's bones, plucked clean. The walls had been breached during the siege; the gates lay on the ground. The refectory was in the corner to his right, the other public rooms aligned in front. The sleeping rooms stretched along the left wall. Every chamber had been pillaged.

Once, there had been an ancient fort here, but it had long since crumbled to dust. Yet, the bright blues and greens of a mosaic floor amidst the air of desertion and ruin was an odd taunt, as if saying that all things Roman would somehow endure.

Sebastian had found it much the same five years ago. Back then, he had been content with his place in the world, not recognizing his own arrogance and ignorance. Now he looked at that man and marveled at the blessings he'd had and never realized. He'd lost his siblings yet remained healthy. He'd won every tourney he'd entered while other men had lost their fortunes. He'd been born free and noble, allowed to learn from the greatest minds. He'd thought himself worldly five years ago. Yet, that young man had been puffed up with his own importance, and the only thing he'd truly known was the depth of his own idiocy. He'd been as pompous as a rooster, as untried as a chick.

The echoes of that man remained, but only in the regret he felt.

Five years had passed for him, but at Montvichet, it was as if there had been no passage of time. The dust upon the courtyard stone was thicker, but undisturbed. A few more stones had crumbled from the walls, barely noticeable among the greater destruction. Yet some hardy vines still entwined among the rocks, and from somewhere close came the song of a bird. And a gentle breeze took the heat from the air and perfumed it, instead.

The silence was that of waiting, as if the mountaintop fortress had stilled and become unmoving in time, anticipative of the perfect moment in the future to awaken itself. If ghosts spoke here, their voices were melodic and easily mistaken for a chime the wind might softly strike against a bell.

He almost stretched out his hand to Juliana before he remembered, so intense was the need to bring her forward, as if to introduce her to all the souls he'd never known. To seek from these long-dead people a benediction for this woman, that she might be spared any pain from him.

"Sebastian?"

Juliana's voice called him back to the present. She stepped closer to him.

"One can almost hear a song." She tilted her head as if listening. "Or the laughter of children."

So, she felt it, too. As if it might be possible to

catch a glimpse of something if he turned his head quick enough. Foolish thoughts.

Those men-at-arms who had not accompanied Jerard entered the courtyard with caution despite the air of abandonment. They searched each room, swords pointed upward until they had determined that Montvichet was indeed deserted.

On the other side of the mountain, the horses were being readied for the journey across the bridge. Faeren took great exception to being led by anyone other than Jerard or Sebastian. He did not like the sound of his hooves striking the logs that comprised the bridge, and reared once. For a moment frozen in time, it looked as if the massive horse would plunge off the side into the gorge, taking with him the man who held his reins.

Sebastian turned and walked swiftly to the edge of the bridge, reached up with a gauntleted hand. He was too far away to grab the horse's reins, and he doubted if the bridge could take the weight of two men and his horse. But Faeren steadied once he called to him, walking toward the sound of his voice. He'd had enough of rebellion, it seemed, once he reached Sebastian, and docilely followed his rider into the courtyard.

"You are perhaps the first four-legged creature ever to see this place," he said, reaching up and stroking Faeren's broad nose with fondness.

Juliana came to stand slightly behind him.

"Why did you bring him here?"

"A good knight is never without his horse."

"Especially if he is being followed by Templars."

"There is that," he said, smiling at her.

Faeren snorted and Juliana stepped back.

"You are wise to be cautious of him. He's old and

perverse." Faeren pawed the ground at that moment, drawing a laugh from Sebastian.

"Has he been with you long?"

"Ever since Cyprus. My own mount had been killed beneath me just before I was captured. I found Faeren there, an outcast just like me." His smile lightened his words. "No one could control him, and I desperately wished to go home. Together we made a bargain of it, didn't we, Faeren?" He stroked Faeren's nose, then led the horse to the side of the courtyard where there was more shade.

Jerard approached through the gateway, a smile on his face. "My lord, the well has not been poisoned. The sides were knocked down, but the water tastes sweet."

"I trust you tested that on a frog, Jerard, and not yourself?"

Jerard's cheeks turned the color of bronze. "There are still a few people in the village, my lord. The information came from them."

"See if they are as generous with their food as their information." He pulled a small drawstring bag from beneath his tunic and handed it to Jerard. As his squire turned away, he called after him. The younger man turned and waited. "Pay them well, Jerard. The people of Montvichet have been ill used."

"Yes, my lord."

Sebastian turned, met Juliana's smile. He should not be so curious, but her eyes sparkled merrily.

"What amuses you?"

"You treat him as a father might."

"He is my squire. How would you have me treat him?"

"As you do at Langlinais. He is your steward

there, with all of the authority you've given him. He uses it well."

"Have I not done so just now?" He frowned as he searched out Jerard's departing figure.

"No. Your demeanor changed with your clothing. You are no longer the monk hiding away from those who might discover you. You are the knight who is sure of your prowess in battle. And poor Jerard has become your lowly squire again."

"Poor Jerard?" he asked, the words too loud for the moment. He discounted that and the fact that several of his men turned to look at him. When had she become so fiercely protective of him?

His words served no purpose but to transfix her with merriment. He loved her laughter, prized it because it was so rare.

Did she know how utterly beautiful she was? She could not, else she would have flaunted those attributes in that way women learned from the cradle. Even now she looked lovely, even with her hair coated with the ever-present dust. Her eyes looked tired, and there was a spot of pink upon her nose where the sun had been too cruel.

It hurt him to look at her.

If he had been wise, he would have sent her back to the convent when he'd first seen her. The instant he'd recognized that this woman with her trembling fingers and stubborn chin was more than what she appeared. He should have banished her from his life back then, or vanished himself. How could he have known on the night that he had first seen her that she would come to mean so much more to him than Langlinais ever had? If there was something he was willing to die for, it was not faith, nor Langlinais, but Juliana.

He had come to realize that during the journey.

So easily that it had occurred without him knowing. Or perhaps it had come that unforgettable night in her room, when he'd voiced his true thoughts, knowing that he would never do so again. Perhaps all this time he'd only been testing his honor or his resolve.

His final gift to her would be a revelation. His life with her had been filled with secrets. He wanted an end to it now. He would tell her as much as he could about the Cathar treasure. And then walk away.

Chapter 29

Sebastian left her a few moments later, having assigned one of the men-at-arms to provide for her comfort. She smiled her thanks as he offered to arrange a pallet in the shade, but declined. She did not want to have to sit and look composed when she was not.

The uncertainty disturbed her, the realization that she had no idea what was to happen from this day forward. During the last days of their journey here, it had felt as if their time together was measured in days. Now, it was as if there were only hours left. She wanted, desperately, to hold back the sun so that the shadows would not move, turn the hourglass over to start again.

How would she bear life without him? She stood straight, head bowed, eyes lowered. Convent posture. There would be time enough to wonder about her capacity to endure. Now was not the time. Not when Sebastian was still with her.

She found herself at a closed door, pushed it open slowly. Montvichet might not be inhabited, but there was still an air of occupation in that room, as if the people had left for only a moment and would shortly return.

The chamber was crafted of the same yellow stone as the remainder of the fortress. The roof was intact except for a large section close to the doorway. Nature had intervened in the guise of a trailing plant that draped over the opening. Juliana stepped into the room, enchanted. Six desks, tall and angled for the greatest ease at work, stood at spaced intervals throughout the room, placed where they might be touched by the greatest source of light. It came from the small openings in the roof, windows of thick glass no wider than her hand. In the afternoon sun they sparkled like the glint of sun off a pool of water.

A table placed against one wall acted as a common work area. Heavy stones weighted down the parchment pages, waiting for the moment they would be needed. A selection of quills, none of them yet cut, lay in preparation for a scribe's hand. Goatskin containers held what Juliana suspected was powdered ink. There was an assortment of knives, novacula and rasoriums, rulers, regula, linula, normas, needle and thread to repair parchment if torn, and a dozen or so assorted covered pots, one of which contained a particularly odious-smelling dried glue. But there were no finished pages here, no diplomae or completed folia.

She walked to one of the desks. The scribe's work space was crafted of wood, once polished with oil. Dark spots on its surface indicated where ink had dropped from a quill, or perhaps soaked through a page.

At the end of the room there was a series of small vertical openings. She bent and looked through one and felt the fast-moving air against her face. A smile touched her lips. They had thought of everything. The openings allowed the breeze to enter and cool the room, but their design would prevent any dislodging of the work.

A scriptorium, tidy and waiting, even after five years.

She sat upon one of the stools, finding it surprisingly comfortable. The sun streamed down onto the surface of the desk, as if a torch had been lit above it. She slowly unwound her bandages, taking care to roll the strips of linen as she removed them.

Her left hand was nearly healed. But the appearance of her right made her wince. There were red lines all along the top of it, places where the bones had protruded from the skin. It was no longer swollen, and the color had returned to it, but she could barely bend her fingers. She turned her hands over, looked at the palms.

She'd touched Sebastian's arm, had felt the strength and the muscles of it. Had threaded her fingers through the thickness of his hair, had touched his face. How odd that she could feel these sensations even now, as if the memory of them was forever embedded in her flesh.

He'd knelt in front of her, his eyes deep with some unidentifiable emotion. She knew its name now. Despair, such as she had never wished to know. Anguish of the soul. Grief and longing so harsh and real that it became almost solid. It would glow crimson, this yearning. Or white like a faded cloud. Nearly invisible, but with its shadow always remaining. She knew, because she felt the same.

She had always loved reading the words of others, had felt that those long dead philosophers and saints spoke to her through their thoughts. She knew why that link had been so important, now. It had brought to her a sense of connection to the world that mimicked companionship.

Had she simply been lonely all her life? It seemed to her now that the occupations of her mind and the skill of her hands had been replacements for something she'd missed and never known. The easy lilting laughter of two people who shared a thought, the conspiratorial smile that bridged words. The ability to seek out and find the face of someone who might ease a momentary loneliness, assuage a temporary ache.

There was no voice within her pages to ask if she was well, to seek her thoughts or reactions. No smile among the laboriously crafted letters. There was no speech, no harshly rasped words or entreaties. No voice that lowered or whispered phrases that intrigued and beckoned and thrilled, that heated blood and dampened flesh. She would never look upon a folia and feel the awe that came from watching Sebastian, her beautiful warrior, a knight crafted of strength and sorrow.

She moved from the stool and went to the table, reaching for one of the Cathar quills. Only when she returned to the desk did she attempt to hold it in her right hand. With some pain, her fingers would curve, but not tightly enough to grip the quill. It fell with a small click to the desk's surface.

The work of a scribe required the most delicate touch. Perhaps in time, she would be able to write again. It was something she must believe, because without that ability she had nothing.

A tear fell on her hands and, surprisingly, it stung.

The sorrow she felt was not for herself. She understood, finally, the enormity of Sebastian's fate. Had such a knowledge been prompted by the quiet of this place? Or had it been born in the certainty that there were only hours left for them? She clenched her eyes shut against the thought of the horrible physical changes to come for him.

Was it wrong to ask God to move time? Would it be a waste of a prayer to beg of Him to allow her to know Sebastian before such a thing happened to him? Please, just a moment in time to kiss his lips, or be enfolded in his arms. *Let him touch me in joy. Once. Please.* She bowed her head and closed her eyes, uncaring that tears wet her hands, small droplets of sharp sensation. *Or if that is wrong, then spare him somehow. Take this from him, God. He is not a saint or so great a sinner.*

Her grief was silent, a moment unplanned. The scriptorium, a place of quiet reflection and studious endeavor, was an odd place to witness such emotion. But then, the thoughts and words of countless minds had been read there, and later transcribed upon parchment. Words conceived in passion remain as years pass, those that speak of the senses, of joy and despair and adoration. Time dispenses with the mundane, but cherishes those of the heart.

The room seemed to sigh in understanding, or silent compassion. As if it were a sentient being and capable of such things.

Sebastian removed his gauntlets once he was alone, wished he could rid himself of his armor. But comfort was a selfish thing to want, especially on this particular quest. He looked down at his hands, blocked out the sight of them.

He knew the path he took well, had walked it but once in actuality, yet often in his memory. He took a deep breath as he neared the area.

The stench had long since dissipated, wafted away in the mountain air. The circle that had once been burned into the earth had been replaced with tall grass. Only he and a few other villagers knew that a Cathar grave was here. Only one marker bore mute testimony to their martyrdom, a small stone pediment with a chiseled circle as its only inscription. His presence here today was not to ensure that it had been erected as he'd ordered, however. He felt a need to be at this spot, perhaps to honor the memory of the woman who had been mother and friend to him. Perhaps to seek approval for the plan he'd devised at Langlinais. Or perhaps to seek the courage to implement it, knowing the responsibility he assumed for doing so.

He knew little of the Cathar religion, only those things he'd read in the scrolls he'd found. He did not know if there was a prayer that was proper for this time or this place, or even if they would wish one said for them.

Magdalene would smile at his confusion, perhaps even tap him lightly on the head as she was wont to do when he was being chastised. He wished he could hear her voice in the gentle breeze that flowed through the grass. Wished, too, that she could offer him counsel in that pragmatic way of hers.

He would be pitting himself against the Templars, and against the faith that had sheltered him.

The silence of the spot worked on his mind like rue, drawing out his thoughts. It seemed as if here, as in no other place, could he confess the depth of his emotions. Fear for Juliana's fate. He'd watched her carefully, had set Jerard to the task of doing so, also, in case her hands began to show symptoms like his.

He could admit, now, that he was afraid of what the future promised him. It loomed before him with outstretched claws, eager and waiting to grip him until he bled. He could only imagine the months and years ahead, yet while his mind did so often, his heart urged him to think only of the past. *Remember those things that brought you joy. Remember when you were a boy and running through the bailey at Langlinais, or challenging Gregory to climb the tallest tree. Recall the moment of your knighting, when your father's blow, so powerful that it knocked you to the ground, was also accompanied by his rich laughter. Remember all those moments when you were victorious in battle. All those days of study, when your mind raced and your heart beat so loud to hear the speech of others mimic your own thoughts. Remember Juliana.*

Memories flashed into his mind with the suddenness of lightning, Juliana, biting her bottom lip as she concentrated upon the perfect formation of a letter. Juliana, standing silent and still before him, as he knelt and confessed to her. Juliana, laughing, smiling, somber, sad.

He wished to be like most men, thought noble and infused with honor. And, like all men, he knew he would not always succeed. But he must accomplish these duties he'd set for himself, to protect Juliana and Langlinais. First, by offering up to the Templars what they thought he had, so that the greater secret of the Cathars might be kept hidden.

And second, by saying good-bye to Juliana. The moment he'd dreaded had finally come. He'd known the morning he'd left Langlinais that such a decision might be reached. Her hope was too strong for his despair. She looked at him with eyes wide-open and accepting, with a hunger in her gaze and a smile on her lips. He would have her sad rather than sickened in horror at the sight of him. This parting must be swift and quick and as painless for her as he could make it. It was enough that memories of her would last him the rest of his life. It must be enough.

He must not fail.

Chapter 30

"I see you've found the scriptorium," Sebastian said.

He stood framed in the setting sun, a man in his prime. She knew how vital it was that she committed the sight of him to memory. There would come a time, perhaps when she was an old, old woman, when she would not be able to recall it. It was the same with her parents' faces. They were only remembered through a scent, a voice, a hint of laughter. Sebastian would exist only as a young warrior, a vision blurred by time and distance and pain.

She studied his face avidly, impressing it upon her mind the way she did a passage she loved and wished to memorize. His lower lip was fuller than the top. His mouth, unsmiling as now. His chin ended in a blunt and chiseled angle. His eyes she would always remember. They were tilted down at the ends just a little. It gave him a slumberous look, or a mischievous one when viewed a certain way. Most of the time, however, she was captivated by their color, so dark they seemed as if they were not blue at all, but black.

She glanced away, before he noted that tears had come again to her eyes. "It is a wondrous place," she said, looking around her as if she had not already studied each object in the room. "Do you think they allowed women to be scribes?"

"I don't know," he said, entering the room. "They were leaders. Why not scribes?"

At her startled look, he smiled. "Magdalene became a perfecti, I understand. A parfecta," he added before she could ask, "was considered worthy enough to go through the Cathar ceremony of purification."

He reached her side, looked down at her hands. She had not replaced her bandages. He rested his hand beside hers on the scribe's desk. His was so much larger, the silver chain links ending at his wrist glinting in the sunlight. His fingers lifted, his thumb stretched closer. Only an inch separated their two hands, but the distance might be measured in miles. The bridge between them, invisible yet strong, was constructed of the bond between their minds, and the fact that their souls felt intertwined.

"Lord," Jerard said, at the doorway. It was clear from his expression that he had not wanted to interrupt.

Sebastian stepped back and motioned him inside.

Jerard entered the silent room, his footfalls the only sound. Between his hands he held a wooden chest, its rounded top elaborately carved. He stepped forward and handed it to Sebastian with a small bow.

He would have retreated then, but for the fact that Sebastian called him back. "Assist your lady with her bandages," he said, his voice curt, the command almost cutting. He walked to the table that held the scribe's implements and placed the chest upon it, his back to the room.

She looked at him, at the stance he maintained,

wondering if these moments were as difficult for him as they were for her. They must be, else his voice would not have been so raspy, his orders so stern. He was not an unkind man.

Jerard bent before her, wrapping her hands quickly.

"Should I not fetch the salve, my lady?"

"My husband does not use his, why should I?"

Sebastian turned. "I have been as faithful as a hound with that vile-smelling grease, lady wife," he interjected.

"It smells of mint, Sebastian," she said, a soft, chiding smile on her lips.

"And so do I. Do I not smell sweet, Jerard?"

He seemed amused by the look on Jerard's face. He relented, finally, and waved him away.

Her bandages tied, Juliana stepped down from the stool, walked to the table where the chest lay. It was the length of two hand spans, and as wide as one. The lid was rounded, the top connected to the bottom by three delicate leather hinges.

Instead of opening it, however, he placed it under the table, then turned to her. He walked to the door, held it open, turned, and smiled at her.

"Would you like to see the Cathar treasure, Juliana?"

She nodded, surprised, and followed him mutely.

There were a series of rooms off of the main hallway, evidently sleeping chambers from their simple design and sparse contents. Sebastian entered the last one to the left, stood looking around him. As with all but the scriptorium, there were signs of disarray. The wooden frame of the bed had been overturned, the single small table lay with a broken leg. A jug and basin lay littered on the floor, shattered. An arched window carved from the stone allowed the sunlight to stream into the room. Upon everything was a thick layer of dust, the signs of invasion and search preserved for all time.

"How do you know it's still here?" she asked, looking around her.

His smile surprised her. "It is here, else Langlinais would not have been threatened. It looks as if they searched well, but they were doomed to failure. I only discovered the secret by good fortune."

He walked to the far wall, counted across the large stones, then down. He pressed the second at the level of his waist. It turned easily as if it rested upon a fulcrum. Juliana peered inside and noticed the rod of iron that projected from the floor. It must fit into the hole at the base of the stone.

Sebastian disappeared behind the stone for a moment, then returned carrying a tightly woven covered basket. He smiled when he saw her face.

"Your eyes are as big as moons, Juliana."

"I must confess to never seeing anything like a secret door," she said.

"Come here and look closer." She peered inside the small space. There was enough room for two people to stand.

"There is no duplicate to it in the other sleeping chambers. Perhaps this niche dated from the earlier fortress, and the Cathars simply took advantage of it in order to hide the treasure. It accomplished their purpose. It was here five years ago, and it's here now."

He placed the basket on the floor, then knelt in front of it. He opened the fastening of the lid gently, as he might handle a newborn babe. No, she thought, watching him. Not gentleness, but reverence. This, then, was the treasure of the Cathars. Not gold, not silver. But the contents of a basket that might be found in a peasant's hut.

A shaft of sunlight created an aura around Sebastian as he lowered the lid to the floor. Neither of them spoke, the moment given up to an odd and eerie silence. Juliana could almost feel the absence of sound, as if the breeze stilled in that moment, or the birds that nested on Montvichet's roof held their songs for the discovery.

She knelt opposite him, her left hand cradling her right. Her breath was constricted, her heart beat loudly and furiously. She suddenly did not know if she wished to learn what he would show her. What could be so precious that it would justify so many deaths, so much secrecy?

There was a folded cloth at the top of the basket. A scent of spices wafted from it as Sebastian gently placed it on top of the lid. Next, there were several small shards of wood, one of which crumbled in his fingers. He placed it beside the others, as reverently as he handled the other object. The scrolls, however, filled the majority of the basket. There appeared to be hundreds of them, packed upright so that they would not be crushed by the weight of the cloth or the wood.

"Of all the things I remember most about Magdalene, it was her quest for knowledge," Sebastian said. He looked over at her. "You reminded me so much of her at first."

"And now?" she asked, the treasure of the Cathars supplanted by another, more personal, mystery.

"Now, you are simply Juliana," he said, smiling. He glanced down at the basket. "Magdalene was the one who taught me to value learning. While my father made my muscles strong, Magdalene worked upon my mind." He placed his gauntleted palm upon the shards of wood and removed it a moment later as if conscious of her regard.

"The treasure of the Cathars is knowledge, first of all," he said, touching the ends of the scrolls. "There are works here detailing all sorts of animals and plants along with the writings of great men."

He looked down at the lid of the basket and the odd things he'd arranged there. He seemed reluctant to continue. The silence increased, so too the feeling that there was more here than she understood.

"But they were not fools," he continued finally, "and they knew how much they were despised for their beliefs. So the Cathars took pains to protect themselves the best way they could. They sent their emissaries throughout the world to gather what they could find and bring it back here to Montvichet."

He looked over at her, his face somber in the face of her confusion.

"They left behind a detailed reasoning behind their actions. You'll find it among the later scrolls. They were being persecuted by the Church; therefore, it was against them the Cathars endeavored to protect themselves. They sought out what was sacred to the Church."

She felt a mingled horror and joy to realize what lay before her.

"The relics of the faith," she whispered. Her left hand reached out, trembled over the scraps of wood, the folded cloth redolent of rich spices. She wanted desperately to touch them, but was too afraid. She drew her hand back, stared at Sebastian wordlessly.

He nodded. "The true cross and the shroud. They held them as protection against persecution."

"And this is why the Templars want them?" She frowned.

"No, because of power, Juliana," he said. "Can

you not imagine the power they could accumulate if they were guardians of the true cross and the shroud of Christ?"

"More than the Church?" she whispered.

His smile was an enigmatic expression flavored with mockery. "There are rumors even now that they intend to claim France. Their ambitions are as great as their wealth. Some would replace the Pope if for no other reason than to curb the Templars. You can be assured he does not know of their demands."

"Yet you could not solicit the help of the Church, because of your disease."

"True enough," he said, placing the relics gently back into the basket.

"But what will happen now, Sebastian?"

"Now we give the Templars exactly what they expect."

They returned to the scriptorium in silence, Sebastian carrying the basket. She wanted to ask him a hundred questions, the most important being how he could distrust the Templars so fervently and yet relinquish the treasure to them. It seemed a betrayal of everything the Cathars had died for, and Magdalene especially, since it was she who had summoned Sebastian to Montvichet.

What was Sebastian planning?

Sebastian remained silent as he placed the basket on the floor and retrieved the chest. He carefully opened it, then turned to watch her reaction.

Inside, nestled in a bed of hay, was a chalice. He picked it up carefully, holding it out for her to see. She was certain it was the most beautiful object she'd ever seen. It was not solid gold, but constructed with small windows of glass of a crimson hue so deeply tinted as to look almost purple. Upon the everted lip of the cup, and upon the stem, was a thin gold line that thickened to resemble a vine studded with thorns. On the bowl of the chalice was an etched figure of a man dressed in a long robe, his face bearded, his hands outstretched. Rays of the sun emanated from behind the man, from his wrists.

Inside the reliquary rested a small wooden cup.

She could feel her breath heat as Sebastian raised the chalice. The sunlight from above seemed to find the golden bowl, extend rays of crimson fire around the room.

"You've wondered what the Cathar treasure is, Juliana." He lowered the chalice, returning it to its chest. "So, too, have the Templars. This chalice will satisfy their longing and assuage their curiosity." He placed his hand atop the chalice. "Sangraal," he said softly, his words nearly drowned beneath the tumult of her heart.

"The Holy Grail," she whispered. "Is it truly?"

"No," he said, shaking his head. "The reliquary was given to me by an old man, in exchange for a service I had done him. It was not long after I was released. He had been set upon by bandits, and I happened to be able to aid him." He lowered the lid of the chest. "The journey home was a dangerous one for me. I had not wished to become involved, for fear my disease might be discovered. But he was no match for the four men who were intent upon robbing him." He remembered that day well, and the fulsome gratitude of the merchant who'd insisted upon rewarding him.

His hand traced the carvings of the chest. "I think of it as a memento of my days in the Holy Land, something that helped remove the foul odor of the prison from my nostrils. I'd hoped to keep it at Langlinais, but now it goes to serve a greater purpose,

242   KAREN RANNEY

to placate the Templars. Enough that they will not search further."

He placed the chest beneath the table, then turned to Juliana.

"Did you think me capable of turning over the treasure to the Templars?"

"No. But I wondered at your plan." His smile seemed to reward her honesty and her loyalty. "What will you do with it, Sebastian?"

"Send the treasure back to Langlinais with you."

There, it had come then. The knowledge she'd suspected deep in her heart. The same knowledge she'd dreaded. His smile seemed infinitely sad, his eyes somber.

The words she spoke were difficult. The truth of their lives had been hurled at her so quickly that she could feel the pain of it lodged in her chest.

"Will you not return?"

He shook his head, his gaze never leaving her. "It is better if I do not."

"What will you do, Sebastian? Where will you go?"

She wanted to know. She *must* know, as if that knowledge would somehow make this easier to bear.

"I will be what I am, Juliana."

Leper.

He was doomed to wander aimlessly. People would not be kind to him, and even a knight needed a touch of gentleness from time to time. They would run from him, cautious because of his size, terrified because of what he represented. No one would touch him. No one touched him now, and here he stood, apart as he always had.

The Mass of Separation would be uttered over

him. She'd had to transcribe it once, and the words seemed etched in the air before her.

I forbid you to ever enter the church or monastery, fair, mill, marketplace, or company of persons. I forbid you to ever leave your abode without your leper's costume in order that one recognize you and that you never go barefoot. I forbid you to wash your hands or anything about you in the stream or in the fountain and to ever drink. I forbid you to touch anything you bargain for or buy until someone gives it to you. I forbid you to live with any woman not your own.

Not your own. But she was Sebastian's own. She was his, but he would never be able to claim her. Sometimes, she thought he was about to touch her, reach out his hand and allow his finger to graze her cheek, or take her hand, or touch her shoulder. But he always withdrew, always clenched his hand into a fist and looked away.

"You could find sanctuary at Langlinais, Sebastian." Her gaze met his. In her look were all the words she could not say to him, words forbidden by the very nature of his courage. But in her mind, she begged him to stay.

"You once planned to remain there," she said, her voice trembling despite her resolve. "There would be no one to disturb your peace."

"No, Juliana. Because to be with you would be to bring you danger." His voice lowered until it was but a soft whisper, no more substantial than a hint of breeze. "Because to be with you would bring me anguish."

His words rang with truth.

She looked down at the floor, shamed by her weakness. "I cannot bear this Sebastian, losing you. I thought myself brave enough. I truly did. But I find I am as much a coward as ever." She glanced up at him, blinking back the tears. That much she could offer him.

"And I cannot ease your way, Juliana," he tenderly said. "If I could, I would change the world for you. I would heal myself and come to you as a whole man. But those are dreams, Juliana, and we are not dreamers." His tone was resolute, each word as strong and as brittle as if it had been chipped from stone. But his voice ended in a shuddering sigh, as if he'd done with courage. It was what stopped her from reaching for him.

"We are real, Juliana," he said, his gaze never veering from her. Would he emblazon the memory of her on his lids as fervently as she did him? This moment was painful and stark, but it would be one of those that she recalled for the rest of her life. Because it was certain that he would not relent. The determination was there on his face, in his beautiful blue black eyes, in the firm set of his mouth.

"We are real," he said again, "and the world is not as we would wish it to be."

No. No, my dearest love, it is not.

But she said nothing as Sebastian left the room.

Chapter 31

E very night of their journey she had slept upon
the ground surrounded by the circle of the
men-at-arms. Sebastian had always remained within
calling distance. A few days the gentle rains had
soaked them and they'd sought shelter in more substantial places like a cave or a copse of trees. But for
the most part, it had not been difficult to find rest.

Here at Montvichet where there was a chamber
tidied for her use and a bed, she found it impossible
to sleep. She could not even bring herself to lie down
upon the thin straw mattress. Instead, she constantly
thought about the people who had lived here. How
had they borne grieving for those they loved?

She stood and donned her clothing, found her
way in the darkness to the corridor and from there
to the courtyard.

Sebastian turned at her approach. Moonlight
streamed across the courtyard, well enough that she
could see the horses at the farside, and between
them, the sleeping figures of the men-at-arms. Even
so, he held a kind of torch, a curved bowl that held
a candle, and surrounding it, a piece of oiled parchment that magnified the light, diffusing it. She'd
seen such a thing in a few of the illustrations in the

books she copied, but never one in person.

She reached out her hand and touched the shade, her curiosity satisfied when she noted the small clips held the parchment safely away from the candle flame, at a curving angle. Only then did she glance up to catch his smile, echoed in the deep night of his eyes.

"Could you not sleep?"

She shook her head.

The horses moved restlessly at the farside. Someone murmured. A snore, a gurgle, a cough, they were all normal sounds to her after weeks of traveling with these men. She knew a few of their names and a few details about their lives. Who had once been on crusade, who had served Sebastian's father, the location of a sweetheart, the number of children, the details about a person's life that is shared with another.

She stepped forward, looked down into the darkness. Instead of the moon-shadowed landscape, it seemed the valley was afire with torches. Small dots of light surrounded a larger encampment.

"They were faster than I anticipated," Sebastian said, not turning his eyes from the scene.

"Who are they?"

"Templars." He turned his back on them, faced the courtyard. "Who else?"

"What will they do, Sebastian?"

He glanced over his shoulder at her. "I've no doubt they wish to challenge us. They know our strength and know we are no match for their numbers."

"But we have done nothing that they should wish to challenge us, Sebastian."

His smile was oddly lit by the oil lamp. "It is not

necessary to be innocent. Only to stand between the Templars and something they want."

The torches seemed to wink at her. "Will they besiege Montvichet again?"

He tilted his head back and looked at the sky. It was a harvest moon, yellow and bright. "I doubt it. It could not withstand another. They have only to ride through the open gates."

"Then what shall we do, Sebastian?"

"Wait until morning. It is all we can do."

"How long do you think it took them to build this place?" Juliana looked around her at the darkened fortress. She sat on the stone floor, her back against the wall. Sebastian sat beside her. Night was full upon them, the glittering stars like tiny eyes winking above, the air perfumed with a slight breeze that carried the scent of pine.

"It depends upon whom you mean," Sebastian said. "I think the Romans came first, or perhaps built their fortress upon another earlier structure."

"Have people always looked for protection, then?"

"In one form or another." His voice was low, sounded like muted thunder. It had entranced her from the beginning.

She bit into a piece of cheese. "This is very good, isn't it?"

"Very good," he said, a smile in his voice.

"The convent had a goat, but we did not make cheese. The abbess thought it a luxury we could do without."

"She sounds like a very practical woman."

"She was."

Silence while Juliana tried to think of another topic of conversation. She'd never had difficulty speaking to him before, but this solemn night was different. There was a paucity of subjects that did not touch, in some way, upon their lives. They had already said all that could be said about futures. His was immutable. Neither her wishes nor hopes could alter it. She could beg him to take her with him, but such words would only mar their parting; they would not sway Sebastian. So she spoke to him of the mundane, simple questions passed between casual acquaintances. All the while wishing to ask those that could not be voiced. Why and how and where, but most importantly, when was he leaving her?

"How do you think they brought the timbers here?"

He tilted his head back as if to count the beams that supported the roof of the sleeping chambers. "I suspect they carried them by wagon. Or perhaps they simply dragged them."

She yawned, an unexpected gesture. Sebastian turned to her in the darkness.

"You should sleep, Juliana."

She had fought off sleep all night, wishing to pass these hours until dawn beside him. Each moment they shared was like a precious bead collected and strung on a cord. But the silence conspired against her, along with the weariness of the journey.

She laid her head back against the stone, savoring the closeness of him. They sat merely a handbreadth apart. Too soon, she felt herself sliding into sleep. His voice spoke to her, a soft whisper of words. "Sleep, Juliana. I'll be here beside you." Permission and protection, all in one.

Dreams haunted her. Not those of the long-dead inhabitants of Montvichet, or of the Templars waiting in the valley for the dawn she dreaded. They were of Sebastian, his words and smiles and laughter. His hands touched her, his lips met hers in a kiss that scorched as it healed. *Intellige clamoren meum. My fingers would make your blood leap.* She awakened to her own soft cry. A sound of yearning.

Dawn had come too swiftly.

Sebastian was not beside her, but she did not seek him out. Instead, she found her way to the bathing room of the Cathars. When she'd first seen it, she'd marveled that they had devised such a chamber. A cistern on the roof, both still intact, held water that was piped down into a basin for washing. Langlinais had such an innovation, but the Cathars had refined it. A pipe led to a large stone bath. Removing a wooden plug at the bottom of the stone released the water, that then sluiced over the stone floor of the chamber and down through the privy hole.

She spent more time than usual on her morning ablutions. She placed a soft wet cloth over her eyes until the pain in them subsided. Tears had made them swell, and she had spent too much time in tears yesterday. She changed her clothes for a soft yellow surcoat she'd not worn before. She brushed her hair vigorously and left it unbraided. Her last act was to rewrap her hands as well as she was able. She would need Jerard's help to tie the trailing ends of the bandages at her wrists.

She hesitated at the doorway of the bathing chamber. Part of her wished to remain in this room, or barricade herself in another part of Montvichet.

The only time the world had truly been kind was when she'd tucked herself into her work and remained there, adrift in thoughts from great and learned minds. She had, like a mouse in its burrow, felt safe as long as she did not peer from her hole. But life was lived at places like Langlinais among the sounds of singing and laughter. It was lived, finally, in each day. Whatever the location, whatever the circumstance.

She walked from the room, closing the door softly behind her.

What had she felt before coming to Langlinais? What emotions had she experienced? It was as if that girl had existed in a timeless limbo, waiting until the first glimpse of Langlinais before feeling anything other than fear. Yet, there was a full range of emotions to choose from now, all of them granted to her by Sebastian.

She did not know what love was, perhaps. But she knew its absence. It was what she would feel the moment Sebastian left her.

He watched as she walked into the courtyard. The sun bathed the yellow rock of Montvichet with a golden light, making the stone glitter. The glow surrounded Juliana as if it approved of her appearance. She smiled, an expression he stored away in his memory for later. For now, it had the power to make him stare at her and savor the picture of how she looked, her black hair shining, her cheeks pinked and her lips softly curved. A spike of pain slid easily through his soul. The price to pay, then, for knowing her and loving her.

She had matured in the past weeks. Her smile was still tentative, but then it had always been rare. But in her eyes was a look that had not been there before, an anticipation, not of excitement, but of pain. It was as if she'd told herself she must be wary, but still retained enough innocence to keep it at bay.

Her black hair was left unbraided, allowed to tumble down her back. The only adornment she wore was a small gold circlet upon her brow. She wore a half surcoat that fit at her shoulders and fell behind her. The soft yellow folds seemed to accentuate the blackness of her hair, as if in her person night met with dawn.

When had he become enchanted by her? At their first meeting, of course. "Are you Death?" she'd asked.

His virgin bride. Of all the things he regretted in his life, it was not that they had not coupled. It was that he had never brought her joy, never brought her to ecstasy.

Perhaps one day she would find someone to love, marry again. A union in truth and not simply in name. There would be smiles again at Langlinais, and laughter there. Perhaps she would name one of her children for him, a sign of her fondness and memory. There might be brothers to play again on the bridge like he and Gregory had done.

He wished for her all that he had never given her.

The woman who greeted him this dawn was not the same one he had married. To this woman he'd relinquish his home without a hint of concern. She would, he knew, be able to maintain Langlinais, provide for the well-being of all those who would come to depend upon her. In her eyes he could see a hint of that woman to come. A woman of wisdom, who would stand at the east tower often and face the world. Would she think about him?

That was the source of the grief he felt. That he would not be able to share each of her days, that he would never see the changes time brought to her.

He saw her shock, her recoil, knew the moment she became aware of what he wore. Not armor, nor monk's robe, but the uniform of the leper. It was of reddish brown wool with a crimson L embroidered upon its back and front. Distinctive and frightening.

It was the first time he'd stood so before the world. Even now, it tasted of hell.

His men-at-arms did not know if such a garment was the stuff of jest, or a ruse to fool the Templars. They had, after all, traveled with him for weeks and had not seen that he was ill. But people will notice what they wish, and often ignore what they do not want to see. He did not doubt that after this morning they would cross themselves while cursing his name.

He wondered what the Templars would do. He would take the chalice to them, and hope that such a gesture would protect Juliana and his men from assault. Then, once he was assured of their safety, he would vanish. It did not matter his destination, only that it was as far away from Langlinais as he could travel.

Jerard brought Faeren to him, but he shook his head. He would ride one of the other horses into exile. Faeren would return to Langlinais and live out the rest of his life in peace. It was scant enough appreciation for the loyalty and skill with which the horse had served him.

Juliana walked toward him, her head held high, her face expressionless. Her eyes were deep pools of green. Soundless tears fell down her face. She did not even seem aware of them. "Need it be so soon, Sebastian?"

"What can time bring us, Juliana?" he asked gently. "Do not weep, my lady. Give me these last moments with you without sorrow."

His words silenced her, but did not stop her tears. Did she know that only by the greatest of wills would he be able to walk away from her?

"The Cathars believed the soul lives again," he softly said. "That our bodies are only vessels to be discarded after a lifetime. Perhaps one day we will meet again, my Juliana. In a place where I might touch you, where I might enfold you in my arms."

"Then let it come quickly, Sebastian," she said, her voice tremulous through her tears. "Not a hundred years or a thousand, but soon. I will wend my way through eternity seeking you."

He gave the signal and Jerard stepped forward, handing him the reins of his mount. He tied the chalice to the saddle. He did not mount, since the horse would need to be led over the bridge. He was nearly at the gateway before he turned. In a voice designed to carry, a declaration meant to be heard so that all of the Langlinais men would hear it and repeat it, he said, "Aristotle was once asked the definition of a friend. He answered that it was a single soul dwelling in two bodies. What is love? I think it is the same. Be my soul, my dearest Juliana."

Chapter 32

"How touching, brother."

Sebastian looked up at the sound of that voice. A quick survey brought him to the source of it. Gregory stood, not at the main gate of Montvichet, but at the ruined wall to the north. Evidently he had scaled the wall just as the final invaders had done, ending the siege.

A moment later, the bridge was swarming with Templar sergeants attired in brown and black mantles. They filled the courtyard, pinning his men against the wall with their swords. They had no choice but to lay down their swords.

It was not alarm Sebastian felt, but a sensation of doomed destiny. That it should be his brother who faced him was not so much ironic as expected. He had been right, then, to think Gregory behind this ploy. A slight nod was his only acknowledgment.

His brother looked well. They were of a similar height and build. Only eighteen months separated them in birth. Age would wear equally on either of them. The last two years had evidently agreed with Gregory, an observation that was met only with a smile on Sebastian's part.

"I was surprised, Sebastian, to discover that you

were headed for this cursed place. I half expected the treasure to be in safekeeping at Langlinais. But you left Montvichet for the Holy Land, didn't you? You'd not enough time to dispose of it otherwise."

"I had no thought to do so, Gregory. In fact, without your threat it would have remained here forever. It was not mine to take."

"How righteous you sound, Sebastian."

"Label me what you will, Gregory. I do not judge a man by his words, but by his actions." He walked closer to his brother. "Was it your treachery that lay behind the attack on us?" His voice was low enough that it could not be heard by others. Inducement for Gregory's confession? If so, he was disappointed.

"Were you set upon, Sebastian? But you know that the roads are not safe."

"And made even more dangerous by you, I've no doubt. How did you obtain their cooperation, Gregory? Torture or gold?"

Gregory only smiled.

"Have you the treasure?" There was a look of such supreme satisfaction on his brother's face that Sebastian was tempted to strike him. But that action would be idiotic, especially since they were surrounded by Templars, swords drawn.

"I will surrender it only upon certain conditions."

"You are hardly in the position to offer conditions, Sebastian," Gregory said, his tone amused.

"Release the woman and my men, and the treasure is yours."

Gregory smiled, looking behind him. "It is too late to bargain, Sebastian. The treasure has been found."

Sebastian turned. The chest that had been tied to his horse's saddle had been sliced free. A sergeant knelt in front of it, his fingers trembling as he raised the lid.

Gregory brushed by him and extracted the goblet. He extended his hand, held it up triumphantly, as proudly as a king would a scepter. The Templars stared in wonder at the sight of the chalice. He lifted it so that the sun's light flowed through the glass. It bathed the stones of Montvichet in a crimson glow.

To Sebastian, it looked too much like blood.

Gregory packed the chalice away reverently, tucked the chest beneath his arm.

"The Holy Grail, Sebastian. A treasure, indeed. If you were less a lover of heretics, you might well be rewarded for such a prize."

"I will allow you the glory, Gregory," he said, his attention on Juliana. One of the Templar's swords pressed against her, pinning her to the wall. Yet, she did not look as fearful as she should have. Instead, his wife appeared angry.

"What ruse is this, Sebastian?" Gregory wore a small smile while appraising him, as if just now noticing the strange robe he wore. "I commend you on the originality of your deception. Did you think to slip by us, then?"

"No ruse, Gregory," he said, his attention reluctantly diverted from Juliana. "The truth, perhaps, unpalatable and raw."

"A leper?" There was derision in the question. Perhaps even disbelief.

Sebastian walked toward his brother, his own smile firmly anchored. The Templar sergeants fell back and away from him as he did so. Evidently they did not think it a trick. He removed his gloves slowly, watching the expression on Gregory's face alter as he drew closer. Amusement quickly changed to revulsion. Gregory held up a hand, then stepped back.

Sebastian began to pull apart the laces that held

closed the neck of his leper's robe. It gaped open, allowing a view of his chest, and the darkening sores there.

"It is not necessary, Sebastian, I need no further proof." Gregory's face had turned ashen.

"You are wondering right now, Gregory, if you touched me. If our breath was shared, or if you can contract such a horror simply by being my brother. Shall we test it?" Sebastian took one step forward, but his way was blocked by the sharp edge of Gregory's sword.

He laughed, and the sound of it, bitter and harsh, echoed through the courtyard. "What, no prayers for me, brother? No wishes for my good health? Did you know that it used to be a sign of good fortune to cross a leper's path? Do you think you shall be blessed, Gregory? Or cursed?"

"You are the one cursed, Sebastian."

"Am I? Do you dream of Cathar children, Gregory?"

"They were heretics."

"Did you tell yourself that when you watched them burn to death?"

Gregory frowned. "Do you think yourself safe to utter these accusations because you are my brother?"

"I do not see you slicing me through with so many witnesses present."

"An arrow can come from anywhere, Sebastian."

"I am dying, Gregory. Kill me or not. It does not matter. I ask only one thing of you, that you spare the woman and my men."

"If I will not?"

"Then I will beg," Sebastian said simply.

"Gather them up," Gregory said to the men in

front of him, his attention never veering from Sebastian.

Two men gripped Juliana's arms, but she wrenched free, only to be restrained again as easily. They dragged her to the gateway. "No!" she screamed. Her feet scrabbled against the stone courtyard as she was pulled forward. Then, impatient with her resistance, two of the Templar brothers lifted her and transported her toward the bridge.

At first Sebastian did not believe what she was saying. Then, the word slammed into his heart with the force of a boulder.

"I am leper!" Her declaration echoed in the sudden lull of the courtyard.

She was dropped to the stone floor.

"No, Juliana!" He stepped forward only to find his way blocked by Gregory's sword pointed at his throat.

"I am leper!" She knelt, displayed her bandaged hands as if in proof. Those men nearest her dropped back, pressed against the wall to avoid her touch.

"I am leper!" she shouted, for the third time. There was no hesitation in her voice, but her lips trembled, her face was pale. Still, there was determination in her eyes. Now, he witnessed the strength always hinted at, the resolve always promised.

She got to her feet, her hands aloft as if her trailing bandages covered sores too horrible to view.

"Prove it," Gregory said, his sword moving from Sebastian to point in her direction.

"You wish me to unwrap my hands?" She looked stunned.

"Do you need help?" He glanced around the courtyard. "Who will help this woman bare her hands?"

No one came forward. The touch of a leper could kill.

"Jerard," Sebastian called out, "aid my lady."

Jerard stepped forward, bowed before her. Juliana looked stricken, as if she could not believe the depth of his betrayal.

"No, Jerard," she said softly. He did not speak, nor look at her face as he reached for her hands.

She glanced at Sebastian. "Please, Sebastian." He knew what she wanted. To be with him, to share his anguish. To spend the nights and days together in a blessed hell comprised of joy and terror. He could not watch her die in front of him, and would not give her the burden of his death. Jerard would unwrap her hands and prove she was not diseased and in doing so would save her from the fate she'd impulsively decreed for herself.

He shook his head and at his gesture, she smiled. It was a smile out of time or place, not at all suitable for this moment of danger. It was soft and spreading as if she began to feel great joy.

He should have known what she would do. But he did not.

She stepped forward, brushing by Jerard when he would have restrained her. She ignored the sword that slid across her surcoat as if it was no more substantial than a spiderweb. She did not appear to hear the muttering of others, Gregory's command, even Sebastian's shout to Jerard. She moved among the men trained for war and they parted for her, silenced not by her taint of disease as much as the look in her eyes and the smile she wore.

He had the thought that she was not unlike Magdalene, her abbess, Hildegard of Bingen, women of intelligence and determination. She was possessed of all that and more, or perhaps it was simply the courage in her face that silenced the men in the courtyard and held them mute as they watched her.

She reached him at last, her smile delicate and trembling, her eyes filled with softness, as if she wept again but the tears had not yet fallen.

"*Hairetikos*. You told me once it meant to choose. I choose you, Sebastian," she murmured. She startled him by laying her hand against his cheek. He felt the scratchiness of the linen of her bandages, inhaled the scent of her. No longer roses, but something else. The smell of spring, perhaps.

Then she stood on her tiptoes, reached her bandaged hands around his neck. Shock held him immobile for a moment, then when he would have pushed her away, she drew his head down and pressed her lips against his.

Chapter 33

I *forbid you to live with any woman not your own.*
The words surged through her with the power
of a prayer.

She had not thought herself brave enough. But it
had not been courage that had helped her walk
across the courtyard to Sebastian, it had been his
earlier words to her. Had she indeed been taught to
fear? *Juliana, you might lose your eyesight with so little
light. Do not touch that plant, Juliana, it will give you a
rash that will scar your skin. Do not go near that dog,
Juliana. He may bite you.* She recognized, now, that
the cautions of the nuns had been because she was
the Langlinais Bride, and as such, to be cared for and
protected. But she had taken their words and transformed them into her fears, and had trembled at life.

She was no longer afraid. So, she stepped back
from him, the taste of his mouth still on her lips and
smiled.

"What have you done, Juliana?" His whisper was
agonized.

She heard the noise around her, horses being led,
the muffled curses as their men-at-arms were led at
sword point through the gate. She cared nothing for
that, or the prick of pain at her shoulder as she was

shoved away from Sebastian. All she knew was that they would not be separated now.

Gregory's sword bit into her skin, enough that Juliana turned, faced him.

Eyes the shade of Sebastian's frowned at her. "You are either a leper or a foolish woman. Do you care so much about him, then?"

"Do you care so little?" she asked.

"Let her go, Gregory," Sebastian interjected. "She is no leper."

"Even if she is not, her actions have now tainted her as well." Gregory studied her. "You meant it to be so. Why?"

Sebastian moved, standing between her and Gregory. "If you want Langlinais, it is yours, Gregory. Take it. But release her."

"You would trade your birthright for this woman's freedom?"

"Yes," Sebastian said shortly.

"Nevertheless, that was not the agreement." Gregory signaled to a sergeant who came forward. Gregory spoke with him and a moment later, he returned, a document in one hand. He placed it on the ground in front of Sebastian.

"Langlinais is yours, brother. Not that it will do you any good. But we are men of God, Sebastian, our word is worthy of trust."

Sebastian said nothing to this pronouncement. It was the ultimate irony, especially spoken there, at Montvichet.

"I will burn the bridge, Sebastian. A wise move to imprison lepers. There are those who would kill you if they could."

"You among them."

A small smile played on Gregory's lips. "I am no Cain. I've no rancor for you, Sebastian. In fact, I can feel only pity for your fate. I do not understand, however, why you would wish to bargain the Holy Grail for a demesne. Nor why you would care so much when you are so obviously dying."

"Langlinais will revert to my wife, Gregory. She will benefit from this trade." Sebastian's tone seemed to warn Juliana to keep silent.

"So, you've taken a concubine like our father." Gregory studied Juliana, but he made no further comment.

At the gateway, he turned, glanced one more time at his brother. It looked as if he might say something further, but he turned and walked over the bridge.

Moments later, the smell of burning wood hung like a cloud over Montvichet.

The moment the Templars were gone, Sebastian ran to the side of the courtyard, dislodged the timbers lying on the stone floor. A square opening revealed a series of stone steps that descended into darkness.

He lowered himself into the opening, feeling for a handhold. There was none. He held both arms outstretched to feel the wall. The steps were mossy and he knew that there must be an underground spring nearby. That would account for the well behind the refectory.

The descent was difficult. Twice the steps angled down and seemed to disappear. He should have thought to bring an oil lamp or torch with him. By the time he was a third of the way down, he was in full darkness. He cursed himself for his lack of foresight and made his way back to the courtyard. Reversing his steps was less difficult than descending into blackness. He found a torch, trimmed the handle, lit it, and returned to the stygian darkness of the tunnel.

At the bottom, Sebastian found what he'd expected. Five years ago, he and Jerard had investigated the valley opening. It had been blocked by large building stones, leading him to believe that it was by this method that the Cathars had been starved in their fortress.

He wiped the sweat from his forehead with the back of his hand. The air here was fetid, the moisture glistened on the stones in front of him. How long would it take to clear a way through the tunnel? Time leered at him from the shadows as the torch flickered.

They had an abundant supply of food bought from the villagers. Gregory's sergeants had not thought to take the supplies not yet loaded on the packhorses. They would be able to survive for a while.

He bent and stuck the torch into a gap of stone between a step and wall, then stripped his leper's robe from his body. He would concentrate on only one task, that of saving Juliana.

The descent to the valley floor could have been made in better time. It was not the prisoners that hampered them as much as it was the horses. His brother's high-stepping horse was the most recalcitrant of all, and Gregory had asked the prisoners who among them was responsible for tending to the beast and had been led to the squire. He released the man that he might lead Faeren off the mountain.

The men he held captive were all from his birthplace, a home he'd not seen in eight years. He did not miss it, but he could not help but wonder if these men had known him when he was a boy. Had he trained with some of them, drunk with them? A strange irony that he was perhaps closer to them than the troops he commanded.

He could kill them all now, or set them free to return home. He chose the latter course. It was one thing to arrange for their ambush by a third party, another to explain killing thirteen unarmed men. What, after all, had they seen? A leper and his woman imprisoned at Montvichet. The Holy Grail being given to the Knights Templar. Nothing that would lead to shame or disgrace.

At their encampment, the Templars mounted their own horses, but still led the men, their hands tied in front of them. All except the squire who led the wild-eyed Faeren. *Only Sebastian would name his horse fear*, Gregory thought.

The chest that cradled the chalice was affixed to his saddle. It would not be far from him until they reached Courcy. He placed his hand over the chest reverently. It was not solely faith that awed him as it was the sense of power he felt at this moment. By such an act, he could rise to become Master of the Order.

They had traveled two hours before he raised his hand in a signal to halt. He rode back to where the prisoners stood, shoulders drooping. He looked past them, to the mountain that sheltered Montvichet. It was far enough.

He sliced their bonds himself.

"You are free to go. Onward, but not back to Montvichet." Their assembled mutters were seemingly in the assent.

When he reached the squire, he studied him. "Will you go on? Or return to him?"

The man did not answer him, only stared mutely ahead.

"He is doomed, you know."

There, that comment elicited some response. There was fury in the man's eyes.

"I will return, Templar."

"What manner of man is my brother, squire, that he would command such loyalty from you? From her?" He gestured toward the mountain.

No answer, but then he did not truly expect one. Gregory turned and walked away.

"A man of honor."

He turned. The squire's gaze was sharp, no longer directed at the scenery, but directly at him.

"He is a man of great honor, Templar. You should count yourself fortunate to be his brother."

For a long moment, the two men stared at each other, Templar and squire.

"Tell him, squire, if you ever look upon his face again, that I was not at Montvichet. That I knew nothing of the treachery that destroyed them. But tell him this, also. That, had I been there, I would have done my duty well."

Gregory strode back to his horse and mounted again, one hand upon the chalice as if to assure himself it was real. He made the signal for the knights to move out.

He did not look back.

Chapter 34

⁓⁓⁓✦⁓⁓⁓

Minutes passed, and still Sebastian did not return. It was as if the ground had swallowed him whole. Juliana retrieved the Templar document, then walked to the edge of the pit. There was not even a dot of light to illuminate the steps. She called out his name once, and had been answered with a faint response, but the nature of it she could not decipher. It was enough to know he was well.

Nothing remained of the bridge that crossed the gorge. Not ashes, not embers. Not even a trailing bit of rope. Everything had fallen into the chasm. Juliana stood at the gateway and measured the distance to the other side of the mountain, then wondered why she took the time to do so. She could not hold a rope and it was absurd to think of jumping it.

She retreated to the scriptorium, her attention caught by the basket of relics below the table. Should she take them back to their hiding place? How odd that the basket looked like a thousand others, equally as innocent and innocuous, yet she knew now that the Templars would kill for such symbols of faith. Yet, if it was truly faith, why would they require such proof?

Sebastian had said nothing to her after she'd

kissed him. Only bargained for her life by giving all that he had. Yet, when the Templars left, not one word did they exchange, not one look. It was as if she had no longer existed.

Slowly she began to unwind the bandages that bound her fingers. In moments, she'd had them exposed to the sun streaming through the small ceiling windows. This morning, she'd begun to bathe them, and instead of discomfort, she'd only felt relief from the eternal itching. It was as if her hands healed while her heart was breaking. She discovered that the more she moved her fingers, the easier it became. Therefore, she didn't see the point in replacing the linen wrapping again.

A noise alerted her. Sebastian stood there. He wore the leper's uniform still, but his face was damp with moisture, his hair wet. His face was set into stern lines.

"I wish you had remained timid, Juliana," he said. "Yet, you have decided to become an opponent as daunting as any I've met on a battlefield. Beneath your trembles rests a will of iron, however misguided it may be. You challenge fate and sneer at Templars and declare yourself a leper with equal belief in your impunity."

She laid her hands, one upon the other, at her waist so that they did not betray her by trembling. "Life is sometimes perilous, Sebastian. May I not choose how I am to live mine?"

"You might have lived in peace at Langlinais."

She shook her head. "For what reason would I have held your estate, Sebastian? For whom would I have guarded it? Our child?"

"For yourself, Juliana. For your own peace and happiness."

"I will not be happy without you, Sebastian." She tilted her chin up.

"You will have to learn to be, Juliana."

"We shared our breaths, Sebastian. I kissed you."

"Do you think I do not remember?"

If he had been standing close, she thought she might have felt the heat of his rage, it seemed to burn so hot. Gone was the man with understanding and compassion in his gaze, the warrior with sorrow in his eyes. This was the avenging angel, who held an arrow that flashed lightning in his hand.

"I will see you free of this place, Juliana. I will see you whole and living and filled with life. I will not watch you die in front of my eyes. Once before you touched me, and we are only fortunate that nothing came of that. But this time, you pushed too far, you dared too much. Despite what you wish and what you do, I will not let this touch you. This is my vow."

She did not speak, simply went to him. Her hands, bare and unadorned, reached for his. It was not until she touched him that she realized he wore no gloves.

Their eyes met.

He slowly pulled his hand away.

"I will not let you be a martyr, Juliana."

"Do not forswear me, Sebastian. Do not send me away or cast me out. I did what I had to do because I do not choose to leave you."

She could battle against ignorance by writing the words of great thinkers, by adding to the store of the world's knowledge. But she could not fight Sebastian's will. That stood between them, a bulwark against any pleas she might utter.

"That was never your choice to make, Juliana."

He stepped back and left the room without saying another word.

*   *   *

Jerard swore as Faeren tried to take a bite out of his rump.

"It's your good fortune that my lord holds you in affection," he said, glaring at the horse. His own mount, of a more even temper, looked up almost in amusement. He'd tied them both too close, but he waited for Templar treachery and wanted to be able to escape quickly.

He had returned to Montvichet as Gregory had taunted, but he did not attempt to find a way over the gorge. Even if he could have constructed some means across, he doubted Lady Juliana could have used it. Instead, he'd come to the tunnel he and Sebastian had discovered, and began to clear it of the rocks and stones that blocked it.

He'd not expected to be released. Why had Gregory done so? At first, he'd thought it was because the Templar regretted leaving his brother marooned atop Montvichet. Then, Jerard had realized that it was simply better for Gregory to dispose of witnesses to his actions. One way had been to kill them. The easiest way, however, had been to send them home to England. Every one of his fellow men-at-arms must have done exactly that. They had disappeared like the morning mist. And they would lose no time telling the people of Langlinais what fate their lord suffered.

The future Jerard had once feared was here.

He would forever remember that moment when Lady Juliana had looked at him as if he betrayed her. He'd wanted to ask for her forgiveness, but his first loyalty had always, would always, be to Sebastian. Still, he recognized courage when he saw it and he'd wanted to commend her in some way, both for that and the expression in her eyes when she looked at his lord.

Love, it had come to both of them.

He had not been unaware of Sebastian's irritation thoughout the journey. It had shown in a hundred different ways. Another man might have thought it had been purely jealousy, but Jerard knew that despair had been present as well.

He bent to pull another rock free of the opening. De Rutger's troops had filled the tunnel well from this side. He only hoped that it was not blocked all the way to the top.

It would make the job ahead difficult, but it would be accomplished. On that, he swore his oath.

Chapter 35

Sebastian avoided her the rest of the day and two days after that. For three days he managed to escape being in the same room with her. He worked in the tunnel, leaving it late at night and beginning again at dawn. She wondered if he ate, then found evidence of it in the room set aside to prepare the Cathar meals. If he slept, it was in one of the sleeping chambers; he never again joined her in the courtyard.

If he meant to wound her, he did. Yet, for all his protests, for all his logic, for all his sacrifice, Sebastian had never said the words that would have dissuaded her from accompanying him into exile. *I do not want you.* She had always been able to see the hint of loneliness in his eyes. Or perhaps it was only the reflection of hers.

She spent the time in chores that occupied the hours. She bathed in the large stone bath. The sensation was odd, that of silky water and scratchy stone. She straightened the empty chambers, as if in silent apology to all those people whose lives had once been so tidily lived in these rooms. One morning, she found a small carved doll beneath an overturned bed. The doll boasted a body of soft down, a face that bore a sweet smile. Upon her cheek was a shiny rubbed spot, as if stroked often. Juliana placed it gently upon a pillow as if its owner would return soon and need it to sleep.

Once or twice she thought she heard the whisper of voices. She could almost believe that, if she remained perfectly still, she might be able to eavesdrop upon conversations, smile at the sound of laughter.

Most of her time, however, was spent in the scriptorium. She had removed the relics from their basket with trembling hands. Her awe and wonder was such that she could hardly bear to touch them. More than twelve hundred years had passed since these objects had been used, yet there was still an aura of holiness about them. She extracted a few scrolls to occupy her before returning the precious objects to their place.

Sebastian had been right in saying that the first treasure of the Cathars was knowledge. There was a collection of bestiaries, each describing strange animals she'd never seen. The tales were accompanied by a series of drawings. One showed an enormous animal with an appendage sagging in front of him like a fifth leg. Another, a spotted beast with an elongated neck and triangular head. There was a series of scrolls entitled *Speculum Divinorum*, and a practicum that appeared to be a text on medical remedies. A few scrolls were filled with the knowledge of plants, almost an encyclopedia of drawings with captions below the illustrations. A few scrolls were in Greek that she could not read, but the majority were in Latin.

She found herself enthralled, delighted, the words whisking her from her misery as nothing else could. Hours passed while she read, her eyes widening at some passages, her smile broadening at others. Evidently, scribes from long ago left personal colophons in the margins, just as she did. A few of them amused her. "It is cold today. It is natural, it is winter." "I feel quite dull today, I don't know what's wrong with me." But her favorite was the self-chiding of a scribe whose sentiments had echoed her own on too many occasions. "He who does not know how to write supposes it to be no labor, but though only three fingers write, the whole body labors." How many times had she ached from head to toe because of being bent over her desk all day?

That day when she emerged from the scriptorium late in the afternoon, Sebastian was in the courtyard. He stood at the ruined wall, looking down into the valley. Because of the steep angle, the road was not visible from there. Nor could they see beyond the thick growth of trees.

At her footsteps, he turned. For a moment he tensed, and she thought he might seize upon any excuse to leave. She would not beg him to remain. It was not pride that made her hesitate, but only the certain knowledge that asking him to yield would only firm his determination to remain aloof. He was determined to free her from Montvichet and from himself.

She looked at the red L upon his back and chest. Loved, perhaps. Her lord. She smoothed her fingers against the initial, feeling the heat of his body through the smooth fabric. It was a coarser weave than his monk's robe, but so much softer. Her hand pressed against his back, and he moved away.

A long moment later, she moved to stand beside him, relieved when he did not move or retreat even farther from her.

"What will happen to Jerard and the others?"

"I do not know."

"Yet, you would have me go with him."

"No. I only selected the lesser of the evils given me." He stared straight ahead.

"Oh, Sebastian, how can you think that?"

"I have seen the proof of it on my flesh, Juliana."

"Did you never think it might not have been a wise decision you made, Sebastian?"

"No," he said, turning to her. "How many hours do you imagine I've thought of it? Weeks, Juliana. That's how long."

"There is nothing I can say, is there?"

"No." He turned away.

"You've found a way out of here, haven't you? That pit."

He glanced over at her. "It leads to a series of tunnels, one of which ends at the base of the mountain. The Cathars called it the Gate of Heaven."

"Why didn't they use it to escape?"

"Montvichet was their sanctuary. Where would they go? The Gate of Heaven was for those who chose to join them. But they never thought of leaving. However, the tunnel is blocked and must be cleared."

"You are going back down there, aren't you?"

He nodded. "I will descend into hell itself if it means freeing you from this place."

"Is there any way I can aid you?"

He glanced at her. "I do not trust you not to pile the stones back in place the moment my back is turned." A quirk of his lips surprised her, coaxed her own smile free.

"I've been reading their scrolls."

He glanced at her sharply.

"I'm amazed at their collection of texts."

"Some are very old."

"I have not read those yet," she said, and her words seemed to ease him in some way.

The afternoon sun seemed lower in the sky. Since they'd left Langlinais, the seasons had changed. Autumn was here. At Langlinais, the harvesting would be done by now. What would Grazide find to occupy her days? How would the castle appear as nature readied itself for winter?

Questions that might be futile. They could be trapped here for the rest of their lives. No, even stone would crumble before Sebastian's will.

She asked another question that had been in her mind for days. "What will the Templars do with the chalice?"

He shrugged. "Allow a rumor to be spread that they hold the Grail, I've no doubt. There might even be a war of wills between the Church and the Order. Whoever emerges the victor will attain more power."

"Will no one ever know that it's a false icon?"

He smiled. "The past abounds with lies, Juliana. The bards would have you believe that God held the sun still in the sky so that Charlemagne could exact revenge against those who killed his nephew in battle. The test is to wean the truth from the falsehood."

"Is that your revenge against the Templars, Sebastian?"

His smile vanished. "I have no reason to avenge myself, Juliana. In truth, they did me a favor by obtaining my release from prison, even if there were other motives behind it. If I avenge anyone, it is Magdalene."

His hands braced against the wall, fingers brushed against a crumbled stone.

It had taken determination and perseverance to withstand the siege that had destroyed this wall. She could not help but wonder what it had been like. She looked down at the valley, captivated by an odd wish to know of those moments. Where would the catapults have been placed? How had the women calmed their children? Had they heard the sounds of the boulders just before they crashed into the stones?

She glanced down absently, her thoughts on those women and their last days. What must it have been like for them?

Her gaze was drawn back to Sebastian's hands. Something was wrong.

At first she thought it was the fact that Sebastian bared his hands. He did not do so easily, even now. He had probably discarded the gauntlets after emerging from the tunnel. The heat and the resultant moisture must render the gloves uncomfortable for him. But it was not the fact that his hands were bared, or even that the afternoon sun illuminated his disease so cruelly.

It was because there were no lesions on Sebastian's hands. They had not merely faded or changed in character. The fingers that rested against the crumbling stone were tanned and free of illness. The sores had not merely been altered, they were gone. Disbelief flared in her chest, followed immediately by a tiny refrain of hope. It seemed to grow, until it sang from her very bones. *Please, let it be true.*

A need to guard this moment, keep it safe and inviolate, prompted her to whisper. "Sebastian, look at your hand."

He glanced down, then remained motionless as if his flesh had become rock. An eternity of moments later, he placed his left hand beside his right, extended both hands in front of him. They trembled.

He lowered them, his gaze now on the far horizon.

He wore no expression, but there was a dawning of something she'd never before seen in his eyes.

Finally he turned, walked with slow and measured steps, as if he were blind and feeling his way, to the center of the courtyard. He viewed his hands by every matter of shadow and light, holding them outstretched, aloft. Both palms were traced with fingers of the opposite hand. Then, he held them closer to his face as if uncertain of what he saw. Finally, he lowered them to his sides and stood there for a long moment, head bowed.

When he moved, it was to fist his hands at the neck of the leper's robe, pulling it apart inch by inch, rending the garment with deliberate force. The material parted, held to his body only at the shoulders. He rolled them and it fell to the ground.

He ran his hands over his flesh as if to test it. He was furred like one of the improbable animals in the bestiary, but there was no blemish on his chest. His fingers flexed and ran from stomach to thighs. He bent and touched his feet, each separate toe, then stood again as quickly.

He closed his eyes, took a long, shivering breath, then opened them again and performed his survey once again. He rubbed his palms hard against thighs and knees and chest, as if to slough off the skin that hid the disease from his sight. But there was no flaw to him, no mark other than that made by war.

She felt a tear cascade over her lashes, fall soundless to the stone of the courtyard.

As she watched, he collapsed to his knees in the bright white afternoon sun. His hands were tightly clenched, resting on his thighs. His head was not bowed, but arched back, as if he sought the face of God in the clear, cloudless day. Only then did she realize that great shudders shook him.

Sebastian of Langlinais was crying.

Chapter 36

She knelt before him, her surcoat brushing his bare knees.

It was as if a thousand candles appeared behind his eyes they seemed so bright. Joy—pure and radiant.

She reached out with fingers that trembled and touched his cheek, the twin of her tears upon his face. He neither flinched nor drew away. Her fingers traced from cheek to nose to temple to jaw, a tender benediction of wonder. He bowed his head, gently held both of her palms against his face as if to encourage her to learn him, the texture of his skin, the warmth of his flesh. As if she gave him life with her caress.

How long they remained kneeling there looking at each other she didn't know. The stone should have abraded their knees, the sun should have burned their skin. Instead, the moment was timeless, a perfect bubble suspended above a silent world. Birth and death are often accompanied with the same awe, as if these moments are a mute tribute to the spirit of life itself. As if some emotions possessed such power that they defied the ability of man to convey it.

Miracle was too small a word.

She whispered it softly, shattering the silence. He did not speak, only traced his fingers upon her lips as she spoke it again.

She closed her eyes, felt his fingers upon her eyelids as delicate as a butterfly. He brushed against her lashes, wiped the tears from her cheek. She opened her eyes to watch him, her heart too full for such a moment. It felt as if it would crack open and tumble to the arid stone of Montvichet.

He had been shunted to dark rooms and black robes, yet now knelt naked and unashamed in front of her in the bright white day. A warrior, whose fingers trembled as they touched her lips.

His hands cupped her face, her fingers touched his chest, trembling as his did. "Juliana."

She closed her eyes at the sound of his voice, felt the soft touch of his lips on her forehead. Another tear cascaded down her face.

Her hands reached up to touch his wrists, to brush against the back of his hands. She had ached to touch him for so long that she felt tentative with the freedom so unexpectedly given her. She wanted to trace her hands where his had been, over the perfect planes and hollows of his body. Not in harsh disbelief but in stunned wonder.

She had never witnessed a miracle before. What the nuns at Sisters of Charity had taught her were less acts of faith than those of practical necessity. Patience was a great teacher, diligence was its own reward, generosity was made null if the gift was given with thought of return. She'd honed her skills at writing and making ink. She'd studied Latin and became adept at deciphering the cramped writing of scribes of another era. She'd transcribed and illuminated, scraped and prepared parchment, rendered ink in different colors. She'd learned how to keep records, and to make candles and soap and oversee servants.

But she had never learned about miracles.

"Should we not pray, Sebastian?" she whispered.

"I am."

His words were so soft that they drifted into the confusion of her mind like feathers. She looked into his face. So beloved, so beautiful. Now matched by the perfection of his warrior's body.

"I heard your prayers once," she confessed. His fingers speared into the hair at her temples, made havoc of her braid. "I did not mean to listen. I've never forgotten the words you spoke, or how sad your voice sounded."

"I will have a lifetime to think of happier prayers."

"Will we have that, do you think?"

"Yes," he said tenderly. "If you are granted the world, how much less to wish for a grain of sand."

"My lord?" The faint echo of Jerard's voice came suddenly and unexpectedly.

Sebastian smiled, stood, and walked to the well of stairs. She heard him shout, but not his words. Instead, she was transfixed with the beauty of him. There was no self-consciousness about his pose, no embarrassment about his nakedness. Once again she was reminded of the statue the villagers had unearthed.

He returned to her side, extended a hand for her. It was the first time he'd done so. She laid her fingers against his palm. She had been united with this man with she was five, had spent countless years as his bride. But until this moment, when he helped her to her feet, she had never felt truly joined. Never wed.

"It seems we've two blessings this day," he said, looking down at her.

She nodded, bemused by mystery and miracles and the wonder of him.

In her left hand she held the straw basket that contained the Cathar treasure. In her right, the drawstring bag that held her clothing, the small store of their food. She had also taken a few pouches of the Cathar ink that she might study it at greater leisure. Sebastian stood just a few feet below her, his hand extended to help her down the first few steps. She handed the basket and the bag to him, stepped back from the opening.

She gave him no explanation, only moved to the center of the courtyard, to the place where Sebastian had knelt only an hour earlier. She turned in a slow circle, her face unsmiling. She could almost hear their voices, sounds of life, now silenced forever. In her mind she could see them, just as she could see Magdalene, a woman with a great heart who was loved even now.

She had thought so much about going into exile with Sebastian that it had startled her to realize they would be returning to Langlinais. There, they would make their futures, not hiding in terror, but living openly.

She doubted this place would be remembered. Or if happened upon, the siege of Montvichet would not be recalled. There would be no one to know what they had gone through, what had happened to these women in the six horrible months they had faced De Rutger in stubborn opposition.

"I will never forget," she said softly, her voice echoing in the haunting silence of the courtyard. It seemed as if the silence smiled.

She turned, and Sebastian stood there, watching her. His chain mail glinted in the afternoon sunlight as he approached her. He reached out his hands and encompassed both of hers in his. He brought them to his lips and gently kissed the tips of her fingers.

She was speechless at his look. There was love in Sebastian's eyes.

Sebastian called once more, and this time, the reply was loud and strong.

A moment later the last stone was pushed aside. Sebastian left the tunnel, followed by Juliana, their eyes blinking in the fading light of day.

He clasped his hand on Jerard's arm. The look on the younger man's face was difficult to decipher. It was comprised of surprise, then amazement as his gaze lowered to Sebastian's hand.

"My lord, you are cured," he said in awe.

"It is true," Sebastian said, nodding.

Jerard held his hand against his heart, fell to his knees. "A miracle, my lord."

"Save your obeisance for saints, Jerard. I am, as you well know, no saint." He looked about him. "Where are the rest of my men?"

Jerard looked crestfallen, as if he'd failed at a simple task. "They would not stay, my lord. They were frightened. I did bring two of the horses, though."

"Tell me one of them is Faeren and I will think you are the one blessed."

At his vassal's nod, Sebastian smiled. "Well done, Jerard. But then, you have always been a faithful man." He studied him for a moment. "My lady wife has reminded me that this is a duty long overlooked. Forgive me for that, Jerard, and for denying you the ceremony you deserve."

Jerard looked stunned as he remained kneeling in front of him.

Instead of a new sword, which he would have prepared once they reached home, Sebastian held out his own. "Bless this sword, so that it may be a defense for churches, widows and orphans, and for all servants of God."

He looked down at Jerard. It was an odd time to feel amusement, but he did so, leavened as it was with fondness. "Now you say, 'Blessed be the Lord God who formeth my hands for battle and my fingers for war.'"

Jerard repeated the words in a clear strong voice.

"Do you serve as my vassal, Jerard, giving me your loyalty and your life?"

"I do, my lord." The words were said cleanly, with no hesitation.

"I swear the selfsame oath. As you swear your loyalty to me, so is mine to you."

Sebastian bent and placed the hilt of his sword in Jerard's right hand, took it back. Then instead of cuffing him across the cheek, he struck the blunt edge of the sword against Jerard's neck.

"Then arise, Sir Jerard of Langlinais, and take up your duties as a knight."

He replaced his sword, then turned as Jerard stood, and held out his hand to Juliana, who smiled mistily at him.

"Now, let us go home."

Words he'd never thought he'd say.

Chapter 37

〜〜◯◯〜〜

"**I**t is magnificent," the Marshal whispered. The chalice stood before them on a small table. A shaft of sunlight illuminated the skill of the goldsmith who had created the reliquary. Inside rested the wooden cup. The Marshal touched it, his fingers trembling as they rested upon the rim.

"Your brother? He relinquished such a thing so easily?" His glance seemed to spear Gregory.

"In return for Langlinais, Marshal."

"He is a fool, then. We would have surrendered all our English fiefs for this treasure." He stroked the rim of the cup.

Gregory did not tell him that Sebastian had been willing to surrender his home for the safety of a woman. And she, in turn, had given up her life for him. A sacrifice he did not understand.

Even as he had pledged his life to the Templars, answered the questions put to him, he had not believed as much in their cause as he had in himself. Do you espouse the faith, are you legitimate and of knightly family, are you unmarried or in holy orders? Are you free of debt, sound of body, and have you used no coercion in order to gain admission to the Order? He had responded with the correct answers, had been led to an oath to obey the Masters of the Temple and his superiors.

An easy oath to swear, one a knight would to his liege lord. They had not asked of him if he believed in the sanctity of the Order more than his own abilities, or if he had believed himself of sharper wit and more talent than most of the men who'd attempted to lead him in battle.

"Your brother, will he speak of this to anyone?" Phillipe's hand rested on the cup as if he drew solace simply by touching it. Gregory had felt the same on the journey back to Courcy.

"What does it matter, Marshal, if he does? We have the Grail. Do we not wish such a thing to be known?"

"But not the manner in which we obtained it. We do not want the Order associated with the Cathars, Gregory. Should we not send our brothers to this home of his in secret? In order to ensure he does not tell the tale?"

It was the perfect opportunity to tell the Marshal that his brother would not speak to anyone. That he was trapped upon a mountain just as the Cathars had been, but that his death would not be as swift, although it might well be as agonizing.

"No, Marshal. Sebastian has kept the secret for five years, he will not speak of it now. Besides, Langlinais is heavily fortified, and the attention we would draw to ourselves by such an action would be to our detriment." *There, Sebastian, by such words have I protected your widow. My conscience is appeased.*

Phillipe stood, replaced the chalice into its casket. "Very well. Prepare yourself for a journey, Gregory."

Gregory bowed. He did not question his destination. To do so would be to show curiosity, and such things were considered faults that interfered with true obedience. Not that his was a character of compliance. Yet, it was better to appear so, for the sake of his future goals.

"We will take the Grail to Cyprus, Gregory. To the Master of the Order."

D'Aubry smiled and clasped his hand upon Gregory's back. A sure and certain sign of praise. Gregory could not help but wonder why it irritated him. Perhaps because he knew that he was the one who had procured the Grail, and yet praise for such deeds would be shared with the Marshal. D'Aubry had sponsored such actions as he'd undertaken but had remained in the shadows, ready to disavow any knowledge of Gregory's activities should something go wrong.

A matter of timing, that was all. He would ensure that those in power would come to realize who had actually obtained the Grail.

"I will prepare for the journey," he said, and bowed his head.

Juliana sat cradled against him on Faeren. His saddle with its raised pommel and cantle had been traded for Jerard's. He would much rather surrender the protection against being unhorsed for that of being able to hold Juliana next to him. Faeren's reins were looped in his right hand, while his left arm circled her waist.

He had wanted her forever, it seemed. Now, he only felt a need so great that he measured the miles to Langlinais in individual breaths.

He had resented Jerard's effortless ability to touch her during the journey to Montvichet, because he knew that he, himself, would never be able to do so. The moment he'd looked at his skin and realized that he had been cured had not been one solely of prayer. It had also been comprised of exaltation, of the knowledge that he could be a man again.

But it had not seemed right to be spared in one moment and become a rutting boar the next. The haunted fortress had not been the place to make her his wife in truth. Nor was their journey, alone and unguarded. He did not wish a furtive coupling with Jerard standing watch.

It was enough, but only barely, to lie beside her at night. Sometimes he watched her as she slept. Once, he'd bent over her, his mouth only a breath from hers. The lure of her had been enough to keep him awake most of the night.

In the morning, he sometimes woke to find her in his arms, as if they had come together in their sleep, each seeking the other. In the dawn light he removed his clothing for his body to be inspected, watching her reaction from the corner of his eye. At first she would barely look at him. Now, she seemed to devour him with her eyes. She never knew that his own breath grew tight as her flush deepened. He always turned away, though, before she could see how her looks affected him.

She leaned against him now, and his head dipped, brushed a kiss against her temple. Her breath hitched. So, too, the beat of his heart. *Juliana.* A breath of a thought, an echo of his need.

She patted him, a gesture she'd begun in the last few days, a small soft pat on arm or knee as if to reassure herself that it was permissible to do so.

He concentrated on the distance to travel, instead of Juliana's soft curves resting against him. That way promised only a journey of acute discomfort.

Jerard called out, pointing ahead to a wooded valley. A stream curved among softly rolling hills, hid beneath a copse of trees. He raised his hand in acknowledgment. They would rest there for their noon meal.

Each morning and each evening Sebastian stripped himself of his tunic and armor and asked that Jerard inspect him for evidence of disease. Once, Juliana had come upon them unawares, and although she'd turned and walked quickly away, she'd retained the shape of his body in her mind. That picture was added to the scene in Montvichet, when he'd stood naked in the sun.

When she allowed her thoughts to dwell on him, she remembered his strong thighs and chest and arms, all the other areas that fascinated her. She wanted to put her hands on him, to stroke his chest and thigh and that place that taunted her ignorance.

She wanted to kiss his skin.

Her breath came tight in her chest even as her heart seemed to slow and her blood to pound.

The man who'd once feared contaminating her now branded her with another disease. One of thoughts and wants and warmth that almost made her wish he would not touch her again. A palm upon her shoulder made her want to curve her face to him. A handclasp urged her to kiss his fingers. A finger trailing along the back of her neck created shivers throughout her body.

She would catch him watching her sometimes, the look in his eyes both fierce and warmly tender. But he never kissed her, and his gentle touches were no more intrusive than a breath of breeze. They enticed; they did not frighten.

There were few moments in which she was free of thoughts of him. In her sleep, she stood on her tiptoes and pulled his head down for a kiss, feeling the warmth of his lips, remembering the taste of their one kiss. Somehow, in this dream state, she had been not untried and ignorant, but sated and sure, a woman, a wanton. Not a girl. She had placed his large hands upon her breasts, and sighed at the feeling of it, turned into his embrace when he'd traced the contours of her hips and belly. She'd been swept away by the thought of exposing her body to his touch, and recalled, too often, the night when she'd sat naked in front of him.

In the morning, she would awaken to find herself within his arms. A smile would brush his lips, and he would look into her eyes as if to see her soul. He was so tender of her that she wished sometimes that she could tell him she did not require such care. But if she would have found the courage to say those words, she might also have told him that she was tired of being a maiden. She wished to be a wife.

She knew the man who dwelled in shadows, who'd whispered despairing words in prayer. She'd understood the lord who had been adjudicator and overseer of his demesne, the student, the man possessed of subtle charm and wit. She respected the man of power, had been the recipient of his will. She'd felt pity and compassion and fear and love for the being clad in monk's black, awe and respect for the warrior.

But this man enticed and beckoned and tantalized.

He dismounted first, held out his arms for her. Without hesitation, she slipped into his embrace.

As she stood in front of him, her hand reached out of its own volition and touched his chest. She had not worn her bandages since Montvichet, and her fingers, ten separate places that measured sensation, trailed up from the center of his tunic to his shoulders.

It would take both of her hands to measure the breadth of his arm. His chain mail felt hot against her fingers. She wished she might again place her palm upon the mat of curly hair on his chest.

Instead, Sebastian stepped back, his breathing just as rapid as hers.

Before she could question him, he was gone, striding to where Jerard was laying out their meal.

Chapter 38

Juliana followed the stream until it curved beneath some large boulders and disappeared. She lifted her skirts, crossed the mossy stones carefully. There she sat and waited.

She inspected her hands in the sunlight. She would always have scars, but she'd been able to regain some use of her right hand. One day, perhaps soon, she would take up a quill again.

"It is not wise to simply walk away like that, Juliana," Sebastian said, his frown forbidding.

She looked up, unconcerned. "I knew you would find me."

"You might have been set upon."

"By rabbits and squirrels?" She smiled at him, but his own smile was not coaxed free. Instead, he stood silent on the other side of the stream. A powerful knight with a face like stone.

Now was the time to fear him.

She could not summon such an emotion, not when she was surfeit with another more powerful feeling. Love. It seemed to surge through her at the sight of him.

She stood, bent down and grabbed the hem of her surcoat, pulled it over her head.

Still, he did not move. *Please, Sebastian, do not rebuff me.* It had taken all of her courage to lure him to her this way, and even more to do what she planned next.

Not a cloud marked the pristine purity of the blue sky. Nothing moved upon the landscape but the gentle sway of leaves in the trees, the stream that flowed at their feet. They each remained silent, Adam garbed in armor and Eve stripping herself bare.

She bent and removed her shoes, stood before him as she never had before, clad in nothing more substantial than her thin cotte. No, once before she'd sat naked while he'd watched. Once before she had trembled beneath his gaze.

"What do you do, Juliana?" The passion of his look was matched by the tenderness in his voice.

"This moment has been long in coming, Sebastian."

"Has it?" He did not move toward her.

She removed her cotte with a swift movement as if daring herself. A moment more and she stood naked before him.

"Juliana," he began, his frown deepening.

"No," she interrupted him. Her hand came up as if to physically stave off his words. "Do not chastise me, Sebastian. Do not tell me that I do not know how I feel, or that I have no choice. It is you who are without choice in this matter."

He stood and stared at her, studying her in the sunlight that streamed over her. Suddenly he was jumping over the mossy stepping-stones, following her path over the stream. His hands were on her waist and she was suspended above him, his laughter echoing throughout this enchanted glade. She braced her hands on his shoulders, looked down at his beloved face.

"Where has my timid Juliana gone?" he asked, his lips curved in a smile, the blaze of his eyes hinting at emotions other than humor.

"She has left forever," she confessed, matching his smile with one of her own. "Will you miss her?"

"In truth I never saw her. Only heard of her existence from you. The woman I know asks if I am Death and tells the world she is a leper in order to remain with me. And now bares herself and tells me I am lax in my duty as husband."

"Oh, Sebastian," she said tenderly, her heart overflowing, "don't you know it is you who have made me brave?"

He stared up at her, the fierceness on his face that of a warrior. The tenderness she felt abruptly tumbled into something else. This emotion was not soft or gentle—it was fueled by a heat that raced through her and scorched where it touched.

He laid his forehead between her breasts. She could feel the warmth of his breath on her skin, the abrasion of his whiskered cheeks. A soft kiss upon the slope of her breast summoned a moan from between her lips. He still held her suspended. Helpless and powerless was not what she wanted to be.

His lips teased a taut nipple just before he mouthed it, then sucked on it strongly. Her breast prickled with a sensation that ran like a fiery cord through her body. Her palms bracketed his head; her soft gasp was both awareness and encouragement.

He lowered her slowly, her naked breasts brushing against his face, then his chest, the chain mail gently abrading. He was armored and she nude. The contrast was startling.

She felt a surge of heat so pure that it rivaled fire.

Her fingers fumbled over his tunic, skidded over the finely crafted links of his chain mail. She wanted to feel him, touch his skin. Thwarted, she slapped her hands against his chest. His smile erupted into a chuckle.

He speared his fingers into her hair, his large, broad hands holding her head steady. His kiss was all the things he'd promised and more, talented and luring and intrusive. His tongue thrust into her mouth, enticing and forbidden. He trained her to welcome him, deepened the kiss until she saw stars behind her lids. She thought she whimpered, but that, too, might have been only another sensation in the maelstrom of the moment.

He pulled away, long enough to pull the tunic over his head. She rained kisses over his mailed chest, stood on tiptoe to kiss his neck, reached up and pulled his head down fiercely when he delayed too long.

She swallowed his smile, changed it into a guttural moan. She bit at his lips, entwined her tongue with his, inhaled the air he exhaled.

He removed the shirt of his chain mail, then the leggings, threw the heavy garments to the other side of the stream. The rest of his clothing was removed as quickly, and he stood before her, naked.

His body was taut with muscle, his skin sleek. A man in his prime. In his arms were ropes of muscles developed to wield a sword, his thighs as powerful from hours of riding. His body had been honed as a battle weapon, his scars attesting to the skill of his opponents. A thin mark ran from his back to trail upward and end beneath his arm. Another sliced from knee to upper thigh.

She had been wrong; he wasn't like the statue the

villagers had found at all. There was a part of him that was much, much larger. A breath escaped her, a soft exhalation of wonder. Her hand reached out and touched him. She jerked her hand back at his soft moan. His fingers curled around her hand, placed it back on his flesh again. Color marked his high cheekbones, and his breathing was almost as rapid as hers. She watched his face as her hand slid over him, their gazes locked and fused by fire.

And were I you, our blood would beat the same, our breaths in tune, our passions high, our love shared in mind and flesh. Who had said that? Or was it a thought formed in that moment? She couldn't remember, didn't know.

He pulled her against the full length of his body. Her nipples brushed against his furred chest, the sensation so sharp it was almost painful. Her breasts seemed to swell, ached to be touched. She pulled his head down, guided his lips to her nipple.

He obliged at once, suckling her, his cheeks hollowing. She threw her head back, her breaths coming in hard panting gusts. Her fingers gripped his hair, kept him in place.

His hands reached around and pulled her even closer. More. She wanted more. As if he'd heard her, he cupped her bottom and lifted her to him, his mouth still locked on her breast.

His skin was hot, every part of him so heated that she thought she might be burned by touching him. But she was mindless, uncaring. She held on to his shoulders with nails grown sharp with need. She stood on her tiptoes, pushed closer to him, his manhood grinding into the notch of her thighs.

She could not breathe, was encapsulated in a fog of passion, stronger than anything she'd ever read or dreamed could exist. She would die of this, she knew it, just as she was aware that her breath was painfully fast, her blood as quick.

He picked her up and carried her to where the moss was thickest, laid her down on the sun-warmed ground. Her gaze never left him. Her warrior. He was limned by the sun, seemed to eclipse it. She reached out to pull him down to her with greedy hands.

He'd readied her for his touch weeks ago, speaking words that had made her blood race. He'd invaded her mind with desire, preparing her for this moment. But nothing, not words, not actions, could have warned her of this, this ravenous desperation that became everything she was and all that she would be.

Her nails scraped his skin. She wanted to absorb him, gather him under her nails, inhale his breath. Become him, if necessary. She was frenzied by this feeling, adrift in it. The bulb of his shoulders, the angle of elbow, his thick wrists and powerful hands, his wide chest, they were all targets for her touch. She rained kisses over him, nipping at his strong neck, his shoulder.

Sebastian seemed as fevered. He grazed his teeth along the underside of her breasts, stroked his hands from her wrist to shoulder, from ankle to hip. His kisses were wild things that tasted of heat.

He widened her legs and knelt between them. She glanced up to meet his gaze. His look was sharp, the blue of his eyes burning like a flame's core.

Then she was being invaded by him, stretched just as he'd once warned her. Molded to become familiar with him. She wanted to scream. It was not enough. The broad head of his phallus was just inside her, but not deeply enough. More.

He kissed her, a sweeping kiss that inflamed her

further. She was on fire, and he was being too careful.

She arched upward, suddenly impaling herself on him. She moaned with the feeling of it, painful pressure and more. It only intensified the ache she felt, did nothing to ease it.

Then he surged fully into her, and she screamed. Just for a moment, the pain was more than she could bear. He murmured to her, words that were meant to comfort, but it was not soothing she wanted. Only something that remained barely hidden. Something close and almost achieved.

He reached down and pulled her legs wider, sank into her still further. She clamped her lips down on the moan she would have made. He parted her still further, reached to brush his fingers over the juncture of her thighs, until he touched a place so sensitive and swollen that she almost screamed again. Not with pain, but with demand. *End this*. It was both entreaty and necessity. She could not live without it and she did not know how much more she could bear. He used his fingers to push aside the folds of her flesh, expose that spot to his strokes. This time when he surged inside her, she felt him there, too, each caress forcing her onward to madness.

Helpless need shook her. Her senses could only measure the pounding of her heart and his body pummeling hers. He invaded and demanded, stretching her, widening her for his use. It was an act of possession, male and hungry and alive.

She hurt with it. Ached with pain and desire. She was weeping, and her nails were tearing at him. Her breath came in surging pants, but the torment went on and on, the pain buried in the core of her body. She felt as if she were being plundered. Besieged.

Her hands gripped Sebastian's arms. His skin was
slick with sweat.

"Juliana." Her name was repeated over and over;
it became a cadence that measured the pumping of
his hips.

She felt herself being ripped apart. Pain ached and
burned in the core of her. But there was another sensation, too. It began between her thighs, where Sebastian's strokes pounded ruthlessly against her
flesh, radiated outward to hips and belly and knees.
Widened still further to encompass her shoulders,
her feet, the palms of her hands. It was a giant blazing star colored red and glowing, into which she had
no choice but to collapse. It was part of her, or she
was part of it, and the only thing anchoring her to
the earth was Sebastian.

His voice was harsh, his words too difficult to understand. Her hands fluttered at his shoulders, there
was a sound like a gasp or a moan that came from
her lips. Another cry, demand this time.

Her hips arched up, her feet planted themselves
on the ground and gave her leverage. Her arms
wound around his neck, every other thought forgotten but this mating, this act, this hunger. She
pressed herself up and against him, inviting his invasion, urging it. And then it happened.

The world turned white.

Her body shuddered again and again. Spasms
wracked her as her hips arched off the ground. She
saw nothing, heard nothing, could only feel the
surge of pleasure so intense it forced a low, throaty
groan from between her clenched lips. The sensation
went on for so long that she became only feeling,
only physical, whimpering her pleasure like an animal lost in mating.

His kiss both urged her on and comforted her,

linked her to him and let her fly. Then, just when she thought she could take no more, Sebastian bucked against her one last time, his body trembling, a low and harsh groan accompanying his release.

"I hurt you."

She lay draped atop him, her cheek pressed against his chest. She raised her head to look at him. Her face was flushed, but her eyes met his steadily.

"No," she said, shaking her head weakly.

"Are you certain?"

A small smile hovered over her lips. "Yes, Sebastian. Very certain." Her flush seemed to deepen as he watched.

"Perhaps it is a good thing our coupling was delayed," he said, threading his fingers though the hair at her temple. "I would not have been able to resist your blandishments had we known each other before."

She scooted up on his chest, laid her forehead against his neck. Sighed against his skin. His lips curved into a smile.

"Do not say you are timid again, my lady wife."

It amused him greatly that the woman who had nearly killed him with her passion now retreated behind silence.

"The rabbits and the squirrels were no doubt frightened away by your screams," he said, hiding his smile with great effort.

She raised her head and frowned at him. There was a fierce look in her eyes that he'd seen only rarely. His smile surfaced.

She slitted her eyes at him, then deliberately pulled one of the hairs on his chest.

He merely rubbed the spot and continued to grin

at her. She shook her head and subsided against his chest, silent still.

"Juliana," he said tenderly. She stirred and would have tipped her head up again, but his hand went to the back of her head as if to keep her pinned against him.

"Only Juliana," he said. He extended his arms around her, held her so tightly a whisper could not have parted them. The sun bathed them in light, the warrior and his woman. She did not stir, nor did he, simply content to feel the magic of this moment.

Chapter 39

Jerard heard their laughter and kept his eyes stoically on the ground. He'd made the mistake of looking up once and had seen his lord kissing his wife, and Lady Juliana enthusiastically responding.

He felt curiously embarrassed. There was such a radiant look on Lady Juliana's face, and such a deeply contented one on his lord's that it was not difficult to determine what had caused their delay. He had long since packed up their noon meal and sat against a tree, knowing that this spot would be their resting place for tonight.

It was odd to be returning to Langlinais this way. Not in mourning or grief for his lord's fate, but with Sebastian healed and his own future bright. While it was true his smile dimmed from time to time, on the whole, the Lord of Langlinais was a changed man. It was not simply the absence of his disease that made him so, Jerard suspected. It was Lady Juliana.

Jerard had lived around lust all his life. As a child, he'd slept in a room with twenty other people. His nights had often been interrupted by the passage of a man to his wife, a woman to her mate. The act had not been done in secret. His own father had made a whore of his mother for lust. It was only at Langlinais that he'd achieved any privacy in order to enjoy his own sport.

He had enjoyed the carnal sports with various women throughout his life, some of them living at Langlinais. He was not as formidable-looking as his lord, matching him in height, but not as broad in chest or arms. His eyes, however, seemed to be a source of wonder to the females of his acquaintance, since they were of an odd shade likened to gold.

He enjoyed women, liked the way they moved and smelled and looked, and perhaps it was that appreciation that garnered him their attention. The gentle laughter of the Lord of Langlinais and his wife reminded him that he had been celibate on this journey, not a difficult feat if a man was concerned for his very survival. Still, the laughter and teasing words and secret kisses reminded him of what waited for him at home.

He'd witnessed the way Sebastian had watched Lady Juliana once when she was not looking, a fierce and protective look not quite masking his despair. It may be lust that flowed between them now, but it originated from a wellspring of love.

His own future was more certain than before. He would remain at Langlinais, not as a former serf in his lord's service, but as a knight. A member of an elite group of warriors. He'd never thought to be knighted; his birth provided a formidable obstacle to being so honored. Nor had his years fighting beside Sebastian on crusade proven him worthy of it. He had fought as well as any man, but without the prowess or the unearthly grace of his lord.

Yet, Sebastian of Langlinais had knighted him, establishing him as a man of consequence. Sir Jerard of Langlinais. He smiled broadly and studiously ignored the couple he served.

*   *   *

The journey back to Langlinais was made slower by reason of the care they took. There was no thundering contingent of armed men surrounding them. But they were not accosted during the return trip, a fact that only led to Sebastian's certainty as to the origin of the first attack. Although Gregory had not admitted it, he'd seen his brother's fine hand in arranging that ambush. He would never forgive him that for one very simple reason: Juliana could have been killed.

The appearance of Langlinais in the wooded valley below them reminded Sebastian of something he had previously forgotten. This homecoming could very well determine the quality of the rest of his life. Langlinais was not only a structure; the essence of his home was its people. The miller whose arrogance he tempered, Grazide who talked too much, but who had a kind and gentle heart, Old Simon who had greeted him every day of his life. The cook and the armorer and the tanner and the boys he trained for trades. All these people and more made up his home, their goodwill aided its cause, their health and well-being mattered to him. His people must be reassured that all was well, that he was free of disease and would bring no harm to them.

When they came to the gatehouse, he dismounted, held out his arms for Juliana. "Remain here with my wife," he said, turning to Jerard.

"What are you going to do, Sebastian?"

"Wait here, Juliana," he said in lieu of answering her.

He walked to the gatehouse. Old Simon was there, his rheumy eyes open and staring, as if he viewed a ghost. The old man had once been portly, but the years had taken his flesh from him and left his sag-

ging skin as a reminder of his girth. Now his face
wobbled when he moved, his dark eyes set into a
frame of apparent sadness. But nothing could be further from the truth. Old Simon enjoyed the nightly
merriment at Langlinais, and most especially Langlinais wine.

Sebastian had always had a fondness for the old
man, despite the fact that he often failed at his post
as gatekeeper. There were always guards set on the
hills that led to the Langlinais valley. For that reason, Sebastian allowed him to keep his post, despite
the fact he often spent the daylight hours sleeping.

"Has anyone passed these gates, Simon?"

"Only those who had business at Langlinais, my
lord."

"No strangers?"

He shook his head, and his jowls swayed.

Then no Templars had come. It was the first of his
worries. The other might be more difficult to alle-
viate.

He walked back to where Juliana and Jerard
stood. He removed his sword first, handed it to Jerard who took it without question. Next he removed
his tunic, then the hauberk, the long thigh-length
chain-mail shirt. He wore a thin gambeson beneath
it, and this, too, he removed.

"Sebastian?"

Juliana was looking at him with the same expression on her face as Old Simon had worn.

Jerard, however, nodded at him, understanding
perfectly. "The Langlinais men-at-arms, my lady,"
he said to Juliana. "They have no doubt returned
with news of my lord's condition."

"And you are stripping yourself of your shirt, Sebastian, to prove you have no affliction?"

"Can you think of a better way?"

"Would not your word suffice?" There was the most peculiar expression on her face. He smiled at the blush that suffused her cheek, then brushed his lips against them, as if to test their heat.

"I want no rumors to accompany us in the future, Juliana."

"But must you show yourself to all the women in the castle?"

He laughed, charmed. Of all the times to express jealousy, this was perhaps the oddest. "They think me a leper, Juliana. I doubt their minds will be filled with other ideas."

"Then should I not do the same? After all, I declared myself a leper before all of them."

He raised one eyebrow. "But you would have become one because of me, lady wife. It is I who must banish any talk."

He motioned for Old Simon to open the gate.

It was no doubt a strange procession they made inside the gates of Langlinais. Him with his chest bared to prove to his people that he did not bring danger or disease to his home, Jerard newly knighted and proud. And Juliana her cheeks a brilliant poppy, her gaze fixed on the women they passed as if she would burn them with her look.

The basket from Montvichet bobbed against Jerard's saddle, a reminder of their danger. What would Juliana say when she learned the true Cathar secret? Not the relics after all.

He had not yet decided if he should destroy it, bury it so that it would not see the light of day for eternity, or make its presence known. All he knew was that it might be a myth, but if it were not, it was perhaps the most dangerous document in the history of the world.

Chapter 40

The convent of the Sisters of Charity was a dreary place, Jerard thought. But its gray stone was enlivened by the green of the grass that surrounded it, even this late in the year. The first time he'd come here, he'd viewed lush gardens inside the tall iron gates. He'd been sent to the convent for something to soothe Juliana's hands and had been gifted with Sister Agnes. She had been an unusual traveling companion. Despite the haste of their journey, the nun had commented upon every plant and bush and tree, and its medicinal properties, between the convent and Langlinais.

He stood now at the gate, waiting for the abbess. He noted the gardens, not as profuse in blooms as before but neatly tended as if it awaited winter with patience.

A bell sounded, the whisper tread of sandals brushing across the floor a summons to worship. An hour passed, but still he waited.

Finally, the abbess was there at the gate, her angular form attesting either to the paucity of rations at the convent or her own form of discipline.

She greeted him with reserve until she remembered him. Then, the lines of her face deepened into worry. "Juliana? She is well?"

"Yes, Abbess. She is well."

"Her hands?"

"They are healing. She is practicing writing each day. It is an effort for her, I think, but she will not desist."

"She was often a stubborn girl," she said, smiling. "Tell me, is she happy at Langlinais?"

"Yes," he said simply.

Lady Juliana hummed and smiled all the time. Sometimes, in walking through the bailey, she would do a little dance, picking up her skirts and skipping not unlike a child. And his lord. Jerard smiled, bending to pick up the chest he'd placed reverently on the ground. Sebastian was like a boy, up to his ears in lust and love.

There was a square opening in the grille of the gate. Through this he passed the chest to the abbess. "There is a missive inside that will explain it all, Abbess. If you don't mind, I will go and sit over there and wait." He pointed to a tree that offered shade.

She nodded, frowning, her attention not on him but on the chest.

He walked over to the tree and sat beneath it, drawing up one leg. The land was carved into rolling hills and shallow valleys, but he could almost see Langlinais.

Gertrude set the chest upon a table in the small chamber that served as hers. She was a curious person, that emotion being experienced every day in her life. There was too much about the world not to feel some interest in it, even if it only be why the bees were attracted to a certain type of flower more than to another. She felt the same at the present moment as she lifted the lid of the plain wooden chest and extracted the letter. She left the top of the chest ajar, concerned now more with the correspondence from the Lord of Langlinais than the contents of the chest.

She scanned his letter quickly. After a few sentences expressing his hope that she was well and that the convent thrived, he continued. His next sentence made her smile, and she vowed to aid him in what way she could. However, her amusement was no preparation for the body of the letter.

I have obtained the items in the chest, and although there is some question as to their validity, I believe them to be genuine. To keep them at Langlinais and hide them from the world would be an act of pride. Juliana has spoken of you often and with fondness, and I myself have witnessed your generosity of spirit in sending Sister Agnes to our aid. I believe, therefore, that there could be no better arbiter as to the destination of these sacred objects.

There will be those who would use what you now have in order to obtain power rather than to reinforce faith. For that reason, I ask that you remove Langlinais from any of your correspondence as to these matters, and that you not speak of how you obtained the shroud or these pieces of the true cross.

Gertrude set the letter aside and reached into the chest with trembling hands. She stood there staring at the cloth beneath her fingers for long moments. Time in which she could not think, thought being buried beneath both reverence and fear.

Indeed, the Lord of Langlinais was correct. Beneath her hands lay the greatest sort of power, that wished by kings and coveted by bishops. Yet there was also the potential for good in this chest, the bolstering of belief, the uplifting of faith. The Sisters of Charity convent seemed a small and humble place for such things. These relics belonged to the world. But who would guard them and hold them sacred in the name of all mankind?

She closed the chest reverently, then bore it to the chapel. It would rest there until she had time to think on these matters. Perhaps she would receive some divine guidance as to where the relics should be sent. Or perhaps they should remain here, in a small convent of women dedicated to good works and joyful duty. Only time would tell.

An hour later, a girl dressed in the garb of a novitiate brought Jerard a large coffer. She also held out a small wrapped parcel. "Food for your journey, sir. And wine, for your thirst."

He took both, smiling his thanks.

"I'm to tell you that the abbess thanks you and those at Langlinais. She sends her prayers with you, and says that she will accede to your requests. She also wished me to tell you that she will pray that you might be forever blessed."

"We have been," he said, smiling still, then turned his horse in the direction of Langlinais.

Gregory kept his face expressionless. Years of being subservient came in good stead now. His smile was pleasant, his eyes downcast. There was nothing about the placement of his hands to show that they trembled, nothing about his look to betray his sudden horrified amusement.

The Marshal was waxing eloquent on some point with a few of the brothers. They, as usual, were listening in rapt attention, nodding where appropriate.

It was not every day the great Marshal visited their monastery, let alone bearing a sacred relic. Moments had been spent admiring the Grail, and it now rested on the table in the chamber given over to the Marshal's use. The sun struck the reliquary and made it gleam gold and red. But the sun also illuminated the small wooden cup so tenderly placed within the gold bowl. He had wondered if a few of his fellow monks were about to drop to their knees in worship at the sight of it.

He, himself, could not remove his eyes from the cup. Not, as a casual observer might think, because he was humbled to be in its presence, but because he was suddenly absolutely certain it was a magnificent example of duplicity.

At Langlinais there was a man who carved all manner of things. He and Sebastian had played with Old Simon's whittled knights in numerous mock battles on the floor of the great hall. The old man had a habit, though, of gouging out a spot to rest the blade of his knife so that he would know where it was after a night of drink. Too many of their wooden knights had borne such wounds.

There was a similar gouge in the wooden cup nestled in the reliquary. It was almost too faint to note, or could easily be explained by its advanced age. Even an object as venerated as the Grail could have been marked accidentally. Or, perhaps, it had been that way from the beginning, a simple carpenter's cup quickly carved to be serviceable, no thought given to ornamentation or lack of it.

Still, he knew it was a fake. When he'd first seen it in the light, he'd known what Sebastian had done. The reliquary was perhaps valuable, but now he doubted even its age or its authenticity.

His brother had fooled the Knights Templar. He'd

made a laughingstock of men who made kings tremble. The temerity of such an action stunned and amazed him.

Why had Sebastian done it? The answer was as simple as the audacious act. To protect Langlinais. He'd given his brother the perfect opportunity, had played into his hands. By suggesting that Sebastian might wish to trade what he'd found at Montvichet for the safety of his home, he'd almost encouraged Sebastian to do such a thing. Just then, a cloud obscured the sun, and the reddish glow became diffused as if heaven itself had heard his thought.

In a few days he and the Marshal were to sail for Cyprus, where the Holy Grail would be taken for safekeeping. The Templar power could only grow with the knowledge that they were the keepers of the Grail.

It was an irony of the purest sort. His advancement would come, not because of his own merits or bravery, but because of Sebastian's deceit. He'd spent the majority of his adult life attempting to climb the Templar ranks. And now he would be mingling with those at the highest seats of power because of something that was not real.

Suddenly, he knew what he had to do.

Chapter 41

Sebastian found her, not in her chamber where one might expect to find a wife, or in the oriel where she spent so much of her time, but in the courtyard. He stopped and watched her. She was bent before a large caldron, stirring something with a branch nearly as tall as she was and earnestly explaining something to two young girls who stood in front of her. He wondered if she knew that she was awe-inspiring to the women of Langlinais. She was their Lady, versed in things foreign to them.

The knowledge of how much he loved her came as a fierce blow to his chest. No, it was a poor choice of word. This feeling he had for Juliana was so much greater than anything a poet could say.

I am hers from head to toe. Forever.

He had never anticipated this moment, of striding through the bailey of Langlinais whole and free of disease. He had sought courage for himself, that he might be brave enough to accept what was his fate. But he had not once believed it might be possible to alter it.

It was, perhaps, not wise to question a miracle. But he found himself doing so. He'd spent the last year preparing for his death, the last few weeks coming to terms with his exile. People would have fled from the sight of him, the sound of his clapper. Doors would have swung shut, little children jerked from his path. Yet, in one moment, his future had been changed. A miracle. Yet, he could not help but study his hands, rub the skin of his chest, wonder why he had been so blessed.

The future spread out before him blank and unwritten. Never even dreamed prior to this moment. Perhaps it was a tinge of fear he felt staring at the void in front of him. He had prepared so diligently for death, now he must make ready for life.

He had sought to obey the commandments of knighthood—not to be a party to treason, to honor all women and be ready to aid them to the extent of his power. He had, until the onset of his disease and his caution for the Church, heard mass every day and he still fasted every Friday. He had attempted to be fair, to be just in his life. But he had sinned, acts for which he asked forgiveness. The knightly virtues such as generosity, compassion, a free and frank spirit, and courtliness were more difficult to attain. He gave to the poor and he would protect Juliana with his life. His compassion was reserved for those weaker and less able to defend themselves. But his spirit was not free, and the secret he held within himself prevented a forthright nature.

He was no paragon of knighthood. He knew that only too well. He despised what had happened to the Cathars, whereas a true knight would have defended the acts of the Church even in thought. He had offered up a false chalice to the Templars knowing it would be revered as a relic. He was willing to bargain what he knew in order to save those he loved and Langlinais. And he had brought danger home with him in the guise of a straw basket. He was no true and noble knight.

Why, then, had he been spared?

Was it because he'd touched the relics? Had they a power beyond their existence as proof of his faith? Or was it the fact that he'd not worn the woolen robe, but his armor, instead? There was but one way to test that, but he could not bear the thought of wearing the monk's garb again. Or had it been the unguent Sister Agnes had given Juliana? He'd been faithful about using the preparation. Could it possess some properties not previously known? Or, perhaps most difficult to bear, what if that physician who first saw him and labeled him leper had not been truly versed in knowledge? What if he had simply been mistaken?

Was he simply doomed forever to wonder? To accept without question? A smile crossed his face as it occurred to him that he had just defined the true meaning of a miracle.

At that moment, Juliana turned and smiled at him. Her young apprentices melted away at his appearance. They were shy, and he was more accustomed to inducing fear than of being pleasing. Besides, he had no patience for those things that separated him from his wife.

He walked closer to the kettle, halted only by a noxious odor. He sniffed. "What is that stench?"

"It is the preparation I use for my parchment," she said.

"Why does it smell that odious?"

She smiled. "You do not want to know, Sebastian."

He raised one eyebrow.

"It is water, Sebastian."

"Water?" He looked into the caldron, one he rec-

ognized from the smith's collection. The contents
were pale yellow and frothy. For a moment he was
speechless. It looked as if most of the castle had
dumped their nightly chamber pots into the vessel.
He turned and raised one eyebrow at his smiling
wife.

"Well, not just any water," she confessed.

"Why would you use such a thing?"

"It aids in removing the last of the hair from the
hide, Sebastian."

"So, we're to have this odor for how many days?"

"A few," she confessed. "But you will become accustomed to it."

"Will I?"

"Well, after the hide is boiled in it. It smells a good
bit, too." She smiled brightly at him.

Her hair had come askew, damp tendrils clung to
her temples. Her eyes were bright with enthusiasm,
her cheeks blushed with color. He did not even try
to hide his enchantment.

"Would you be willing to take a moment from
your vile chores?"

As he watched, the color of her cheeks deepened.
He laughed, pulled her into his arms, and kissed her
until her ears were scarlet.

He did not speak further, just grabbed her hand
and pulled her with him, nodding at the smiling
faces he passed. He knew full well what they
thought, and he had plans for that, too, but first he
wished to give her his surprise.

"Why must I keep my eyes closed?" she asked as
he led her into the chamber that had once been hers.
He did not answer, simply pushed her into the center of the room.

"I know you've been practicing," he said gently,
"for that day when you will be able to write again.

And when you do so, you should have the finest surroundings."

Her old bedchamber had been converted to a scriptorium, but not any place where a scribe might work. This was a room alight with the sun's rays, captured from prisms mounted in the ceiling. But that was not the only Cathar wonder that had been duplicated. The window that had once overlooked the kitchen garden had been replaced with a series of openings to allow fresh air into the room. But where the ones at Montvichet were open permanently, these had small louvers that could close during cold weather.

The desk, however, was the greatest innovation. Instead of being simply a smooth surface on which she could write, the structure was formed in three parts, a center unit and two flanking areas of the same height.

Slowly she walked around it, then sat on the padded stool and looked about her. On her right was a place to store her powdered inks. On the left, a long shelf for blank parchment. The surface of the main desk was divided, one side for the parchment she was copying, the other for the original, both gently slanted. There were two holes carved into the top and inside these rested twin reservoirs crafted of glass. One would hold the ink she mixed for the day, the other her quills.

On top of the desk rested a large coffer. She looked at him questioningly, but he only smiled. She slowly opened the lid. Inside was a tray, separated into sections. She lifted the tray free, and laid it aside. The body of the coffer was filled with a square box. He said nothing at her glance, only shook his head.

He leaned back against the wall, folded his arms,

as enthralled as she. Not in the gifts, but in her reaction.

The box was enameled, its corners rounded. She removed the top cautiously. A thin parchment sheet lay on the top. A gasp of wonder escaped her. "Goldbeater's skin," she whispered in awe. Beneath the thin, hardened membrane were more than a hundred leaves of beaten gold.

She glanced over at him, the look on her face one he wished he could hold forever. Amazement and joy, both contained in her eyes and her expression of wonder. "How did you know, Sebastian? How did you know I've always wanted to work with gold?"

"Your abbess arranged it. I asked her to send me all that a scribe would dream of having."

"But I've never worked with gold, Sebastian. I might waste some of it."

"Then you'll learn," he said, his smile coming from deep inside him. She looked so earnest, so sincere. What did it matter if she wasted a few sheets of gold? He would have given his life for her.

"It was a good harvest, Juliana. And my ransom is fulfilled. Don't tell me you are going to turn into a nagging wife, telling me where to spend my money?"

She shook her head, her eyes misty.

"You haven't seen the rest," he said, the words having to travel around the boulder in his throat in order to be voiced.

She looked inside the tray. There were five drawstring leather bags, each one of them contained a different powder. "Vermilion," she whispered as she opened the first one. She glanced up at him. "Sebastian, do you know how costly this is? Only the abbess was allowed to use it."

He raised an eyebrow. She smiled and turned back to the tray. "Lapis and orchil, azurite and orpiment," she said, after she'd opened all of them.

"What colors do they produce?"

"The lapis and azurite are blues, the most beautiful shades of blue. And the orpiment is yellow. The vermilion, of course, is scarlet."

"Orchil?"

"Purple," she said softly. Her fingers played upon the tray, and when she turned finally to him, her smile was radiant.

"Have I made you happy?" he asked, and took a step toward her, pulled her from the stool and into his arms.

"Oh Sebastian, I am happy even when you do nothing."

"Allow me the pleasure, then," he said, turning her cheek against his chest.

The day was bright, the weather fair, the harvest was in and there were no Templars on the horizon. He had pleased his wife.

He closed his eyes. A man should be content with such a day. But then, there were the scrolls, and the codex that pulsed its presence louder each day like a living entity.

Chapter 42

⁓✦⁓

"I suspected as much, my lady," Grazide said. She bustled into the scriptorium carrying a tray. She bumped the door shut with her backside, frowned at Juliana. "When I don't see you or the lord at the noon table, I know it's one of two things. You've either got it into your head to make Langlinais an heir, and right about time it is, too." Juliana could feel her face flaming. "Or he's in the tilting yard and you're in this place."

"Then I take it that my husband is practicing with his squires?"

Grazide set down the tray on the wing of Juliana's desk. "No, it's too wet and raw a day for that. I've no idea where he is, my lady. In truth, I thought he was with you. No doubt he's with the masons or fiddling with that special door of his." It was no secret at Langlinais that Sebastian had explained the Cathars' secret door to their masons in an effort to duplicate it.

"But just in case you were holed up here, my lady, I've brought you something to eat. Some bread and cheese and some good Langlinais beer. It will line your womb and make you fertile."

Juliana blinked at her, but she dutifully picked up

the cup from the tray. Sebastian laughed at the notion she'd ever been timid, lauded her occasional ferocity, yet before Grazide she still felt as defenseless as a child.

Now her attendant stood before her, tapping her foot and frowning at her, so that Juliana had no choice but to tear off a bit of the bread and begin to nibble. Juliana sighed, albeit silently. Each day brought her closer to being able to form her letters. So much so that she ached to practice. Even now she could grip a quill at just the right angle, and she'd been able to draw a glyph, although it was more clumsy than her usual effort. But perhaps the respite would make the writing easier when she returned to her task.

"I thought I would find you here," Sebastian said as he opened the door. "I'd not constructed this to be your cage, Juliana." Grazide smiled approvingly at that comment before leaving the room. Juliana only rolled her eyes and continued eating.

"You sit within this chamber for too many hours. You need a change from your reading."

She slitted her eyes at him. "Why do I think you not altogether truthful, Sebastian? I suspect you wish a rematch of the chess game we played yesterday."

He smiled slightly. "If you have the time."

"You do not like it when I win."

His current frown mimicked the one he'd worn all day yesterday. "I am a better man than that, Juliana. Besides, it was only once."

"Then why did you walk away when I won?"

"Jerard needed my counsel."

Her smile could no longer be hidden.

He came closer, leaning over her plate. She held a bit of cheese against his lips and his bite encompassed both the food and a portion of her fingers.

She laughed and pulled her hand away.

"You have the beginnings of autocracy in your nature, Sebastian," she said softly.

"Indeed?"

He circled her desk, pulled her from the stool. She fell into his arms. He bent, and in a move that startled her, released her girdle, then grasped the hem of her garment and pulled the surcoat over her head.

She gasped. "Sebastian, Grazide . . ." That was as far as she got before his lips closed over hers.

"Autocracy?" he murmured when she surfaced from the kiss. "Perhaps you are correct, Juliana. I'm feeling despotic at the moment."

He stepped back and fumbled with her quills, selecting one that had been newly sharpened. His fingers pinched a fold of the linen of her cotte; the quill pierced the material easily. He inserted one finger and slowly pulled the fabric apart until there was a gap of more than a hand's span. Her eyes widened as his fingers reached in to play on her skin. A gasp escaped her as a warm palm cupped a heated breast.

"Not chess, then," she softly said, "but another game."

"You cannot fault me, Juliana. I have a wife who enslaves me like Circe."

Her head fell back as his fingers caressed her flesh.

His two hands rent the material of her cotte to its hem. Another quick tug and that was ripped apart. The cotte hung by her shoulders, and he reached in through the folds, his palms sweeping over her skin.

"Did you know I used to dream of you?" he asked, his attention directed to the flush that enveloped her breasts. One finger toyed with a nipple, as if encouraging it to lengthen.

She shook her head. Her hands gripped his arms. "Should we not retire to our chamber, Sebastian?"

He smiled. "Indulge me, Juliana. Have you never wished to be naughty?"

"Only children are naughty," she said. Her eyes watched him, widened as he picked up the enameled box and opened it slowly. He held it only an inch from her body, bent and blew softly. A sheet of gold leaf fluttered from the interior to be caught on his open palm. He laid the sheet of thinly hammered gold across her breast. A gentle breath was all it took for the gold to splinter, glittering dust bathing her skin. A touch of a finger spread it from sloping curve to nipple, turning it coral and gold.

"You are no child now, my lady wife."

She shook her head, her eyes fluttering shut as his gold-tipped finger brushed softly between her breasts, coating her skin. "Sebastian, I truly believe we should retire to our chamber."

"You've never been timid in my arms, Juliana. Is it your wish to be so now?"

Her eyes flew open. "We've coupled in almost every room at Langlinais, Sebastian. A timid wife would not do so."

"Oh, but that was my naked Juliana. Devoid of clothes she is a siren. Garbed, she is timid and quiet." He bent to capture her mouth with his. Their kiss was heated and carnal, luring her to feverishness. As it was every time he touched her.

"Perhaps she is only conspiring in silence," she said, pulling back from him, a small smile lifting her lips. She reached for his hand and pressed it to her breast. His smile broadened. "Perhaps she is reading Ovid again and thinking of all manner of things she might do to a husband who is a knight with a wicked grin and talented hands."

He extended his hands to her shoulders. His gold-tipped thumb brushed against her neck, leaving a glittering trail.

"Then do with me as you will, Juliana. In the meantime, I will satisfy a dream I had."

"You dreamed of me?" Her words felt heated, but he had that ability to stir her, to encapsulate her in thoughts only of him, to entwine her in passion. She sometimes grew breathless simply remembering how she felt when he entered her, her body welcoming him, easing for him.

"You have filled my nights since you came to Langlinais." His fingers curved around her breast. He bent his head and kissed her shoulder where his other hand lay, then trailed his lips down her chest.

A tremor seemed to skitter over her skin at his touch. Her breath quickened.

"Warm and enticing." His tongue sampled her glittering skin between her breasts. His palm brushed against a nipple that felt hot and tight. A thumb brushed against it as he bestowed a delicate kiss to the side of her neck.

He kissed her again, brushing her mouth with soft strokes. Tiny flecks of gold glittered on his mouth and she reached up and traced her tongue over his lips, cleaning him.

She pulled the ruined cotte from her shoulders, stood naked before him. Her smile felt daring. His eyes seemed to darken as he looked at her, but she did not move to cover herself.

"The vision in my dreams is a poor replica of you, Juliana," he said, his voice harsh.

She knelt before him on the floor, gathering up her ruined cotte to serve as their mattress. It was she who reached for his hand and urged him down to her, propriety and timidity forgotten.

He kissed her, leading the way into a vortex of

darkness and desire. He removed his tunic and she kissed him again. Each successive bit of clothing he removed was marked and rewarded by a heated kiss.

He laid her down, then thrust gold-tipped fingers into her hair, holding her immobile while he plundered her mouth.

She held herself still, her breath captured on a sigh as he sat up, reached for the enameled box, opened it. A breath dislodged another sheet of gold. It fell to her belly in a tremulous quiver. His fingers broke it apart, his palm smoothed it over the curve of her hip, then halted at the juncture of her thighs.

He watched her as a soft touch of two of his gilded fingers brushed the gold dust over the delicate curls, touched her intimately.

A soft, helpless gasp escaped her. She closed her eyes as he painted her with a breath and the exquisitely delicate touch of fingertip. Her legs widened, welcoming him without a word. But he continued softly stroking her. His fingers were gentle but demanding. She opened her eyes to find him smiling at her.

The passion was building, the moment soon here when the world turned heated and white and she shattered into a hundred pieces. But she'd never felt it without him.

"No." Her head moved from side to side.

His small smile was wickedly charming, but resolute.

"Yes."

"Please, Sebastian." Her breath was coming too fast, there was that feeling like fire in her blood, heaviness between her thighs, anticipation too intense to be endured for too long.

"Now?"

"Yes." A soft gasp, but he did not enter her. Instead, his mouth came down to bestow the most intimate of kisses. A stroke of intrusive tongue threw her into the white void. She called out to him and he rose up and held her tightly, was there when it ended and she became whole again.

She trembled, but not from fear. Her sobs unmanned him; her effortless soaring into ecstasy enfolded him in pride. She came apart in his arms, and it entranced him.

He had been married to her as a boy. Had not known her until a few short months ago, but in that time she'd changed his life, made it brighter. She'd brought him joy and acceptance and curiosity. Would he have always loved her, or had it taken the knowledge of his own mortality to change him from the youth he'd been to a man worthy of Juliana? Would he have seen past her beauty to the soul of her? Would he have known that when she laughed it was almost with a note of surprise, as if the sound of it astonished her? Would he have seen that she had such passion about her work? She had wept for the Cathar women and children, with a generosity of spirit he'd witnessed and that had humbled him. Would he have appreciated, this man who had been untested, that she was a woman who loved deeply, without restraint? Or perhaps such questions were not important after all. She was here and so was he, whole and untainted.

"Are you pleased, Juliana?"

"No," she said, her voice somber. Surprised, he raised his head to look at her.

"Not as much as when you are in me, Sebastian." Her eyes were lambent, her face flushed, and there was a small smile that played upon her lips. Had he ever believed that she would be capable of saying such words to him, or that her glance would be filled with remonstrance? Timid Juliana? Had she ever truly existed?

She pushed him to his back and held him there, a palm placed on his chest. The box was open again. She licked two fingers and pressed them against the sheet of gold leaf. It clung to her fingers.

He wanted to be in her, but he slowed himself, curious as to what she would do. She draped the gold between his thighs, over his erect and straining flesh. He closed his eyes at the feeling of her fingers brushing against him, coating him just as he had done with her. A hesitation of touch had him opening his eyes again.

She seemed to study him, examine her adornment of him as closely as she would one of her manuscripts. He raised his head and looked at himself. He glittered like an idol.

Her fingers curved around him, lightly squeezed.

"I had the oddest thought, Sebastian," she said, her fingers trailing in delightful torture over his flesh. "Your phallus is not unlike a quill, I think." Her soft, daring smile startled him. So, too, the bubble of laughter in his chest. The moment seemed so filled with passion that humor was a strange emotion to feel. But he choked it back, gave her soberness instead.

"Am I not substantially larger than a quill?" His smile released some of the silly happiness he felt.

Her head bobbed down and her soft, intimate kiss banished his humor. A wordless groan occupied its space.

"You write beautiful love poems, Sebastian." Her gold-tipped smile teased and promised.

"If that is a result of your reading, my lady wife,

I shall send to the abbess," he said, the words pushed through a cloud of exquisite agony, "and beg her to send me some more of her most audacious texts."

She returned to her task, and he was treated to the oddest sensation of smiling lips brushing over his flesh.

He raised up and flipped her on her back, hovered over her.

She undulated beneath him brushing her breasts against his chest, hips and thighs arching, a teasing touch.

He looked down at her, frozen into wonder by the sight. Her eyes were closed, her face flushed. Upon her cheek was the beginning of a glittering trail that led to the generous slopes of her breasts. Her nipples were engorged and tinted golden, her open thighs sparkled with gold.

He tried to hold back, to make the moment last, to make their joining even more fervent and desired. But somewhere in between the words of that thought crept another—he must be in her now or die.

He moved back, kneeling, and pulled her onto him, her legs curving around his hips. The position thrust him deeper into her, but she was slick and ready for him.

Her arms wound around his neck as she hung from him. She whimpered, not in distress as much as yearning. His hands pressed down on her hips as he rose up beneath her.

He covered her breasts with kisses, anointed her neck with soft bites, breathed into her ear words he'd once thought with such ferocity. "Mine, Juliana. You're mine."

Her inarticulate murmur was appeasement

enough for his sudden, fierce possessiveness.

When she cried out in joy, he covered her lips with his, to keep her sound of rapture secret and his. Only too soon he joined her, his lips clamped over a shout that demanded to be heard. He was lost in the feeling of her, adrift in the undulations that united their bodies and splinted together the raw ends of their souls.

Later, a very long time later, he lowered himself to the floor, pulling her close. Her head was tucked against his shoulder, her arm lay atop his chest. He stroked his hand on her belly, trailed gold-dusted fingers to her quivering breasts. They were both too weak to move.

She breathed the words across his skin. "I will not feel so guilty now if I waste a sheet or two of gold."

His laughter was reborn again and echoed throughout the room.

Chapter 43

⌒⌒◯◯⌒

She was cold, even though the room was warm. The chill came from inside her and was only hours old.

Juliana slipped from the stool and took the spiral stairs to the top of the tower. She could now stand at the battlements and relish the view.

The autumn wind swept her skirt around her ankles, brushed her hair back from her face. Langlinais was bathed in the light of a late-afternoon sun, the orange glow giving the stones a yellowish tint. From somewhere came the sound of laughter, a shared jest, a ribald joke.

Sebastian was in the exercise yard, training some of his would-be knights. He was using poor Jerard as an object lesson. Jerard was wiry and tall, but he was not the match of his lord in strength or breadth. What made Jerard valuable was not so much his skill with a sword as it was his loyalty.

The abilities of Sebastian's mind enchanted her, his humor surprised her. His strength of will humbled her. When he touched her, all thoughts other than those of him flew from her head. She would die for him. But he had not asked her to. Instead, he had challenged her mind and enthralled her body.

Sebastian of Langlinais was no ordinary man.

The inhabitants of Langlinais did not seem to mind that he was no longer as devout. He laughed a great deal, and his smile was almost constantly upon his face. He spent a good amount of time among the villagers, helped them draw up a charter, invited a few members of the growing guilds to make their homes there. He took in the poorest lads for training, and had promised them positions as squires and eventual knighthood if they proved worthy. It was not that he did not see the line between noble and serf. It was as if he moved it subtly from time to time, allowing those of the inclination to advance as they would.

He seemed to revel in the strength of his limbs, in the fact that he could go abroad without being garbed in a concealing robe. The men at arms he practiced against were eager to demonstrate their own ability, but it was obvious who would be the winner.

There were, however, still moments in which he grew too quiet, when he appeared trapped in thought. Too many times, he stood at the tower and faced south, as if he waited for the Templar army to invade his land. It was a sad fact that they would always need to be prepared for unrest. And, perhaps for the Templars.

Arrogance had surfaced from beneath his despair, and no one but she had the courage to tell him when he was being overbearing. He would lift his eyebrow and look very much the noble on such occasions, and she would tremble, but not in fear of him. Rather, with how much she loved him. The feeling, she knew, that was echoed as strongly in him.

There were times when she simply watched him. Sometimes, he would be in the middle of a conver-

sation and look up as if sensing that she studied him.
He would find her immediately, their gaze meeting
among the throngs of people who surrounded them.
There would be an expression on his face she was
sure she wore, one of startled wonder that such a
thing should have happened to them. And at those
times, she thought as she had once before that it
might be possible to speak to him in her mind. *Beloved.*

He looked up now, as if he'd heard her.

Sebastian had known, of course. He had to. This
was the true secret, the real treasure. Not the relics.
But the document she'd read wide-eyed and disbelieving.

She closed her eyes, forced a deep breath. Was this
the reason De Rutger had been so desperate to kill
the Cathars? Not for the treasure, not because they
were heretics, but for what they had believed? If so,
then the same danger had been transported to Langlinais. She shuddered, a movement more of the
mind than of the body.

She looked down at the exercise yard. Sebastian
was no longer there. With a sense she'd come to accept, she knew he was coming to her. Had he seen
her atop the tower? Had he known, somehow, what
she had found?

She returned to the scriptorium, sat at her desk
again. The codex remained on her desk, the wooden
cover closed. She'd found it, buried beneath the
scrolls, had slammed it shut when she'd read the explanation for a long list of names. She opened the
book again, read the Latin words that began the
work.

*O reader, in spiritual love forgive me, and pardon the
daring of him who wrote, and turn his errors into mystic*

good. A colophon she'd read before, a sentiment espoused often by conscientious scribes.

The codex was a series of parchment pages bound together and contained within a wooden cover. The preface stated that it was the Latin translations of the oldest of the scrolls, those written in Greek and Hebrew. Those same scrolls had been kept in a sealed coffer in their chamber. Only for the last week had they been close at hand, remaining in the scriptorium that she might study them.

The scroll in front of her was one of the oldest of the more than hundred originally tucked into the basket. Somewhere in its past the parchment had become wet, and was consequently stiff on the corners.

She did not read Greek. There had been no one at the convent either to find the time or with the knowledge to teach her. The other language she also did not know, an involved series of curving letters beautiful in their regimentation. She surmised that it must be Hebrew.

She did not even dare to place her fingers on the scroll. It was so brittle that a piece had flaked off in her fingers. How old was it? A thousand years? Less? More?

Was that why the Cathar scribes had copied them, because of their fragility? Or because most of the ecclesiastical world could read Latin?

One of the scrolls consisted of writing that was superimposed over the original writing, a palimpsest. The newer the ink, the easier it was to remove. She'd reused parchment herself by simply sponging off the ink, then wetting the surface carefully, allowing it to dry, then scraping it gently. That same procedure did not work as well with old ink, because it had a chance to eat through the parchment. It looked as if this scroll had been saved not because of the later words written, but because of the earlier text not quite obliterated.

She lifted her head and Sebastian was there, covered in dust, his hair sweat-dampened against his head, his helmet somehow discarded on his way to her side.

He reached out for her and for a moment she did not think at all. Only that his mouth descended to hers, the cold of his lips rapidly turning to heat.

He pulled back, looked beyond her to the scrolls that lay open upon her desk, at the codex beneath her left hand.

"You've found it, then."

She looked at him without surprise. "You knew I would."

He nodded.

"Do you believe what you have read?" he asked.

"You once asked me what I would do if I noticed the sky was green. That it had always been green, even when I thought it was blue. Is this my green sky, Sebastian?"

He smiled. "Yes. I had kept the secret for too many years. I brushed the edge of danger asking you that question."

"But the bloodline of Christ, Sebastian." She gently touched the edge of the scroll. The shock she'd felt initially had deadened to numbness.

"From what I understand about their religion, the Cathars believed that man is intrinsically evil. And so, Christ as a man, could never be divine. Such a tenet of faith placed them on a course of opposition with the Church."

"Do you believe it?"

"No, but I doubt it matters what you or I believe, Juliana," he said. "The Cathars did, and went to great lengths to prove that Christ married and that his wife and child escaped from Jerusalem. They believe they traced the lineage almost to the present day."

"Why didn't you tell me before, Sebastian?"

His smile was tender. "These scrolls could rock the very foundations of the world as we know it, Juliana. Even a hint of their existence is enough to bring us danger. I did not wish for you the fate of the Cathars."

"Then why tell me now?"

"Because you are Juliana," he said, the smile vanishing, a somber look replacing it. "Because you are my wife. Because you deserve to know the danger I have brought to Langlinais. Because if anything happens to me, you must be prepared. And for the greatest reason of all. There has been too much deception in our life together. I want no more secrets between us."

"Do you think they know about the scrolls?"

"The Templars or the Church?"

"Either. Both."

"I doubt the Templars know, else they would not have accepted the chalice so easily. As to the Church, I have my suspicions, but no proof."

"Did you go on Crusade in order to find your faith, Sebastian?"

"Perhaps," he said, tracing his finger across the bottom of the curving parchment. "Has this shattered yours, Juliana? Or just made you more certain than ever that what you believe is true?"

She thought about his question, "My faith has not been shaken, Sebastian. Faith is a belief that does not rest on proof. It exists on its own, stands on its own."

"Yet people seek out objects," he said, "in order to bolster that faith. Pieces of the true cross, the shroud of Christ."

"Relics that remain in our chamber."

"They are not there, Juliana." At her look, he smiled. "I removed them from the coffer. Your abbess has had them for a few weeks now. They belong to the world, not to us. Eventually, I'm sure, they will find their way to being known."

"Why not send them to the Pope?"

"And fuel the battle that is brewing, Juliana? No, your abbess will make her decision when it's time. I've no doubt she will choose the proper place for the relics to belong."

"And the scrolls, Sebastian? Where do they belong?"

"Where did they come from?"

His question surprised her.

"I doubt the Cathars created them. I suspect, in their travels to obtain relics, that they stumbled onto their existence. Their scribes compiled the codex, but the scrolls are much older. Where did they originate?"

She shook her head. "There are nothing but questions, are there, Sebastian?"

He smiled. "More questions than answers, Juliana. The Cathars would have every reason to foster a myth, especially since it matches so precisely their own beliefs. Or perhaps they considered it truth. My guess is that whatever they believed they planned to use it to discredit or even confuse the Church."

"Why didn't they trade the scrolls for their safety?"

"I think they knew it was too late. Why surrender their treasure when they were certain they were going to be killed? Remember, by that time, the men had already been burned at the stake."

"Is that why Magdalene sent for you, so that the secret would be preserved?"

"I asked myself that question all during my imprisonment." He smiled, an odd expression for this moment. "Why had she entrusted their secret to me? Even after a year, I was no closer to an answer."

"Perhaps she knew you valued knowledge, Sebastian. And that you were not as intolerant of those who thought differently."

His hands were braced on his hips. He had removed his gloves, but otherwise still remained armored. His sword swung easily against his body. He was comfortable with it, at ease with the fact he could bring death with a slice of it.

"I am as flawed as any man, Juliana. But Magdalene's death made me wish that such an act not be repeated. And perhaps I could not destroy them because of her."

He glanced at the paragraph she had studied for so long. It began a nearly thousand-year lineage, a carefully written record of births and marriages and deaths ending two hundred years earlier. "I found the codex first. It was on the top of the basket, as if Magdalene had wanted me to discover it. I remember the moment I read these words."

She stared down at the desk.

"What do we do with them, Sebastian?"

He smiled. "The choices have occurred as easily to you as they did to me. Send them to the Church in secrecy, but be prepared for the answers never to be known. Send them to the Templars and watch them be used to feed their power. Destroy them."

"Or hide them again."

"A coward's way, perhaps."

"Or one of wisdom."

"It would be my choice," he said somberly.

"It's why you kept them at Montvichet, isn't it?"

"I could think of no better place. An abandoned

fortress is not a place one expects to find a treasure."

"Then why didn't we leave them there, Sebastian?"

"You wish a confession from me? Very well." He walked to the vents on the wall, closed now to keep out the autumn wind. It was not yet cool enough to utilize the oversize fireplace that would heat the room in winter. "For a long time, I thought that I would simply extract the relics and leave the scrolls at Montvichet. But just before we left the fortress, I changed my mind again. I, too, wish to use the Cathar treasure." He glanced over his shoulder at her. "I've not the purest of motives, Juliana. Although I value knowledge, it is not for that reason I would keep the scrolls safe. I will do whatever I must to protect you and to provide for the well-being of those who entrust themselves to my care. A hint of their contents will provide that protection should either the Church or the Order come to Langlinais."

"Will they come, Sebastian?"

"Yet one more question I cannot answer," he said.

Juliana held the codex in her hands. She had read it through four times after she and Sebastian had decided to hide the scrolls again.

A dangerous document, one that endangered them.

She lived in a world of divisions. Noble and serf. Faithful and heretic. Scribe and unlearned. Lines drawn to separate one man from another. She, herself, had felt the bite of that careful delineation. "You are a woman, weak of mind. You cannot succeed in such fine work." Words to her from the priest who had visited the convent often and questioned her ability as a scribe.

It was difficult to move from one world to another. Jerard had passed from serf to knight, a distinction awarded because of his loyalty. She had progressed from unlearned to scribe, only because of a stubborn will. Did she endanger herself now, traversing from faithful to heretic, by refusing to destroy such work?

A great many of the Latin texts she'd transcribed had been written by men who had worshiped gods and goddesses. Yet their work had been diligently preserved through the ages. Why? Were they not heretic, too?

Sebastian was not the only one who was concerned for their safety. She would not live without him, could not bear the idea that he might be endangered. She was going to do her part to safeguard him and the people of Langlinais.

Again, the words she'd whispered to Sebastian in the Montvichet courtyard came to mind. *Hairetikos means to choose.* Once again she made a choice. Only the future would determine if it was the right one.

She laid the codex down, and gently flexed her fingers. The work would take more time than it would have in the past, but she would be careful and as diligent as the Cathar scribes. Not one word would be omitted, and in addition to their explanation of the scrolls, she would add a codicil of her own. She would tell the story of the true relics, of the Templar chalice, and of the ruse perpetrated in order to protect both the treasure of the Cathars and Langlinais castle.

Chapter 44

The large green window of the chapel had been replaced with a stained-glass work of art. The artisan who had crafted the window had come from a family of such men, his grandfather and father having worked on a cathedral in France. It depicted a monk kneeling before a blazing sun. On the ground beside him lay a sword and a covered basket. It would be the only public record of the miracle of Langlinais, and the secret they would forever keep. The window's placement had been finished just the day before, and the odor of lead and clay was almost as strong as the wax of the candles. The winter day did little to illuminate the room, and their glowing light added an otherworldly air to the room.

An altarpiece, tripartite in form, lay open, its newly painted image that of the Garden of Eden. On one side was the image of Eve's temptation. On the other, the scene of Adam and Eve being expelled from the garden. But it was the middle panel that attracted her gaze. It showed both Adam and Eve upon their knees in devotion to God. Both were smiling, as if welcomed back into the garden. When it had been placed upon the altar, Juliana had been surprised, then embarrassed to note the resemblance of Adam and Eve to Sebastian and herself. Sebastian tweaked the nose of the Church in subtle ways.

The chapel was crowded, the people had assembled there at Sebastian's request. It was to be a surprise for Jerard, a blessing of the sword Sebastian had ordered prepared for him. The entire populace of Langlinais was aware of this honor just as they had been Sebastian's gift of her scriptorium. As they had with her, they had taken great pains to deflect his attention from what was obvious. Yesterday, the smith had finished the sword, a result of steady hammering night and day for nearly two weeks in order to have the weapon ready.

A man attired in black monk's garb stood at one side of the altar. Brother Thomas was new to the village, new to Langlinais. He had wise blue eyes for one so young, and a smile that Juliana doubted would ever be thinned in censure. He came forward, his tonsured head bared in one sweep of hand upon cowl.

Juliana thought back to the first time she'd seen Sebastian, hidden in the darkness of such a garment, isolated in loneliness. She placed her hand in his and he seemed to understand because he pressed it tightly.

Jerard stepped forward, the look on his face one of caution. They had evidently been successful at keeping such an event a secret. Sebastian retrieved the sword hidden behind a pillar. An emerald the size of a thumbnail was embedded in its hilt, and below that the word *trewe* etched into the metal. Trustworthy. It was more than an apt description for Jerard.

Jerard knelt, the look on his face one of disbelief. Sebastian held the sword up until the candlelight bathed the blade, then laid it before Brother Thomas.

"Bless this sword," he intoned, "so that it may be a defense for churches, widows and orphans, and for all servants of God against the fury of the heathen. I command you, Sir Jerard, to perform your duties faithfully and devoutly. Will you do so?"

Jerard nodded.

Sebastian smiled, then whispered to him to stand. He stepped forward, girded the sword belt around Jerard's waist.

"Wear it in honor, Jerard."

"I will protect it, my lord. With my life."

His vow signaled an end to awed silence.

Sebastian closed the door behind Jerard. Below them were the sounds of merriment, as the inhabitants of Langlinais celebrated. Juliana remained in the great hall, a reluctant but radiant hostess. The two men were now alone, as they had often been in other times, days that seemed gray now in retrospect.

"You have served me well over the years," Sebastian said, his smile not as easy as he would have wished.

Jerard dropped to one knee before him. "My lord, I am overwhelmed. To bestow upon me knighthood when I was but a bastard serf is a great honor. But to give me this magnificent sword is too much."

Sebastian smiled. The youth he'd first seen in France had grown to be a man of loyalty and humility. Too much humility at this moment, however.

"As I said, you have served me well, Jerard." He clapped his hand on his vassal's shoulder. "Because of you, Langlinais remained prosperous and its people happy during my imprisonment. You've held the secret of my disease and been my friend when the world would have shunned me. I care not for your birth. You are a man of Langlinais, and as such you will be forever known."

Jerard looked down at the wooden floor.

"But I need you to evince your loyalty once more."

He looked up. "Anything, my lord."

Sebastian sobered. "Do not promise so easily. The boon I ask of you will not be an easy one."

He moved to the other side of the room where a small table and two chairs were placed, sat, and waved Jerard into the adjoining chair. "I want you to leave Langlinais," he said, and at the stricken look of his vassal, his own smile slipped.

"Have I done anything to offend, my lord?"

"On the contrary, Jerard, you are the only man to whom I could entrust this task." His fingers drummed on the edge of the table.

"You know of the Cathar scrolls," he said, "but you do not know what they contain." For the next hour, he explained their contents, answering Jerard's questions with as much knowledge as he had. It was only right, the man who would possess them must also know their danger.

"You are only the third person alive to know the secret," Sebastian said. "Such knowledge might prove dangerous for you. I do not make light of this, Jerard."

The other man looked stunned.

"I've land north of here." The only property other than Langlinais that he had left after paying the ransom to the Templars, but he did not tell Jerard that. "Build your own castle upon it, create your own demesne. Take the scrolls there and guard them. It is a sacred task you assume now, Jerard. One of more import than being my vassal or my friend. Do you accept it?"

Jerard cleared his throat twice before the words emerged. "Yes, my lord, I will. And my sons and my daughters. It will be their inheritance to guard the scrolls."

"Is there anyone at Langlinais you wish to go with you? A woman you might take to wife?"

Jerard shook his head. "No, my lord."

"Think carefully, Jerard. If you do, she may go with you with my blessings. And a dower, to assist you both."

"No, my lord."

Silence, while Sebastian weighed Jerard's response. "We have always jested about your prowess with women. There are none among your conquests you would wed?"

"No, my lord. The woman I would take to wife must be learned and loyal. She will be intelligent and courageous, and have the kindest heart."

Sebastian raised an eyebrow. "You have just described my wife," he said, forcing his tone to be calm.

Jerard's face blanched, then just as rapidly his face bronzed. "No, lord," he said. "I revere her as my lady."

"See that you always do so."

He stood, clasped Jerard on his shoulder. "I will miss you, my friend. Remember that, too. And now, it is time to join the others. I'm sure Old Simon has already begun his own celebration."

Chapter 45

"**W**hat is that noise?" She looked up at the ceiling of the great hall. Sebastian extended his goblet to her instead of answering. She shook her head.

Langlinais wine was famous for its potency. It was not a product of the castle, merely decanted and seasoned until the bitterness was made mellow and sweetness was the lingering aftertaste. The recipe was a closely guarded secret of the brewers, who were also responsible for an equally acceptable ale.

The evening had been set aside for celebration. The fruit in the orchards had been harvested, and firewood, acorns, and beechnuts gathered from Langlinais's forests. For days the air had been thick with dust from the wheat threshing. Normal preparations for winter.

But it was not only the harvest that was being celebrated, but the elevation of one of their own. Jerard had come almost full-grown to Langlinais, but he had served it well, been a fair steward. It was not every day that a man born serf could rise to the rank of knight, and be gifted with three horses and a magnificent sword.

A loud thud shook the ceiling again, but not one

person in the Hall seemed to notice but her.

"Did you not hear that, Sebastian?" She stood and would have left the dais to investigate had he not pushed her gently back in her chair.

He motioned with one hand and a jongleur came forward and bowed to the table at large, then sat upon a stool facing the other diners. He idly plucked the five strings of an ud, a short-necked lute, as he told his version of a chanson de geste of Charlemagne and his twelve great peers.

Every single person in the hall looked intrigued with his story. Except for Juliana, who was still curious about the noises she'd heard, and for Sebastian, who was performing deeds not normally ascribed to knights.

"What are you hiding from me this time, Sebastian?"

His right hand held his goblet, his left was wadding up the material of her embroidered surcoat and cotte. His fingers were suddenly on her bare skin.

"Sebastian!" Her whisper did not seem to disturb him one whit, and as an admonishment, it was useless. His expression was that of a man contented with his lot; a small smile played around his mouth as if he were well pleased with the tale he was hearing. A lock of hair was dislodged upon his brow, giving him a youthful, almost mischievous appearance. But it was the look in his eyes that warned her she would have no success in deterring him from his actions. They held a lazy, almost sleepy expression, one he wore often. Not the look of a predator, but that of a man wishing to bed his wife.

She could feel her skin warm. If she was a wanton to wish his touch so much, then so be it.

"You have the strangest look on your face, lady

wife," he said, his whisper no louder than a breath against her ear. "Are you hungry?"

She shook her head from side to side. Even his voice had power, made it appear as if the air was hotter and thicker around them. As if she could barely breathe.

"Are you sure? You look almost ravenous. Come," he said, standing and extending a hand for her. "Smile your apologies for quitting our banquet too soon, my lady wife."

She did so, not questioning the need that flowed around both of them. *Touch me. Touch me.* It seemed a song she sang in her mind, one he seemed to hear as easily.

He led her past the floor that held their chamber. It had been easier than she'd thought to share a bed. He was so large, however, that several times during the night she awoke with him crowding her to the edge. One fingertip was all it took to dislodge him, and he would roll over to his side of the bed. Sometimes, however, his eyes would open at her touch as he came instantly awake. Then, he would reach for her and the thought of sleep vanished from both their minds.

At the top of the east tower, he pulled her into his embrace, his mouth covering hers before she could speak. He had a way of kissing her that stole her breath. All she was conscious of in those moments was Sebastian and his talented mouth. He rained kisses over her face, his breath harsh, his grip in her hair not at all gentle.

He pulled back, traced the shape of her face with his fingers. Even now she marveled at the touch of his skin against hers, no barriers between them.

"I used to sit and watch you here, Juliana, and

wonder what it would be like to touch you."

A rush of warmth flowed through her at his words.

He placed both his hands at her waist, then turned her in his arms so that her back was to him. Pulling her close to him, he wound one arm around her waist. His other hand went to unbraid her hair.

When he was finished, and her hair lay like a cloud around her shoulders, his hand cupped her breast. "I used to wonder if your breasts were as pale as the rest of your skin, if they looked like snowy mounds tipped with delicate rose." His thumb slid over her breast, and when it peaked and rose in concert with his touch, he laughed softly. "Then I discovered one night that they were. Soft and snowy white."

She reached up her hand and arched it behind her until she touched his face. He kissed her fingers, then bent to place a small kiss at her temple. Her fingers threaded through his hair.

"I thought I would die, I wanted you to touch me so much." A soft confession. It was the first time they had spoken of that night when he'd interrupted her bathing.

"I came too close to it."

He turned her in his arms and bent to touch his lips to her neck. "You taste of roses, Juliana."

He raised his head, his breath as fast as hers. She ground her forehead against his chest. He moved one of her hands to place over him. She felt him hard and heavy against her palm. Had it not already transpired, she would have been sure the act was impossible. It was no wonder, then, that she'd felt stretched and filled with him when he entered her.

Her fingers began a slow exploration of his flesh. She had already discovered that she could make him tremble, or draw in a low, shuddering breath.

He laid her down on the wooden floor of the tower, an unlikely bower for their tryst. But the rains had come earlier in the day, and the air smelled fresh and clean. There was no dust, and in the way it happens sometimes, the night seemed clearer after the storm. She looked up to see a thousand winking lights, like torches seen from a distance. But no fire in the sky could capture her attention once Sebastian lay beside her.

He propped himself up on one elbow, and one by one, divested her of her garments, ripping out the seams of the fitted sleeves when they could not be easily removed. She did not bother to protest; one did not gainsay a crusader. The moonlight created shadows on his face, rendering it beautiful in a stark fashion. She brought her hand up to rest against his cheek. He halted in his determined campaign.

"What is it, Juliana?" He turned his head, bestowed a soft kiss in the center of her palm.

"Only that I would hold this moment safe forever, Sebastian. Until the end of time." The words came from some place deep inside her, a secret spot kept hidden and vulnerable.

His smile was blazing white in the moonlight, his kiss was invitation to lose herself again within his embrace, be lured to passion once again.

He had only hoped to divert her attention from the noise the masons were making. It had been easy enough when her scriptorium had been built; he'd simply kept her occupied in the bailey or in their chamber. But the oriel was being converted into a bathing room, complete with a stone bath similar to the one at Montvichet.

All thoughts of diversion had slipped through his

mind at her look and he'd found himself falling into lust quickly enough. So deeply that he did not care if smiles followed their exit, or they were spoken about with ribald comments.

He was a man well versed in his power. A warrior must know his strengths, work to eliminate his weaknesses. Why, then, did he feel like an untried boy when she smiled at him, or lay in his arms? Perhaps what he felt at this moment was not so much lust, he thought, looking down at her. Love? Too small a word, too puny a thought. He knew he would feel this way about this woman for the rest of his life, and perhaps into eternity.

He could not wait to touch her, so the final seam on her cotte was ripped rather than unlaced. She lay, naked, her garments strewn around her like a foil for her beauty. The moonlight bathed her in a glow, gave a mysterious curve to her lips, a beckoning glint to her eye.

It seemed somehow right and fitting that they should come together here, in this place that was the scene of his greatest yearning. How many nights had he sat and watched her and felt physical pain that he could do no more?

For the shadow of that man, he bent and kissed her breast, tasting the stiffness of a nipple. Because that man had wished to know, had dreamed about such things, he drew it between his lips, heard her soft gasp as he grazed her delicate flesh with his teeth.

The man he had been knelt beside him, a ghost of longing and need. He heard the commands in his head, the urging, and stroked his hands over Juliana's body. He knew her flesh as well as he knew his own. The indentation where waist met hip was especially sensitive to her. Her toes curled when he brushed the tops of them. Her breath halted as his fingers traced up one thigh and then, to their juncture. Instead of holding herself tight, her legs fell open, wordless invitation.

He divested himself of his tunic, his waistbelt, the patterned hose. Soon he was naked, his figure draped in shadow as night fell over them like dust.

His fingers seemed acutely talented at this moment, imbued with instinct or perhaps the coaxing of the man he had been, who had spent too many hours envisioning just such an occasion. He touched her gently, with restraint born of wishes. His lips covered her breasts, neck, arms. He loved her with his mouth, her skin anointed with kisses and sighs, as if his breath could not come deeply or quickly enough.

She gripped his arms, her hands reaching out, her head twisting from side to side. Eagerness and protest, all in one. He felt her, swollen and wet, and touched her softly, then with more insistent strokes.

"Sweet Juliana," he said, against her lips.

The siege was forgotten, the need paramount. He slid into the depths of her, heard the shuddering breath she took. He leaned back, supported only by his knees, placed the heel of his hand upon her, just above where they joined. He pressed gently, as she arched beneath him. Then again, as a soft sob emerged from between her lips.

"I want to hear your screams," he said, watching her. "I want you needy and hungry, Juliana."

He rocked with her, the thrusts shallow and fast. Her body arched to take more of his. Her hands clawed at his arms. He reached beneath her with one arm, thrust her clothing beneath her, then raised himself again. The angle of her body now brought him closer to the core of her. Again, he rocked, his need a battering ram, his fingers a key.

Small sounds emerged from her lips, moans or entreaties, he didn't know. He lowered himself, began to make longer strokes, withdrawing almost entirely, then thrusting forward to the depths of her.

Her eyes opened, the look in them helpless and wanting.

He abruptly recognized the significance of this moment. He could give her passion but it would be because he'd conquered her. He did not want submission from Juliana.

He was too close to shattering in her arms. His breaths came in gasps, the need ran through him in shuddering waves. He lowered himself, and rolled over until she was atop him, their bodies still joined.

"Take me with you, Juliana," he whispered.

Her nails skittered over his chest, her head arched back as her entire body seemed to shiver.

"Sebastian." His name was a sigh.

His hands gripped her hips, raised her, lowered her against him. A lesson she learned quickly. The next movement was hers, as she braced her knees against the floor, rose up and teased herself on him. The sensation was too much, pushing him closer to the edge.

"Take me, Juliana," he bit out. He closed his eyes, his body demanding that he surge even deeper into her, finish this. His mind urged restraint. He didn't know which would win, flesh or intellect.

She widened her legs, wedged herself farther on him. How had he never before discovered that ecstasy could border on torment?

She arched up one last time, the demand in her grip as ruthless as his had been. Her nails almost pierced his skin. He felt her shudder around him, as her body urged his on to completion.

Finally, her cry announced her release. It was so sharp as to be pained, but filled instead with joy. A moment more and she slumped over him, her kiss swallowing his groan as she accompanied him into bliss.

The man he had been, wraithlike and lonely, vanished forever, his flesh appeased and his soul complete.

Chapter 46

O ne of the benefits of his new position as aide to the Marshal was the ability to be absent from the brotherhood on D'Aubry's business. But Gregory's return to Montvichet was not on the Marshal's business but for his own. He wanted to discover the truth about the Grail, and the only person who could substantiate his suspicions was his brother.

He stood on the other side of the mountain, called out across the gorge, "Sebastian!" The sound of his brother's name ricocheted back to him. Either he was refusing to answer him, or was too weakened by lack of food and water.

It took him nearly the whole day to form a crude ladder, After several tests to ensure himself it would hold his weight, he laid it across the gorge. He threw his sword into the gateway of Montvichet, then crawled slowly across his ladder.

Once there, he pulled the ladder to safety and left it leaning against a stone wall. He bent to retrieve his sword, then walked slowly into the courtyard.

"Brother!" No response, only the sound of flapping wings as a bird was disturbed from its nest.

He held his sword in front of him, bulwark

354

against what he might find. But there were some things against which a sword was no protection. Whispers, soft and faint, the sound of a child's cry. It was the wind, the gentle breeze that soughed through Montvichet. Even as he told himself that, he doubted the truth of it.

He walked through each sleeping chamber, noted how neat and tidy everything looked. A doll rested upon a pillow, and he looked away. The refectory was empty, there was no sign of food or even recent occupation. Finally, he walked through the scriptorium. The dust there was not as thick as elsewhere, and it looked as if the table to the side of the room had once been cleaned and used.

He walked back to the courtyard, his confusion deepening. Sebastian was not there. Nor was the woman.

When he saw the opening, he walked toward it, his smile growing wider with each footfall. He descended the curving steps slowly, feeling his way in the darkness. Halfway down weak sunlight illuminated the way. A few moments later he emerged at the bottom, near the place where he'd left his horse tied.

He retraced his steps, walked to the gateway, and tossed his makeshift ladder into the gorge. This place needed no intrusion, no casual visitors. Indeed, if he could have covered it with dust and blocked its existence from the world, he would have. There were hints of things he did not understand and an air of sadness that threatened to seep into his bones.

He turned and headed for the hidden steps again. Before descending, he turned and looked around him. He was grateful that he'd had no part in the siege of Montvichet.

Had the leper's robe and disease been another of

Sebastian's lies? He felt a reluctant admiration for his brother's cleverness. He had fooled them all.

Should he send men to England to force the truth from Sebastian? If he did so, others would discover that he had been tricked. He had nothing to gain by telling the truth. Instead, he would be a laughing-stock. No, worse. He would be sent on some endless round of inspections again, making a tally of sheep and cows and lecturing the monastic brothers in how to keep better records.

If he pretended the Grail was real, his own career would be advanced, and the honor of the Templars would be enhanced. Only he and Sebastian would know that the Grail they revered was a false relic. And who would believe Sebastian, a lover of heretics, over the word of a Templar? It took him less than a moment to come to that conclusion, and the decision, once reached, drew a broad smile from him.

Gregory descended the steps and disappeared from sight.

The breeze began to blow, catching dust and fling-ing it into the air, swirling the bits of dried leaves and fluttering the stems and flowers of late-blooming plants that grew on the roof and between the stones.

From somewhere came the sound of laughter, a faint and reminiscent echo. Then there was only si-lence enveloping Montvichet again.

There was such a look of disgust on Sebastian's face that Juliana laughed. He frowned at her amuse-ment, then scraped another gall from high atop the tree trunk.

"You do not have to eat them, Sebastian," she said.

"At least you do not ask me to help you scrape your hides. Has that been done yet?" There was such a look of repugnance on his face that her lips trembled in amusement. Who would have thought that the great knight Sebastian of Langlinais had no stomach for certain things?

She nodded.

"There must be a better way to make parchment. And to make ink. Nor can I understand why it needs to be made so often."

She shrugged. "It goes bad, Sebastian, just like wine."

"But these are bugs." He scowled down at the mess in his hand and shook his fingers over the basket.

Her laughter echoed through the wood.

"We'll see how much you laugh when we go falconing this afternoon."

It was a bargain between them. She would overcome her dislike of the mews and the birds, and he would help her fetch some oak galls from the trees.

"Must we?" Juliana had vowed to avoid the mews, a separate building built with high-arched doors and airy slits that made it appear larger than it was. She had never been around hunting birds before, but the gyrfalcons, the sakers, the lanners, all used to pluck ducks and geese from the sky seemed like fierce, angry creatures. There were two falconers in attendance, an old man and his apprentice, who spent more than an hour introducing her to all their charges and explaining their various stages of training. Though she smiled and thanked them for their information, she was grateful to leave the building.

"We must," he said, smiling down at her. He grabbed a branch and swung himself up into the tree. "Care to join me, my lady wife? It is a good sturdy branch." He rested against the trunk, one leg aligned along the branch, the other dangling. His grin was infectious, his invitation too tempting to resist. She placed the basket on the ground, extended her left hand to him and found a toehold in the large burl of the oak. Sebastian simply pulled her into place, grabbing her waist and holding her steady until she was in position.

She sat on the branch, her legs dangling before her. A posture not fitting for a chatelaine of a great castle, surely. But the Lord of Langlinais sat beside her, idly twirling the end of her braid.

"What is Ned building, Sebastian?" She watched as the carpenter, his wife, and his son gathered branches from the forest floor.

"Nothing. He's gathering the wood to make charcoal."

She frowned, perplexed. "What does a carpenter need with charcoal?"

"He provides it to the smith, and in return, the smith keeps his tools sharp. There is nothing about our demesne that isn't linked in some way, Juliana." He settled himself into the notch of the tree, staring out at the view before them. The denuded branches of the large oaks allowed them to see the sweeping vista of Langlinais, the upper bailey, the first bend in the river, all three tall towers. "The millstone is kept sharp by the people of Langlinais, and the miller, in turn, charges only a small fee to grind the wheat brought to him. The weaver provides good quality cloth for the castle and in return his loom is kept in good repair by the carpenter. Every person has a duty, and every duty leads to another person. Even if a man has no trade, he's put to work thatching roofs, spreading dung, or whitewashing the castle walls."

"And the Lord of Langlinais? What duty has he?"

He smiled down at her, swung his legs beside hers.

"Perhaps the most onerous and difficult. Pleasing his lady. My present obligation, besides harvesting bugs, is to convince her to share our new bathing chamber."

She turned her head to look at him. There was a boyish grin on his face, and his eyes seemed dark with mischief. She shook her head and looked away from him. "I'll tell Jerard not to make the water too hot. That together we'll warm it," he said in a coaxing voice.

She reached over and pinched his thigh.

He only laughed.

"You are a lusty man, Sebastian of Langlinais. I see that now. Perhaps even a satyr." Her mock frown made light of her words.

He pulled her to his side, bent and kissed her on the nose, a tender gesture that surprised her. She smiled at him.

"Are you happy, my lady wife?"

His voice had changed so quickly from amused to somber that she knew the question was a serious one. She reached over and placed her hand on his sleeve. "I do not see how anyone can be happier than I am."

He seemed to study her in the afternoon light. "I remember once, at Montvichet, thinking that I would never be able to see your smile or hear your laughter again."

"Is that why you are so generous to me? Why you give me things like rare ink and a scriptorium and build a bathing chamber?"

"To see you smile? Any gift is a paltry expense."

"Will such generosity excuse me from the mews?" she asked, her smile returning.

He shook his head. "You'll come to respect the birds, Juliana."

"I respect them now."

"Then you'll come to like falconing."

"Will I?"

"You must trust me in these things. You do not mind sitting in a tree do you? Despite your fear of heights?"

She looked down at the ground beneath their feet. In truth, they were not all that high.

"I've given up my fears, Sebastian. I think you were right all along. I think being afraid is something I learned."

"I am a wise man," he said smugly.

She made a face at him. His laughter made her frown.

"There she is, the child I knew." His fingers framed her chin as he turned her face to one side and then the other. "I knew she would come again if I was patient."

"She has grown, Sebastian, and now possesses a husband who is arrogant and lofty-headed."

"Come with me falconing," he said in his most persuasive voice. "You may grow to love the sport. But at the very least, you should attempt it." He smiled again, and the place in her chest that was once hollow expanded again with love. "I wish to share my life with you, my joys, my interests."

She looked away. There were some things they could not share. Not now, not yet. She felt a measure of guilt for not confiding in him. He had said that he wanted no more secrets between them. But this secret needed to be kept hidden for a day or two more. That's all she needed, and then she would tell him everything.

"Juliana?"

She glanced back at him. "Very well, Sebastian, but before we go to play with your precious birds, my entire basket must be filled with galls."

His look of disgust kept her amused as he helped her down from the branch.

Juliana avoided the presence of the master mason, a sober man with a face that appeared as quarried as the stone he chiseled. She skirted the north tower, entering through the door now framed in timber. For months the mason and his apprentices had been shoring up the north tower. Now the structure, once used to store armament, stood empty.

The workers, like the rest of the people of Langlinais, were sharing their noon meal in the great hall. She must hurry. Any moment, Sebastian would be looking for her to join him at the dais. Today Jerard would leave Langlinais forever, and she must be there to bid him farewell.

But first, she must find the perfect spot.

One way to correct the damage done by the flood was to demolish the tower completely and build it over again, an expensive undertaking. Another alternative would have been to allow the tower to remain empty, but even that was not acceptable, since eventually the structure might topple. The easiest way to solve the problem of the crumbling foundations was to build an interior wall. It would be like slipping one quill inside another, thereby strengthening both.

A few moments later, she found what she needed. The stone was thicker behind the first flight of stairs. The space between the new masonry and the old stone was wide enough to conceal the coffer she held. Inside was her own version of the codex, with notes as to how the original had been found and the tale of the chalice. She knelt and wedged it into place, then smoothed the mortar where her fingers had rested.

Grazide frowned at her as she entered the great hall. "My lady, you are cold, and such things are not good for you. Come into the warmth and have your ale. I have told my lord that you were about the castle, but didn't know your destination nor your purpose, and he has not stopped asking me this quarter hour."

She pulled loose the toque from her chin, handed it to Grazide, who took it, then extended a hand to rearrange Juliana's braid.

"Not that I wish to know, my lady, but I am counseled with your welfare. What you do is your concern, of course, but when my lord asks of me so often, I feel foolish not knowing."

Juliana walked beside Grazide, headed for the dais. Sebastian sat there, his gaze fixed on her. She warmed at his look. They'd had little sleep last night, the hours given over to laughter and love. His sudden smile reminded her of it.

She was no longer the girl who had sat in the great hall frightened of her future. Juliana the Timid, Juliana the Mouse had been replaced by a woman who knew herself well. She loved her work, and would always be thankful for the ability to continue it. But it was no longer all that she was, would no longer be the only way she measured her life.

Instead, there was Langlinais, and the people she'd come to know and love. There was the future, promising despite the threats they faced. But above all, there was Sebastian.

She felt a surge of love for the man who sat watching her, a small smile playing over his mouth. He was ennobled not only by birth but by honor. It was not a banner or a series of tourneys won that made him a great man. It was his character, his nobility. Sebastian had sacrificed his freedom that a vassal might escape, had planned on exile rather than imperil her, had been willing to give away his birthright in order to shield her.

She would have done anything for him.

"And I told him that I'm sure you weren't near the river, my lady, but we looked through the upper bailey and you were not to be found."

Juliana turned, smiled down at her attendant. Her tone was soft, the words curious. "Grazide, do you never, ever hush?"

The shorter woman looked taken aback, but only momentarily. "My husband used to ask me the same thing, my lady. Why, he would sometimes sit and stare at the fire while I spoke with him, not saying one word. It might have been that he was not in the same room, for all that I saw his body. Up until the day he died he looked just so. There were times that I despaired of him ever answering me." The rest of her words trailed off into a rambling monologue.

Across the table, she and Sebastian exchanged a look of amusement. Evidently, there were some things that never changed, despite how courageous she became.

Chapter 47

"Where will he go, Sebastian?" Juliana stood at his side atop the east tower, watching Jerard ride through the gate of Langlinais. He rode slowly, despite the cold weather, looking around him often as if to sear into his memory the sight of the home he'd known for the last seven years. Old Simon stood at the gatehouse, reached up to lay a hand upon his knee, then stepped back and watched him, as they all did, pass through the gate.

Juliana felt tears mist in her eyes. Sebastian held her hand in his, their fingers entwined. "I have given him property north of here. A section of land I won in a tourney and was going to surrender to the Templars."

"I will miss him."

"Loyalty is a virtue much espoused, but difficult to find. He is the most faithful of knights," Sebastian said, watching as Jerard turned and was lost from sight.

She pulled her hand free from his, stepped back. Would he think her actions disloyal? She would know in the next moment.

"I have done something, Sebastian, of which you will not approve."

He turned and looked at her, his lips curved in a smile. "Have you lain with another?"

She frowned, then shook her head.

"Stolen my money?"

"No, Sebastian."

"Then what have you done?"

"Is that all that matters to you, that I might have taken your money or been adulterous?"

"In truth," he said, one arm extending around her waist, "the money does not concern me as much as the other. I should hate to spend my days kneeling before the altar praying for forgiveness."

"Why would you do that, Sebastian?"

"Because I would have to kill him, my lady wife." He leaned down, kissed the tip of her nose. "Your eyes are so wide, Juliana. Did you not think I would guard those I love?"

"If I felt much the same, would you be as understanding?"

"What have you done?" His smile had not diminished.

"Copied the scrolls."

At his silence, she modified her statement. "In truth, only the codex."

He glanced away from her, looked out toward the north, in the direction Jerard was to travel.

"Why, Juliana?" He spoke into the distance. Was he displeased?

"Because something might happen to Jerard. Or the scrolls might be destroyed. Or, we might be besieged and need them close at hand in order to bargain."

He turned to look at her. "Why did you not think of all these arguments before we decided to send the scrolls with Jerard?"

"Is it not better to have a copy, Sebastian? For the same reasons?"

"It was not an option I'd considered," he said, picking up her right hand. "You were able to do this? Without pain?"

There were scars upon her hands. She could not deny their existence; she would always bear them. Nor did she have as much strength in her fingers as she had before, but that was not something she would mention to him.

"I am slower than before," she admitted, "but it was not that difficult. Even if it had been, I would have completed it." She stood tall before him, looked at him directly. "I will not have you harmed, Sebastian."

"My fierce Juliana," he said, bringing her fingers to his lips and brushing a kiss over them. "When you first came into my life," he said softly, "I prayed for your safety, that you might be guarded against the Templars and from me. I am a knight, trained for war, and yet you would stand between me and harm."

He touched her cheek with a fingertip. "I am not sure I agree with what you have done, Juliana, but I cherish the reason behind your actions. If there is a true miracle in my life, it is you."

"Sebastian, how can you say that? You have been spared exile and a living death."

"What if I had not had leprosy?" he asked softly. "What if the physician who examined me and declared me a leper was wrong?"

"You would question the nature of a miracle, Sebastian?"

"I have done so endlessly," he admitted, looking down at her. His eyes, those lovely blue eyes of his, seemed to darken as he studied her. "I ask myself if such a thing happened because I touched the relics. Or was it the sun upon my skin for the first time in years? Or Sister Agnes's unguent? Or perhaps because I had worn my armor, instead of that cursed robe?"

"Is it important that you know, Sebastian? What if you never do?" Her left hand cupped the side of his face.

He picked up her hand again, turned it over, bent, and placed a kiss upon her palm. His smile altered in nature, seemed to hold only the purest joy. "Then I will live each day and bless our deliverance, whatever the cause."

He extended his arm around her, laid his cheek on the crown of her hair.

The moment was silent, the thoughts each held remarkably similar. Perhaps it wasn't important to gauge a miracle, to mark it and record it and prove it. Perhaps the greatest wonder was the touch of a hand in friendship and the joy of a heart. They belonged together, and the fact that they stood linked in each other's arms was proof enough that sometimes events happened that defied explanation. In mind and body and spirit they were joined and would be, perhaps, until time ceased to measure the passing of decades and the onset of centuries.

You my life, promise that this love of ours that we share will last forever. Great gods, arrange for this truth to be spoken, and to say this sincere and from the depths of a loving heart, so that it is granted us to continue all our life this treaty of inviolable friendship.

Catullus
84–54 B.C.E.

Epilogue

Gertrude received the missive with mixed feelings of curiosity and alarm. Did the Lord of Langlinais wish the relics returned, then? She'd grown accustomed to having them at the convent these past months, had grown familiar with the feeling of awe she felt when viewing them, had drawn a great deal of comfort from their presence.

She opened the letter with some trepidation, but smiled as she read it.

I trust you are well and that the gift we have presented the convent has posed no problems for you.

Thank you for aiding me in providing me with inks for my beloved wife's scriptorium. She has used them ably.

My purpose in writing to you is to commission the convent to supply my wife with a few garments of rich color and fine detail. Something to match her loveliness and enhance the color of her eyes, but with short and loose sleeves that she might continue to work in the scriptorium without them trailing in her ink.

I would like, also, a set of christening garments for our child.

But most importantly, I would beg your forbearance in sending Sister Agnes to us again, this time in August. Our child is due to be born during that month, and I wish my wife to have someone versed in the healing arts to be with her in her travail. Please assure Sister Agnes that I will assist her in any way that I can, even to the extent of remaining silent. But please prepare the good sister with the knowledge that I will not be separated from my wife under any conditions.

Gertrude smiled. Perhaps the mystery of Juliana had been solved at last. The girl's talent might lie in the scriptorium, but her greatest blessing was the ability to love. That was evident in the tone of this letter. The Lord of Langlinais was obviously deeply in love with his wife.

The last two sentences of the letter amused her. She read it again.

Would there be any manuscripts of Ovid that you might send to me for my library? Or any works by a poet named Catullus?

She folded the letter, stood, and walked down the silent corridor, her destination the large and sunny solar where the sisters who did such things embroidered. She would deliver the commission and then arrange for the volumes to be sent to the Lord of Langlinais. She smiled again, certain that both errands would please husband and wife.

Afterword

History is littered with lies. Rumor is often converted to fact with only time as its validation. Therefore, where there was rumor, or supposition, or conjecture, I have played with "what if's" because fiction allows for interpretation. *My Beloved* is as historically accurate as I can make it within the framework of my imagination.

The Cathars, also known as the Albigensian movement, were real. There were various sects of the religion, each of which varied in their interpretation of accepted belief, probably not unlike the Protestant denominations we know today. The siege against the Cathars and their ultimate fate was unfortunately real. And although Montvichet is fictional, there are historical models such as Queribus and Minerve. While there were rumors of Templar involvement in the betrayal that condemned the Cathar women and children, it cannot be proven true or false. Therefore, it must remain one of those mysteries of the ages, along with the persistent hints that the Templars actually possessed the Holy Grail.

The Poor Knights of the Order of the Temple of Solomon—the Knights Templar—are often conveyed as being heroically knightly. I believe that they were a devoted and devout group of men whose leaders lost sight of the aim for their ambition. They were for the most part misogynist, few of them were actually knights, and few could read. The expression "he can drink like a Templar" had roots in truth. But they were great fighters, and were helpful in establishing the banking, currency, and credit systems we know today. Perhaps the almost legendary aura that still surrounds them is due mainly to the way they were rounded up on Friday, the thirteenth and the Order systematically eradicated.

Hildegard of Bingen actually lived. A German abbess, she was consulted as a prophetess by heads of state. In addition to her visions, she was renowned for her musical compositions such as *Ordo Virtutum* (written before 1158), one of the first examples of a morality play, for her poetic works, and her studies on natural history and medicine.

One of the earliest known female scribes was Ende, who assisted in the preparation of a Spanish work of the vision of St. John the Divine in 789. Documentation from the ninth century lists a number of manuscripts attributed to women scribes, their work mostly done in convents.

Leprosy was not easily diagnosed in the Middle Ages, and was often confused with eczema, psoriasis, scrofula, skin cancers, and even allergies. Therefore, people could be—and were—condemned to being one of the living dead when their conditions were relatively minor. The Mass of Separation was also, regrettably, real.

Any errors in translating the poetry of Catullus are mine.

It is impossible to write a book using the historical backdrop of the Middle Ages without considering the impact of the Church. Not one facet of medieval life was free of its influence. The convents and the monasteries that dotted the medieval landscape achieved what could not have been accomplished by kings or emperors. By teaching the same words and practices throughout the world, the Church brought people together, gave them one set of beliefs. Faith alone had united Europe. But it was vital for the foundations of that faith to be forever considered sacrosanct and inviolate and not open to interpretation. Seven hundred years later, however, I am able to do so.

Dear Reader,

So many of you have been patiently waiting for Lori Copeland's next Avon Romantic Treasure, so I'm thrilled to say you don't have to wait any longer! Next month, don't miss *The Bride of Johnny McAllister* — it's filled with all the wonderful, warm, western romance that you expect from this spectacular writer. Johnny McAllister is on the shady side of the law, and never in a million years would he believe he'd fall for the local judge's daughter. But fall he does — and hard. You will not want to miss this terrific love story.

Contemporary readers, be on the look out — Eboni Snoe is back, too! Your enthusiastic response to Eboni's last Avon contemporary romance, *Tell Me I'm Dreamin'*, has helped build her into a rising star. Next month don't miss her latest, *A Chance on Lovin' You*. When a stressed-out "city gal" inherits a home in the Florida Keys, she thinks that this is just what she needs to change her life...but the real changes come when she meets a millionaire with more than friendship on his mind.

Gayle Callen is fast becoming a new favorite for Avon readers, and her debut Avon Romance, *The Darkest Knight*, received raves. Now don't miss the follow-up *A Knight's Vow*. And sparks fly in Linda O'Brien's latest western *Courting Claire* — as an unlikely knight in shining armor comes to our heroine's rescue.

Don't miss any of these fantastic love stories!

Lucia Macro
Lucia Macro
Senior Editor

ael 0899